THE WORLD'S GREATEST HIT

THE WORLD'S GREATEST HIT

— UNCLE TOM'S CABIN —

By

HARRY BIRDOFF

ILLUSTRATED WITH OLD-TIME PLAYBILLS,
DAGUERREOTYPES, VIGNETTES,
MUSIC-SHEETS, POEMS, AND CARTOONS

S. F. VANNI
Publishers and Booksellers
30 West 12th Street
New York

Copyright 1947

by

HARRY BIRDOFF

CONTENTS

                                                          Page

Prologue   1

PART I

I   The Book of the Play   13
II   In the Beginning —   20
III   Mr. Howard and the Foxes   27
IV   Captain Purdy and His Argosy   60
V   The War of the Cabins   107
VI   The Rehabilitation of the Stage Negro   127
VII   Of the Tomitudes Abroad   144
VIII   On the Continental Stage   166
IX   The Cathering of the Forces   186

PART II

X   Wild Turkey Tommers and Sweet Jubilee Singers   213
XI   Further Adventures Abroad   238
XII   Cavalcade of Tom Shows   257
XIII   The Play That Went to the Dogs   292
XIV   The Double Mammoth   306
XV   Grand Pavilions of the Nineties   329
XVI   The Twentieth Century   357
XVII   Uncle Tom Goes to the Movies   392
XVIII A Good Play Needs No Epilogue   411
       Appendix   423

ILLUSTRATIONS

George L. Aiken 39
His Directing Genius Set the Course of the Play 50
The Precursor of a School of Topsies 52
Her Precocity Was the Wonder of the Fifties 55
Chatham Square in the Fifties 63
Playbill with the Original Cast 68
A Black Joke 71
One of the Many Inspired Songs 78
"Captain Purdy" 92
The Olympic Version (1852) 145
Diogenes, on His Search for an Honest Man... 150
An English Conception of Haley 153
The English Topsy 154
Playbill of Theatre Royal, Oldham (1856) 160
The English Marionettes 164
La Case de l'Oncle Tom (1853) 168
Uncle Tom Begins To Worry about His Great Popularity 170
L'Oncle Tom (1853) 173
Endowed with Too Much Sensibility, Uncle Tom Abandons
His Dramatic Career 177
Manager—Come, hurry, hurry...the curtain is up! 179
The Play Captures the German Stage 181
Transatlantische Skizzen 184
Last Appearences of Little Cordelia 193
Topsy! 212
Lotta as Topsy 221
David Belasco as Uncle Tom 222
How the South Enjoyed the Play 228
Jubilee Furor of the '70s 233
This Ticket Admits a Scholar 237
The Prototype of Uncle Tom 239
Between Performances 272
Eliza Crosses the Ice-Clogged Ohio... 294
They Introduced Dogs into the Play 296

In the Days of the Doubling Fever 308
When Tom Shows Outrivaled the Circus 319
The Next Best Thing in American Grand Opera 324
When Uncle Tom Married Little Eva 327
As It Will Have To Be Played If Johnson Wins 330
The Back Stage Tragedy 334
At a One-Night Stand 338
Off Stage Amenities 343
The "Uncle Tom's Cabin" Season 345
Harbinger of Spring 358
Theodore Roberts 361
A Tense Moment in the Folk Play 376
The Duncan Sisters in *Topsy and Eva* (1924) 383
The Earliest Movie 395
Shirley Temple as Little Eva 404
Judy Garland as Topsy 406
Jane Withers Sings "Uncle Tom's Cabin Is a Cabaret Now" 408
Betty Grable and June Haver as Double Topsies 409
The Players' Revival of the Perennial (1933) 412
A Stylized Production 413
In Leningrad (1933) 414
Queenie Smith 415
Sold down *Sweet River* (1936) 417
Parade in *Bloomer Girl* (1944) 418
The Thrill That Comes Once in a Lifetime 420

TO BERTHE

Well!—*A show once came to Cedarsville,*
Uncle Tom's Cabin, so it said on the bill,
They had a mule and a dog to boot—
Durn my buttons, but the critter was cute!

Well!—*After dinner we did up the chores,*
Washed the dishes, and locked the barn doors;
And Ma and Pa and Sis and all—
We started out for the old Town Hall.

Well!—*When we got there we found an awful crowd,*
More than fifty people, Dad allowed;
"Gimme my ticket," I loudly cried—
So we grabbed our tickets, and we wint inside.

Well!—*They had a melodeon, a fiddle and a horn—*
The grandest music since I was born!
They played a little while and then
They rang up the curtain, and the show began.

Well!—*First fellow on the stage was a man named Legree,*
The durndest cuss I ever did see!
He had a blacksnake whip about three yards long—
We was all mighty glad when he was gone!

Well!—*Out comes a nigger, and his name was Tom;*
He was mighty nice, I swan;
He was sold to the man named Legree—
The durndest shame I ever did see!

Well!—*Out comes a woman, and her name was Lize,*
You could see she was scared, by the look in her eyes;
And Legree comes arunnin', and he yells "Come back!"—
And he sets the bloodhounds on her track!

Well!—*Up goes the curtain, and there was a river,*
So doggorned cold, it would make you shiver!
And in jumps Lize, and something broke—
And we all knew the river was boxes of soap.
. . . .
Well!—*Out comes a little girl with Uncle Tom,*
She was mighty sweet, I swan!
Her name was Eva, and she'd cough and she'd sigh—
We all knew that Eva was agoin' to die.

Well!—*She died all right, and the niggers sang,*
Giminy how that Town Hall rang!
Eva died all right, about a quarter past eleven—
We all knew that Eva was agoin' to Heaven.

Well!—*We all got up for to walk out slow,*
When a fellow comes runnin' and says "Folks, don't go!—
I advise you all just to stay and wait
And see Little Eva go through the Golden Gate."

Well!—*The Gate of Heaven was there all right;*
Up so high 'twas almost out of sight;
And there was little Eva way up in the air—
She looked mighty purty with her yellow hair.

Well!—*They rang down the curtain and the show was done,*
So we all grabbed our hats, and we all went hom'.

—Popular Ballad

PROLOGUE

I've been a good boy to my dear mamma;
I never tried to deceive her;
So I think she orter give me a quarter
To see Uncle Thomas and Eva.
—Air

WITH THE COMING OF SPRING they blossomed forth —
covering barns and fences, and in flaming colors overrunning
stone walls; the "three sheet" lithographs could not be read
from a distance, but there wasn't a boy who didn't recognize
immediately the familiar figures: Little Eva ensconced in
old Tom's lap, Eliza pursued across the ice by the hounds,
Lawyer Marks striking that grandiloquent posture, and
Topsy doing a breakdown! Never, never was a traveling
Tom show known to curtail its lavish posters, for they outdid
the circus. Only the elements and malicious boys might
destroy them.

A week before the arrival, the countryside was plastered with:

REWARD!!!

GEORGE HARRIS, *Absconded from My Plantation,*
Is Reported Headed for Canada.
Reward for His Return. SIMON LEGREE (*owner*).

With the crack o' dawn came the little caravan, wagons
with gilded gingerbread, the sides depicting draperies of
scrollwork — and a legend in red and gold letters. Proclaim-

—1—

ing its massive scenic allegories, one was embellished with the Apocalypse scene, Eva surrounded by chubby cupids and overflowing cornucopias; another, the tableau that unfolded as the greatest American drama reached its terrifying climax: Legree whipping Tom in a sulphurous red light! More wagons, with golden sunburst wheels, for the baggage, for the Tommers' living quarters, and for the accessory menagerie.

The grand, gala free street parade was advertised for 11:45 A.M., but it never really got started before the noon hour. Agile boys shinnied onto the roof of the grocery sidewalk shed, and had the best view, gazing enthralled at the long ceremonial procession. Two uniformed bands came in the strident wake — one white, one colored, often supplemented by a Ladies' Drum Corps; a strutting figure in scarlet twirled a drum-major's baton. They played "slave melodies," and also "There'll Be a Hot Time in the Old Town, To-night," with plenty of ginger in it.

A carriage drawn by spirited white horses, decked in spangled nosegays, carried a famous trio: Old Tom sandwiched in between Mr. St. Claire and Simon Legree, the raiser and purchaser both looking proud and self-satisfied as if they had calved him between them. Often an open barouche held golden-haired Eva, at her father's side, facing Topsy, whose topsails shivered in the wind, and strait-laced Aunt Ophelia, who kept calling folks, "Shiftless!" Sometimes Little Eva rode her beplumed Shetland pony; or she appeared in an "Apocalypse" on wheels, in virginal white, with a papier-maché halo, in all the moving splendor of a gilded float, from which vantage point she worked havoc in the hearts of her youthful admirers.

An avalanche of hisses and catcalls greeted that old terror, Legree. Gargantuan in his small mule cart, with slouch hat at a rakish angle — (S-s-s-s!), he glowered (S-s-s-s!), snarling half-muffled oaths at the would-be upholders of virtue and truth (S-s-s-s!), cracking a great blacksnake whip at them (S-s-s-s-s!), and he made it work overtime on their invisible hides. It only wanted somebody to say the word to the youthful lovers of humanity on the sidewalk, and they would have lynched the infernal slave-monger. Surprisingly, his fellow actors vouched, "Hard though he is, even he was once rocked on the bosom of a mother!" It was difficult to believe *that*, and although the Mayor of the town was enlightened, other officials argued, "It doesn't matter — he must be wicked to be able to play such a character!"

In Legree's cart rode Eliza, displaying her charms. And if she were put up on the auction block, there wasn't a citizen who willingly wouldn't have put in a bid toward her purchase.

Lawyer Marks, with his famous umbrella, sat astride a docile, mouse-colored donkey, dragging his white-legginged feet on Main Street, offering everyone his card from an accordion-pleated wallet. The crowd echoed, "Yea-a-a, veri-lie!" when Phineas Fletcher, the Quaker, greeted his host of imitators. He placed the ends of his fingers together, pausing to rise slowly on his toes, with a teetotally this and a teeto-tally that. Gumption Cute, hard by, chawed tobacco, whit-tling away on half a tree with his Barlow knife.

Most climactic of all were *"The genuine bloodhounds: 12—Count Em — 12."* As pale green programmes of long ago put it, they supported the rest of the cast as "the full strength of the Company." Boys in faded, oversized overcoats led them in the parade and excited the envy of other boys, who traded apples, marbles and candy for the privilege of holding the leash.

A feature in the parade was a log cabin on wheels, real smoke issuing from the chimney, and Aunt Chloe washed clothes on the doorstep, while Uncle Tom gidapped the horses. Then a belching calliope, the old steam fiddle, chant-ed Foster melodies, but chronically afflicted with the croup, frightened the horses on Main Street.

The Tommers later waylaid the innocent bystanders. On the sidewalk Simon Legree cracked a whip fearsomely, thundering out, "I'm looking for a likely-looking yaller gal named Eliza.... She belongs t'me, an' I want her.... I want t'find Uncle Tom, tew.... They tell me they're both with this hyer show that's at the — (here naming the local theatre), an' I wish ye'd tell me whar that is." A shabby-genteel figure rubbered into windows, entered stores to wander aimlessly about, and buttonholed passersby to ask, "Can you tell me, please, where the Theatre is? I understand that they're showing there a great play called *Uncle Tom's Cabin*, and as I, myself, am Marks, the lawyer, I'd like right well to see it."

One caught a glimpse of the classic features of St. Clair in a lithograph in a saloon window, close to the stodgy goat of the brewery advertisement. The soda fountains in town hung up signs: "Try our Topsy Tipple," "Try our Uncle Tom Special," "Taste the little Eva Sundae," and "Special — with Eliza Icing." At the schoolhouse gates, an individual in ante-bellum dress offered the pupils, with magnanimity, "This Ticket and Ten Cents" pasteboards.

Blazing away, the Tom band's concert before the theatre, at one o'clock, drew a throng. Then it entered, and became the orchestra; when the plantation scene went on, the same musicians donned "slave" clothes, as Jubilee singers.

From the rise of the curtain until the final tableau, anything might happen. Invariably the mechanical equipment was crude, the drops neither dropped nor lifted, but caught in some of the other scenery, and refused to be extricated. A curtain came down on a horse (that drew the barouche) amidships, as she turned her hind quarters squarely upon the spectators. On the creaking pulleys Eva was drawn up to Heaven feet first, or got stuck en route; while the red fire in the Ascension wouldn't burn, and if it did, made everyone in the audience cough. In the whipping scene Legree would catch hold of Tom by the slack of his blue shirt, pulling it out of his belt and exposing a wide spanse of white skin. "The street in New Orleans" fluttered in every backstage breeze, yet worked its own illusion. A stock curtain of Leutze's famous painting of Washington Crossing the Delaware might rise on Eliza and the "prop" floes. She often outran the hounds, had to wait for them, urge them on, and they chased the wrong people; she lost her balance, as the hounds bounded up, sympathetically licking her face. Critics made much of these mishaps.

The play was never like Mrs. Stowe's novel, but native as a patchwork quilt. Bits of "business" from generations of Tommers had developed the "sure-fire" stuff, the ad libbing making permanent the bristling lines. Some charac· ters were built up into flesh and blood and sinew, others cut down to the grim essentials, or jettisoned. The original connecting passages were altogether cut and lost, but the scenes beat forcibly upon the heart and brain. Like Topsy, it "just grow'd" — giving us the true folk play.

With the traditional text lost sight of, any number of Tom companies claimed they were giving the "only original." A verbal form was handed down. Stock companies failed when they put on the piece — no, what kept the play alive wasn't in any printed script: It was stuff that came down by word-of-mouth from generations of Uncle Toms, Markses, Topsies, Legrees.

The intense rivalry among Tom troupes, playing with gusto in their brassiest days, exacted a fierce vitality. Often a performance lasted five hours, embracing six acts, fifty scenes and eight tableaux, an elaborate chorus of two hundred Jubilee singers, a mother-of-pearl Apotheosis, and an "ice-gorged river" — Nature herself imported! It brought a decade of "Double Mammoth Productions," all the characters in pairs — as if one mammoth was not sufficient!

They traveled along every tank-water line and gave it at every whistle-stop, stepping from the wagon flap onto the platform, before flaring acetylene torches. They were born in the show-wagon, named after the early parts they were to play — "Harry" or "Eva," and when only a few months old Eliza carried them across the ice as gurgling infantile "property." Little Evas grew to Topsies, Maries, Elizas, and then to Aunt Chloes. Gangling boys attempted the irrepressible Topsies, went on to Markses, then to Legrees, and in old age achieved the epitome — Uncle Toms. If some were arrested in their dramatic growth, they at least attained some degree of perfection in a given part. Steeped in the lore, they spent their lives as Tommers, and finally shuffled offstage without ever having appeared in any other play. You did not find their names in the Who's Who on the Stage. The newspapers found it economical in space to refer to them merely as "U.T.C." companies, but to the actors themselves they were Tom shows, or Tommers.

The *legitimate* held them in derision because the hardy perennial traveled to the remotest parts, known to the profession as the tall-grass tanks, the kerosene circuits, and to the farthest fork of the creek. As the apple-knockers of the red clay crossroads, and those from the highweed hills and the tall-grass territory, had no theatres, the Tommers set up improvized stages in the prairie way-stations, in the fraternal halls like the Odd Fellows' Hall and the Volunteer Fireman's Association, in livery stables, in dining-rooms, in courthouses. The *legitimate* scenery- chewers laughed about the "sticks" and the tank-towns of Ohio, about Kennebunkport, Me., where the folk play was enacted on a twelve-foot platform with no footlights at all, and where Eva stood on a pickle keg. The pioneering Tommers journeyed to the Rockies, in what was rip-roaring territory then, and achieved the Coast. Then only — in their wake — did the *legitimate* reach out for the ripe plums.

The American cross-roads expected the play, with its touching morality, at least once a year, and it did appear with the regularity of an almanac. Their sole contact with the "the-ayter," the hinterlanders came in wagons from miles around to mingle their tears with Little Eva and the old colored gentleman. There were, also, the semi-annual and monthly arrivals, called "ragtime Tom shows," because the tents were worn to rags.

After the Civil War, critics tried to explain away the early furor of *Uncle Tom's Cabin* on the ground that the whole thing had been carried on the lift of the antislavery movement. They insisted that the play was rapidly outliving its popularity, that its glory had waned. Yet an excited admiration swept the country anew, and the dramatic chestnut ripened over-night — it was "all the mustard!" *Uncle Tom's Cabin* was commonly supposed to have died — for the last time — during the '60s, the '70s, the '80s, the '90s, and in the early decades of the Twentieth Century.

The healthy old barnstormer remained ever an enigma to the critics who wondered about its hold on those who seldom went otherwise to the theatre. Now, it wasn't Art; the play was badly constructed, and — alas! — did not follow the ancient Aristotelian unities. Worst of all, it ran more than one consecutive season!

When all the famous "hits" went the way of the Biblical grass, the passionate heights to which our sole folk play aroused audiences compelled its perpetuation, and the Tommers' lithographs were more than justified in advertising: "A Version of a Play That Has Defied Time." When Little Eva, then Uncle Tom, died nightly in a hiss of blue-white calcium light, those coming to scoff found themselves making surreptitious use of handkerchiefs. If the Tom show was a circus in miniature, as critics claimed, what did it matter? The play was big enough to hold animal talent. If, during the *entr'actes*, a Tommer appeared before the curtain, while the scenery was being shifted, and gave bird imitations and the progressive sounds of a railway train in the distance — was there really anything wrong about that? By far, it was more honest than the literary subterfuges in the closet dramas of the day.

It is unaccountable why modern sticklers for the so-called fixed laws of Elizabethan times and the Globe Theatre did find fault with the raw chunks of morality in our native play. If *Uncle Tom's Cabin* had three unrelated parts, so had Shakespeare's dramas. Moreover, the very line of established tradition went into what the critics now called "the best bad acting" of the Tommers. The outcast, so unworthy of their notice, kept the humorous weeklies supplied each year, and inspired a host of burlesques. Yet, *Uncle Tom's Cabin* triumphed over them all with the longest run in theatrical history: beyond the million mark.

Now, if a playwright produces a single drama which runs for two seasons or more, it is a remarkable feat. Consider then a play that ran not for one or two seasons, but *continually* for over ninety years! Not a year passed that elaborate revivals weren't usurping the boards in the large cities, while a score of Tom companies carried the folk play to the provinces. Abroad, it was produced in every language, from Czechoslovakian to Polynesian, and had a phenomenal run in Great Britain.

When all else failed, managers were quick to realize the fortunes to be made in its destined popularity, and tapped its old vein. Beginners got their start with *Uncle Tom*, became enriched, then promoted Classical plays that failed. The Topsies and St. Clairs acquired fortunes, the Legrees became property holders, and Evas without number achieved both wealth and distinction — as did Mrs. Edwin Booth; while poor Uncle Tom, like the faithful old house servant he was, "has lost everything in *this* world" — but he, too, like the others, made many a dollar from the play. "Turkey actors" gave it during the holidays, and they were of the type of Edward N. McDowell, who recalls a time when he produced it at the Bijou Theatre, Pittsburgh, with the colossal sum of fifty cents — playing two consecutives weeks at a profit of $1,200. As one manager expressed, and it was the last word in tribute, "You generally find money on a Tommer."

How many were launched on their theatrical careers by seeing it as their first play! One began auspiciously by witnessing Eliza clatter across the "prop" ice in Oskaloosa, Ia; another became ever so determined when Uncle Tom was flogged to the portable reedy organ accompaniment in Showhegan, Me. If you study the faded pink programmes, you will find few of later prominence who did not at one time or another attempt a role in it. They all cut their eye teeth on its woodwings; yet search their memoirs — little trace of how they really spent their apprenticeships. Nor have the historians given our one indigenous folk play, authentic Americana, its full share of recognition. If a thousand people were chosen at random to name the play that had the right to be called "The Great American Drama," the chances are that not one would pick the lowly *Uncle Tom's Cabin.*

The powerful play, vibrating with its note of sympathy for the enslaved, set many precedents: It was the first ever given as an entire evening's fare; it established, once and for all, the matinees and popular prices; it brought Spirituals to the fore, with Jubilee singers from the ranks of the Negroes; and it was the pioneer of long runs.

In a period when all playacting was anathema, and theatres condemned as "citadels of hell," *Uncle Tom's Cabin* broke the severe Puritan strait-laces. It brought Christians to the theatre in such flocks that the ministry had to yield to the early, picturesque playbills that proclaimed: *"A Great and Moral Play, Coming with All the Grandeur and Magnitude the Mind of Man Ever Conceived!"*

Part I

AN INFORMAL AND AFFECTIONATE HISTORY OF AMERICA'S FOLK PLAY

CHAPTER I

THE BOOK OF THE PLAY

> *Know her! Who knows not Uncle Tom*
> *And her he learned his gospel from,*
> *Has never heard of Moses;*
> *Full well the brave black hand we know*
> *That gave to freedom's grasp the hoe*
> *That killed the weed that used to grow*
> *Among the Southern roses.*
> —Oliver Wendell Holmes

UNCLE TOM'S CABIN APPEARED as a squalling infant when the nation was at the crossroads. The Fugitive Slave Law had just been passed, and the novel came at the psychological hour. The social forces long stirring crystallized, at last.

That winter, Edward Beecher, up in Boston, had fought the Law from his pulpit. His wife wrote to friends of tragic cases: slave families broken up, Negroes frozen to death in their attempt to reach Canada. She pleaded with her sister-in-law, "Now, Hattie, if I could just use the pen as you can, I would make this whole nation feel what an accursed thing slavery is!" Mrs. Stowe read it to the family gathered in the small parlor in Brunswick, Maine, and rising from her chair, she crushed the letter in her determination:
"I will write something — I will if I live!"
Mrs. Stowe had just borne her seventh child, was diverted by household duties, and — to make ends meet — tutored a group of students. Her husband was away in

Cincinnati. But she kept assuring her sister-in-law, in December, 1850, "As long as the baby sleeps with me nights, I can't do much at anything; but I will do it at least — I will write that thing if I live!"

Harriet had to do it — she could do it!

Lyman Beecher, her father, preached on the Missouri question, and since her childhood, Byron's poetry had been a passion in their household. When the poet fell fighting for the enslaved Greeks, the pastor burst out in his grief: "My dear, Byron is dead — gone." Silent for a while, he added, "I did hope he would live to do something for Christ — what a harp he might have swept!" As for Byron's digressions, he was firmly convinced that had he only talked with the poet, "It might have got him out of his troubles."

Harriet's earliest writing reflected the frowning books in her father's library. At twelve, she wrote, "Can the Immortality of the Soul Be Studied by the Light of Nature?" defending the negative. At the school exhibition, as the childish, cramped handwriting was rendered aloud, the preacher asked, with a theologian's concern, "Who wrote that composition?" Without realizing it was his daughter's, he took issue on a few minor points.

A year later, Harriet attempted a play, *Cleon!* She furtively filled little copy books with blank verse about a Greek pagan lord living at the court of Nero, who saw at last the true light of Christianity. Her sister Catherine caught her at it, and Harriet was assigned the proper study of Butler's *Analogy* to discipline her mind. In those innocent days the theatre was considered the workshop of the Devil, and plays were never, never enacted beyond the few parlor "reading recitals," and then only with proper emphasis on the poetry.

Even novel reading was regarded as evil in the little Litchfield home. The foremost novelist of America suffered, in her childhood, the stern discipline of a Calvinist father, and endured such works as the ponderous *Toplady on Predestination*: This may have been the very germ for the name Topsy — not yet born in this world, but destined to "just grow'd up" in little Harriet's mind.

A great change came when the Beecher family moved to what was regarded then as the capital of the West — Cincinnati. The long trip began in the Fall of 1832, and on the way Harriet had an unusual experience. Her father made an appeal, in New York, in behalf of a poor student, Calvin E. Stowe, who sought a Biblical professorship. Harriet wrote breathlessly to a Hartford friend, "Father is to perform tonight in the Chatham Theatre! positively for the last time this season!" That was her most immediate contact with a theatre, and, coincidentally, the first *Uncle Tom's Cabin* was produced in a Chatham Theatre.

Once in Cincinnati, the Beechers really found themselves. Catherine established the Western Female Institute, with Harriet as a teacher. The latter continued to unfold creatively, and in the winter, when the editor of a new magazine, the *Western Monthly*, offered fifty dollars for the best short story, Harriet carried off the prize with *Uncle Tim*, a momentous event in her sheltered life. The title was changed in reprintings to *Uncle Lot*, but it anticipated a later and more famous character.

The poor professor of Biblical Literature in her father's seminary lost his wife, and Harriet's sympathy for the lonely, grief-stricken man culminated, after two years, in love and marriage. Her career as an author seemed to have ended, for with the exception of a few insignificant sketches and a geography, she produced almost nothing until 1851.

The eighteen years in Cincinnati, however, revealed to her the realities of the American local evil. Her own servant had been raised as a chattel in Virginia, auctioned off, then carted away to the Louisiana sugar plantations. Harriet often wrote letters for this Negress to the slave husband in Kentucky. Although traveling on business for his master

— 15 —

between Kentucky and Ohio, his pledge of honor was never broken, yet the master's promise of freedom was deferred time and again. Here the portrait of Uncle Tom kept growing more definitely in the mind of the future authoress.

Once, in the company of an associate teacher, Harriet crossed the river into Kentucky — and there the virus of slavery struck her with its full force. They stopped at an estate depicted later in the novel as Colonel Shelby's. Another time, she witnessed a Negress' separation from her husband, and her sale. The description of Legree came from her brother Charles, a clerk in New Orleans, who reported on a brutal overseer's methods. One wild night Harriet's husband and brother Henry drove to safety a fugitive and her infant, and that adventure provided Harriet with material for Eliza and the Senator Bird chapters.

Mrs. Stowe hoped to relate these episodes dramatically some day, but the impulse for the actual writing came years later. In February, 1851, while seated in a little church at Brunswick, Maine, listening to communion services, there came to her suddenly a forceful insight into the Negro's suffering. She visualized clearly a slave dying under blows of a whip, and it seemed to her that Christ was speaking: "Inasmuch as ye have done it unto one of the least of these My brethren, ye have done it unto Me!" Quivering in every nerve, Mrs. Stowe hastened home.

That Sunday afternoon she locked herself in her room, seizing writing paper and pencil. When the foolscap gave out, she salvaged scraps of coarse brown grocery wrapping. The first part committed to paper was Uncle Tom's death.

She put the manuscript aside for several weeks, as domestic cares called her elsewhere. She was afraid, too, that Mr. Stowe would not approve her literary labor. But she discovered him, one day, leaning over it; he had found the brown wrapping paper by chance. He read it avidly, excited by curiosity, admiration — tears. At his suggestion

Mrs. Stowe decided to make this material the climax for a much longer story.

The *National Era*, an abolition paper in the heart of Washington, printed it on June 5, 1851, intending to serialize it for three or four numbers only. It was as though the Mississippi levees had burst wide open, and the momentum carried Mrs. Stowe on and on and on. She confessed later, "I could not control the story; it wrote itself." And it ran through fifty numbers, not being completed until the following April.

Then Mrs. Stowe submitted it to several publishers in New York and Boston. They were apprehensive of a "nigger" book, as it was then called, and feared the odium of its publication would ruin them.

A Boston publisher's wife became greatly interested, having followed the installments in the Washington paper, and she importuned her husband, John P. Jewett, "Bring it out in book form."

He refused, "These abolition novels are ever unpopular — and unprofitable."

The disreputable bookstalls on Chatham Square, indeed, were tangible witness to these liabilities; the dusty discount morgues held many earlier failures.

"They have no sale whatever," he insisted. "No novel about slavery can be expected to sell."

"The story was so compelling in the newspaper," continued his wife.

"Now, periodicals are different. Take Greeley, for example. He can carry that slogan, 'Spread the Truth,' in his weekly — and do it for years. But how many readers will be sufficiently interested to buy his wildcat reforms when placed between hard covers?"

He meant a four-page weekly, *The Log Cabin*, which Horace Greeley launched a decade before, and which may have suggested to Mrs. Stowe, indirectly, the title for her novel.

"It served its purpose in electing General Harrison to the Presidency," went on Jewett. "But I cannot for the life of me see why Greeley keeps on publishing it."

Mr. Jewett refused to run the risk. But his wife's nagging efforts made life so unbearable that he, poor henpecked man, was driven to accept Mrs. Stowe's story. The unhappy publisher then found it difficult to sleep.

As her literary mentor, Mrs. Stowe's husband suggested that she drop the *e* from her name ("it incumbered the flow and euphony"), but beyond that he was as helpless as she. They then consulted a friend, Philip Greeley, the Congressman from the Boston district, who predicted, "You will be lucky if you get enough out of the novel to buy yourself a new silk dress."

When the two-volume novel, with frontispiece depicting a cabin in woodcut, appeared, the Congressman studied it dourly.

"It has very little chance of success," he prophesied, "being as it is on an unpopular subject — and by a woman at that!"

But unlike the abolition tracts of the period, Mrs. Stowe's novel was charged by an inner, exciting power; there seemed to be involuntary promptings impelling its very action. To many critics she had no talent at all; they said she lacked classic restraint, that she was all instinct. Her prose had bewildered even the editors, who pooled their abilities in disentangling her syntax; the proofreaders wept over her punctuation. Mrs. Stowe's upbringing may have precluded the theatre, but — by some strange agency — she possessed all its peculiar qualities: pathos, sharply-drawn types, tense conflict, melodrama.

The novel reached out and gripped the hearts of readers. Turning the pages, they heard the cracking of the slavedriver's whip; they sat up nights, tense and disturbed by grief, fear, hate, love, religion. One woman wrote that she could no more leave the novel than she could abandon a dying child!

Boys hawked the book in the street, their apple baskets filled to the top. Three thousand copies were sold the first day, then ten thousand — a second edition went to press the following week. The demand could not be met by the eight power presses, running without a letup, day and night. Within a year one hundred and twenty editions were issued!

As for Jewett — who had feared loss of prestige for his publishing house — he completely lost sight of the risk in the amazing windfall. And it came to be as Lowell said, "Consider yourself to be in the position of all the world before the Mansion of our Uncle Thomas (as I suppose we must call it now), it has grown so respectable."

Nothing like it had been known before. During the first five years half a million copies were distributed in the States. And *Uncle Tom's Cabin* became an emotional torch for scores of theatrical troupes, lighting up the far distant corners of the nation.

Chapter II

IN THE BEGINNING —

*Would not go down as part and parcel
of the burnt-cork melodrama of the Bowery.*
—*South. Lit. Messenger*, Oct., 1852

A FEW BOYS WERE "playing theatre" in a stable loft on South Street, Baltimore. Scrawled on the outer door, facing an alley, was the stark feature title: *The Shivering Idiot*!!! a doleful tragedy in seven acts. You could get an idea of the patrons from the range of admission: "Boys, three cents; little boys, two cents — Come early, and bring your fathers and mothers!!!"

The "all-star" cast — it couldn't have been otherwise — was gaining a foothold in the profession. Among them were the future comedian, Stuart Robson (in whose barn the stage was rigged up), the ill-fated John Wilkes Booth, John Sleeper Clarke, and Edwin Booth. The last two, insurgents of the group, held out for "terms"— something they had heard around the Baltimore Museum, to wit, "one-fifth of the gross receipts."

Alas! there were no receipts for the principals that day, for the performance ended abruptly — at a critical moment, too. Robson's mother swooped down upon them:

"My Stuart is intended for the pulpit—not the theatre!"

This necessitated refunding eighteen cents to the audience, who scampered out, believing that the added attraction outstripped by far the rest of the performance.

However, S. Robson soon had the satisfaction of seeing his name actually *printed* on a playbill. A great comedian, John E. Owens, was then managing the Baltimore Museum and Gallery of Fine Arts, and the novice, John Sleeper Clarke, got a small part with him. Aided by Clarke, the would-be tragedian, Robson, aged sixteen, persecuted Mr. Owens until an opening was secured.

Robson's first engagement fell on the evening of January 5, 1852, a day unusual for more than one reason. Advertised was the very first dramatization of Mrs. Stowe's novel, under the flamboyant subtitle, *The Southern Uncle Tom!*

How this came about, and what inspired it, went back a few weeks previous. The manager was then called from rehearsals backstage by an odd-looking, excited visitor, who introduced himself:

"I'm Prof. Hewett."

"We don't have many scholars dropping in," Owens admitted.

"As a citizen of Baltimore, I'm using every means to counteract a vital danger. I have here—" his hand reached into a deep coat pocket, producing a mysterious package.

"What is it?"

"A version from the slavery viewpoint, an answer to Mrs. Stowe's libel. Her novel has not yet appeared in its entirety in the *National Era*, but I have lifted certain scenes from it."

Owens studied the script, "Well, it might make a good dramatic offset — might catch the Baltimore public."

"My Uncle Tom is not portrayed as a martyr, nor shown in less piety, but with absolute devotion to his master."

"I get the flavor in this—" Owens read aloud one of Tom's excessive speeches: " 'Sha! I was born a slave, I have lived a slave, and, bress de Lord, I hope to die a slave!' "

"That's when a sanctimonious Northerner urges Tom to break his shackels."

"I see you have no title for your play."

"You know the theatregoing public better. I left that for you. Can you suggest an infallible title?"

"Well, Mr. and Mrs. Barney Williams won audiences with *Ireland as It Is*, Chanfrau enjoyed popularity with *New York as It Is* — now, *Uncle Tom's Cabin as It Is* should be another drawing card!"

In this curious dramatization, *Uncle Tom's Cabin as It Is*, young Robson played Horace Courtney. He had all of twenty lines to speak, one of the scenes calling for him to strike Uncle Tom — whereupon Uncle Tom was to wrest the lash free, and lay it over Courtney! The lines were affectingly tender, meant for the display of any dormant tragic power in the performer. And Robson was determined to be a great tragedian. The first line he spoke was pure pathos: "Farewell, my mother,—farewell, perhaps forever!" This line was most gratifying to Robson's taste as he embraced every variation, every delicate shade of tragedy, and he expected to make a great sensation that night.

But as Robson stepped before the footlights, his stable-loft *sang-froid* deserted him suddenly, and he stumbled on his first stage fright. He had overstudied the line; the high-pitched voice, quavering with ludicrous tremolo, touched off the audience.

He decided to sever his connection with the Baltimore Museum that night, but Owens, observing his plight, came over. "That was, indeed, the finest piece of acting, sir, that I have ever seen in all my life!" he said.

Robson was young enough to believe it. When the prompter told him that he had brought the wrong kind of tears to their eyes, it is a matter of record that the actor replied: "I am aware, sir, that I made myself sufficiently ridiculous without your reminding me of it. But as they laughed so much at my tragedy, I will give them an opportunity to honor my comedy—for I intend to become a low comedian." And a low comedian he became.

As for the rest of the play, the slaveholders seated in the theatre couldn't swallow it, sugar-coated as the black pill was.

The manager, while enacting Tom, whispered to the actors, "You can see them turn around, wink, and smile, all over the house!"

It was a flat failure. Afterward it was done at the Marshall Theatre, in Richmond, Virginia, receiving the same cold reception.

Soon other playwrights became interested in Mrs. Stowe's novel. The *Southern Literary Messenger* first called attention to its dramatic possibilities: "Mrs. Stowe reminds us of the ventriloquial vaudevilles of the facetious Mr. Love, who, individually representing the entire dramatic personæ, is compelled to withdraw as Captain Cutandthrust, before he can fascinate his audience with Miss Matilda Die-away."

When the novel was published in the Spring, a gentleman named Asa Hutchinson, a popular temperance concert singer, asked permission to dramatize it. Out of a New England Puritan conscience Mrs. Stowe replied: "I have considered your application and asked advice of my different friends, and the general sentiment of those whom I have consulted so far agrees with my own, that it would not be advisable to make that use of the work which you propose. It is thought, with the present state of theatrical performances in this country, that any attempt on the part of Christians to identify themselves with them will be productive of danger to the individual character, and to the general cause. If the barrier which now keeps young people of Christian families from theatrical entertainments is once broken down by the introduction of respectable and moral plays, they will then be open to all the temptations of those who are not such, as there will be, as the world now is, five bad plays to one good. However specious may be the idea of reforming dramatic entertainments, I fear it is wholly impracticable, and as a friend to you should hope that you would not run the risk of so dangerous an experiment. The world is not good enough yet for it to succeed. I preserve a very pleasant recollection of your family, and of the gratification I have derived from the exercise of your talents, and it gives me pleasure to number you among my friends."

The frustrated playwright was perhaps consoled by his family, "Well, what can you expect? She's the daughter of a minister, the wife of another, and the sister of a half-dozen preachers — her whole background will not permit it."

A "first production" took place soon, in New York, five months after the novel appeared. Charles Western Taylor, an actor in Purdy's company at the National Theatre, dashed off a "catch-house" adaptation, which opened on a Monday, August 23rd, sharing the bill with a variety of specialties. The great Herr Cline, a tight-rope walker, performed; and — to the spectator's astonishment — made three changes of character without leaving the swaying rope! T. D. Rice appeared in the burlesque, *Otello*, in which was heard Desdemona's fantastic retort to Othello's request for her handkerchief: "Blow yah nose on yah sleeve, nigger, and git on wid de show!" And we must remember here that Rice was the creator of *Jim Crow*, bringing Negro minstrelsy to the fore. As for the feature, *Uncle Tom's Cabin* — it was condensed to one hour's acting time.

Of all audiences, those attending the first night of Taylor's drama were the most puzzzled. Many were familiar with Mrs. Stowe's novel, but had the greatest difficulty recognizing the characters.

"I read the book," said one man. "But these names listed in the programme—who are they? Except for Uncle Tom and Chloe, I can't say they are familiar to me."

"The names have been changed," whispered another.

"Then why is Uncle Tom mentioned?"

"Because, properly, he is mentioned in the title. That's the playwright in the role."

"They say he's a skillful adaptor."

"Right! There are three plots in Mrs. Stowe's novel, and what we see tonight is evidently the romance part."

"The fortunes of George and Eliza Harris?"

"Right! Only their names have been changed to Edward and Morna Wilmot."

"I see it now. Which ones are St Clair, Eva, and Topsy?"

"It has been found necessary to delete them altogether."

In the play, as spectators soon discovered, Uncle Tom was depicted as a sort of Caliban to the Little Ariel; the martyrdom was left out, and it all ended happily.

That inept affair, in fact, bore no more similarity to the novel than did Prof. Hewett's. The Baltimore play, however, was not called *Uncle Tom's Cabin*, but Taylor's was. The New York *Herald* accepted Taylor's attempt as a true dramatization, and warned the public of its inflammatory possibilities.

A critic from the New York *Sunday Dispatch* went to the theatre fully expecting to behold benches torn from the floor by a furious mob. He had in mind an earlier riot at the Bowery Theatre, when a ballet-master, George W. Smith, was driven from the stage because the audience clamored for Julia Turnbull, and would not tolerate Signora Ciocca's dancing. The critic now left C. W. Taylor's drama, commenting, "The piece is perfectly harmless, in fact, there is nothing in it whatever." He found the dialogue "dull," the audience "listless."

As business fell off, more numbers were added. T. D. Rice introduced other Ethiopian specialties, and Herr Cline leaped higher and more energetically on the *corde elastique*, supplying the suspense which the drama sadly lacked. But the play slumped so badly that it was withdrawn on September 4th. It had been performed exactly eleven times. It saw a few, scattered additional performances, but failed signally.

A month and four days later a history-making version opened at Troy, New York. The following year, this same version came to the National Theatre where Taylor's play had failed, and set a precedent with its extraordinary run.

CHAPTER III

MR. HOWARD AND THE FOXES

> *The question has been asked would it be improper for clergymen and church members to visit the National Theatre during the performance of this piece? Our answer would be, as there is no other theatrical representation given with it, there would be no impropriety in the religious portion of the community witnessing it. It is a moral, religious, and instructive illustration of the justly celebrated work of Mrs. Harriet Beecher Stowe and is most faithfully dramatized. The representation of Little Eva, by little Cordelia Howard, should be witnessed by every lady in the land. We are informed that the Manager has taken every precaution that no disorderly person be admitted to the Theatre during the performance of this great production.*
> —Advertisement

IT WAS A PERIOD WHEN PURITANIC influences made up the stuff of everyday life. The New England conscience had misgivings; so much — that pants were referred to discreetly as "unmentionables," and rosemantled the cheek of modesty upon the mention of a mother about to give birth, even when expressed so subtly as in a "delicate condition," or "great expectations," or about to place herself in the hands of the *accoucheuses* — meaning midwives. Locofoco matches were preached against as an invention of the devil. Such a depression of spirits distinguished Calvin's followers that if the true believer of predestination succeeded in being as miserable as possible, it was accepted as proof of his rectitude; but if he smiled, it became an unbecoming levity, and laughter was sinful. Promenading in cemeteries was the popular diversion of the day.

Playacting, of course, was anathema to the ultra-religious background. If Shakespeare was read, it was for his moral worth; but if enacted in a "the-ay-ter," it was shunned. The house of Satan pandered to the vices of the weak brothers unable to resist the seductive lure. One celebrated preacher at Indianapolis, in 1846, classed together "vagabonds, fiddlers, fashionable actors, strumpet dancers, dancing horses, and boxing men." With admirable naiveté he asked his congregation if they knew a theatre in which a prayer at the beginning and end of the performance would not be considered an intrusion! In Brooklyn, where Mrs. Stowe joined her brother Henry after the publication of her novel, there had been no theatre over a long period. When the residents of the City of Churches — as Brooklyn was called — decided to build its first playhouse, the edifice was called an Academy of Music. A firm stand was taken against the installation of a curtain, the solemn citizens arguing, "A curtain is intended to conceal something — and concealment suggests impropriety."

Although Boston, in the early forties, had long since repealed old restrictions from the city's ordinances, the inbred prejudice against matters theatrical still prevailed. One shrewd manager, Moses Kimball, hit upon a subterfuge that at last attracted a great number of hostile potential theatregoers. In June, 1841, his establishment, at the corner of Tremont and Bromfield Streets, underwent a redecoration, and the puzzled Bostonians, who stopped to study it on the sidewalk, wondered at the meaning. A large van drew up near the curb one afternoon, and into the building poured an odd assortment of stuffed mummies, fowls in glass bells, minerals in glass cases, wax figures, and other curios. The designing manager announced the formal opening of "The Boston Museum and Gallery of Fine Arts," and appealing to the intelligent classes, he invited them to these "branches of learning." The spacious music-saloon, seating 1200 persons, had been converted into an auditorium; *and here dramatic performances could be given without the disreputable word "theatre" being connected with the enterprise.* The Museum was closed on Saturday evenings so that the eve of the Lord's Day could be observed.

Those who avoided the moral impropriety of visiting the theatre now formed the habit of going to lectures on animal magnetism, table-rapping seances, and what became most popular — Public Temperance Concerts, or revivals. Manager Kimball met the demand with a realistic portrayal of a drunkard's downfall, reproduced in wax, in the gallery of the Museum. Here were drawn Boston's morbid audiences. When the sights of stuffed birds and beasts had exhausted their educational faculties, a thrifty New England conscience caused them to ascend the stairs, to a lecture hall where a great moral idea was expounded on a bare platform!

The all-engrossing topic of the day was Temperance, for the panic of 1837 resulted in austere abstinence. In Boston public sentiment was aroused to such a pitch, by 1844, that pedestrians were stopped on the streets, and it was not unusual for them to sign the pledge several times in a single afternoon.

The proprietor of the Boston Museum was very much impressed. He pondered not a little, in turn, at the density of the crowds before the wax figures, in the uncertain candlelight, illustrating the evils of an inordinate appetite for the wine cup. As Kimball gauged the public temper, he sought out a playwright, William H. Smith, to capitalize on the situation. Then he engaged a company of all the available players in Boston, and impatiently awaited the opening night, February 26th, of *The Drunkard! or the Fallen Saved!* It was purely didactic, of a flowery verbosity, and designated on the bill as a "new moral and domestic drama of great local interest (written expressly for this Establishment)." It was divided into "parts" instead of acts, and visitors believed that attendance at the "Deacon's Theatre," as the Museum was soon called, was quite different from going to a playhouse. In the programme a tactful reference was made to the experienced taxidermist at the Museum, for the convenience of patrons who wished to preserve pet birds or quadrupeds.

Wonder of wonders! *The Drunkard* saw one hundred performances, phenomenal in those days, and on the occasion of a temperance parade, it played five times in one day. Public sentiment was stirred to such a height that rabid drys marched through Boston streets advocating prohibition and urging people to see the drama. The movement died down, however, when charges were brought that the Museum proprietor himself had inspired the demonstration.

What interests us in *The Drunkard* is that most of the cast were connected with the earliest successful dramatization of *Uncle Tom's Cabin.* The directing power was the soft-spoken, twenty-four-year-old Nova Scotian, George Cunnabell Howard, who enacted the part of Farmer Stevens. He had left Halifax, where his future had been promising enough, because his gentle nature was set against the whole mercantile life. He wrote verses, setting many to music. As a boy, he had come in contact with some wandering actors who set him on his course, and, in 1838, at eighteen, he came to Philadelphia, where he made his theatrical debut. Then he struck Boston. He dropped the middle name Cunnabell because he did not wish to wound the pride of his family, and further, a dramatic instinct warned him that Cunnabell would do him mischief by appearing in print as Cannibal — leaving him wide open to the wit of his critics. As Mr. George Howard, therefore, he enacted many walking gentleman parts. Extremely handsome, he was called the *jeun premier* of the Boston Museum.

Aloof and scholarly, he nevertheless took time out from his studies to fall in love with the reigning favorite, Caroline E. Fox, a fifteen-year-old girl, playing Sally Lawton in *The Drunkard*.

In those days, a young suitor was expected to lay siege first to the mother's heart. Accordingly, he directed his attentions to Mrs. Fox, who was Thoda in the temperance drama (she was listed as Miss W. Fox). In green-room conversations, young Howard soon learned that Mrs. Fox had been Emily Wyatt before her marriage. Left a widow, with four children, an animating spirit made her organize her brood into a troupe called "The Little Foxes," or "The Fox Children." They traveled through bleak New England towns, doing concert turns on dining-room tables in country hotels. Their entire orchestra was John B. Hough, later famous in his own right, who stimulated their talents with a shrill fiddle.

"The little troupe, while it lasted," Mrs. Fox recalled, during one of Howard's visits at her home, "assured us a comfortable income. Then they grew up — 'Laff', especially, stood too tall in his stocking feet to be a bonafide infant prodigy."

" 'Laff'?"

"My husband was very patriotic, and named our eldest son George Washington Lafayette Fox. It was shortened considerably, later, by other members of our family — to 'Laff'."

"And Miss Caroline —" with intense interest.

"Did I tell you that she made her first stage appearance right here in Boston, when only four years old? The Kembles selected her as one of the children in *The Stranger*, during that Spring of 1833."

The mother untied a precious bundle of playbills in her lap.

"In the *Forty Thieves* she went on as a fairy, and in *Rip Van Winkle* she was the little daughter so many times.

Whenever a child was needed, my little Caddy was always called. These show her with Edwin Forrest, J. R. Scott . . . ."

The young suitor was lost in reflection.

"I was saying," Mrs. Fox continued as she poured tea into two little cups, "Caddy has come thru for us gloriously, and we owe most of it to Mr. Kimball. You remember those three performances of *The Golden Axe* spectacle?"

"When Mr. Kimball lured the Bostonians from their Christmas dinners? I certainly do."

"Caddy's engagement began then. As long as they're eager to see her dance hornpipes and Highland flings between pieces, we'll stay in Boston."

Whereupon the *jeun premier* of the Boston Museum breathed freely.

"It's all remarkable," he declared, once more in stride, "especially with all of you in *The Drunkard*. Your son excels as Henry Evans. I understand you have other ties in our company."

"Mr. G. H. Wyatt—I hope you like him as that villainous Lawyer Cribbs. However, Mr. G. C. Germon holds up the more philanthropic aspect of our family in the Arden Rencelow role. Now, his wife as Marie Wilson . . . ."

"Quite a family!"

It was really a short courtship. On October 12th, the newly named Mrs. G. C. Howard made her last appearance under her maiden name, supporting Mrs. Barrett in an appropriately entitled play, *Love's Sacrifice.*

Beyond doubt, the earlier experiences of his mother-in-law left a deep influence upon G. C. Howard. Caroline came home breathlessly, one day, "Mr. Kimball is vacating the Bromfield Street house and moving to a new building, and George has decided not to go along!"

"Why?" asked Mrs. Fox.

"He wants to try his luck in the outlying towns."

"Good for him — my boy!"

"He's obtained the rights to *The Drunkard*."

When Mr. Howard arrived, later, his pocket held the prize.

"But isn't the play too long — I mean the way we gave it at the Museum?" asked Mrs. Fox.

"We'll condense it."

"Even if we pool our two families, we'll still be short in casting —"

"We'll omit many characters. I intend to change the names of the remaining ones. By the way, we'll also put on *The Gambler, or Lost and Won*."

The Howard company started out, visiting the isolated towns of New England. They made a swing of the general store circuit, hanging up strange playbills under flickering kerosene lamps, and selling tickets over a cracker barrel. Mr. Howard was convinced that the inhabitants wanted irreproachable entertainment, and that the theatre could convey as worthy lessons as the pulpit.

Later, they settled in Providence, Rhode Island, where, from 1846 to 1850, they gave regular performances. Afterwards, with two of the Fox brothers as co-managers, Howard leased Brown Hall in South Main Street. The continuing success encouraged him to move into larger quarters farther north, occupying Cleveland Hall. The admission price was low, only twelve and a half cents, and so respectable their offerings that a story was then current about the conversion of a Providence citizen.

The old gentleman — so ran the story — brought up under the strict tenets of the day, regarded the theatre as the most perilous gateway to Erebus, and he often expressed this conviction to his family. But one day, news of a dreadful nature reached him: his son had gone clandestinely to "Howard and Foxes!" Hurriedly, the panic-stricken parent ran to save the lad at all costs. He reached the Hall, and entered. He glanced about him to rescue his offspring from his impending downfall—when lo!—the curtain rose, the play commenced, and his interest was riveted. Soon all reverential fear left him, he was fascinated by the acting, and forgot completely the object of his mission. And when the performance was over, he walked home with his son, arm in arm. He could not find it in his heart to censure his son for that which had equally captivated himself!

One day, unfortunate news came to Howard and Foxes. "The Providence Museum is opening in opposition to us!" a troubled actor informed them. "And they say there's unlimited capital backing it!"

"We'll lose all our customers, I'm afraid," Howard said, gloomily.

Because of this formidable rival, Howard and the Foxes had to relinquish their lease in July, 1850. With the dispersion of the company, many decided to try their fortunes in New York.

"The National Theatre has an opening for a Yankee type comedian," said Laff Fox. "There's a Christopher Strap character in a play to be put on in October, and I've been promised the part. How about coming along?"

And the Howards joined him.

Two plays in which they appeared, during the stay in New York, bore prophetic titles. G. W. L. Fox enacted Rideout Ruggles in *The Fugitive Slave*, on March 19th, about three months before Mrs. Stowe's first installment in print. In the other, during the second week of July, Mrs. G. C. Howard took the lead in a play called *St. Clara's Eve* — similar to Eva St. Clare.

In the Fall of that year, 1851, the Howards picked up a rich plum. All the way upstate, Peale's Troy Museum needed a manager, and Garry A. Hough, the lessee, came to New York for the purpose of engaging George C. Howard. As a lure, the lessee took from his pocket a few interesting advertisements, with which to prod him. One of the "bills" described the Museum's assets: "Curiosities of every description including beasts, birds, reptiles, minerals, fossils, works of art from the heads of the native savage, and the more finished from civilized artists, — Grand Cosmoramas, fifty Burmese figures in their native costumes and different castes, superior electrical machines and admirable paintings of the Great Sea Serpent." Another, which the proprietor knew would drive home his point, conveyed: "Theatrical performances and scenic exhibitions; on Saturdays, the play. . . . adapted to the taste of juvenile visitors."

This was an irresistible offer. To the sound of the dinner bell, Howard selected his company: his wife, his brothers-in-law, Mrs. Fox, George L. Aiken and h's brother Frank (cousin of his wife), and others. One member of that company might have been classified as actor's baggage, namely, "Little Cordelia," almost three years old, born to the Howards in Providence.

On their arrival in Troy the Howards boarded at the American Hotel. The Museum, Mr. Howard learned, was in Boardman's building, on the northeast corner of River and Fulton (Elbow) Streets, and was crammed full with dusty curiosities.

On his first visit to the Museum the lessee pointed out their moral worth:

"No one can traverse these elegant rooms," he bragged, with proper solemnity in his voice, "and thru the medium of old-time relics hold communion with past ages, without coming away, if not better, at least a wiser man. . . . Mr. Howard, that's what I tell'em."

Indeed, ranged around the rooms were stuffed birds and beasts of every description.

"From the smallest humming bird t' the American eagle," intoned Hough, dominated by his possessions, "and from the monkey t' the rhinoceros."

There were likewise strange fish, fossils, minerals, shells, sharing one common quality — they were rare, curious, and in great abundance. When Mr. Howard drew back at the sight of one mysterious creature, the lessee, smilingly, assured him,

"That's a duck-billed platypus."

Mr. Howard at once took cognizance of what Hough claimed, that it was "second to none" — in Troy, at least. The lessee was tireless in pointing out its beauties and verities. Howard seemed to agree, not because of the different specimens of the flamingo, crocodiles, or the cosmoramic views, but because he was ruminating on his first posters for a repertoire in accordance with Hough's wishes — "adapted to the taste of juvenile visitors." The new manager aimed to win a reputation.

One afternoon, while looking about for other dramatic pieces for the approbation of Troy audiences, Mr. Howard came unexpectedly upon a small bundle of talent. An adaptation of *Oliver Twist* had been announced, with Mrs. Howard as Oliver. Little Dick, the sick pauper child, usually omitted from popular versions, was retained; those familiar with the novel may recall the tiny lad who bids Oliver such a tearful farewell when he runs away from the poorhouse. Someone suggested to the manager that his little daughter be dressed as Little Dick and placed behind the paling, to whom Oliver could talk. It was without any idea that she would be more than a "dummy;" but when, during rehearsal, the mother caught the baby up and went through the scene, they were all taken unawares by the response, just in the proper place, too: "Dood-by—tum again."

"Well, now," said Mrs. Howard, "if she is going to do anything like that, better teach her the lines."

The story of that production has been told so well by the wife of C. K. Fox, that it can hardly be improved. Little Cordelia, accordingly, during the day, was taught in her mother's lap the speeches of Little Dick. When night came the fat baby face was painted skilfully to represent consumption; duly clad in her brother's suit, and a little spade in her hand, Cordelia Howard made her first appearance on any stage.

On came the fugitive Oliver, while Cordelia, according to direction, dug vigorously at the pile of dirt dumped in the corner.

Mrs. Howard, as Oliver, said: "I'm running away, Dick."

"Lunning away, is you?" replied the tiny chit, with an immediate perception of the character, and an utter disregard of the words taught her, imparting the sense of the scene.

"I'll come back and see you some day, Dick," continued Mrs. Howard.

"It yont be no use, Olly, dear," sobbed the little actress. "When oo tum back, I yont be digging 'ittle graves. I'll be all dead an' in a 'ittle grave by myself."

This in a voice tremulous with feigned emotion, yet clear as a bell, and distinctly heard by everyone in the theatre. Such a shower of tears as swept over that house! Actors and auditors were alike affected. The Oliver, naturally enough, broke down completely, but Cordelia's and her parents' fortunes were made that night.

Cordelia was advertised as "The Youthful Wonder Generally Called the Child of Nature." It became a practice with managers in later years to print "The Child of Nature" after the names of all infant prodigies who attempted Little Eva. The phrase may have meant, originally, a role of naiveté, in which the little actress was all innocence, totally ignorant of certain facts of life never mentioned in a mixed gathering of the sexes. But what Cordelia's proud father really meant was: that his daughter was a *born* actress, that an audience had never seen anything more natural and beautiful than the way she played Little Dick (later Little Eva); that she had acquired no training for it, that she could not have helped acting it. And perhaps the managers of the thousands of Evas of the future meant the same thing.

The Howards, naturally, felt that such infantile emotional talent should not be wasted, and decided to exhibit "The Child of Nature" in the outlying towns. In those days few companies ventured to these remote places, and Little Cordelia's visit was an unforgetful occasion. Many stories are told about those early audiences. Once in Lowell, Mass., the curtain fell at the end of *Oliver Twist*, but the audience remained strangely quiet, retaining their seats for a few minutes. The manager had to step out before the curtain, and announce, "Ladies and gentlemen, I wish to inform you that the play has terminated!"

The proud father ransacked other plays to exploit the little actress's capabilities. It is not recorded who first suggested that the precocious child be cast as Little Eva, but the whole country was discussing Mrs. Stowe's novel just then, and tears were being shed for Eva everywhere. Howard, too, like most Canadians, was interested in the abolition cause. Here, then, was the very role for Cordelia! His four-year-old daughter would shine in it most brilliantly!

At that time each stock company carried a playwright of its own, and generally useful in this way was George L. Aiken, a twenty-two-year-old cousin, who, like the Foxes, came from Boston. He had made his first appearance as an actor in June, 1848, when the Howards were in Providence, as Ferdinand in *The Six Degrees of Crime*. He was listed as a "juvenile man" in the company.

"Pode," called Mr. Howard, dismissing the rest of the players for the day, and young Aiken, who answered to the peculiar nickname of "Pode," listened to the manager. "How long ago did you first try your hand as a hack-dramatist — of novels, I mean?"

Courtesy of Harvard Theatre Collection

George L. Aiken

"Well," came the answer, "there was *Orion, the Gold Beater*, in January, last year."

"How much weight did your gold beater have with audiences?"

"Only a few performances at the National Theatre, in New York."

"Then I must be thinking of that play of last June," said Mr. Howard.

"My blank verse tragedy?" eagerly.

"I refuse to antagonize you, my boy."

"Sir, *Helos the Helot, or the Revolt of Messene* was advertised as a 'prize play.'"

"And ran but a night or two. What was it about?"

"It dealt with a noble Grecian who was slave to a Spartan general...."

"That's it! I've something a great deal better for you now. You can do it within a week."

And in a week Aiken completed the dramatization of *Uncle Tom's Cabin*. It was not difficult, for the novel was mostly in dialogue, and he faithfully copied entire speeches; thus were the local color, the Sunday-school beatitudes of Little Eva, the fervor of the devoted slave retained — Aiken's pen moved swiftly.

"What is embarrassing," confessed the young adaptor, when he showed it to Mr. Howard at the American Hotel, "is that the novel has enough material for three distinct plays."

"That's interesting," said Howard, studying Aiken's script in the kerosene lamplight.

"See here — I've marked the various chapters — these deal clearly with the personal fortune of George and Eliza Harris. Now here we have the account of Uncle Tom and Eva. And here — the history of Emmeline and Cassy."

"Rather ambitious for one novel," commented Howard.

"Worse! George Harris and his wife flee by way of

underground railroad to Canada, but Tom goes down the river to New Orleans...."

Young Aiken found that the play would have to jump from plantation scenes in Kentucky, through the Ohio River country, leap abruptly to the Quaker colony of Pennsylvania, on to New Orleans, featuring the St. Clare mansion, up into staid old Vermont, then to the murky byways of Simon Legree's Red River plantation — and to end by way of conjecture — at Heaven's own door, with Eva seen in a far better world by the dying Tom.

"The little stage of our Museum will have to capture somehow that passing, large geography," said Mr. Howard.

"But how?"

"We'll find a way out — if the characters can't. How have you divided the play?"

"Into four acts. With plenty of Eva for Cordelia."

The script handed to Mr. Howard was not the drama that became known later as "the" version. It was now left to Manager Howard's judgment and experience to make a wise selection of episodes, fitting them together in a more practical way. He knew "good theatre," and embodied all the salient points of the novel, linking together disjointed portions, and bringing out — in the staging — each character in bold relief.

The few incidents capable of dramatic treatment were scattered loosely in the two volumes, connected by three irregular plots. Now Howard altered the play radically, to form a consistent or plausible plot. New scenes had to be introduced, others cut short; many situations shaped themselves out in rehearsal. Ineffective lines were deleted, too, and many enhancing effects suggested. Oddly enough, several new characters — unknown to the novel — began to emerge. The active manager spent many sleepless nights. He also wrote verses for the play, and composed the music.

Manager Howard's troubles were not over. When casting time arrived, several members were hostile to the roles assigned them.

"I refuse to play Uncle Tom," said G. C. Germon, the leading man.

"Why?" asked Howard.

"I'm not going to play a Jim Crow darkey. It will jeopardize my reputation."

"How?"

"My very make-up as a Negro means burlesque, and Uncle Tom will make everybody laugh. I want to be a straight actor."

"But Uncle Tom is a new type," insisted the manager, "a type that will bring out the leading man's genius. It has to be created; it has so much pathos, and you will be the first to play it."

"Still, it's a Jim Crow part. It will ruin your play," the other stubbornly maintained.

"If you could only submerge yourself in the straight interpretation of the Negro," pleaded Howard, "there is no telling to what heights you will reach."

Germon yielded, his decision bringing him a success so great that he played nothing but Uncle Tom for the remainder of his life.

Topsy was quite a problem, too. Aiken had drawn her as a boy.

"That won't do," said Howard to the playwright. "You know the only man in our company who has appeared in Negro parts and whom we can cast as Topsy is six feet tall! I think the part should be rewritten for a girl, and assigned to Mrs. Germon."

But the manager found to his distress that Mrs. Germon, the ingenue, also refused to play Topsy because no woman had ever been asked to black up in the theatre.

Howard was at his wit's end.

"Who will play it?" asked Aiken, fearing that Topsy would have to be changed back again to a boy.

Then, in desperation, Howard suddenly turned to his wife. No one expected that the demure little figure at his side would attempt it.

"I will," she said.

And one rehearsal freed the manager from any uncertainty in the matter. Thus, largely through chance, Mrs. Howard created the role which embodied the very spirit of sportive mischief — and later became world famous.

Another member, William J. LeMoyne, also kicked at his traces. He had begun his career that same Autumn, playing in "stock" under Howard, as utility man, at a princely salary of six dollars a week. Now to advance in the profession, at that time, meant that he had to go through three successive grades: general utility, respectable utility, and responsible utility; the first corresponded to the "extras" of today; the second were rewarded with a line or two; and the third achieved a small part commensurate with their talent. The season had hardly begun when LeMoyne got the part of "old man," plus a visible increase of two dollars a week.

When the role of Deacon Perry was assigned to him, he balked,

"I won't play another 'old man.' I'm tired of them. I want to play low comedy."

Howard directed Aiken to rewrite the part *expressly* for LeMoyne's talents, and surprisingly, the actor made a comedy "hit" of the supposedly straight part of Deacon Perry.

When the difficulties of Manager Howard were smoothed out, the drama had its first public showing on September 27, 1852. That day the newspapers carried this advertisement:

TROY MUSEUM

Corner River and Fulton Streets

Manager . . . . G. C. Howard
Treasurer . . . . R. Cruikshank
Scenic-artist . . . . S. Hayes
Musical Director . . . . Prof. Barnekoy

MONDAY EVENING, Sept. 27, 1852

the new drama from Harriet Beecher Stowe's popular work
entitled

UNCLE TOM'S CABIN, OR LIFE AMONG THE LOWLY.

Uncle Tom. .Mr. G. C. Germon   Topsey. . . .Mrs. G. C. Howard
St. Clair. . .Mr. G. C. Howard   Aunt Ophelia. . . . .Mrs. E. Fox
Geo. Harris. . .Mr. G. L. Aiken   Eva. . . .Little Cordelia Howard
Eliza. . . . . .Mrs. G. C. Germon

to conclude with

THE FIRST NIGHT

Mr. Peter Paul Pearlbutton . . . . Mr. C. K. Fox

*Doors open at 7. To commence at 8. Admission, 25c.;
children half price; boys to gallery, 12½c.; box seats,
12½c extra; orchestra spring seats and cushioned armchairs, 25c. extra. Seats secured during the day.*

The curtain rose on a four-act drama faithfully retaining Mrs. Stowe's story at its best, and concluding with the
death of Little Eva. The running time was three hours and
fifteen minutes. Manager Howard dared not break entirely
with the practice of the day which held that a play must be
preceded by a curtain-raiser and followed by a farce. That
came later.

The dramatization may have had all the advance publicity of a best-seller, but there were, alas, many disadvantages: An earlier adaptation was a failure; Negro minstrelsy had to be bucked, besides. Worse, the coming presidential election, with Pierce the favorite candidate, engrossed the citizens of Troy. The *Daily Whig* did not even send a reporter to the theatre.

Aiken's name did not appear on the early programmes. Soon there were "last nights" and "benefits" for the principals, as was the fashion then. "Dely" had her farewell performances on October 18th and 25th, with printed notices, "Last appearance and benefit to Little Cordelia Howard, the youthful woman of four years, on which occasion she will play in both pieces. This evening positively the last night of the new Drama from Harriet Beecher Stowe's popular work." The manager advertised that he was compelled to withdraw the play after a few evenings more to make room for other pre-arranged attractions. Theatregoers, of course, rushed to the Museum — before it was too late!

"It has lived thru and survived several of the most exacting days preceding and succeeding the election, drawing houses," commented the *Budget* of November 6th, six weeks later, "and since that event has passed off, 'comes out' stronger than ever."

The play kept growing, day by day, and lines were incorporated from the predecessor, *Oliver Twist*. We heard Eliza saying now, "I'm running away, Uncle Tom...." And Cordelia, as in her portrayal of Little Dick, repeated, "I'm going there." When Tom asked, "Where, Miss Eva?" she pointed to the sky, "I'm going *there*, to the spirits bright, Tom; I'm going before long." The catch-lines had never been used with so sure a touch.

One day, a body of Troy citizens descended on the theatre.

"We want a further dramatization," they demanded.

The manager replied, "We're doing our best to satisfy you."

"But what we have here," complained one citizen, "is only the first volume of Mrs. Stowe's novel. We want a further account."

"Yes," chimed in others. "We want to see Uncle Tom's life on Legree's plantation."

"Wouldn't that be more fascinating!" they agreed.

Stimulated by the suggestion, the manager and the young playwright prepared a supplementary four-act play, which was advertised as:

Another New Drama on the Subject of UNCLE TOM'S CABIN
Dramatized by G. L. Aiken

Entitled, THE DEATH OF UNCLE TOM, OR THE
RELIGION OF THE LOWLY

The following characters will appear:

George Shelby . . . . G. L. Aiken
Deacon Perry . . . . L. Moyne
Legree . . . . C. M. Davis
Gumption Cute . . . . C. K. Fox
Topsey . . . . Mrs. Howard
Cassy . . . . Mrs. Germon
Emmaline . . . . Miss Emmons

The sequel ran several weeks, and then ceased to draw.

"I realize it a little too late," confessed Howard to his company. "It lacks coherency. It is too detached from the first volume. Perhaps" — he turned to Aiken, "if the two plays are combined, the story can be carried over the action of both."

Aiken welded the two short plays into a six-act drama, the form we have known since.

In those times an acting company was very small, for expenses had to be kept at a close minimum. With misgivings, therefore, the playwright brought the enlarged drama to Manager Howard. Accompanying him was his younger brother, Frank E. Aiken, visiting for a few days.

"It necessitates all of twenty-five roles," he said, hesitatingly.

"We'll leave the minor parts to the remaining members of our stock company. Now, Mr. LeMoyne can double Deacon Perry with Wilson, and Mr. John Davis will have to do the same with Legree and Haley. If Mr. Salter has no objection to blacking up as Quimbo —"

"The Tom Loker part should be in good hands."

"Mr. Asa Cushman has been with us since our days in Providence, in Cleveland Hall. Made his debut, you remember, as one of the villagers in *The Maid of Croissy* and was about the best talent we could draw from the town. It's about time we rewarded him with something he desires — the part of a 'heavy.' "

"Whom will you get for Eliza's child?"

"There's a Master Groat, who's caught Little Cordelia's fancy. She will not play with dolls any more. . . ."

"There's another insignificant bit, and it's not more than a 'feeder' — the part of Lawyer Marks. No possibility of doubling it with any other character."

Mr. Howard reflected a moment, then glanced at the younger Aiken.

"How old are you, Frank?" he asked.

"Seventeen."

"Then you will go on as Marks."

Frank Aiken thus became the original of what later developed into one of the foremost comedy roles on the American stage.

All the principal actors were closely related. The phenomenal success of *Uncle Tom's Cabin* became identified with one family, in so far as the original cast held three generations in one line. Little Cordelia's grandmother, Mrs. Emily Fox, played the New England spinster, Aunt Ophelia; papa enacted St. Clare; and mamma was Topsy, who, with padded shoulders, also doubled as Chloe.

And there was a sprinkling of uncles and cousins. Charles Fox, Mrs. Howard's brother, represented both Phineas Fletcher and the Yankee character, Gumption Cute. Mrs. Fox's nephew, George L. Aiken, did George Harris and George Shelby. The Germons were related to the Howards through Joseph Jefferson, the first; his granddaughter now enacted Eliza and Cassy, her husband portraying Uncle Tom. The Germon's two daughters, Nellie and Effie, in turn, also won reputations in the play; the latter was the original Aunty Vermont in Conway's version in Boston. With nine members of the family in the cast, it came near being a family reunion.

On November 15th the Troy newspapers carried this announcement: "Grand Combination of the two dramas on the same evening. The last week of *Uncle Tom's Cabin, or Life Among the Lowly, and Death of Uncle Tom or Religion Among the Lowly*. Little Cordelia Howard as Eva. The desire of the entire community being to see the work from beginning to end, and the manager wishing to gratify all patrons, is why this immense work is undertaken in one evening. Owing to the length of the drama, no other piece will be played. Change of time, doors open at 7, to commence at 1/4 to 8."

This exigency, as we shall see, brought a radical change to the American stage. In those days an evening's entertainment began at seven, or seven-thirty o'clock, at the very latest. It consisted of a five-act tragedy, a melodrama in two or three acts, "The whole to conclude" with the afterpiece, usually a burlesque, rounding out the fare toward one in the morning. The several *entr'actes* regaled the audience with singing, dancing, etc. The public certainly got its money's worth — at twenty-five cents for the dress circle, and twelve and one-half cents for the pit.

Later, when Manager Howard's play began its amazing run in New York, his innovation became permanent. Howard was right, afterward, in claiming: "I was the first, I may say, to introduce one-play entertainments. That is, till the advent of *Uncle Tom* in New York, no evening at the theatre was thought complete, without an afterpiece, or a little ballet-dancing. When I told the manager *Uncle Tom* must constitute the entire performance, he flouted the idea; said that he would have to shut up in a week. But I carried my point, and we didn't shut up, either. People came to the theatre by hundreds, who were never inside its doors before; we raised our prices, which no other theatre in New York could do, and we played *Uncle Tom* over three hundred times during that engagement."

At last! the curtain rose on the newly completed version, six acts, eight tableaux and thirty scenes. Many a die-hard may have felt that Manager Howard did not at all uplift the American drama in Troy, for he offered no Elizabethan blank verse and completely disregarded the Greek unities. Moreover, the characters used the idiom of the day, which must have nonplussed the followers of the classical school in Troy.

But Howard knew his business. The orchestra contributed generously at vital moments: when Eliza was pursued, hurried melodramatic music intensified the chase; and when Legree's whip struck Tom, each of the three blows was accompanied by a crashing chord. The beautiful songs were Howard's, with the exception of that sung by Uncle Tom in the third scene of Act V, "Old Folks at Home," which came from the pen of an unknown composer, one Stephen Foster. There were many comic interludes. Mrs. Howard's dancing as Topsy was the precursor of a school of Topsies doing "breakdowns."

Mr G. C. HOWARD,
IN
HIS ORIGINAL CHARACTER OF "ST CLARE"

IN
"UNCLE TOM'S CABIN"

Courtesy of Harvard Theatre Collection

His Directing Genius Set the Course of the Play

In true chromo style, the eight tableaux composed splendid pictures in a drama packed with lurid action. As the curtain descended, the characters held their positions for a minute, *frozen* — congealing them in the memory. When Legree raised his whip to strike Tom, he stood over him for a full sixty seconds; the respite taken out for gloat-ing made his crime the more heinous. Many of the tableaux were really Holy Pictures. Little Eva sat on Tom's knee, hung a wreath around his neck, and Tom allegorized, "Look yer; I'm the ox, mentioned in the good book, dressed up for the sacrifice." A scene later the two were under a large tree, the setting sun tinging the distant waters with gold — a Bible open on Eva's lap. When George and Eliza were saved by the Quakers, they knelt in thanksgiving, their child between them. One of the most famous tableau-curtains came at the end of the third act, when Eva, in virginal white, coughed and perished to sacred music; with protecting arms, a convoy of angels hovered over her from the "fly," and lifted her bodily to a better world. That tableau was rivaled only by the death of Uncle Tom, the playwright's directions calling for: *Clouds work on and conceal them, and then work off.* The very essence of allegory was in his description of the grand finale: *Gorgeous clouds, tinted with sunlight. Eva, robed in white, is discovered on the back of a milk-white dove, with expanded wings, as if just soaring upward. Her hands are extended in benediction over* St. Clare *and* Uncle Tom *who are kneeling and gazing up to her. Impressive music — Slow curtain.*

Howard's production was indigenous with the New England environment. That its sacred character greatly helped the play can be seen in the comment of the Troy newspapers. The *Budget*, on October 19, described the crowded house at the Museum when the drama was in its fourth week, and was convinced that the thrilling scenes "have drawn a class of auditors to the Museum who heretofore have rarely witnessed dramatic performances. They have been amply repaid, — and many who have heretofore opposed the stage, after seeing *Uncle Tom's Cabin,* have gone to their homes with better impressions in regard to it." The Troy *Daily Times*, the morning after the play's first performance, described the copious tears shed by the audience, "The play is

The Precursor of a School of Topsies

a good rebuke to those ranting abolitionists who are continually talking about slavery, yet who do not do anything to either free the slave or better his condition." It commented, two or three times a week, on the fact that "the most respectable" and the "best people" were seen at the play. "The Museum is thronged nightly with the most respectable audiences who witness the play with great satisfaction," the *Times* reported on October 11th; and three days later, "This play has brought out our first citizens, many of whom have never before entered the Museum. Manager Howard is reaping a great harvest."

Many were won over, further, by the Museum's canny manager. This letter, appearing in the *Times* of November 6th, conveyed his line of strategy:

MR. FRANCIS,—

I take pleasure in acknowledging the receipt of $5.00 from Miss Cordelia Howard, daughter of G. C. Howard, Esq., for the benefit of the Troy Orphan Asylum.

It appears to me that the imagination never conceived of a sweeter character than Little Eva, and it is exceedingly pleasant to find its living representation in the person and moral qualities of little Cordelia Howard, the truthful personator of that interesting and benevolent character.

Yours ob't. servant,

S. K. STOWE, *Treasurer*.

The play began to attract the clergy and thousands of devout sectarians who had never crossed the threshold of a theatre. And it may be mentioned here that G. C. Germon, through constantly playing the role, later caught some of the spiritual qualities of Uncle Tom, and became a very devout man.

Everyone in Troy went to see it. The play held the boards for ten weeks, and in a town of only 30,000 inhabitants. The *Budget*, on November 26th, described the furor: "Now in its 9th week, *Uncle Tom's Cabin* continues to draw its crowds of admirers nightly to the Museum. Never before did any play have such a run at this establishment. Its performance had been witnessed by over 25,000 people and the cry is still they come! Since the several parts have been united into one harmonious whole, the play has received an additional avalanche of admirers. Uncle Tom, Little Eva, Topsey and others taking characters in the play are nightly gathering fresh laurels in a field already brilliant with numberless theatrical triumphs."

On December 1st, *Uncle Tom's Cabin* closed in Troy. The amazing one hundred nights "was equal," Mr. Howard told a friend, "to about seven years' run in New York, when the population of the cities is considered." The record set by the play is still unbroken in Troy, although the population has doubled many times since.

Afterward Howard took the drama to Albany. Among the pleasant events in that city was the appearance of Madame de Marguerittes. At her suggestion copies in fresco of Night and Morning — "two immortal inspirations of the genius of Albany" — were placed over the proscenium of the otherwise dilapidated, old Green Street Theatre. Her "finished education" (as awed critics affirmed) shone forth in bright little pieces, written by herself, all dealing with dukes and duchesses. The great Madame de Marguerittes was determined now to demonstrate the "grand manner" in her own interpretation of Little Eva. She wanted to be Topsy, too, but the frantic pleas of playwright Alfred B. Smith made her relinquish it.

When her play opened, on January 17, 1853, the Albanians were frankly puzzled by her conception of Eva: the Madame was short, very stout, and gray haired, and

"*There are a great many things here that make me sad.*"
Uncle Tom's Cabin, Chapter XXIV.

LITTLE CORDELIA HOWARD

THE CHILD OF NATURE, AGED 5 YEARS.

In the Character of

EVA.

The Original personator of the part.

Courtesy of Harvard Theatre Collection

Her Precocity Was the Wonder of the Fifties

panted stertorously with a French accent. It was the first and most odd-looking Eva they had seen!

The arrival of the Howard company showed Albany the complete difference in the two Evas. Little Cordelia's education was not quite as "finished" as the Madame's — it had scarcely begun. Mr. and Mrs. Howard had become a little anxious about the education of "the Child of Nature," but the press notices somewhat relieved them. The Troy *Times* said: "Little Cordelia as little Eva has been the chief attraction in the Drama of *Uncle Tom's Cabin,* and by her truthful child-like representation has won the hearts of all our citizens. In course of the scenes in which she appears one can scarcely believe but that little Cordelia is *really* little Eva, so truthfully does she perform her part. She beats all youthful prodigies, *les petites,* etc., that we have ever seen."

However, the watchful parents became concerned about "Dely." Her schooling now began in earnest, but it was a routine consisting of the school day and a performance in the Museum at night. One of her schoolmates, the late Major Elihu R. Rockwood, frequently accompanied her in the trip from school to Museum for rehearsals (the play was still undergoing revision).

When the Howards left Albany for New York, they lost several members of the original company. Young Frank D. Aiken, for one, felt that he lacked sufficient training, and joined the traveling company of his uncle, George H. Wyatt, who advised him, "These are the days of wandering for actors, and they wander by the year, not by the week." William J. LeMoyne, the original Deacon Perry and Mr. Wilson, gave the play in the provinces. He married the Marie St. Claire of his cast, Sarah Green; then, crediting rumors of the Tom vogue, moved to Canada.

Now the Howard family was en route to New York, to capture the great city's patronage.

Against the backdrop of the eventful year, there was riven, adumbrated significance. The decade before the Civil War saw an unprecedented rush to our shores — a thirty-five percent increase in population — with the high-water mark in 1854; the potato famine was on in Ireland, while hard times gripped Germany. In 1852 we had twenty-three million people, three and a quarter millions of whom were slaves. The country began to be drawn closer together: A celebrated clipper ship, a year before, had made its record run between New York and San Francisco — by way of Cape Horn — in eighty-nine days and eighteen hours; now the lean steel rails, converging in Chicago, joined those of the East; the following year a route was surveyed for a railroad to the Pacific Coast.

The native genius of 1852 ushered in a great many innovations: the first national agricultural convention, the American Geographical Society, the Women's State Temperance Society, sprinkler installation, intercollegiate boat racing, the shoe pegging machine, the whale electric killing machine, authorized U. S. postage stamped envelopes, and the cast-iron bath tub. Workshops in the southern cities of New England, and the greater ones in New York and Pennsylvania, hummed with the impulse brought by Yankee ingenuity; the change from agricultural to the newer, industrial activity reached out as far as Ohio. In Philadelphia department stores began to hire women clerks, then the fair sex monopolized type-setting. Godey's, in 1852, originated the department headed, "Employment for Women;" the same year marked the opening of the first college for women, and the publication of the first book on obstetrics. A new word appeared — "lingerie," displacing the mysterious "white sewing" and "the white wardrobe" heard in parlors; if it added an inkling to the inner nature of things, it was fated to remain mysterious as ever (today department stores advertise them as "intimate apparel"). Advocates of a strange ample pair of pants devised by Amelia Bloomer gave it a trial in public, and the notoriety lasted five years.

The masculinity of the times, alas, was such that it cost one man the presidency. Although a hardened Indian fighter, and the conqueror of Mexico, General Winfield

Scott let slip in an unguarded moment that he was to have soup for supper; as no "red-blooded" man had anything to do with such a dainty dish, the ridicule that followed was a contributing factor to the General's defeat in the 1852 campaign.

Mrs. Stowe's novel, although creating much discussion, still seemed to have missed fire in the presidential election. One observer, Ticknor, complained bitterly of the apathy of the times: that the novel deepened the horror of servitude but did not affect a single vote. An election law, passed that same year, limited voting to "Every man of color, possessing freehold estate of the value of not less than $250, and qualified by residence as in the case of white voters." Rev. Calvin Fairbanks was found guilty that year of "stealing" Negroes at Louisville, and sentenced to fifteen years imprisonment.

However, the public was more interested in such news items as: the marriage of an eighty-year-old man, weighing three hundred pounds, to a nineteen-year-old girl, at Floyd's Fork, Kentucky; of a dog, its feet tied, being thrown into the Niagara, and going over the Falls uninjured; of a duel between a State Senator and an editor at Oak Grove, Sacramento, the law-maker killing his political opponent; and of the sensational arrest by the Cincinnati police of a man counterfeiting dimes. It was the year of the discovery of the planet Aquarius, whose brightness equalled a star of the ninth magnitude and could be seen with a telescope of very ordinary power, yet no one was much impressed. Something, that year, did have a noticeable effect on the public. There passed away in the primitive wilds of Chicago an old man, David Kennison, 116 years old, the last survivor of the "Boston Tea Party." That same Fall anti-renters up in Nassau, New York, following in the footsteps of David Kennison, disguised themselves as Indians, and threatened their landlord with violence unless he complied with their demands. He dispersed them all, killing one and wounding several others.

Considerable attention was focused on the usual disasters: rising of rivers, loss of crops, hailstorms, and gales at sea. Many steamers exploded with great loss of life, since steam was still in the experimental stages.

Ironically, the country sympathized with political fugitives — but only with those from abroad. Kossuth came over, and everyone went wild. They held a Congressional banquet in his honor, and he was presented with money and arms to free the Hungarians. In behalf of Irish exiles, President Fillmore received deputations from the various States; in New York many attempted to rescue a fugitive claimed by the British Government. Wild acclaim greeted the ninety-five Americans of the Lopez expedition in Cuba, who had been captured, sent to Spain, and then released because of popular feeling.

In the meantime, a group of citizens from South Carolina and Florida were seeking permission from California to colonize each rural district of that State with "no less than 2,000 slaves."

The political situation would not permit a subject in the theatre that might stir up an ill wind, at the least.

Chapter IV

CAPTAIN PURDY AND HIS ARGOSY

Oh, for a glimpse of the olden time,
When we sat in the National pit—
When Scott and Allen and Jones in their prime,
With such critics as we, made a hit!
When lean Fox and fat Herbert merry made
To gain them our boisterous praise,
And drown'd was the music Peterschen played
In the racket we would raise.
—Edwin De Nyse's "An Old-Timer's Lament"

During the sultry summer of 1853, if you strolled towards City Hall and reached Chatham Square, you came to one of the dirtiest streets in the City. Streams of refuse stagnated in the gutter — dregs of the markets, the butchers' especially. The smell of oysters frying in pork fat intermingled with the débris, for several dozen oyster houses vied for customers.

Chatham Street seemed to be closely drawn together as if in some sort of obscene conspiracy. It was narrow, the pavement worn out, the wooden blocks of the gutter rotting away — scarcely worthy to be called a street, and respectable citizens could not be blamed for going out of their way to avoid it. The few barber shops, with floors well sanded, catered to the shabby-genteel; one of the signs bore the legend: "George Washington Jones, Physiognomic Operator and Professor of the Tonsorial Art." The greater income came from painting black eyes, cupping, and blood-letting of leeches. There were a few daguerrean galleries for Chathamites not above vanity, which bore descriptive names, such as the Sun Daguerrean Sky Light Gallery, for the likenesses taken were limited to the conditions of the sun and produced only on glass or metal. Of the hat stores — someone sized up the situation with the observation, "One would think that the Boweryites were a many-headed race." Elbowing each other were the six-cent eating houses, the numerous pawn-brokers, poulterers, livery stables, saddleries, and "old clo' " shops. The street, moreover, had the reputation of reselling costly gratifications as well as the lowly necessities of life; on auction day, which was every day, sidewalks were rendered impassable by the bankrupt furniture thrown up like barracks, and offered to public bidding under red flags. To many a passerby it seemed like a city in the act of pillage during a rebellion.

The slovenly Square attracted many outsiders, especially green country cousins, for notorious establishments pandered to their vices. Here they fell victim to a sharper's felicity, the mock auctions, the pocket-book "droppers," and other mantraps. Saloons were invitingly open, too, selling three-cent brandies midst the glaring gaslights. If the visitor was not swindled outright or insulted by rowdies, the chances were ten to one that he would succumb soon enough to other perils of the quarter: Cumbersome omni-buses bespattered the pedestrian with the mud of broken-down, rutted cross streets, while recklessly endangering life and limb; bulls, led to the slaughter houses, ran amok; many fat sows — grunting, bristling porkers — roved about at large, tripping up many a sightseer; but the worst peril of all — the allurement of the National Theatre! In the eyes of the devout the latter was the more contingent evil, because of its magic appeal.

The National was located on the east side of Chatham Street, at 145-147, near James, its grimy stage door facing an open alley, Roosevelt Street. This "devil's workshop" was known more popularly to the Square's denizens as "the new Chatham," for a good reason; it was not to be confounded with the prior Chatham. The latter, in better days, had been a drinking-garden, but having no permanent company it could not be classed professionally as a theatre. About a dozen years before, an anti-theatre crusade blazed out, and under their pastors' exhortations, many congregations openly prayed for the souls of actors. They bought the sinful old Chatham and converted it into the Chatham Temple, which became a shrine for rural evangelists visiting the City. The zealots, however, did not exult long over the theatre's downfall. An indignant patron met them in open defiance, and happening to own some land nearby, erected a larger playhouse in close proximity to the old, on the more attractive side of the street. And out of sheer spite he bestowed upon it the name of its predecessor.

Soon the popularity of "the new Chatham" was unequalled. A great favorite with the gallery "b'hoys," who shook the rafters with unrestrained applause, was a certain actor, Kirby, who had a genius for realistic death scenes. Whenever it was announced that he would appear in a new blood-curdling melodrama and afford further mimic death struggles, the house was sure to be packed. His followers hung on with veneration; sometimes, during a dull lapse in the performance, they would fall asleep, but with an injunction to their more wakeful neighbors, "Wake me up when Kirby dies." It became an apothegm.

Under the aegis of Alexander H. Purdy, in the Fall of 1850, the National was launched on a prosperous season. The new lessee was very fat, short, and his great face, strikingly cherubic, beamed with good humor. His advertisements boasted, "Grand performances every evening, with sterling Dramas, Comedies, Burlesques, Spectacles, &c., &c., supported by the best company in the city, and where a greater variety of novelties are produced than at any theatre in the Union." He became known as "Captain Purdy," and the crackling excitement created by such local dramas as, *Nature's Nobleman, the Mechanic; or, the Ship Carpenter of New York,* was unsurpassed.

The Bowery Theatre felt the competition. In fact, both places were "the select home" of the blood-and-thunder school, where melodramatic chains and ghosts and dungeons were the prevailing properties; both had pits, whereas other theatres had *parterres* — indicating at once the kind of patronage they enjoyed. And if East Side audiences were attracted to the National, it was because the latter offered the better bill.

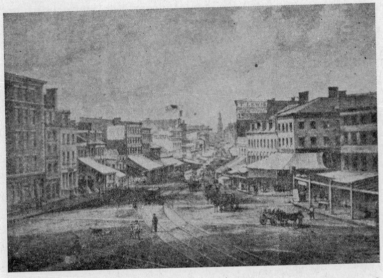

Valentine's Manual

Chatham Square in the Fifties
At the Left, the National Theatre Is Seen with Flags

"Captain Purdy is on his pins all the time, and is going ahead, and no mistake!'" said the critics. Others agreed, "Enterprise and industry command many things in this wide, wide world!"

But the year 1853 proved unfortunate for the Captain. The Crystal Palace was going up, and the first great Exhibition ever held in the country kept patrons away from theatres.

Backstage of the National this was heard, one day:

"They have their money sewed up for that opening on July 14th."

And:

"What makes matters worse, it's the hottest summer in years."

In a quandary, the genial proprietor approached his manager, George L. Fox.

"Now, Laff," he said, "we customarily draw good houses with your Yankee take-offs, but I'm afraid nothing will see us through this summer."

"Why not put on *Uncle Tom's Cabin?*" was asked.

"But I need you for Yankee types."

"There's a Phineas Fletcher in the play, and I'll undertake that."

Fox's suggestion, however, proved unpopular with the rest of the company.

"It failed here last year," said Mrs. W. G. Jones, who found the idea distasteful. She had enacted a wild woman of the woods, while her husband had assumed the character corresponding to George Harris of the novel. "It is an absurd thing."

"That was Mr. Taylor's dramatization. Now, Mr. Howard's enjoyed a great success in Troy, and in Albany."

"We know this —" said Mr. Toulmin, the Rory Marks of the failure. "None of us have great confidence in its fate in New York. The City is Democratic."

Indeed, Tammany controlled at that time the wards comprising the Five Points' district, and the section south of Chatham Square, and was sworn to anti-abolition. Hatred of the Negro was so intense in the City that it burst out, years later, into the Draft Riots of wartime.

"Now," the little Captain put in his licks, "the play really did fail here. But we all know — *Ingomar* divided honors at the Broadway and the Bowery, but it hardly lasted *here* a week, a season or two back."

"You can't draw any comparison."

"Isn't Mr. Fox the brother-in-law of Mr. Howard?" someone asked insinuatingly.

"Now, now! I won't have that. If there are any family interests here, they're beneficial. Charlie Burke [the half-brother of Joseph Jefferson] first recommended Fox to me. Well, both cousins are reigning favorites with National audiences!"

The final decision rested with the Captain.

"We'll hazard it."

From upstate came Mr. Howard, his wife, and daughter, and many of the original cast. At rehearsal none of the National company talent suspected that they were to act in the greatest success that the City — as well as the Nation — was to witness.

As the Captain was low in resources, the run began without any splendid accessories. The only extravagance in the eyes of members of the National cast was the amount Purdy agreed to pay Mrs. Howard.

"Imagine! Mrs. Howard is to receive the sum of *one hundred dollars* a week for the services of herself and little Cordelia!"

"I never acted with anybody who received so much!" exclaimed Mrs. W. G. Jones.

"And you left your position as leading lady at the Bowery Theatre because they threatened to reduce your salary from eighteen to twelve dollars a week!"

The National Theatre set out on its memorable run

just a week after closing a play with another domestic title, *Harvest Home*.

The evening of July 18th brought discomfort to the habitués of Purdy's. The theatre's loft was called "the sailor-man's delight," for when Jack Tar landed he would hail his Susan, fill his innards with grog, then shape his course to Purdy's — and go *aloft*, where it reeked of odors of pickled pigs' feet, tripe, strong drink, and peanuts. Those who perched high consumed peanuts by the quart, shucking them audibly during the most thrilling scenes, stepping on the discarded shells. The corrupted breaths of quid permeated all, for the habit of tobacco-chewing and squirting in all directions was universal. Stewing in the hot and vitiated atmosphere of the gallery, the "b'hoys" divested themselves of their coats. Revealing the lack of a shirt to an acrimonious neighbor, one demanded "that sixpence" he had loaned his friend on Saturday night; another, "Hi, Jack, come over here, will yer?" and made room for his pal by shoving his neighbor aside. Some of the older, ragged boys raised objections to sitting near "a bloody shoe-black." The unsavory occupants in the front row had secured their seats in the first general rush, and dangled their legs over the gallery balustrade, exhibiting boot soles for general inspection.

The gods in the gallery held themselves beyond reach of ordinary discipline, and governed Purdy's at their pleasure. They made free use of a vocabulary of their own, using the rich overtones of oyster venders. The first thing heard was the gratuitous loud whistling, which soon gave way to stamping on the floor and on backs of seats. The guardians of order, the "M.P's" or "posts," as the boys called them, would descend, give admonitory taps with rattan canes, and haul out the worst offenders. The noise subsided, then another part of the house took it up, with convulsive ejaculations of "Hi! hi!" and resounding thumps of sole-leather. There was a sprinkling of respectably dressed persons, attracted, of course, by *Uncle Tom's Cabin*, and not a few of them seemed to enjoy the fun of the "b'hoys." When the property man tried to set something right, he was greeted, "Make a bow, Bobby!" and when that much-abused attendant — whose duty it was to regulate the hooded footlights for the first scene — bent over the row of smoking gas-jets, a shrill voice from the gallery warned, "Take care, Johnny, you'll singe your whiskers!" If it was said once, it was said a thousand times, yet it always brought the house down. The raising of the curtain was delayed, and their mandate was carried out by the peremptory order, "Hoist that rag!"

The evening began with a mélange of Negro airs, to a boot-heel accompaniment marking time to the music. When the old drop curtain, picturing the epic grandeur of Cleopatra embarking to meet Mark Antony, rose, the members in the cast felt quite apprehensive. The first scene was a short one — just a few minutes — in which Eliza, in her natural whiteness, met her husband. The flickering gas-jet footlights revealed that George's countenance was made up in red, and Little Harry (seen later) also appeared red-faced. The scene was similar to most dramas where lover and mistress part.

In the unclean boxes ladies munched apples, or sucked oranges, and dropped various favors below. Amid the faded finery and tarnished gilding the gentlemen kept their backs turned to the pit, sitting on the rails, the better to engage in audible conversation with their female companions. From the gallery came the traditional sarcasm and raillery, "Shame!" and "Really, it isn't right!" in spite of threatening rattans.

Then the curtain rose on Haley and another slave buyer, Shelby, discussing the purchase of a slave. And now the play really began, for the first scene had been a kind of prologue. Anticipating the possible hostility of the listeners,

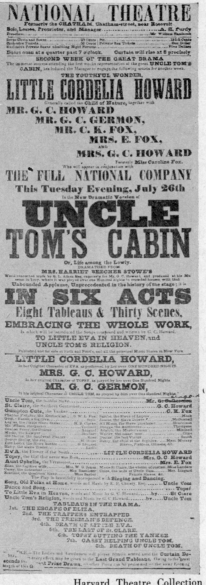

Playbill with the Original Cast

the two actors forgot their lines. Low rumblings came from many parts of the stuffy house; a few handclaps (doubtlessly from the actors' personal friends) were silenced with "psts!" and catcalls. It became apparent to the two actors that the audience would not brook any anti-slavery sentiments. Shelby was to open with the line, "This is the way I should arrange the matter"—but found himself speechless, and Haley, equally flustered, could not utter a single coherent word. While they hemmed and hawed, the prompter could be heard all over the house. Finally, the manager emerged from the wing, and escorted them both off the stage. And the Gods above showered down orange pips very lavishly on the mortals below!

The play did not continue long in this peculiar manner, for the next scene set it all right. The Bowery theatregoers had not been applauding much thus far, but when the old black woman, Aunt Chloe, in nightgown and carrying a candle, came out and spoke in a high, screeching voice, it set them roaring and applauding vociferously, "Hi! Hi!" At the appearance of Uncle Tom they expected to laugh once more, because a black man meant only one thing to them, an ignorant comic. Now their unaccustomed ears heard something unknown in the theatre: A good actor had the part of Uncle Tom, and his very first words were delivered with *the* accent — broad and guttural — but spoken so earnestly that the first laugh died away into deep silence. The voice, through some strange providence, seemed to come from the dark, unknowable places of the earth. . . .

The popeyed pit audience had never seen nor heard of Mrs. Stowe's novel; in fact, they never had read a single good book in their lives. They were riggers, hucksters, stevedores, harness-makers, shoulder-hitters, park loungers. Most were youngsters out for a lark: apprentices, chip-boys, butcher boys, newsboys, short-boys, and bootblacks. In the upper gallery Lize plied her profession, as no woman was permitted in the first gallery or the main floor unless accompanied by a male, her guarantee of respectability. A young mother suckled her baby in the dress circle. They were recruited from the very dregs — frequenters of the low saloons in Chatham Square, and the lower classes swarming through the shadowy byways of the Notorious Five Points. They knew very little of church or school, so it seemed strange that at the National, usually termed the most disreputable in the City, the finer feelings could be invoked.

At the end of the scene, the women in the boxes fluttered white cambric handkerchiefs, surreptitiously removing all traces of emotion; the gentlemen, shifting their position, commented in audible tones. The coldest listeners in the gallery had shown the closest attention to the plot, and there was a multiplicity of "Hi! hi's!" They called out, "It isn't right!" and gone were the offending boots over the railing.

More surprising, the new version kept packing Purdy's theatre, in the furor overshadowing the Crystal Palace. It was impossible to get standing room fifteen minutes after the box office opened early in the morning.

The happy proprietor hunted out the crannies in the old structure, a small theatre, only 136 by 60 feet, and hit upon a plan:

"We'll move the musicians into the wings!"

This large orchestral box occupied a space 60 by 20 feet, which Captain Purdy carpeted handsomely, furnishing it with cushioned armchairs, and three hundred additional persons were accommodated in what became thereafter the most comfortable location in the playhouse. Ladies and gentlemen clamored for these seats, even at the exorbitant admission of fifty cents.

The dress circle and boxes sold at twenty-five cents, and the gallery at twelve and a half cents, so the enterprising Captain proposed, "I know it has never been done before, as it is considered a ruinous policy by other managers — but we'll raise the admission price."

When Purdy, thereupon, increased his prices — three times — he raised the box-office standard considerably for those days.

Two more significant changes occurred at the National. First, on August 15th "a neat and comfortable parquette" was installed in the lower part of the theatre, for respectable colored persons; and in order to protect the women from insult or annoyance, Purdy reserved the front seats for "females accompanied by males, and no female admitted unless with company." He charged twenty-five cents. This parquette was entirely separate from the rest of the house, with a special entrance and ticket office under the first circle. Although the colored folk who went to the National were not permitted to sit where they wished, like the whites, it was perhaps all that could be expected at the beginning of a break with a traditional practice. The Old Bowery Theatre

A Black Joke

*During the run of "Uncle Tom" at the National, some wags one
night as the audience were leaving the theatre, altered the card
which is put upon the benches, by substituting a W for the letter
B so that the announcement read: "This Wench is taken." This
they pinned upon the shawl of a sable damsel, coming out, who
could not imagine what "de nasty white trash was laffin at."*

waited until 1860, when its top gallery introduced a pen in
the centre roughly fenced off for Negroes, who paid thirty-
five cents for a hard bench.

Captain Purdy's innovation became the fount of humor
of the weeklies, especially *Yankee Notions* and *The Lantern*.
The latter was edited by the actor-producer, John Brougham,
whose attitude can be best explained by a story. In one
play, *John Bull,* he enacted the character of Dennis Bulgrud-
dery, and when directed to do a certain piece of stage
business, refused. Then he was asked to do it for the sake
of his posterity. This seemed to stagger him an instant, but
he recovered himself, and blurted out, "Do it for the sake
of my posterity? And phwat did my posterity ever do for
me?" He had no intimations of immortality.

Apprehensively, Purdy had objected when Mr. Howard insisted that the play constitute an entire evening's bill. He feared the doors of the National would close within a week, for in those days a playbill was a document of some dimensions — a yard long; anachronistically, advertisers called them "small bills," for the public's attention was called to certain "particulars." "Laff" Fox assured the hesitating proprietor, "The entr'actes and afterpiece will be replaced by rounds of applause."

The play soon attracted a better class of people, and it became imperative to give matinees for the accommodation of women and children. After the lamps were lit any women seen walking on the street were immediately considered of dubious character, demireps who took possession of the pave. The matinees were on Wednesday and Saturday and soon a third matinee had to be added, putting a telling strain on the cast. Performances increased from twelve to eighteen a week, and the company ate their meals in costume behind the scenes, not leaving the theatre from early morning to midnight.

Up to that time there were no regular matinees, the phenomenal run of *Uncle Tom's Cabin* instituting the practice as permanent markers in the American theatre. Hitherto, an afternoon performance implied Sabbath-breaking, since throughout the whole New England region a restriction held that the Sabbath began at sundown, and in Boston the theatre was forbidden to stay open on Saturday night. Thus, if a manager did not wish to incur a loss, he resorted to a substitute performance in the afternoon. And now! the popularity of matinees swept in once and for all, breaking down this New England prohibition. When Saturday evening performances were finally allowed, in 1855-6, many in the profession believed these would naturally abolish the Saturday matinees, but they were to learn otherwise. Managers grasped clearly that they paid no more for seven performances a week than they had paid formerly for six, and so held on to the matinee.

Captain Purdy received many petitions from suburban towns and villages, from people who never in their lives had been inside a playhouse, complaining that try as they would nightly, they found it impossible to gain admittance. How the matinee shaped itself as it did, at a definite hour, can be discerned from an early advertisement in the City's newspapers, in October: "The Manager of the National Theatre announces to the citizens of Morrisania that in compliance with their request, and at the request of heads of families and principals of schools, the wonderful drama of *Uncle Tom's Cabin* will be performed on Saturday afternoon, the 15th inst., commencing at 2 o'clock, which will conclude about 5 o'clock, thus giving ample time to return by the 6 o'clock train of cars."

The matinees contributed greatly to the financial sinews of Captain Purdy's dramatic temple.

The cherubic proprietor, not a little awed himself, tried to figure it out. He would stand pompously on the steps of the National, appraising the "Temple of the Muses" and its immediate sordid surroundings. At the right, Peck the furniture dealer occupied No. 139, and on the corner, Brundage's eating house, better known as "the Theatre Restaurant." From that corner, too, you could not fail to see the dilapidated row of blowzy porter houses on Roosevelt Street — "Hackett's, "O'Reilly's," "Leonard's," "O'Calahan's," "Ramsey's," "Whittey's," "Ma Martin's," "Hart's" — all catering to the spirited toughs of the street's gas house, stave yards, distillery, and livery stables. The aroused moral sense of Captain Purdy may have directed his steps to the Theatre's left: There Chatham Street slanted erratically inward, and cheek by jowl was a clutter of run-down stores: McKee the clothier; "Mike" Kerrigan's furniture; Stam the carpet-dealer; Hall, with feathers for beds; Buhler, more furniture, who rented half his quarters to another

Hall; No. 163 was empty, dusty windows displaying *Uncle Tom* sheet music and playbills; further left, Resch's, where the Captain stepped in for a segar; and at the corner, "Mike" Morris' cutlery. However, the Captain preferred the view down James Street: children playing "one-old-cat" and "duck-on-a-rock" before Ward School No. 10, diagonally across the church; a few short blocks off stretched the East River waterfront — a forest of masts — and the James Street slip, where the ferry disgorged eager Brooklynites to *Uncle Tom's Cabin*.

Captain Purdy, having aimed at the lowest classes, now discovered his theatre filled by society's élite. They accepted the embarrassment and discomforts, such as the lack of antimaccassar splendor, which a visit to the place entailed, all for a glimpse of the anti-slavery drama. Daily and nightly, the ladies usurped the entire dress circle, ladies who rarely went to a playhouse, except to hear Jenny Lind sing or to see Fanny Elssler dance. The men, too, knew little more of theatregoing, aside of the popular diversion of lectures on mesmerism, animal magnetism, and phrenology. Very respectable Christians occupied whatever seats they could obtain, and overlooked the proximity to certain rather repulsive-looking individuals attracted to the theatre solely on worldly principles. One saw Quakers, wearing hats of most orthodox breadth, who had arrived at a decision to depart from the sect's rule prohibiting attendance at "places of diversion."

The anti-slavery drama made them forget their prejudices. Its effect upon the faithful is left to us in a vivid account by a contemporary journalist, Adolphus M. Hart: "Had he.... witnessed the representation of *Uncle Tom's Cabin* at the National Theatre in New York, he would have been struck with the marked peculiarity of the audiences that were brought together on those occasions. There was an air of sanctity in the upper tiers, which betokened that the work had a powerful influence in awakening the religious feelings of certain classes of the people, whilst in the balconies and pit, there was another class intent on every scene in the drama that could gratify their morbid love of cruelty, and make them gloat over pictures of human wretchedness and misery. In those secluded corners of the theatre, called private boxes, might be seen some demure looking gentleman, who had never been at a theatre before, and who drew out his white pocket handkerchief and applied it to his eyes, as the black apostle of liberty, Uncle Tom, was reading the Bible, or Little Cordelia Howard was suffering, perhaps her hundredth martyrdom on the boards of the New York National Theatre. Finding himself, perhaps for the first time in his life, in such a novel position, he carefully lays aside the half-drawn curtain, and reveals to the audience his dark colored garments and starched neckcloth, indicating, that his mission was one of peace and brotherly love, and that he had descended for the nonce from the pulpit to the theatre. The transition did not appear as easy to him as it did to the unwashed boys of the Bowery, for whilst he was conscious, in the innocence of his heart, of the error he was committing by his fruitless attempts to conceal his person from the gaze of the audience, the boys were shouting and holloing as Eliza was crossing the Ohio, or George Harris was shooting his pursuers."

Fully one-third of the audience was composed of church members and their pastors, of many sects and denominations, who looked upon *Uncle Tom's Cabin* as in the line of Biblical education, and the tableaux, especially, were to them like many religious paintings. Clergymen from every State attended the matinees, including Henry Ward Beecher, Dr. Bellows, and many other eminent divines. Edified and delighted, they recommended it later in their pulpits, where all praise was accredited to the proprietor. The lobby of the National was thronged daily, a rendezvous for consistent church members who wished to meet their clergymen.

In those piping days Purdy began to consider himself a crusader. He advertised the National as "the Temple of the Moral Drama," and to show how well the lambs were protected, the public was assured that every precaution had been taken to exclude all bullies and pickpockets. The year of the great "moral drama" became known as the long season of repentance and sackcloth and ashes.

Much to the amusement of his employees, the kindly, round-bodied proprietor hung the lobby with framed scriptural texts of the theological highpoints in the conversations between Eva and Tom. Soon after, in the entrance, near the box office, he also added a large idealized portrait of himself, a Bible in one hand and a copy of *Uncle Tom's Cabin* in the other!

The National inaugurated a series of Sunday evening meetings. The Bowery and one or two other playhouses, of course, followed his example, and for the next three or four years the Sabbath was consecrated by secular nights, the Stanton Street Baptist Church leading off at the National.

Never had the abolitionists expected to find the stage their advocate, and enthusiastically they helped aggravate the housing problem of the National. Horace Greeley held out for a long time, attacking all playhouses as dens given over to the indulgence of degrading appetites, where the better thoughts were expressed only to be parodied. Now even he opened the columns of his newspaper to glowing accounts of the drama.

William Lloyd Garrison, in disagreement, felt that Uncle Tom exemplified the duty of non-resistance to his white owner. The end of the story, particularly the plea for African colonization, dissatisfied him altogether. He preferred the inspired examples set by the Hungarians, the Greeks, the Poles, and our own Revolutionary sires. However, after witnessing the play on September 3rd, he wrote in the *Liberator*: "I went on Saturday evening to see the play of *Uncle Tom's Cabin*, at the National Theatre, invited thereto by the description of the *Times*, which appeared in a late *Standard*. That description does no more than justice to the play. It is better by one hundred percent than the version of the Boston Museum. If the shrewdest abolitionist amongst us had prepared the drama with a view to make the strongest anti-slavery impression, he could scarcely have done the work better. O, it was a sight worth seeing those ragged, coatless men and boys in the pit (the very *material* of which mobs are made) cheering the strongest and the sublimest anti-slavery sentiments! The whole audience was at times melted to tears, and I own that I was no exception. It was noticeable that the people, after witnessing the death of Uncle Tom, went out of the house as gravely and seriously as people retire from a religious meeting! I wish every abolitionist in the land could see this play as I saw it, and exult as I did that, when haughty pharisees will not testify against slavery, the very *stones* are crying out!"

The play was spontaneously subtitled, "Abolition Dramatized!" Ironically, a few years previous, a mob had stormed the Chatham Street Chapel, driven out a peaceful abolition assembly, and forced the two speakers, Rev. Cox and Mr. Tappan, to hide from their violence. Since then anyone bold enough to get up such a meeting in the City invited martyrdom. Nightly, the gallery was compact now as a barrel of mackerel. When the slave escaped, the "b'hoys" shouted and used their feet as auxiliaries of applause, and when Fletcher confronted Loker on the rocks, and the fugitives were saved, the gallery leaped upon benches in wild enthusiasm. The resistance to the Fugitive Slave Law was met with triple salvos of approbation, and vociferously they applauded all allusions to human rights.

They left the theatre humming tunes. The warblers of Chatham Square whistled them in the street. They were tortured out of pianofortes in back parlors of nearly every

LITTLE EVA;

UNCLE TOM'S GUARDIAN ANGEL.

COMPOSED AND MOST RESPECTFULLY DEDICATED TO

MRS. HARRIET BEECHER STOWE,

AUTHOR OF "UNCLE TOM'S CABIN."

POETRY BY

JOHN G. WHITTIER.

MUSIC BY

MANUEL EMILIO.

Price, 25 cents net.

BOSTON:

Published by John P. Jewett & Company.

CLEVELAND, OHIO:

Jewett, Proctor & Worthington.

1852.

One of the Many Inspired Songs

home, and a critic confessed that he expected yet to witness *Uncle Tom* transfigured in a grand Italian opera, perhaps with Mario as Uncle Tom, Grisi as Eliza, and the latest successful *debutante* as the gentle Eva. About that time news came from Italy that the play was being made into a ballet in Milan.

If you took a walk through Chatham Square, you spied the sheet music in many shop windows. The melodies were not all Howard's however. Mrs. Stowe's publisher issued "Little Eva; Uncle Tom's Guardian Angel," words by John Greenleaf Whittier, music by Manuel Emilio. Stepping into Millet's, at 329 Broadway, you could get Watt's Nervous Antidote for which he was an agent, but he also carried music and musical instruments, and had just published a new song, "Uncle Tom's Cabin." Two doors ahead, 333 Broadway, the enterprising Horace Waters, G. C. Howard's publisher, displayed in handsome style the latest song hit, "The Ghost of Uncle Tom," composed by Miss Martha Hill. Scenes from the play appeared in verse set to music. A collection of thirteen ("Eliza's Flight," "Eva's Parting," "Uncle Tom's Grave," etc) under the heading *Lays of Liberty, or Verses for the Times,* was printed in Boston.

Heard, too, at the popular Hutchinson Family concerts at the Tabernacle were songs like "Little Topsy's Song" and "The Fugitive." The first, composed by Eliza Cook, was set to music by the very man whom Mrs. Stowe had refused the privilege of dramatizing her work. Although vocalists in the Temperance cause, they sang on themes from *Uncle Tom's Cabin,* and sold the pieces at the door. One proslavery cynic observed that it was hard to say whether the greater amount of moral courage was displayed in the Hutchinson choice of songs or in their execution.

Those in the habit of visiting the National Theatre discovered, on September 1st, that several members of the Howard-Fox ménage were missing. Occasional changes had been made in the play, and now Mr. Howard was gone. No one else fitted the character of St. Clair better than Mr. Howard, answering the conception of Mrs. Stowe's idealized Southern planter — with "the noble cast of head." He made it a practice to wear in public the black broadcloth frock coat, with its collar of satin piping, brass buttons, the stylish neckcloth, and always the lavender trousers. His conspicuous figure was recognized everywhere — in the hotels, on the street, in the shops. Those who caught sight of him exclaimed, "There goes little Eva's father!" He was seldom called Mr. Howard.

Purdy did not know whom to get for the new St. Clair because all the available talent in that line had already been snatched up by visiting managers from other States. Moreover, the part involved a song, and S. M. Siple, who temporarily filled the role, sad to say, could not sing.

One day, a short, ungainly man approached the Captain. The visitor had a cadaverous face, and was obviously down on his luck, yet he did have the finest black, curly hair ever seen on a man's head — at least, so thought the Captain.

"I am J. B. Howe," said the stranger. "I have just landed after a voyage of forty-three days in the steerage of an English sailing ship. I went to see the stage manager of the Bowery Theatre, Mr. Stevens, but they are full. He gave me this letter of introduction to you. Have you an opening?"

"Here's an easy-going and money-making establishment," boasted the generous lessee. "Our houses are good, and so are the plays."

Prosperity was ostentatiously evident on the flashy person of Purdy, now given to the wearing of immense watch-chains and weighty gold rings. His sharp contrast to the seedy-looking actor must have made him feel like Mr. Pickwick encountering Jingle in the Fleet.

"Always ready to augment our forces," continued the

good-natured Captain. "Scarcely a week passes that some new and telling addition and improvement is not made to the play. Have you any playbills?"

"Yes," replied the actor, eagerly. "My lodgings are nearby. I'll fetch them in a few minutes."

Purdy's curiosity was piqued by the uncouth figure. Perhaps he had even then a hasty notion of the rumor that dogged Howe's later career: that he had mounted to the stage from a Chatham Square oyster bench. The same had also been said of the talents of N. B. Clarke, in private life Mr. Belden, owner of a large boarding house on the corner of Madison and Catherine Streets; now his very successful conception of Simon Legree was attributed to that fact alone — for he filled the role with all the traditional ferocity of the hard-hearted landlord! Both Howe and Clarke were actors by intuition, and the stage has known few of their type, for they differed from the more certain stars of the period; always erratic, their uncertain courses in the roles they assumed often made them veritable planets. They were "all round" men, and after playing Hamlet they did not think it unworthy to black up as Christy Minstrels.

In less than ten minutes the proprietor was handed a batch of playbills, from which he learned that Thomas Burdette Howe was called "J. B" because he had been so described through a printer's error.

"You may be a fairly good actor," agreed the Captain, "but what we need for St. Clair's part is someone with a strong baritone voice. And the song has to be committed to memory by next Monday."

The eager aspirant was led into the deep recess of the theatre, where an orchestra struck up the first verse of the ballad St. Clair sings in the act following Eva's death:

Childless, desolate this heart,
Naught on earth is left to cherish;
All is lost, since we must part,

Every hope and joy will perish.
Eva! Eva! lovely daughter;
Are those bright eyes veiled in death
That so fondly smiled in gladness
Upon all at parting breath?
Are thou gone from me forever?
Shall I never more behold thee?
Bud of life, my heart's fond treasure,
What is now this world to me?

Hardly had the opening chords been struck, when Howe exclaimed, "I know that tune!"

"You do?" asked the orchestra leader.

"Yes," went on Howe. "That is 'Can I e'er Forget the Valley,' an old English song."

"I beg your pardon," the musician cut him short. "This is an *original* song—words and music by Mr. G. C. Howard, the father of the little girl who plays Eva."

"Oh! I beg your pardon," as Howe grasped the whole situation. "I must have been deceived."

But it was note for note the melody Howe knew, and he had no difficulty *learning* it. The next morning he had his first rehearsal, and when the following Friday came around he was judged letter-perfect. Purdy's faith in instinctive acting was affirmed.

Howe opened on Monday night, and made a hit. The song was encored twice. In less than six weeks his career was firmly established. Purdy raised his salary voluntarily, and his daguerreotypes appeared in shop windows. Further, success went to the actor's head in an unexpected manner, when a placard in the window of Deucey's hat shop, in Chatham Square, announced: "The St. Clair Hat, as worn by Mr. J. B. Howe, in that admired character at the National Theatre, in the Great Moral Drama of *Uncle Tom's Cabin*." That set the fashion for a popular hat, which became known all over the City as "the St. Clair hat."

One other incident of that time, in which Howe had a share, is rather outstanding. Solicited by Henry E. Stevens, the manager of the old Bowery, to play *Michael Earle* for his Benefit, Howe received permission from the Captain to do so. There was at least an hour and a half between the scene where St. Clair dies in the fourth act and the "Apotheosis" in the last scene where he reappears, and Howe figured that he could make it in time that night. But the compliant Captain laid down one stipulation: that he come back in time for the "Ascension" at the finale.

Returning, Howe rode quickly past the front of the National in his brougham. He was on his way to the stage door when, with misgivings, he saw crowds issuing from the porticos, and knew at once that the moral drama was ended for the night.

To avoid meeting the Captain he entered Brundage's eating house on the corner, at 137 Chatham, where the cast customarily assembled after the show. The Captain usually went home after the last performance, but this night he happened to ramble into the restaurant. Howe had hardly time to collect his wits. .

"Why were you not in Heaven tonight, J. B.?" asked the Captain, with a twinkle in his eye.

Howe tried to explain.

"Well, if I have heard it once," continued Purdy, beaming, "I've heard it at least fifty times as the people were coming out: 'There was no St. Clair ascending to heaven tonight!' "

Howe's misadventure suggested to the Howards that little Cordelia could be sent home much earlier each night. If those in the audience were concerned because the "dear little girl" was kept up very late, ready to serve until the final curtain, when she was revealed robed in white behind a scrim drop on the back of a milk-white dove with expanded wings — they did not guess that Cordelia Howard was safely in bed, and that the child soaring upward among the sun-tinted, gorgeous clouds was her double.

With the play all the rage, it became obvious to other managers that Purdy's fortune was rising to its zenith. Then suddenly, four versions leaped into the field! — the Bowery Theatre's, another at Barnum's Museum, a third at the Franklin Museum, to say nothing of a burlesque by Christy's Minstrels.

Mr. Howard had anticipated the rivalry. He left his role to protect specifically his dramatization in Philadelphia, and George L. Aiken, too, notified the public in newspapers: "It having been asserted in some of the New York papers that my version of the drama with the above title yielded me but twenty-five dollars, I beg leave to contradict the statement and assure the public that Mr. G. C. Howard (for whom I dramatised the work, for the purpose of presenting his wonderful daughter in the character of Eva,) paid me most liberally. I would also state, in consequence of the many applications for the piece, that Mr. G. C. Howard, of the Troy Museum, and Mr. A. H. Purdy, of the National Theatre, New York, are alone authorized to sell copies of the drama, and none are genuine unless procured from them." He informed the New York *Herald* critic, on September 26th, that he had received forty dollars in the first instance, and later a splendid gold watch.

Of all the competitors Mr. Howard was most apprehensive of one—Phineas T. Barnum. The King of Showmen had made his first contact with Chatham Square some twenty years before, as a "drummer" for several establishments. Within six months he started in show business exhibiting a withered, old Negress, Joice Heath, as the one hundred and sixty-one-year-old nurse of George Washington, "the first person who put clothes on the unconscious infant who was in after days to lead our heroic fathers on to glory." Barnum added another feature — a white Negress. In the Spring of 1841, the year Moses Kimball discovered that people who shunned the fearful theatre could be made to enter a "lecture-room," Barnum quit the show business, and settled in New York as agent for Sear's Pictorial Illustrations of the Bible. Within two months, however, he was bamboozling the public again. He leased Vauxhall Garden, left it in the Fall for a position as "puff writer" for the Bowery Amphitheatre, and in December bought up the contents of Dr. Scudder's Museum. He moved to Broadway and Ann Street, where he scored his first success with a Fejee Mermaid. Now Barnum rose to the demand — and began humbugging the world in earnest. He pursued Kimball's strategy, fitting up his freak hall with the appendage of a lecture-room, and the accessory "fixins" of Biblical waxworks. Out of deference to the prejudiced, Barnum invoked a tender sympathy by addressing them as "the congregation," and to children accompanied by their parents he lavishly distributed peppermint lozenges.

During the season of 1850-51, Barnum's American Museum saw a definite transformation of its lecture-room, and audiences acclaimed the stirring preachment of *The Drunkard*. The philanthropist who promotes Middleton's regeneration was made up to resemble Barnum, and the actor affected the black clerical coat and high, black hat which Barnum wore to win the public's confidence. On display at the box-office was a pledge, which many thousands signed as they left. While a force in breaking down the theatrical taboo, the showman surely did fool them in many ways.

The American Museum stressed Biblical offerings. Never was villainy triumphant, never did the ballet profane that stage, and the stock company became comfortably quartered by the success of such dramas as *Joseph and his Brethren*, *Moses*, and now *The Drunkard*. The moral plays were given in a moral manner; the leading lady, Mrs. J. J.

Prior, who portrayed the boy Joseph, was known by her matrimonial title, since Barnum felt that it chaperoned, so to speak, the whole performance, and besides kept suitors at bay.

The crowded houses at the National had provoked Barnum, and the Great Showman felt that *Uncle Tom's Cabin* undoubtedly had elements of perpetuity. He looked about for a suitable script, and his attention was called to a dramatization by Henry J. Conway, which had opened at the Boston Museum on November 15, 1852, a month after the Troy production. The playwright had prepared almost the same version expressly for the Eagle Theatre, about eight months before its initial appearance at the Boston Museum, but the management lacked the moral courage to make use of it. Nor did Conway preserve the fidelity of Mrs. Stowe's story, for he softened what he termed "the many crude points," and effectively removed "the objectionable features which meet the eyes of the reader while perusing the book." It was presented as a more truthful portrayal of Southern life than even the original. Further, Topsy was a pointless caricature, and the lightest hand touched the scene of the slave auction. The dramatist omitted the final tragedy, and added a happy ending, with Uncle Tom rescued by George Shelby from Legree.

Conway's work, shorn of its salient points, derived new interest through excellent scenery — "scenes in living pictures." A grand panorama by C. Lehr, in the second act, representing a moonlight view of the Mississippi (a reverse movement of the canvas giving apparent motion to a steamer on her way to New Orleans) surpassed anything the Bostonians had seen in years. It had such a lasting effect upon two members of the cast, John Davies (Simon Legree) and J. P. Price (Drover John), that when they retired from the stage they both hit upon the idea of lecturing with panoramas.

Mrs. Stowe later saw this same Conway adaptation at Hartford. She went with a neighbor, Charles Dudley Warner, and occupied a free box (her only profit from the dramatic rights). As the drama unrolled before her eyes, she sat profoundly surprised. When Penetrate Partyside made his colorful entrance, she was taken aback, and overwhelmed by his strong language, she left the theatre in disgust. Warner afterward said that she couldn't follow the plot at all — that he had to explain it to her.

When the Conway adaptation began performances at Barnum's American Museum on November 7th, it was advertised as "Originally dramatized, upwards of eighteen months ago, expressly for this establishment" — that it had been in preparation at Barnum's and under rehearsal during the last twenty weeks. The public was invited to see the giraffes, the Bearded Lady, in fact, all the other curiosities "without extra charge."

The Great Showman emphasized a panoramic view of the Mississippi River from Natchez to New Orleans ("which alone is worth the price of admission"). One beheld a steamer gliding in the most palpable moonlight, with a thin blue haze rolling up from the majestic river, set to quivering melody. The triumph of Delamere, whose brush followed the dictates of Barnum's heart, was an unforgettable, gorgeous dream. Smoke puffs rose from the steamer, and miniature rotating wheels were heard clearly; then gradually, with the coming dawn, the lights on the boat and in the saloons blinked out, the sun threw its beams over the rippling waves — first clouded in — and appeared in full radiance!

Eva's fall overboard, while the steamer was in motion, and her rescue by Uncle Tom, caused intense excitement in the audience.

Barnum claimed that his play was sustained by some fifty talented performers, plus the *tout ensemble*, but many actors really doubled. The direction was by Corson W.

Clarke who, with an eye at the National cast, also played St. Clair. One of the actors, cast as George Harris, suspected that the sole reason he had been engaged was because his name (Mr. Howard) was similar to the rival manager's — and soon took to drink.

As Barnum owned about half a dozen traveling menageries, he was afraid of the sentiment in the South, and with admirable discretion avoided all the argumentative portions of Mrs. Stowe's work. A bit of dramatic criticism carried by the *Liberator* on December 16th had this to say: "To make amends for the manner in which the New York theatres have set the South at defiance, and the humanity they have inculcated, Barnum has offered the slave-driver the incense of an expurgated form of *Uncle Tom's Cabin*. He has been playing a version of the great story at his Museum, which omits all the strikes at the slave system, and has so shaped his drama as to make it quite an agreeable thing to be a slave. 'Verily, he will have his reward.' "

Barnum advertised in this grand manner:

This is acknowledged to be the only just and sensible dramatic version of Mrs. Stowe's book that has ever been put upon the stage. Precisely the same version has been represented in Kimball's Boston Museum over

TWO HUNDRED SUCCESSIVE NIGHTS,

and received with the most lively satisfaction and unqualified applause of more than

THREE HUNDRED THOUSAND CITIZENS
OF NEW ENGLAND,

It represents Southern Negro

embracing all its abhorrent deformities, its cruelties, and barbarities.

It does "nothing extenuate nor set down aught in malice," while it does not foolishly and unjustly elevate the negro above the white man in intellect or morals.

It exhibits a true picture of negro life in the South, instead of absurdly representing the ignorant slave as possessed of all the polish of the drawing room, and the refinement of the educated whites.

And instead of turning away the audience in tears, the author has wisely consulted dramatic taste by having Virtue triumphant at last, and after all its unjust sufferings, miseries and deprivations, conducted to happiness by the hand of Him who watches over all.

In a word, this drama deals with

FACTS, INSTEAD OF FICTION.

It appeals to reason instead of the passions; and so far as truth is more powerful than error, will the impressions of this drama be more salutary than those of any piece based upon fanaticism without reason, and zeal without knowledge.

On the other afternoons of the week, at 3 o'clock, remarkably diverting and comical performances, for which see the bills of the day.

To which the National answered, "Which is the humbug version of *Uncle Tom's Cabin?* Not that played at the National Theatre!"

Barnum retaliated. A critic on the *Morning Express* voiced his argument: "There is no good reason why Uncle

Tom should be whipped to death by a brute in a moral drama, because from the popular character of the drama itself, such a closing triumph for vice and defeat of virtue would leave a most pernicious impression upon the general mind. Hence the astonishing success of the sumptuous version of Uncle Tom at Barnum's Museum, where the hero, after all his tribulations, is restored to his freedom and his family."

In this newspaper war a sharp distinction was drawn between the rival attractions. The New York *Atlas* saw the Conway dramatization as violative of the original spirit. "It may be well enough, perhaps, for the mendicants of the state," it declared on November 20th, "if they belong to the 'home squadron,' to vitiate the works of authors of *their* own country; but, is it to be endured that an imported scion of Cripplegate should be allowed to falsify and misrepresent such an author as Mrs. Stowe, to pander to the appetites of a few mercenary toadies, who would misrepresent a moral and enlightened community. *Uncle Tom's Cabin*, as played at the American Museum, has few charms for us; and yet, it is the popular drama of that establishment. It calls in immense audiences; and, of course, is most vociferously applauded." On the other hand, the Aiken version was accepted as the one that confined itself to the dialogue and dramatic purity of the original work. The faithful readers of Mrs. Stowe's book were warned that if they had no desire to see it misrepresented then the National Theatre was the place; in so many words, there it did not "pander to the fears of the timid, nor gratify a perverted taste."

The battle reached the stage itself, in full view of the spectators. The actors at the National made direct references to their rival, and some of the improvized lines stuck to the drama long after the feud was over. For example, Gumption Cute (in the second scene of the fifth act) exclaims suddenly to Topsy, "I've an idee in my head that is worth a million of dollars." Topsy is puzzled, and he continues: "I'm a man of genius. Did you ever hear of Barnum?" Topsy answers, "Barnum! Barnum! Does he live in the South?" Here the audience roared. Then Cute would take up the thread again, "No, he lives in New York. Do you know how he made his fortin?" And so the mischief went on. Cute found time in the regular business of the scene to interpolate, "Well, as I was saying, Barnum made his money by exhibiting a *woolly* horse; now wouldn't it be an all-fired speculation to show you as the woolly gal?" Topsy hesitates, "You want to make a sight of me?" "I'll give you half the receipts, by chowder!" Topsy hesitates again, "Should I have to leave Miss Feely?" "To be sure you would," is the reply. Topsy runs off with, "Den you hab to get a woolly gal somewhere else, Mas'r Cute." Then Cute observes, "There's another speculation gone to smash, by chowder!" pointing in the direction of the American Museum.

Simple folk gaped in open-mouthed amazement before the American Museum and the National Theatre. The hyperbole lavished upon them was beyond the wildest imaginations. The redoubtable Barnum called his place that "Wilderness of Wonderful, Instructive and Amusing Realities!" Purdy enticed them with the "Great Allegorical Tableau of Eva in Heaven, a Spirit of Celestial Light in the Abode of Bliss Eternal!" The National had two ticket booths, one for whites, another for colored. The Museum raised the ante — with three!

Intense patriotism was the order of the day. Barnum's white stone edifice, five stories high, its outer walls embellished between the windows with medalion murals of beasts, birds and fish, now went into the spread-eagle business, displaying a panorama of gaily colored flags. The National countered with the American Eagle and the Star Spangled Banner, and both hung transparencies outside after the manner of the European traveling booths.

"Captain Purdy"
The Advance Agent of the Civil War

Then Barnum dug deep into his pocket. High along the cornice, some fifty feet, the title of the play was blazoned forth in ornamental letters. Below floated some five hundred yards of cotton muslin, representing on one side a Negro dance, and on the other the anti-fugitive slave law fight between runaways and pursuers.

Fortunately for Purdy, a new style of art had been imported just then — and he was the first to seize upon it — tinted lithographs! Thereafter they became associated in the minds of all who saw them with but one play.

To offset the "World Renowned and Absolutely in-the-Universe Unparalleled" American Museum, Purdy hit upon another idea. Three days after the opening of Conway's version at Barnum's, the National celebrated its one hundredth night with a "Grand Jubilee Festival." At nine o'clock in the morning, the powerful National Brass Band — thirty performers under the direction of John Schiebel, Esq. — began playing marches and quicksteps from the front balcony of the Theatre, way into the evening. At two o'clock in the afternoon, the great drama was performed for the accommodation of ladies, families, schools, etc. At six o'clock Messrs. J. G. and Isaac Edge, popular pyrotechnists of Jersey City, set off a grand display of fireworks in front of the Theatre, showing a favorite scene from the play, at the conclusion of which Professor Grant exhibited his celebrated Drummond Light from the roof-top. At six-thirty, the doors opened for the one hundredth representation of *Uncle Tom's Cabin* with additional new scenes, music and allegory. In the course of the performance Captain Purdy presented to Little Cordelia Howard a gold tea set, manufactured by Messrs. Brown & Atwood, No. 148 Chatham Street, as a testimonial.

The rivalry was further enhanced when Purdy produced, on December 5th, C. W. Taylor's *Little Katy, or the Hot Corn Girl*. Another adaptation had been performed for the chaste and delicate ear at the American Museum, and now the National thought it would vary its bill by giving it on afternoons other than Wednesday and Saturday. The new play was called "a religious and moral drama," and

dealt, in its gas-lit genre, with New York low life. What it
set out to accomplish was lost somehow, for the worst abuses
of the notorious Five Points had already been removed;
besides, the Old Brewery, warren of vice, had been razed
the year before. The new play was strangely reminiscent of
the regular fare at the National. The same Grand Allegory
was used: Little Katy, affectingly catching pneumonia while
selling "hot corn" on the wind-swept streets, sings her last
song and floats upward to the realms of bliss, attended by
seraphim. Mrs. Bannister, who played Wild Meg, resembled the Wild Mag the playwright had introduced a year
before in his unsuccessful adaptation of *Uncle Tom's Cabin*:
the Sedleys family, also, reminded one of the Shelbys.
Little Cordelia enacted Katy.

Before the drama's opening Purdy publicized an
incident supposed to have occurred in the Howard family:
"Father," says Cordelia one day, "I have just been reading
that beautiful little story in the *Tribune*, under the title of
Hot Corn, and the death of Little Katy, and I tell you what
I want you to do. I want you to set apart one dollar every
night as long as I play Little Eva, to give Mr. Pease, for the
benefit of some other Little Katy. Will you, father?" To
which Mr. Howard was supposed to have answered, "Yes,
my child, I will; and I hope your example will be followed
by a great many others who have the power to do so much
good by such gifts."

However, this announcement suddenly brought the
wrath of a proslavery newspaper. "There is not a greater
rendezvous for prostitution and iniquity of every sort than
this same National Theatre," the New York *Observor*
accused. "Undoubtedly the moral character of the play
which has for the last few months been nightly exhibited on
its stage, and with so much success, has been the means of
enticing hundreds of innocent souls within its halls and on
the road to ruin. But Satan has indeed put on the double
garb of an angel of light when, as a means of alluring a

still larger number of them into his snares, he clothes himself thru the column of that same N. Y. *Tribune* with the eminently righteous work of devoting a dollar a night for the support of a charity to which the National Theatre with the above zealous aid is nightly adding its victims."

For a time bitter contention raged over "Satan transformed."

"Some innocent strangers," came the charge, "very likely Western readers of the *Tribune*, and led there by its advice, have been inveigled by bad characters, and robbed of money and reputation."

The National Theatre was defended not only by those citizens living in the Tenth Ward (and Allen Street had more than its share of actors), but by those in the best residences in the section, from Bleecker to Fourteenth Street. If nothing was heard from Gothamites further uptown, it was because the City limits did not extend that far; the sites of our present-day skyscrapers were piggeries and shanties then, and as the City grew they were driven further uptown, and Central Park was a wilderness inhabited by squatters and goats. Many took up cudgels against the National, some admitting that the place, as formerly conducted, was amenable to the charge brought by the *Observor*, others insisting that the harlotry formerly so conspicuous had been exorcised completely by the spirit of the anti-slavery drama.

"Females of improper character are not admitted in any part of the house!" challenged Purdy.

The editor of the *Sunday Atlas* volunteered to go in person and brave the temptations. He had the misgiving of having entered the wrong place, because the people he saw at the National were of the highest respectability, and religious looking folk, too. To one man, who, from the warmth of his applause, seemed somewhat of a republican, the editor said,

"It seems to us, Sir, from the aspect of things, that there are no wantons in this theatre."

"No—*sir—ee!*" came the prompt reply. "Them's the women and gals that don't come here. No, *sir—ee!*" he reiterated emphatically. "These 'ere gals and women go where trade is kept up. This 'ere theatre is one that goes in for religion, virtue, morality — and *liberty!*"

Later, the editor reassured his disquieted readers, "There was not, in the whole establishment, unless she was under sanctified hypocritical protection, which we do not believe was the case, one of those frail sisters of the *town* and *pave*, who nightly seek a market-place in the corridors of other theatres."

The sudden opposition attracted greater numbers to the National. Excited visitors gathered on the pavement in a demonstration, each day, freely giving way to their Northern sentiments. The police force was something new in the history of the City, having been formed but the year before, and Mayor Westervelt was inordinately proud of their brand new uniforms, the blue coats with beaming brass buttons, and spotless gray trousers. Now he lay awake nights, worrying over the political animosity that taxed the energies of his force to the utmost at the doors of the theatre.

Upon the descent of the final curtain, the restive auditors made the lobby a heated forum! If blows were exchanged, it was in the street only, where glaring gaslights blinded eyes and senses. Conveniently near, around the corner at 4 James Street, was Izzy Lazarus' saloon, where his sons, Harry and Johnny, taught the manly art of self defense. The spectators of the anti-slavery drama argued until the gas lamp posts in front of the National went out, and the gray dawn broke over the East River, when they would, at last, go home to apply fresh Croton water to fevered brows.

Everywhere there were "two sides." In Chatham Street, for instance, two clothing stores — one at No. 194, the other at No. 200 — contended in rivalry for the American Museum and the National Theatre trade. The first called itself Horton & Barnum's, and the other Brown & Purdy's, each emphasizing latest fashions of the North and South.

And so it went on, by day, and far into the evening. As the shops began to close for the day, the last to give up were the tobacconists and public-houses, the light of the Publican's lantern showing where oysters were pried open. You stepped into "Sweeny's," on Chatham Street, to get a cup of coffee for threepence, or a penny segar. The poorer classes ordered their favorite — Indian cakes — and arguments flew back and forth on the Purdy drama. If you joined the earlier Broadway throngs, turned the corner on Spring Street, you came face to face with the sumptuous Prescott House. This first-class hotel, in all its opulent grandeur, was lit up with the splendor of its magnificent cut glass; and entering its inviting bar — where the fashion and luxury of the day assembled — you heard one topic only: *Uncle Tom's Cabin!*

Nor did the rising generation miss it. This play determined the future careers of more than one youngster. Little Ida Vernon was twelve when her parents, spending the Christmas vacation in New York, took her to see the drama everyone was discussing. "The best people in the City used to drive there in their carriages," she recalls. "The play was *Uncle Tom's Cabin*, which was greatly in vogue at that time. I saw a wonderful little Eva. Then it was I decided I wanted to become a little actress. I told my family so when I arrived at home. I was laughed at, but the laughter was not as loud as my ambitions."

How they idolized the golden-haired Cordelia! She was the very embodiment of the gentle Eva, "too pure for earth, just fit for heaven." Her acting had a strange effect on children. A little girl in Brooklyn — a popular story went — lay dying. The twilight was fading in the hushed room, one after another the stars shone in the sky, and she was so absorbed that her father asked, "My daughter, what are you thinking of?"

She started, as if suddenly aroused from sleep, and answered: "I was thinking" — and her little eyes sparkled, "I want to be an angel."

The father leaned over and wept. She wept too, smoothing the soft hair of his head, and kissing his forehead. The grief-stricken father took her parting kiss, and the innocent child, with smiling lips, whispered in his ear: "Papa, I'm going now where Little Eva is."

Those were very sentimental times, indeed.

Old men now, small chips then, tell us that no more consummate acting than Cordelia's had been seen on the American stage. When her carriage clack-clacked along the street, a large, smudgy-faced "guard" of admirers would converge to escort her home to 51 Allen Street. In their boyish hearts it was a token of high rank to be near her, to be selected to walk beside her, or to open her parasol, and he who carried Little Cordelia's brown paper parcel was one of the immortals. A few sometimes actually succeeded in gaining admittance to the National stage where, with black-corked faces, they attended the divinity of Eva. And often many a one of the young rival "angels," upon whose pinions she rested, was set apart from his companions by a blackened eye.

When the little actress undertook *Katy*, her followers, in the intensity of their blind devotion, rioted in old Chatham Square. One of the participants, Arden Seymour, a veteran of the stage, recalls: "Many and bitter were the contentions as to in which character, Eva or Katy, the fair Cordelia's histrionic genius found the greater scope. Soon the clans crystallized, and clashed in combat in the Square after the show; and sometimes the Eva clan was victorious in enforcing its views, and then, again, the Katy clan had the best of the argument all to the great distress of the ancient constable who kept the peace in those then quiet purlieus of the town, and who often shooed the strenuous contenders into side streets and blind alleys there to conclude their battles over nice questions of art."

Nor was this wild admiration confined to the young ones only. Poets like William Cullen Bryant, and weathered actors like Edwin Forrest, were moved to tears listening to Cordelia Howard. They all agreed: it was not art, but nature, that made her performance so nearly perfect. The New York *Atlas* commented on the child's precocity: "We shall not admit that we are extravagant, if we avow that little Cordelia executed the part assigned her with wonderful taste and nature. We have little if any faith in prodigies. Indeed, we have usually regarded them with the contempt that was manifested by Hotspur when he rebuked the pretension of Glendower. But we cannot refrain from saying that the enacting of Eva by little Cordelia Howard, was one of the most delectable and affecting specimens of the *art dramatique* we ever beheld. This little girl apparently throws into the character of Eva the very life and soul and spirit that was intended by its author. She is of course a well trained child, subjected to discipline. Little Cordelia is one of those precious gems of intelligence and intellectual precocity which sometimes leap into existence to delight and astonish the world."

The National Theatre now rode the full tide of this prosperity. A steady concourse of vehicles streamed in the streets that radiated from the Square. Nassau Street had its junction with Chatham Street; another artery, the Bowery, emptied here as the great carotid from the heart. One placed his life in jeopardy when he tried crossing the thicket of horse-drawn vehicles: double and single, all sorts of stages — public and private, hacks — ancient and modern, carriages, carts, omnibuses. How they thundered over the cobblestones! "Going up! going up!" cried the coachmen, clanging their bells. "Hi hi! G'lang — whoa! you son of iniquity. . . ." In the tremendous surge, the men annoyed women passengers, ogling and squeezing them, and the protests were lost in the loud rumble. If Broadway was destined to become greater, with such elegant stores as Stewart's — still, the year brought such an invigorated rush of traffic to Chatham Square, that it became known as "the cab-in." The railroad made its terminus at Chatham Corners; four-horse passenger cars were drawn to and from Madison Square, where a little steam locomotive was hooked up, making the rest of the trip northwards. Also getting into operation were two stage lines running through Chatham Street, the Second and Third Avenue horse railroads; the play proved a boon to them, raising the value of their stock. During the winter, great sleighs with jingling bells, pulled by six or more horses, drew up before the National Theatre.

When the new year 1854 rolled around, the critics did not know what to make of the antislavery drama. Purdy desired to present the play in more magnificent style, and now invested two thousand dollars in the project, engaging two eminent scenic artists, S. Culbert and J. Whytal, to prepare these gorgeous new pictures: A Grand Panoramic View of the Ohio and Mississippi Rivers; A Splendid Saloon and Sale Room at New Orleans; Little Eva's Bed Chamber; A View of Lake Pontchartrain by Sunset; a Winter View of Uncle Tom's Cabin; a Winter Scene near the Ohio River; The Suburbs of a Village on the Ohio River, in a Storm; Perspective Ice Scene on the Ohio; New Ice Scene on the Ohio; A Handsome Drinking Saloon and Reading Room at New Orleans; A Grand Allegorical View of the Regions of Bliss.

The entire interior of the National was redecorated, the seats cushioned, and the house carpeted in a superior manner, a great contrast to the former rows of long, bare benches, and cheerless, cold walls. The circle was finished in matching style. In the lobby a placard bore the legend: "No females of an improper character will hereafter be admitted to any part of the house, as it is the manager's intention to make this a strictly moral theatre." Purdy commissioned Alanson Fisher to paint a portrait of Mrs. Stowe from life, for $565.00. About four feet high and three feet wide, the picture was enclosed by a splendid gilt frame and another of polished mahogany, with a plate glass to protect it. It was placed on exhibition in the Theatre, together with a letter from Mr. C. E. Stowe stating his great satisfaction with the likeness.

Of interest to a close historian of the famous play may have been the circumstances of the January 9th performance. Seen at the National was a completely overhauled version, by Charles Western Taylor, which consisted of seven acts, twelve tableaux, and thirty-four scenes. Two whole scenes were added to the original Howard-Aiken representation: that of the Ohio Senator and his wife, the former apologizing for the Fugitive Slave Law and the latter denouncing it — when Eliza's arrival puts the Senator to the test, and shows his heart to be sounder than his head; and the other, a steamboat passing down the Mississippi, when Eva falls overboard. These were afterward deleted, nor do we find them in the later authorized acting edition.

In fact, the play at the National Theatre had been revised so much by 1854 that it hardly resembled the one compiled in Troy. Taylor added so much new material, that George L. Aiken protested vigorously. The latter was in Detroit, stopping at the St. Charles Hotel, when a copy of a New York paper caught his eye, and he immediately wrote to the New York *Atlas,* on February 12th, and besides claiming the play's paternity, insisted, "The *first person* who played the drama in the New England states was your humble servant; who, in conjunction with a portion of the old National Theatre company, Boston, produced it in Nashua and Dover, N. Y., and in Haverhill, Mass. It has since been played in Worcester, Hartford and New Haven."

The newspaper commented that *Uncle Tom's Cabin,* seen at
the National, was entirely different from Aiken's, and that
the present version, with the exception of a few original
retentions, was the handiwork of Taylor, "a veteran dramatist, whose good taste and discretion, in connection with
theatricals, are readily recognized and admitted." Further,
"In justice to Mr. Howard, we think fit to say, that he never
claimed its paternity. No one is entitled to any great credit
for dramatizing *Uncle Tom's Cabin.* The work of Mrs. Stowe
is exceedingly dramatic from beginning to end, and anyone
who will divide it into dialogue, will find a perfect drama
at his hands. All who have dramatized it, have detracted
from its merits by lugging in expletive characters, such as
Yankees and Dutchmen. Play the book as it came from the
hands of Mrs. Stowe, and it will best suit the wishes and
tastes of the public."

On January 16th the Bowery Theatre joined the rivalry
with a third adaptation, which departed from the National's
dramatization with one notable exception — the introduction of a Yankee and a horse. The new play drew immensely
because Uncle Tom was portrayed by the father of Ethiopian
minstrelsy, "Daddy" T. D. Rice. Regarded as *the* pioneer,
his personation of the Negro was expected to lure audiences
from both the American Museum and the National.

As in the case of Barnum, Purdy launched another
"Grand Uncle Tom Jubilee." On the morning of January
26th, at eight o'clock, Professor Koop's celebrated National
Brass and Clarinet Band evoked a series of new and fashionable music in front of the Theatre, which continued all
day, lasting into the night. At two o'clock came a performance of *Little Katy, the Hot Corn Girl.* Then in the
evening the outside of the Theatre was illuminated brilliantly, and Professor Grant exhibited a powerful calcine light
from the roof. At six-fifteen precisely, the Edges, of Jersey
City, covered the full front of the National with a grand

exhibition of fireworks. And fifteen minutes later the doors opened for the 200th representation of the record-breaking piece.

Captain Purdy had weathered the opposition of two rivals. In addition, not far from his playhouse, at 175 Chatham Street, the Franklin Museum displayed magic-lantern views of the play. As one theatregoer observed, many a "country cousin" found himself beguiled into entering the place thinking that it was the famous Purdy's. Strategically, a brass band stationed on the balcony facing the street drowned out all the barker's cries, except the one magic word — "Purdy's."

This deception naturally caused the Captain to lose some of his avoirdupois, for he had spent great sums spreading the fame of the play throughout the Union. Now many managers were traveling about with dioramas, reaping the benefits of this publicity.

What grated the Captain most was that the Franklin Museum, up the street, claimed, "It is far superior to any dramatized play now being performed at the different theatres in the United States." The dissolving views comprised twenty-five tableaux, beginning with Mrs. Stowe surrounded by garlands, and ending with George's idyllic home in Canada, where were seen Madame de Thoux, Cassy, Emmeline, and the good Missionary.

"Get a celebrated artist!" commanded the Captain. "Get Mr. Rogers, and commission him for a mammoth Mississippi River!"

It was to be gigantic! It took a considerable time to paint, covering over ten thousand feet.

"That canvas is enough to rig out more than half of the Nation's navy!" observed Purdy.

It was late in March, 1854, before he could unroll it in the drama. By then his rival, George Lea, had retired from business at the Franklin Museum.

Purdy found that, panoramically, he could not offset his mobile competitors. Worse still, no longer did Philadelphia boats, tying up at Pier No. 1, in the North River, discharge excited passengers. Two theatres in Philadelphia were showing the drama.

"And across the Hudson," the stout Captain was heard to complain, "Mr. Marsh and his company have been playing it at the Newark Theatre since August 15th of last year, and to immense audiences!"

With the passing months came the historical enactment of the Nebraska-Kansas bill. The question of slavery was now on everyone's lips, and partisans of Negro freedom couldn't get enough of the play, and didn't care who gave it.

As the attendance kept falling off alarmingly at the National, Purdy advertised, "A few more lessons to all humanity at large!'" He selected for Monday and Friday afternoons a drama whose very title suggested at once his own plight, *Lost and Won, or the Gambler*. Little Cordelia was cast as Brother William, and her mother as Sister Mary. On other afternoons *Little Katy* bid for further emotional responses. A later matinee lure, *The Six Degrees of Crime*, made it obvious that something more potent was needed to hold the old audiences. Although Cordelia Howard's benefit on March 18th proved a drawing card, business remained ruinous throughout the season. On April 17th the proprietor presented for the first time in America, *The Child of Prayer, or Thirst for Gold*. Purdy figured, "Since Eliza and a cake of ice are thrilling, the Polar regions — the aurora borealis, the terrific storm, and the breaking up of the ice — should be more so." Despite the talents of Cordelia as Marie Little, the play failed miserably. It became better known as *The Sea of Ice*, and three years later was the turning point in Laura Keene's career.

Uncle Tom's Cabin on May 13th reached the three hundred and twenty-fifth representation, something until then unknown in long runs! Of the original cast that had set out in 1853, Little Cordelia alone possessed the stamina to carry on to the very end. The last performance was a grand benefit farewell to the Eva who had captured all New York.

At the close of the epoch-making run Purdy was reputed to have amassed a gigantic fortune. Certainly, he had increased the size of the display on his shirt, his gold watch and chain were larger, and he was stouter. But when Mr. Howard and "Laff" Fox inventoried the gains at Purdy's home, 34 Mott Street, they discovered the Captain's predicament. He had been making money so fast that it did not seem possible it ever would cease. He had converted at a great cost a slovenly playhouse, located in the dirtiest street in the City, into "The Temple of the Moral Drama." And the season, so propitious to Purdy, revealed — when the final figures were added — alas, a far-reaching loss!

The competition of four other dramatizations proved a drain on Purdy. He had spent enormous amounts advertising, carrying more newspaper space than all the rival playhouses combined: Advertisements by Aiken warning the public that the National alone performed his version; notices disarming religious people of their anti-theatre antipathy; public statements to the effect that little Cordelia was certainly as young as claimed, etc., etc. Then, too, there was the costly innovation of colored lithographs, with their blow and buffing.

When the money was flowing into his pockets by the bushel, the prodigal bought a new house, presented little Cordelia with rings and sundry silver sets, and generously rewarded the entire cast with worthy gifts. The portraits in the lobby, the gigantic panorama, all the added features, and the periodic jubilee celebrations — the Captain's liberality left but $30,000 after the memorable run.

This money he soon lost. In some measure the following season was also unfortunate to other managers because of the financial stringency of the times. But Purdy's failure was due to a most deplorable lack of local dramas with sufficient drawing power. He fell back on the National's old routine of former years, and resorted to the blood and thunder element, the claptrap of the worst raw-head-and-bloody-bones affairs contrivable. When Cony and his dogs returned to their old stamping grounds, once more were heard the hoofbeats of *Mazeppa*, and the strident cries of the auditors, "Say, Jack, heave over some more peanuts, will yer?"

The playhouse saw a brief flurry or two. On June 14th a revival was attempted, with Taylor as Uncle Tom, Mrs. W. G. Jones as Topsy, little Lavinia Bishop as Eva, and the rest of the cast just about the same. Another effort, on June 19th, did not survive beyond a night or so. How keenly Purdy felt the absence of Cordelia Howard!

Alas! the Captain's veering away from the ultra-melodrama to the "moral" had so alienated old gallery frequenters that no public notices could bring them back. In the days of its fallen fortunes the National degenerated into a variety house, with occasional religious revivals on Sundays. In 1857 it finally succumbed to the march of trade, and under the carpenter's hammer was reconstructed into a large furniture warehouse. And that was the end.

Captain Purdy then went to live in retirement in Brooklyn. He became known as the man who had financed and advertised the play which crystallized feeling against slavery, which fired audiences to such a pitch and to such applause *that the nation split apart to the echo!* He was the advance agent of the Civil War.

CHAPTER V

THE WAR OF THE CABINS

When Latin I studied, my Ainsworth in hand,
I answered my teacher that sto *meant to stand;*
But if asked I should now give another reply,
For Stowe *means, beyond any cavil, to lie.*
              —*South. Lit. Messenger*, Jan., 1853

WHEN THE PLAY WAS FIRST ANNOUNCED at Welch's
National Amphitheatre, in Philadelphia, shortly after the
novel's publication, organized opposition met its initial performance.

Old Joe Foster was the manager there at the time,
and he had a friend in London who would send him, every
little while, all the new plays published. In one of the
bundles he thus received was an early adaptation, a crude
affair in three acts, and written by one who evidently knew
little about the Negro character. Anyhow, Foster thought
he had found a bonanza, for the novel was attracting some
attention, and he decided to put it on.

The theatre was just across the street from the Girard
House, where the Southern medical students of the Quaker
City made their headquarters. Not a stone's throw away,
they saw the bills announcing *Uncle Tom*. Immediately,
they got together, and formed a scheme to make the production a failure. The opening performance saw the house
sold out.

When the green baize curtain rang up pandemonium
broke loose.

"No English playwright can libel the South!" they cried.

Each reference to slavery was greeted with jeers, and in the din the actors could hardly hear their cues. After struggling through two acts, the manager was compelled to ring down the curtain. Then he announced a change of bill for the following evening. The City of Brotherly Love had no further opportunity to see the play until the great run of Purdy's.

In the interim there appeared at the old Walnut Street Theatre, on March 3, 1853, a professed answer, *White Slave of England, or the Age We Live In,* which stressed the Negro's being better off than the poor coal miners abroad. In the same vein, *Cabin or Parlour, or a Picture on the Other Side of Jordan to Uncle Tom's Cabin,* a melodrama adapted by B. Young from a Philadelphia book, was shown a year later.

While the famous anti-slavery play was in its ninth week in New York's National Theatre, S. E. Harris, proprietor of a Philadelphia playhouse bearing the same name as the one in New York, announced his new production of *Uncle Tom.* Many coincidences began to surround the play of the Philadelphia usurper. Rather an old hand at the abuses of diplomacy, his newspaper letters to the public were couched as follows: "The undersigned has been surprised or rather amused, at reading in the New York *Herald* an article purporting to be issued by one 'A. H. Purdy,' in which said Purdy claims the exclusive right of dramatizing the world renowned novel of *Uncle Tom's Cabin.* Verily, the modesty of some individuals is refreshing. That Mr. A. H. P. was a dramatist until this moment we were not aware, but presume that his 'light was hid under a broom' until now. Who is A. H. Purdy? Is he a reality, or is he some imaginary 'phantom of the brain?' When we learn whether there is such a person as A. H. P. in existence, we will answer the individual."

From this distortion one got the impression that Aiken had *written* the novel, and that Purdy *dramatized* it!

Harris emphasized that his play was attracting houses "crowded from parquet to dome by the élite and fashion of the City." Harris himself enacted pious Uncle Tom, and advertised his portrayal as "the great original" — a statement far from the truth.

Whereupon Purdy enlarged further an unusual advertising bill to clear up Harris's circumlocution. He claimed Aiken, Howard and he alone were authorized to sell the piece, and that they had *not* disposed of any copy in Philadelphia. The one performed there was *not* the genuine copy of the great adaptation, and Purdy then announced: "The respectable portion of the Philadelphia public will soon have an opportunity to behold the true piece!"

On September 26th, two months after the eventful opening in New York, the Chestnut Street Theatre opened its doors to the Howard-Aiken version. Entrusted to two cousins of the Howard family, Mr. and Mrs. Joseph Jefferson, were the Gumption Cute and Marie rôles.

Philadelphia now had two rival plays, which were received in quite a different manner from that early unfortunate presentation at Welch's Theatre. The slightest hiss at either theatre was drowned out by a united roar of "Order!" One spectator, at Harris's National, expressed this feeling: "On the whole, the Play was eminently successful, and one may infer a hopeful change in public sentiment, when they see three thousand persons unconsciously accepting anti-slavery truth; hundreds of boys — incipient rowdies, growing up to become the mobocracy of another generation, but preparing unwittingly to 'mob on the right side'; and I could not help thinking, that before we hold our third decade in Philadelphia, abolitionists may have to intercede to save slaveholders and slavehunters from the fury of the mob, so long directed against us."

The two plays on a single theme left a deep mark on all Quakers. Further, the custom grew in the Quaker City, for those oddly encased in drab shad-belly coats and wearing remarkably broadbrimmed beavers, to take a promenade that led — sooner or later — to either playhouse. They debated inwardly, on the sidewalk, the problem of the Theatre as it *is*, the illegitimacy of its art, and the balancing conviction that it *could be made* — somehow — Humanity's special appeal for its former abuses. Then arguing that the popular heart had transmuted the materials, that the old misdirection was gone, they would seek a true means of acknowledging their obligations to human freedom. They fulfilled them by entering the theatre — where they met the rest of the parish!

Moreover, the Philadelphia theatrical era of *Uncle Tom* influenced a great many boys like John S. Wise, long before they admitted it. When *Graham's Magazine* ran counter to the new spirit in the City, attacking the novel as "Black Letters, or Uncle Tom Foolery in Literature," and appraising the drama, "Uncle Tom is played at two theatres, and everything is *Topsy*-turvey in regular dramatics," the puns were like the finishing strokes of a coup de grâce. The great magazine's circulation immediately decreased, and it went out of business.

Philadelphia, as a matter of fact, did not care whether Harris's or Purdy's was "the great original." They packed both playhouses.

Curiously, the relation of affairs between Harris's and Purdy's rival versions in Philadelphia was similar to the plight in which the Howard family found itself later. When the Howards left New York they took the play to Boston, where, on June 19, 1854, they opened at the National Theatre. They encountered an opposition *Uncle Tom* at the old Boston Museum, which had already won the Hub. And none other than the influential Theodore Parker had praised that Museum production at the annual meeting of the Massachusetts' A. S. Society: "....But now theatres have come up again; and while the work of that venerable Doctor's daughter is read out of the churches, while its doctrine cannot be preached there, Mr. Kimball opens the doors of his theatre, and *Uncle Tom's Cabin* is played to large audiences, eight times a week (Loud cheers). I thank God that when Humanity is excommunicated from the Boston church, she can yet find a resting-place for the sole of her foot in a Boston theatre! (Cheers). Some years ago, my friend Brother Spear, (who sits at my side,) asked Mr. Kimball why he did not have some play that touches the humanities, and was moral and elevating in its tendency? 'Why don't you have an anti-slavery play?' asked Mr. Spear. Whereupon, Mr. Kimball said—'I can't get the audience; but soon as you get the people outside ready to come in and see an anti-slavery play, I will perform nothing else.' (Cheers). Now, *Uncle Tom's Cabin* has got the outsiders in favor of humanity, and Mr. Kimball opens his doors. In due time— when the wind blows long enough in that quarter—I suppose humanity will get even to the churches (Applause)." The Howards did not find their stay in Boston too lucrative.

Mr. Howard decided to take the play in repertoire on the road. The family went south, appearing at Baltimore and Washington, and continuing on to St. Louis. In none of these three cities, strongly proslavery, did they meet with any discourtesies.

However, to produce the play in Baltimore was as much as a man's life was worth. John E. Owens, famous for his characterization of Solon Shingle in *The People's Lawyer,* was managing during 1855. When the Howards arrived at his theatre in March, of that year, their carefully chosen pieces, *Fashion and Famine, Hot Corn,* and *The Lamplighter* were failures with the public. Only slim houses could be drawn, and Owens lost money rapidly. The parents of little Cordelia, claiming that she was ill, withdrew.

Then Owens thought of *Uncle Tom's Cabin*. He had once given, as may be recalled, the very first adaptation, *Uncle Tom's Cabin as It Is;* concocted at the time with a shrewd Shingle view of "a bar'l of apple-sass," it had been beyond the credulity of the most zealous slaveholders. He now reasoned, "So, seeing that neither the blissful spectacle of radiant orange groves, wherein the Negro reclined, whilst fruit was showered upon his head, nor the rhapsodies of Uncle Tom, would attract the public, I'll bring out the Simon Pure article!"

It was, of course, a risky bit of business.

"Can the *Uncle Tom* you play be so adapted and softened in its style, without losing much of its interest, as to be made not only acceptable but telling to a Baltimore audience?" Owens asked Howard, shrewdly. "I would not hesitate, if you concluded to play here, to announce the piece as 'The Great New York Uncle Tom, &c.' "

Howard was uncertain about how close he could come to the original costly staging.

"Our expenses at the present time are one hundred dollars a night," Owens anticipated him. "But if we produced *Uncle Tom* they will necessarily be somewhat increased." Then he stated proudly, "Our theatre, albeit called the Little Charles St., will hold four hundred dollars!"

While the drama was being announced to the public, Owens met his lawyer on the street, one day, who warned him, "You will ruin yourself with the South, and get into all sorts of trouble. The citizens will tear the theatre down, and do you a personal injury!"

To avert the expected riot, Owens warily modified the play script even more. He called his players together:

"Mr. Edwin Adams will tone down his Legree. And Mr. Colin Stuart will do the same with George Harris. And you, Miss DeVere, make the Marie role more sympathetic."

"How about Eliza?" someone asked.

"I've already instructed Mrs. Parker."

"You're not going to implicate the Howards," said Mrs. Jane Germon, the Aunt Ophelia, who had the family's welfare at heart.

"Oh, they'll assume their old parts."

Then the comedians in the company were singled out by the manager:

"Mr. John T. Raymond, see what you can do with the Gumption Cute lines. Mr. Joseph Parker, I have you down as Deacon Perry."

"Isn't it all rather on the comedy side?" the puzzled members asked one another, going over the lines.

"I've raked up all sorts of situations from old farces, and so on — anything to cover up the real drift of the play," admitted Owens. "Where's young John Sleeper Clarke?"

"Here, sir."

"I am assigning you the part of Lawyer Marks."

"But my *forte* is tragedy!" the boy complained.

"You're like your companion, Robson. I believe he used those very words when I gave him an opportunity in *Uncle Tom's Cabin as It Is.*"

"But the part is a mere 'feeder'!"

"I have built the character up to the foremost position in the play. We'll launch you on the career of a popular comedian."

"But isn't that in your line, sir?"

"I'm undertaking Uncle Tom."

"That can't be, sir!"

"Besides strengthening the bill, I'll be on the spot if trouble breaks out."

When the play opened, on April 16th, advertisements proclaimed it as a first production south of the Mason and Dixon line.

The town was set on its ears! The theatre was jammed nightly, and how they laughed over that scream of a fellow in his misadventures as Lawyer Marks! The Tom they beheld was faithful in all detail, to their way of thinking then. In the impersonation Owens, for example, had blackened heavily the toes of his boots, leaving the heels yellow with mud. When Howard asked him, later, why he didn't clean up the back of his shoes, the knowing answer came: "Howard, a Nigger never polishes more than the toes!"

In relating this incident in the dressing-room, afterward, Howard was corrected by little Cordelia, who suggested "colored gentleman."

When the Howard family left Baltimore, they ventured into St. Louis. And this was about as far into the deep South that their play had gone.

Earlier, however, through the efforts of one Colonel Robert E. J. Miles, of Culpepper Court House, Virginia, the anti-slavery drama was shown in Cincinnati, which touched Kentucky. By chance, the Colonel had been attracted to the play that was creating a furor in New York, and sensing its destined popularity, became determined to obtain it. He knew that the only available copy was guarded zealously by the prompter, and that it was not for sale. But he haunted the National night after night, and on small cards jotted down surreptitiously the outlines of the drama, scene by scene. Back at his hotel, he filled in all he could recall of dialogue and stage business, often resorting to Mrs. Stowe's novel to refresh his memory. He was unfamiliar with the technique of play-writing, his only experience being that of a circus ring master and four-horse rider. He hurried off to Cincinnati, where he organized a company, and brought forth the play at Melodeon Grand Concert Hall on December 5th, 1853.

From an old diary left by the George Harris of this company, Harry Watkins, we can trace the circuit of this successful venture in Ohio. On one occasion, they were diverted by the début of a very temperamental Eva. The three-year-old daughter of Harry Chapman had been carefully coached by her grandmother, Mrs. S. Drake, who wished to perpetuate the dramatic line in the family. All went sufficiently well with the new Eva on the opening night — that is, until the very last scene, the wonderful apocalypse. The child had been permitted to slumber for an hour, until the scene of her ascension to heaven on a cloud. Abruptly aroused, Little Blanche sleepily repudiated any idea of putting the finishing touch to an otherwise perfect performance. Nor could she be prevailed upon by a threat of private injury in the offing, or the greatest plea of dramatic tradition: The show must go on! She repeated explicitly, "I won't go to heaven on a board," and nothing could sway her. Fortunately, the audience was not much the wiser — the play was then in its nascent period — and as they left the theatre they did not realize that they had been cheated of a good slice of paradise.

The following night, Little Blanche still held her ground. When St. Clair affectionately asked her what she saw, he expected to hear, "I see the angels bright." Instead, Eva, supposedly dying of consumption, yelled with all the full power of her healthy lungs, "I want to see my grandma!"

"Hush!" said Uncle Tom, sotto voce, and bowed down in solemn prayer.

"She's going to heaven!" said St. Clair, loud enough to drown her appeal.

"No, I ain't!" shrieked Eva. "I don't want to go to heaven without my grandma!"

Never did the mourning doves witness such a spectacle. The devoted darkies, gathered to do service in a beautiful spiritual ensemble, harmonized, "Tell Me Where My Eva's Gone" — for Miss Eva's safe journey across the river Jordan, but this unforeseen "misfortune" in the St. Clair family busted up the whole works. To make matters worse, the prompter was raw in his calling, and slavishly carried

— 115 —

out orders not to ring the curtain down till Eva was dead all over. The paroxysm of laughter that seized the spectators violently shook the rafters of the playhouse. Those related to the gentle Eva, and such faithful slaves as were gathered about her bed, constrained their emotions by burying their faces in the bedclothes, until someone mustered the necessary intelligence to ring down the curtain on what proved to be the second and farewell appearance of the widely heralded "WORLD'S WONDER, LITTLE BLANCHE CHAPMAN."

Certain little Evas did not "take hold," but others did. No small share of the historic play's success was due to the players who created the characters. As had been true with the Lawyer Marks of John Sleeper Clarke, minor rôles grew in stature, and now we may glance leeward to one such development — or maturity — of another famous part.

When the Howard family first took their play to New York, the lessee of the Troy Museum, Mr. Hough, also left the scene of that first triumph. He produced another dramatization of Uncle Tom, by Robert Marsh, at the Syracuse Theatre.

The rival adaptor, one day, approached Manager Hough: "Would you like to go along with this company, during the summer, and enact the part of Gumption Cute at Oswego for one week?"

Mr. Hough glanced at the sixteen-line part, and laughed at the idea, "It is the very fragment that Mr. Howard had."

"My dear Hough," urged the other, "take hold of the part, and build it up. The play needs some humor, and you can put it in that part. If you do, I'll conform the rest of the play more to Howard's version."

Hough elaborated the role into fifteen lengths, or 800 lines, and played it with Marsh's company in Oswego, Auburn, and Utica for four of the five weeks. A decided hit, Mr. Hough soon realized that he could do better by playing it in his own company.

Marsh's troupe, likewise, found their lines cropping up, unwittingly, in odd places and odd moments. They had never played one drama so continuously, being accustomed to stock. Once, upon the request of citizens in a small town, the standard fare of *Charles II* was substituted. A young actor, Martini, (the Uncle Tom in the anti-slavery drama) personated Charles II — and made a most amusing blunder. In the first act the roystering monarch, accompanied by Rochester (both disguised as sailors), visits the tavern of Captain Copp, an old sea dog living in the suburbs of London. After a merry time of it, during which they knock things around generally, they call for the bill.

"What is the reckoning?" asks the King.

"Two pun ten," says the host.

"Two pun ten?" repeats the King, feeling for money in his pockets, but finding none. "Shipmate (to Rochester) give us your purse."

Rochester protests that he has not a shilling. Captain Copp becomes incensed: "Wot does this mean? You comes to my 'ouse, an' horders us 'round as if you was the king of Hengland. Best supper, best wine, dance a 'ornpipe on my table, an' rumples my niece. Hit's my opinion that you're a couple o' swindlers. Wot's the name o' yer ship?"

But neither the King nor Rochester can remember the name of their ship, while the Captain berates them fiercely with many sarcastic questions about the sea, reiterating, "Now, har'n't ye asham'd o' yeselves!"

Martini hung his head, forgot his part, now fancying himself abused by Legree, and lapsed into Southern Negro dialect: "*Y-a-s, mas'r!*"

The effect was like lightning, and sent the audience into gales of laughter.

The play held the boards in many parts of the country, but principally in the larger cities. As was the custom, the stars traveled from place to place, alone and unattended.

When they reached the theatre, they depended upon the local company to be letter perfect in the various supporting roles, arriving just in time for a single rehearsal before the opening performance. Journeying troupes like Hough's were rare, indeed. Furthermore, in those days the expense of travel was prohibitory, and it would have been impracticable to transport combinations and elaborate. scenery.

The Fall of 1854 found the determined young G. L. Aiken in Detroit. Two years before, on October 2nd, according to Col. T. Allston Brown, a dramatization by Clifton W. Tayleure was seen there which represented Southern political sympathies; it was subsequently acted, with very slight success, in Cleveland and in a few other Northern cities, with Tayleure in the part of George Harris. Now Aiken was in Detroit, bent on letting it see his own. Accordingly, he opened on October 2nd, himself enacting George Harris, supported by the local stock company.

Chicago saw an early dramatization about the time the Howard family was closing the Troy engagement. On December 13th of that epoch-making year, John B. Rice's theatre performed it in a wilderness numbering less than 5,000 souls. Chicago was a mud hole in those primitive days. There wasn't a paving stone, just plank sidewalks; it was common for teams to stall to the wheel hubs, churning in this wonderful world of mud. Often a mule sank deeper and deeper, its cries growing fainter and fainter — as it was sucked into the Great Lakes. On the slippery loam the first citizen was on an equal footing with the town pauper. Without a single street lamp in the town, the citizens, in the darkness, lit their way to Rice's theatre, carrying flickering lanterns on long sticks.

To reach that far outpost of American civilization meant many days in travel-worn stage coaches, especially from the Eastern seacoast.

One day, toward the close of the year 1852, a little

woman stepped down from a dusty coach, and asked her way to Rice's theatre.

"The old one burned down," said a heavy-booted man. "You'll find the new brick one on the easterly side of Dearborn Street, a little way south of Randolph. Mr. Laundry's livery stable stood there once."

When another offered to carry her portfolio, her face implied deliberation.

"Popular man — Mr. Rice, yes-sir-ee! If Chicago ever has a mayor, it'll natcher'ly be him."

When she entered the theatre, she was instantly recognized by fellow actors, "Dan Marble's widow is here!"

"Wasn't an abler comedian. If the cholera hadn't swept the country that Spring, three years ago —"

"Now, sister-in-law," Mr. Rice greeted her affectionately, "once here, you're required by the nature of things to get along without such luxuries as tea and coffee. We use a substitute for tea, and it's concocted from the herbs we pick in the neighborhood. Moreover, you'll eat wild turkey."

"How barbaric!"

"In New York State —"

"In Buffalo, you mean. And that is not far from Troy, neither, dear brother-in-law. You have heard how the Howard family and their play are taking the city by storm?"

"What play?"

"*Uncle Tom's Cabin*, of course!"

Mr. Rice became interested.

"The Boston Museum is crowded, with its competing adaptation. And you should see how my brother is making them laugh there!"

"William Warren?"

"Yes. He has the interpolated character of Penetrate Partyside. It's not in the novel at all."

Then Mrs. Marble opened her small, precious portfolio.

"What's that you have there?" asked Rice.

"My very own dramatization of Mrs. Stowe's novel."

"Let me see it."

"I have left out Topsy and Eva altogether."

In that manner, the prize was brought to the wilds of Chicago. Actually, it ran all of three consecutive weeks. This was an unusual triumph, for up to then swift changes were the order of the day in the tiny town. Mr. Rice's only serious competition was Colonel Wood, who had rigged out an empty store on Lake Street, where he exhibited a collection of live snakes, a double-headed rooster, etc., adding a hand organ to beguile the curious, all billed as "The Greatest Show on Earth!"

A year later, on December 10th, Chicagoans saw the drama again, this time with the full grandeur of R. D. Smith's Mississippi panorama.

And event of events! The Howards arrived in February, 1854. With the company were William J. LeMoyne, in the part written in for his special talents, and Greene C. Germon, the creator of the Uncle Tom rôle. The visit to the Windy City proved fatal to Germon. He was found dead one morning, a victim of consumption. On a cold, cheerless day in March, they buried him on the North Side, not far from the Lake, and John Rice with his little band of players attended the funeral.

Most notable of all, in Chicago, was James Hubert McVicker's production of 1858. His own début had been made at the time that Dan Marble departed, and he filled the gap left by that comedian, purchasing the plays and costumes from the widow. Mr. McVicker followed closely the Howard-Aiken dramatization, himself undertaking Gumption Cute, and for Deacon Perry he secured John D. Dillon. The latter had an ingenious way of finding quaint and absurd coats and other mirth-provoking bits of attire, that fitted the Deacon Perry personation as well as the lines did. He shunned publicity, and refused to be advertised as "America's greatest comedian." His manager pleaded with him, "Well, you *are* America's greatest comedian, aren't you? What's the use of concealing the fact?"

Dillon answered, "I'm willing to assume to be the greatest anything you say, but I think it would be much nicer to surprise the audience...."

Many in the McVicker cast became quite famous later on, notably Mary McVicker, who made her début as Eva at the age of nine. Her personation caught the attention of Edwin Booth, who visited Chicago at the time. They were betrothed nine years later.

Meanwhile, over the rest of the continent, a foundation was being laid which all the masons in the world could not dislodge. Along with the serious dramatizations were many take-offs. Mr. and Mrs. Barney Williams made an Irish holiday of it in H. J. Conway's *Uncle Pat's Cabin*. Another, also put together with a shillalah, was *Uncle Mike's Cabin*, at Purdy's National Theatre, a month before the New York opening of the Howards. The Bowery Theatre boasted an *Uncle Crotchet's Parlour*, and minstrelsy was responsible for such burlettas as *Uncle Dad's Cabin*, *Happy Uncle Tom*, *Uncle Tom and His Cabin*, and *Aunt Dinah's Cabin*.

Mrs. Stowe was lampooned in H. Plunkett's *Black and White, or Abroad and at Home*, at Burton's Theatre, in New York, toward the close of 1853. The scene was laid in England, and contrasted English miseries with the so-popular Southern variety. One of the characters, a Mr. Crab, resented his wife's concern for the Negroes rather than for the home-grown wretches. Mrs. Stowe was caricatured as Mrs. Skreecher Crow, and when the Duchess of Thunderland fell passionately for the American "dear negroes," and rushed to embrace a black boy, Cornet Cologne, his coloring rubbed off accidentally — and exposed the imposter!

Another, *Uncle Tom in England*, saw the lamps of the Richmond Theatre, with a long subtitle, *A Proof that Black's White; a echo to the American "Uncle Tom."* This flubdub purported to be the dying confession of Emmeline, whose ultimate fate, in the playwright's opinion, should have been left to the reader's imagination.

In the Fall of the year, fun was rampant below the Mason-Dixon line with *Uncle Tom's Cabin, or Freedom at the North and Service at the South.* The Charleston *Standard,* commenting on the performance scheduled there by the Nightingale Troupe, said: "We hear already of a great demand for tickets. Aunt Harriet Beecher's *toe* will, we anticipate, be entirely dislocated." The following year, in February, New Orleans, too, borrowed the idea, and the play was rather modified from the original form in the Northern States, but tailored to suit the locality.

That was about the best the South could do to contravene the effect of the play. Newspapers like the Ohio *Anti-Slavery Bugle* reported glowing eye-witness accounts of the great dramatic success up north. A sample of the reviews that aroused Southern speculation was Parker Pillsbury's on the Conway dramatization: "....And now a prominent and wealthy Boston whig, the proprietor of the most popular, and deservedly popular Theatre in the City, has just placed a dramatic representation of *Uncle Tom's Cabin* upon the stage, in a manner to bring the whole subject of slavery before the community as never before.... And now, the Theatre is openly, where it has long been *actually; before and better than the Church.* Let the terrible fact be told in thunder round the world. In the Play, the slave-holder declares boldly, '*Slavery is the Devil.*' In most of the forty thousand ecclesiastical Theatres and Playhouses of our country, the ghastly performances solemnly say, *it is of God.* In the language of one large Presbytery, 'It is the Lord's doing, and marvellous in our eyes.' Now we have the Theatre *versus* the Church, on the question of slavery. The Theatre says it's of the Devil. The Church claims it is of God. Let us wait patiently for the verdict. The question is before a jury comprised of the civilized world.... It was

Uncle Tom's Cabin, on the stage, and before one of the largest and best looking audiences I ever saw in any theatre. And five hundred people bought tickets in the forenoon for *secured seats, at double price* — and excepting those seats, the house was almost literally crammed, nearly an hour before the rising of the curtain. And the most radical sentiments, together with the shooting dead of the kidnappers in pursuit of George and Eliza, were most loudly applauded: -—and one thing more, the Play will, doubtless, from present appearances, be a. fortune in the pocket of the proprietor of the museum. *Vive la agitation!"* No puns there, but enough to awaken the curiosity of Southerners, who wanted to know what it was all about.

A Mississippi pilot, better known later as Mark Twain, went to see it, and thought it a masterpiece, as did Senator Lyman Trumbull, friend and rival of Lincoln, who viewed it with Stephen A. Douglas in Springfield, Illinois.

Oddly enough, not a single play which tried to show that *Uncle Tom's Cabin* was a misrepresentation ever won an audience. This is the more amazing because the theatre-going public was in the prosperous slave-holding cities, like Baltimore, Richmond, New York, New Orleans; while the abolition movement centered in New England towns, where all playhouses were subject to taboo, and shunned. Those plays that did procure patronage for a while were takeoffs or minstrel burlesques of the drama then sweeping the nation. The case for the South, moreover, could never be stated adequately on the European stage, and the matter of winning sentiment abroad was an important one. Adaptations of Mrs. Stowe's novel enjoyed even greater popularity there than in the States.

The growing strain between North and South, especially in the Presidential race, had its repercussions in the theatre. At least to one actor the eve of conflict brought a harassing experience. J. B. Howe's dramatic instinct may have gotten

the better of historical accuracy, but such was the concate-
nation of events that we can forgive him errors in dates and
the forced closeness of the events. He was in Richmond at
the time — Lincoln had just been elected — when, a day
later, he found himself drawn into a peculiar bit of business.
He received a message instructing him to appear at the
theatre immediately, and when he arrived there, he was
ushered into the private office of the manager, George Kunkel, whom he found peculiarly disturbed. Kunkel warned
the actor of the shocking condition in which the South would
be, now that they had elected Lincoln, and repeated: "The
country will run rivers of blood; the business will begin to
fall off — and I intend to end the season three weeks from
now. But before doing so, here is a drama (flinging the
MS. on the table) which I intend putting up for next Friday,
and there is an awfully long part for you to study. So you
had better take it at once."

Howe picked it up, glanced through the pages, and was
struck by one curious circumstance — the speeches were
eighty and ninety lines long! He looked up at Kunkel, "This
must be some amateur author."

"It is by Mr. Bricken, the editor of the————, and
is called *Parlour and Cabin*," continued Kunkel. "It is in
opposition to *Uncle Tom's Cabin*. And, no doubt, as the
Anti-Abolition feeling is strong, it may prove a card for a
week or so. Do what you can with the part, as this is
Tuesday, and we can only have three rehearsals."

To do justice to a part of such extremely long, political
speeches in so short a time, would have taxed the most extraordinary mind in the world, and Howe asked permission
to "cut the part," or he would relinquish it altogether. He
complained to Kunkel's associate, Thomas Moxley.

"Do your best with it," urged Moxley. "I leave it to
yourself, but I do not want Mr. Bricken to find fault with
us. His paper is very powerful, and might do a great
amount of harm."

Irresolute, Howe left. At the first rehearsal he found that the role was even more involved and obscure, and when Kunkel came on the stage, Howe renewed his protestations: It was impossible to commit to memory a part of thirty lengths in such limited time! The manager told him to do the best he could under the conditions.

On the opening night the theatre was jammed. The audience gave free rein to their emotional judgments, applauding and hissing the questions of the hour as expounded on the stage. When the curtain came down, Howe breathed more freely.

As he left the stage door, he recognized a faithful patron. It was the custom to exchange compliments of the evening, but this night when the actor said, "Good night," in his usual manner, the gentleman turned aside brusquely, muttering something indistinctly, which Howe knew was anything but complimentary. The actor tried to disregard it, and proceeded to his lodging.

The next day, however, he was awakened early by a mysterious tapping on his door. The visitor was William H. Bailey, who enacted the "first old man" parts in the company, and known as "Old Man" Bailey to all. Now he was a study in excitement, as he whispered, "Howe, you have to clear!"

"What do you mean?"

"Look at this," the other answered, producing a notice of the play in the very paper of which the playwright was editor. Howe read with quickened interest, and realized his unfavorable position in the City when he came to the lines: "Mr. Howe, the original St. Clair in that filthy tissue of lies and misrepresentations of our glorious Southern institutions, which emanated from the diseased brain of the notorious Harriet Beecher Stowe, should not allow his political bias to influence his professional abilities, as an actor; it is time we were rid of all such sympathizers of purely Northern feelings from our part of the soil."

"Good heavens! what can it mean?" Howe asked. "I am no politician. I have never—" In fact, the English actor hardly knew what the term meant. But Bailey interposed with further disquieting news: He had been drinking at a hotel with some friends, when he saw some gentlemen draw up a paper of some sort, setting forth that, if the actor Howe did not get out of Richmond there and then, they promised to make it pretty hot for him. "I know you can't go on the stage again," advised Bailey. "Kunkel and Moxley also have come to the conclusion not to let you. Even now, Bob Meldrum has the MS. studying your part for tonight."

"Tonight," said Howe, recalling the ineffectuality of committing the part to memory. "Why, he could never .."

Bailey interrupted him, "He is to take it on and read it."

"Oh! if that's the case, I must leave."

In less than two hours, Howe left Richmond on a steamer bound for New York. But before it reached the pier, two men boarded it in the Sound — bringing news that the first shot had been fired on Fort Sumter in Charleston harbor.

CHAPTER VI

THE REHABILITATION OF THE STAGE NEGRO

> *"Hulloa, Jim Crow!" said Mr. Shelby... "Now,*
> *Jim, show this gentleman how you can dance and*
> *sing...Now, Jim, walk like Uncle Cudjoe, when*
> *he has the rheumatism," said his master.*
>   —from the Novel

OF THE EVENTS SHAPING THEMSELVES in the early history
of *Uncle Tom's Cabin* this became most salient: the Negro
— for once — was recognized as serious stage material;
hitherto, he had belonged to travesty.

Up to this time the colored unfortunates had been
depicted rather sporadically. The Moor that Shakespeare
drew was never acknowledged as the typical African, notwithstanding the fact that Othello shows acute distress, in
the third act, when he is referred to as "black, and has not
those soft parts of conversation that chamberers have."
Roderigo describes Othello's thick lips, and doubtlessly
Shakespeare held the conviction that the Moors belonged
to the Negro race. In 1696 appeared a five-act tragedy,
Oroonoko, by Thomas Southerne, based on the kidnapping
and bondage of a real African prince, who was sold as a
slave in the West Indies. The hero had dark skin and
kinky hair, but alas, his stilted blank verse would have bewildered the original darkies of the West Indies!

When the Negro did begin to emerge half-recognizably
on the stage, it was in mere bits, and then only as an adjunct
to the song and dance. One of the earliest Negro imper-

sonations goes far back to 1767, in New York, when a farce, *The Enchanted Lady of the Grove*, listed in the programme: "End of Part the Third, a Negro Dance in Character by Mr. Tea." But it is really Mungo, a year later, whom we accept as the progenitor. He figured in *The Padlock*, a comic opera by Isaac Bickerstaffe, performed at Drury Lane. The rôle had been written in at the suggestion of John Moody, who had lived in the Barbadoes, and knew at first hand the Negro dialect and manners. In the course of the action, Mungo sang a ballad, setting the style for his burnt-cork descendants. The following year Lewis Hallam, the younger, introduced Mungo in America, and it is claimed that Negro minstrelsy had its first inception when the play opened in Boston on December 30, 1799. Gottlieb Graupner was seen "in character," in the second act, singing "The Gay Negro Boy." Although the Federal Street Theatre was draped in mourning for General Washington, the audience was lifted up with a new joy: the performer came forth from the wings, again and again, with his little bench and banjo.

About the time of the Revolutionary War the Negro was introduced into legitimate drama. There were fragmentary parts in *The Candidates* (1770) by Colonel Robert Munford, and in *The Fall of British Tyranny, or American Liberty* (1776) by John Leacock. In the latter play Virginia slaves were kidnapped aboard a man-of-war, and promised their freedom if they murdered their masters. But there is no evidence that these two pieces were ever produced.

J. Robinson's *The Yorker's Stratagem, or Banana's Wedding*, in 1792, concerned a New Yorker who wooed a West Indian heiress; Mrs. Gray, who played the mulatto, had lived in the West Indies, and therefore, may have reproduced the dialect faithfully. The American public was entertained by the two-act farce, and did not take exception to the novelty of colored characters, perhaps because they were not native Negroes.

Three years later Philadelphia saw a four-act comedy, *The Triumphs of Love, or Happy Reconciliation*, with a scene containing an early protest against slavery. A philanthropic master, George Friendly, Jr., freed his Negro servant, Sambo, and this marked the first approach to the problem of the American Negro. The author, John Murdock, introduced in his next play, *The Politicians* (1795), four more delightful Negroes: Cato, Caesar, Sambo and Pompey; but the play, replete with realistic touches, was never enacted. Another playwright, twenty-five years later, followed the example of Murdock's earlier play, for the first act of David Darling's farce, *Beaux Without Belles, or Ladies We Cannot Do Without You*, performed at the Fredericksburg Theatre, contained abolition sentiments.

Only in a fortuitous manner did the Negro appear as dramatic material, and on the rare occasions when he could not very well be left out. Such was the pantomime *Robinson Crusoe*, at Drury Lane, in 1781, where Friday was very necessary to the action; in coffee-colored tights and blackened face, he always figured as Harlequin. The spectacular thriller, *Obi, or Three-Finger'd Jack*, stressed, later, a Negro dance, the inside of a slave's hut in Jamaica, and extensive views of plantations. More sympathy was evidenced when the setting was far away from home, as in *Slaves in Algiers, or a Struggle for Liberty*, given as an afterpiece at the John Street Theatre in 1796. Frequently, in lurid Gothic plays like *The Castle Spectre*, at the Park Theatre in 1793, Negroes were cast as villainous slaves aiding their wicked lords in the abuse of dungeon victims.

Perhaps Negro delineation became a little more perfect, a little more realistic, in the course of time, but intelligible Negro dialect was very slow to evolve. Take, for example, L. Beach's *Jonathan Postfree* (1807), where Caesar says: "Me no muchee fear the weight of your cane, massa, such a little tick no hurtee me much—and me didn't expect to feel the weight of your money — me only try to see if you had any soul or no." We immediately hear the sentiments of the future Uncle Tom, just as we recognized George Harris' opening lines in the ballad which Mungo sang years before in *The Padlock*. However, the dialect is not that of a Negro, but of a Chinese!

The ear for Negro speech was ever faulty; many Caesars took a foothold on the American stage as type-characters, one in an adaptation of Cooper's *The Spy* in 1822. They were intended primarily for humor, and frequently were shown drunk during their master's absence. In A. B. Lindsay's *Love and Friendship* (1809), a Negro boy, Harry, belonging to a South Carolina family, spoke after the fashion of someone struggling with a word-for-word translation: "Heigho! what wicked worl dis white man worl be for true do! No like de negur country; no do sich ting der; no hab run for git drunk and fight. I wish neber bin blige for lef it. I bin happy dere.... no de hab massa for scole, no lan bad ting, and hear him ebery day so much.... But why me de no happy? He bess be happy I can, now I here poor slave, and no can git backa my country again."

Curiously, through the efforts of the Negroes themselves we finally got something approaching the genuine dialect of the race. In 1821 a small group of New York colored citizens rented a place in back of a hospital, at the corner of Bleecker and Mercer Streets, known as the African Grove, and here tried to imitate the whites in the City's larger gardens, where Negroes had long been denied access. In the little boxes a determined effort was made to pursue the coquetry and causerie fashionable among the paler belles and dandies. A partition in the back marked off an inclosure for white visitors, and this latter adjunct proved disastrous to the whole venture. The black corps drama-tique fell victim to the raillery of the town wits who, out for a lark, found diversion in scaling crackers onto the stage, picking off the principals with apple-cores, chestnuts and potatoes, and the lesser supernumaries with a barrage of hissing peas.

During this civil dissension, the "African Company" attempted *Richard III* and *Othello*. The critics refused to see the performances except in the light of a laughable absurdity, an attitude carried on later in the extravaganzas of minstrel shows. One critic of the day observed: "A little dapper wooly-haired waiter at the City Hotel personated the royal Plantagenet in robes made up from discarded curtains of the ball room." Another covered the performance of *Othello*: "The curtain was raised, and behold! — a street in Venice — it more resembled a dirty kitchen — enter Iago and Roderigo — Iago was dressed in blue satin pantaloons, and a cap, which appeared to have been in the Revolutionary war, by the many shapes it now assumed; he wore a kind of roundabout jacket, or an old coat with the skirts turned up; he wore an ancient looking sword, well clad in a coat of rust. Roderigo wore for a sword, the part of an iron hoop! his whole dress resembled that of a patent sweep's." The minstrel cakewalk of the future can be discerned in the offing.

Before the little establishment broke up, unable to withstand the raids upon it, several more plays were subjected to trials. One of these, *Tom and Jerry, or, Life in, London*, a "burletta of fun, frolic, fashion, and flash," added an extra scene, the slave market in Charleston — the first attempt at a realistic portrayal of the American Negro. Eventful, again, were the few performances advertised as "the Drama of King Shotaway, Founded on facts taken from the Insurrection of the Caravs in the Island of St. Vincent, Written from experience by Mr. Brown." We may call it the first Negro drama.

It was not until almost thirty years later, with *Uncle Tom's Cabin*, that the native Negro again became the subject of a serious full-length play.

Meanwhile, Thomas D. Rice's impersonation conferred upon him the title of founder of Ethiopian minstrelsy. There may have been others before him, but his portrayal of a human crow hopping along with a broken wing won a sensational popularity both here and abroad. While a member of Samuel Drake's company in Lousville, in 1828, he accidentally came upon the original. Back of the theatre was a livery-stable, where an old, decrepit Negro lamely made his way about. The actors often watched his queer movements, the twitching-up of the arm and shoulder: Deformed, his right shoulder was drawn up high, and his left leg was crooked at the knee, which made it rather painful to get around — overbalanced, he limped in an exaggerated manner. He crooned a peculiar old tune, to his own words; at the end of each verse he had recourse to an erratic step, "rocking de heel," in the enactment rendered afterward by "Jim Crow" Rice. None but Rice saw the possibilities of the ungainly, shambling character. He studied the Negro attentively, and hired him to teach him the words. Rice added a few more verses to the refrain, with many witty local allusions, and somewhat altered the air. When a local piece, *The Rifle*, was produced in the Louisville Theatre, Rice persuaded the manager to permit him to introduce a song and dance. He received more than twenty encores on the first night, and "Jim Crow" soon jumped into national fame. The popular impersonation gave rise to new terms, "Jim Crow cars" and "Jim Crow laws," which later meant Negro segregation and legislation.

With the imitators of Rice, who wheeled about on their heels all over the nation, came a demand for more of this lively entertainment. A "Dinah Crow" was done by Dan Gerner. The youngest imitator in burnt-cork was Joseph Jefferson, who, at the age of four, was carried in a burlap bag by Rice himself onto the stage of the Washington Theatre, where little Joe hopped about as a miniature "Jim Crow." As others tried to emulate the Rice success of the phenomenal ditty and dance, the American stage suddenly beheld a wild, dark flower blooming — Negro minstrelsy.

"Jim Crow" Rice, like many before him, appeared as an individual performer between the acts; but now, by the 1840's, they began to organize. The first blackface band made its début at the new Chatham Theatre in 1843, consisting of "Dan" Emmett, fiddle, "Frank" Brower, bones, "Bill" Whitlock, banjo, and "Dick" Pelham, tambo — the familiar shortening of the names was indigenous with minstrelsy. Using the instruments of the Southern plantation slaves, they formed a nondescript band, playing new songs set to the most precious gems of Negro melody, such as "The Essence of Old Virginia" and the "Lucy Long Walk Around." Soon after, Emmett wrote the most famous of all minstrel songs, "Old Dan Tucker." In the late fifties he devised "Dixie" as a walk-around in a New York minstrel show, and it was introduced by Mrs. John Wood into a burlesque in New Orleans. The Confederacy later adopted it for its rallying song, and when Richmond fell, President Lincoln ordered that bands everywhere play it, insisting that with the capture of the Southern capital the song, too, was captured.

As the minstrels sang, cut capers and clogged about to the bones, banjo and tambourine, Thackeray, during a visit here, was moved to write: "I heard a humorous balladist not long since, a minstrel with wool on his head, and an ultra Ethiopian complexion, who performed a negro ballad that I confess moistened these spectacles in a most unexpected manner. I have gazed at thousands of tragedy queens dying on the stage and expiring in appropriate blank-verse, and I never wanted to wipe them. They have looked up, be it said, at many scores of clergymen without being dimmed, and behold! a vagabond with a corked face and a banjo sings a little song, strikes a wild note, which sets the heart thrilling with happy pity."

In the craze that swept the country, such minstrel bands as Emmett's helped to send into obliquity the formal *classical quartette concerts*. The burnt-cork order took hold especially in the beer gardens, then in many halls, or "rooms" of its own. The lower classes stormed the doors for a glimpse of the plebeian entertainment, the lowly Black Opera kept growing, and soon it enjoyed a larger patronage by far than conventional opera houses. The triumph of minstrelsy was reflected in the miserable failure of the Astor Place Opera House, where four marked unsuccessful efforts were made between 1847 and 1852 to attract patrons, and the house had to be turned into a public library.

But in the development of Negro extravaganza an opera bouffe was borrowed from abroad. And here Negro minstrelsy, full of promise in its humble beginnings, began to decline; for the original pathos compromised with the grotesquerie of English burlesque. Minstrels now sang such parodies as "Lucy Did Lam a Moor," and in such plays as the *Othello Travestie*, Iago hailed from the country of Tipperary, while Othello was listed as an independent Nigger from the Haytian republic, a "jealous nigger." Pickaninny was confused with Piccadilly, and laughable absurdity, incongruity — these replaced the tear. In the farce, *The Darkey in Livery*, appeared one Garrick Kean Forrest Pompey, and in *The Black Ghost, or, the Nigger Turned Physician*, a character was called Black Joke. The pomposity of the cakewalk began strutting into plays like *Rehearsal for a Negro Ball*, and gone were the genuine sketches of plantation life!

Indispensable to extravaganzas were the many "specialties." The slaves now wore small knee breeches of canton flannel, then colorful velvet, later a great deal of gold tinsel and cheap lace. They ransacked the dictionary to cripple the long word, rolled their eyes like moons, and flung up their arms as if afflicted with St. Vitus dance. They assumed a remarkable obesity; indeed, became rather romantic-looking old grayheads, and added a subtle whine to "Massa," and "Bress de Lawd!" They expressed devo'ion and intense felicity with their condition on "de ole plantation." They no longer did the jig and breakdown with awkward jumps and wild breaks in time to the music — the spontaneous expressions of joy — but executed neat shuffles and breaks in a gliding manner, in low-cut, highly polished soft shoes. In their fancy neckties, fastened loosely, their striped shirts, and lavish display of "sparklers," they became stereotyped professionals, known as "heelologists," or "the professors of heelology." They strove after nothing more than eccentric novelties, finding that a burnt-cork countenance assured immunity for any kind of song, and introduced Swiss yodeling and other falsetto tricks. Their days on the true stage were certainly over.

As minstrelsy became the class of mixed entertainment known at first as variety, then vaudeville, the black-face entertainers swarmed upon the variety boards, losing much of their old-time minstrel savor in the new caricature. The songs lost their inspiring mournfulness — the sad interest in bondage, and the humor lacked the childlike artlessness. The professional "niggers" lost altogether the power of viewing the slave in a semi-poetic, semiquizzical light; instead, they lavished affection on the provender of ham and 'possum fat, little concerned with the genuine essense of plantation life. They could not go back to the legitimate, and the theatrical world soon evolved a term expressing fittingly such performers who were behind the times — "hams." It was a shortening of what was once original with and peculiar to minstrelsy: the practice of rubbing ham on the face as a base and insuring easy removal of blacking; in the quaint cover lithographs of the earlier songs you can see their faces glowing with the fat. The term "hamfatters" arose. Moreover, as Ham happened to be the son of Noah, and the progenitor of the colored race, the association became even more fixed. The contracted form was a term of contempt for all low grade variety people, indeed, for any cheap performer, and especially for those worthless habitués of the Rialto yearning after Hamlet.

A true portrayal of the Negro was left to the legitimate theatre, but such instances were insignificant until 1852. The Bowery Theatre, in 1839, had an opportunity when there hove into view with widespread, dark wings *The Black Schooner, or, The Private Slaver Armistad,* but the African captives in the play were mere wax figures. The Zeke in Mrs. Anna Cora Mowatt's *Fashion, or, Life in New York* (1845) belongs to minstrelsy rather than to drama: in dashing red livery, he committed a great deal of malapropism. The same year, Mr. Baker's skit at the Olympic, *Peytona* and *Fashion, or, North Against South,* treated of two young gentlemen, Harry North and Charles South, who were engaged to the Misses Races; the Negro servant was called Sweepstakes. In 1850, Edwin Booth and John Sleeper Clarke, each seventeen years old, gave Negro impersonations at a court-house in Belair, Maryland, "using appropriate dialogue and accompanying their vocal attempts with the somewhat inharmonious banjo and bones." There was little else on the horizon.

In 1852, *Uncle Tom's Cabin* represented the first serious portrayal of the Negro, in sharp-cut contrast to former characterizations.

Just then, Wood's Minstrel Hall, at 444 Broadway, between Howard and Grand Streets, was giving "a new serio-comico-tragico-melodramatical negro version of Macbeth." In early August, a new, beautiful, and plaintive song, "Poor Uncle Tom," was heard at the Hall. The real composer was unknown, for in those days songs became identified with the minstrel performers, seldom credited to the poor "hacks" who wrote them. It was the work of a young man, one Stephen Collins Foster, who had been working as a bookkeeper in his brother's shipping office in Cincinnati, about the time Mrs. Stowe was there. Familiar with the Ohio-Kentucky background, he was moved to put down the haunting words of a song, "Poor Uncle Tom, Good Night," when Mrs. Stowe's novel was published, and this is how the original chorus appears in Foster's manuscript book:

> Oh good night, good night, good night
> Poor Uncle Tom
> Grieve not for your old Kentucky home
> You'f bound for a better land
> Old Uncle Tom.

When *Uncle Tom's Cabin* became identified with the anti-slavery movement, pressure was put upon Foster's talents; his family were ardent Democrats. Since his very means of subsistence depended on the ten dollars apiece E. P. Christy paid him, the poor composer created Ethiopian melodies suitable to the demands of Christy's troupe, and he had to make changes in the theme; the song now became "My Old Kentucky Home, Good Night," and in the final form, the new refrain, "Weep no more my lady," no longer fitted the original words. The evidences of his debt to Mrs. Stowe could not be completely obliterated: we still have in the song the description of Uncle Tom dying, as Master Shelby, finding him at last, exclaims, "Uncle Tom! my poor — poor old friend!" One slave greets Master Shelby, "Hard times here, Mas'r," and Foster borrowed the idea with "....hard times comes a'knockin' at the door." The composer could not resist the nostalgic "Kentucky home," that appears elsewhere in the novel, and later drafts of the song reveal a reluctance to part with the old title, while the last line of each verse ends: "Den poor Uncle Tom, good night." As the composer set out to remove all traces of the original hero, he placed an emphasis on the habitation. Years later, old mansions by the score erected

memorial tablets, all claiming to be the inspiration of
Foster's song.

It is noticeable that Foster abandoned in the song the
authentic crudity of his earlier Negro compositions. Although the emotion stemmed from the heart it no longer came
from the lips of a Negro, but was couched in white man's
speech. Except for two insignificant efforts, he never again
used the genuine Negro dialect. "Old Black Joe" proved
successful, but it, too, was phrased in the white man's language; compared to his earliest work, "Nellie Was a Lady,"
the loss is apparent at once. He later wrote "My Loved One
and My Own, or Eva, a ballad," which St. Clair could have
sung appropriately in the drama. The theme evidently kept
haunting him, for it reoccurs again in two other compositions
— in the thinly disguised "Little Ella," and in "Little Ella's
an Angel." What an opportunity was lost for an early production of *Uncle Tom's Cabin* with original music by Stephen
C. Foster! There is left for posterity, at any rate, four of
his songs to make up such a score. Perhaps Mr. G. C.
Howard alone recognized the parallel of "My Old Kentucky
Home," for he had incorporated it almost immediately into
his drama at Troy, and carried it on to New York.

In the Spring of 1854, Christy & Wood's Minstrels
were responsible for a so-called "opera" of *Uncle Tom's
Cabin, or Hearts and Homes.* This extravaganzical burletta
started its run on April 10th, and to dispel any doubts of
those who felt the undertaking too ambitious, posters plastered on the town's fences proclaimed its complete triumph,
its reception by perfect thunders of applause, and that of all
theatres in the world Christy's alone could present such a
unique triumph! This was a typical advertisement: "WHO
HAS NOT SEEN IT? — THE OPERA OF UNCLE TOM, We
mean, as performed by George Christy & Wood's Celebrated
Band of Minstrels. It is a novel performance, and as gratifying as it is novel. The part of Uncle Tom was never per-

formed until Sam Wells took hold of it. It has been attempted, but never actually performed as it should be. There is
not exactly a dozen acts in THE OPERA OF UNCLE TOM, which
it would take a whole evening to perform, but there is enough
in it to awaken admiration, touch the heart, and bring down
spontaneous applause...." The versatile George Christy
was Topsy, and a dance, "Pop Goes the Weazle," concluded
each performance.

The burnt-cork order felt that Tom and his sentiments
verged closely on a metaphysical disquisition, and that it
might be augmented to advantage by the bones and banjo.

Since minstrelsy preceded the anti-slavery play by
some years, veteran performers claimed that they alone were
the Simon Pure, the regular Old Tom — no "flam," and
advertised themselves as "the original Uncle Tom." Claimants to having cut the umbilical cord of the play were
many, but the most remarkable was Manager George Kunkel,
who maintained that he dramatized the play in 1848, four
years before the novel was written!

Kunkel organized his Nightingale Serenaders in 1853,
and while traveling through the South, observed the passionate opposition to Mrs. Stowe's book. Surreptitiously, he
got hold of a copy at Wilmington, North Carolina, and spent
the whole afternoon in his hotel room, after double-locking
and bolting the door. So cautious was he, that he even hung
a towel upon the door knob to shut out any chance keyhole
peeper. The more he read, the more he was entranced, and
when he came to the last half he resolved to produce it on
the stage right there in the South! He prepared a sketch in
one act, whose running time was about three-quarters of an
hour. It opened at the next stopping place, Charleston, South
Carolina, at the conclusion of the regular minstrel performance, with Kunkel as Uncle Tom.

The Charleston citizens expected a burletta based on
the novel. They anticipated something similar to what
Kunkel had offered them in 1850, John T. Ford's farce

dealing with local matters, *Richmond As It Is*. Ford became business manager for the minstrel troupe on the strength of it. Now taken unawares by the new play, excitement gripped the city. A meeting of the City Council was called, and resolutions passed forbidding all colored persons to enter the hall. Parson Brownlow, of Tennessee, reproached bitterly the people of Charleston for having even permitted the walls and fences to be desecrated by Uncle Tom posters. Secretly, Negroes came to the performances, paying as much as five and ten dollars — fortunes to them. Kunkel managed to conceal them, slipping some "Stowe-aways" up into the flies. But it soon got altogether too hot for him, and at Savannah he had to give it up.

He left behind him a trail of old Spanish quarters, taken in at the box office each night. Kunkel had a sharp die made, notified his treasurer to stamp on them, "Kunkel's Nightingale Minstrels," and to hand out the defaced quarters as change.

The best Uncle Tom by an Ethiopian performer came some time later. T. D. Rice, the "daddy" of Negro minstrelsy, attracted everyone, especially when he was through jumping "Jim Crow" and about to accept the lead in the Bowery Theatre version on January 16, 1854. The National Theatre was then in the sixth month of its amazing run, competing against Barnum and the Franklin Museum. A very large painting of Little Eva crowning old Tom with flowers soon hung over the Bowery's facade. Several weeks after that eventful opening, tragedy overtook the dramatist, Henry E. Stevens, who had boasted to William Hamilton (Aunt Chloe) that he — Stevens — could not be thrown in any wrestling match, especially by one impersonating a woman. On landing off a Williamsburg ferryboat, they began the sport on the sidewalk, where Aunt Chloe divulged her lack of effeminacy by laying the dramatist out cold.

Stevens struck the curbstone, his neck broken, and he died a few days later.

The Bowery Theatre substituted a far different version on May 8th, with two well known burnt-corkers in the leads, Frank Brower as Uncle Tom and John Mulligan as Topsy. As the junior member of the original Ethiopian band formed by Emmett, "The Virginia Minstrels," Brower gave an original performance, to say the least. In the Fall of the year, while with Wood's Minstrels, he had regaled the public with a sketch of Ethiopian eccentricities called *Happy Uncle Tom*, featuring his "Uncle Tom Jig." The flavor of that burletta is disclosed in one scene where the title character enters excitedly, and W. Birch, as Bones, asks, "Why, what's de matter?" "Ain't got no use fur such old gemmans — We wur talkin' bolitics, an' he differ'd wid me, an' dar I call'd him a cake!" answers Uncle Tom. "Et's insultin' t'call a gemmans a cake," Bones goes on. Tom clarifies, "Dat all wur berry true, but we wur all cakes." "Wal, what kind ob cakes wur we?" "Jis black cakes." "What kind ob cake is Little Eva?" "An angel cake." "An Massa St. Clair?" "An eclair." "What kind ob cake is Lawyer Marks?" "He's a sponge cake." "And Gumption Cute?" "He's a loaf." "What kind ob cake would yuh call Eliza an' Little Harry?" "A choc'late float an' shortenin." "An' Aunty Ophelia?" "She's a lemon cake, an' mighty hard t' squeeze!" Happy Uncle Tom then made his exit, limping, assuming a posture as if his backbone were broken. The frequenters of the Hall were warned to come early, and to "give happy Uncle Tom a new Leg-i-see."

Further mischief was contributed by White's Ethiopian Opera House, opposite the Bowery Theatre, where with the new year, 1855, such architecture was banged together as *Uncle Dad's Cabin* and *Old Dad's Cabin*. Perham's rivaled it with the farces, *Aunt Dinah's Cabin* and *My Aunt's Cabin*.

Another burlesque was advertised, in Newark, on April 25, 1855: "Remember, Sanford is the original author of

the Burlesque of *Uncle Tom's Cabin,* and not the person who
has represented himself to the New York public. Due notice
will be given of the first representation of the correct Burlesque of which the public will have the pleasure to comment upon its merits." *Happy Uncle Tom* had been performed, indeed, by the New Orleans Opera Troupe, in Philadelphia, under Sam S. Sanford's management, where it
attracted fashionable audiences since the day of its inception, the middle of October, 1853. Sanford sold manuscript
copies to other minstrel troupes, which he regretted later
on. His own was called *Sanford's Southern Version of
Uncle Tom's Cabin,* and glorified slavery with song and
dance. One of his playbills, of August 18, 1861, four months
after the outbreak of the Civil War, bore this rime at the
foot:

> *Oh! White folks, we'll have you to know,*
> *Dis am not de version of Mrs. Stowe:*
> *Wid her de Darks am all unlucky,*
> *But we am de boys from Old Kentucky.*
>
> *Den hand de Banjo down to play,*
> *We'll make it ring both night and day;*
> *And we care not what de white folks say,*
> *Dey can't get us to run away.*

Recognizable as a corruption of T. D. Rice's song,
"Jump Jim Crow," it was now, alas! a sorry scarecrow.

Sanford experienced a change of heart at the end of the
War, and thereafter enacted the role straight. He advertised:
"Sam S. Sanford as Uncle Tom! In which character he
stands without a rival in the World. The late EDWIN FORREST,
witnessing Sanford as Uncle Tom says the stage has few such
Actors. The late CHAS. DICKENS says Sanford's Uncle Tom
is inimitable and unapproachable. MR. JOHN E. OWENS
says Sanford was born for the character. Praise from the

above superior judges is sufficient guarantee of SANFORD'S EXCELLENCE." He insisted that his alone was the original.

With the War, developments piled one on the other and so rapidly that their full import was lost. What ordinarily would have been a sensation of the first order became almost a footnote to the mighty surge of events. A tragedy occurred in a cheap Bowery hotel, as an instance, the significance of which was overlooked at the time. On a cold morning in January, a derelict, ill with fever in his drab surroundings, attempted to reach for a drink of water, and in his weakened condition fell, struck his head against a broken pitcher — and gashed open his neck. He was taken in an unconscious state to a charity ward in Bellevue Hospital, where he died from fever and loss of blood. Unidentified at first, his shabby belongings disclosed a pathetic little pocketbook holding thirty-eight cents, and a scrap of paper bearing the pencilled words — intended probably for the title of a song — "Dear friends and gentle hearts." During the last days of his troubled career Stephen Foster was alienated from his wife, from his proslavery family, and from his proud relatives. He could forget them in a disreputable bohemianism, especially in the alcoholic habit, but it proved his undoing. He was but thirty-seven. At last, a friend traced the body of the composer, where it lay in the morgue awaiting a pauper's grave. The name was misspelled on the hospital register, and there were no big headlines in the newspapers about the passing of America's greatest writer of folk-songs. The single obituary notice that did appear was printed days after the funeral, with none of the sordid details. But for that, Stephen Foster's death would have gone totally unnoticed.

Chapter VII

OF THE TOMITUDES ABROAD

Wherever you travel, wherever you stop,
Uncle Tom his black poll's sure to show:
With his songs, polkas, waltzes, they fill every shop
Till, like Topsy, "I 'specs they must grow!"
The stage had enough of Jim Crow,
A jumping and a "doing just so;"
And 'twould be quite a blessing if poor
Uncle Tom
Would after that poor nigger go.
        —Sung at the Haymarket, 1853

AWAY FROM THE NATIVE EXCITEMENT, *Uncle Tom's Cabin* was enjoying a furor abroad, and the English coined a word to describe it — "Tomitudes."

England had no Negro problem. Wisely, she had years before taken some twenty million dollars and purchased the freedom of her slaves. And now, when the London stage in December, 1852, was crowded with eleven different competing dramatizations, she was reminded forcefully of her sound step.

What a deep wave of excitement surged over the Atlantic! All along the London streets the wagons of retail shops rumbled on, carrying Tom's face on placards, and named after him were a great variety of articles: "Uncle Tom's pure unadulterated coffee," "Uncle Tom's improved flagelots," "Uncle Tom china," "Uncle Tom's paletot," "Uncle Tom's new and secondhand clothing," "Uncle Tom's shrinkable woolen stockings." From these thriving commod-

ities one would suppose that Uncle Tom was rather gain-
fully employed, and even rich enough to buy out all the
slaveholders in America.

Named after the humble abode of Uncle Tom were
many creameries and eating places, pastry shops, dry-goods
emporiums, and cameo shops. A Liverpool store exhibited

London Illustrated News

The Olympic Version (1852)

*An Effective Scene, Where the "Man of Humanity,"
Haley, Feels First a Touch of Generosity That Per-
mits His Negro Subjects To Enjoy a Dance, and
Then Directs Tom To Inflict the Lash upon George
Harris, Whom They Have Captured*

wallpaper patterns which represented in panels the most striking scenes: Eliza wore the latest Parisian fashion, while the
male slaves were attired in such costume that wontedly fell
to the unfortunate lot of Don Juan's man, Leporello. Staff-
ordshire ware was decorated with the Cruikshank illustrations. Pictures inspired by the story were exhibited in the
Royal Academy, and the humorous weekly, *Punch*, serial-

ized "The Political Topsy." Young ladies of the period worked fancy sketches of Uncle Tom's physiognomy in black worsted, while infants toyed with woolly-headed Topsy dolls. Mrs. Stowe's heroine added many pages to the Registrar-General's list of Evas.

Typical of those days was the man who complained that he was being "hunted down!" His home was cluttered up with fresh editions of *Uncle Tom's Cabin,* and *Aunt Phillis' Cabin,* and *Southern Life as It Is,* and *Southern Life as It Isn't.* He had no peace — morning, noon, or night. His Indian cake at breakfast suggested sympathetic allusions to the thousands of poor Uncle Toms who must eat hoe-cake or die. He was pestered every evening after tea by his oldest daughter to hear "that last sweet song about Little Eva" dinned into his ears. He hadn't read the book, and didn't doubt that it was remarkable; he felt that if it weren't, it never would have set all creation agog. Nevertheless, he kept thinking of it all day, and dreaming of it all night. He was certain it would be the death of him. Yet, he was determined *not* to read the novel — no, not even if people pointed him out in the streets as *The Man Who Has Not Read Uncle Tom's Cabin!*

In September, 1852 — while the Howard-Aiken play was being given in a two-by-four upstate town, more than half a year from its sensational New York opening — no less than a dozen adaptations were waiting to be licensed by the Lord Chamberlain. Three London theatres, the Great National Standard, the Olympic, and the Royal Victoria, stole a march on less fortunate managers, and they caused greater excitement than the death of the Duke of Wellington, who was being mourned just then.

All London went to see the plays, with but one exception — and a famous actress, too — Fanny Kemble. She, moreover, could have enlightened the public further, for at that time she was in possession of a diary disclosing an eye-witness account of the slave evils on her husband's

Georgia plantation, but had not the courage to release it for publication until the second year of the Civil War.

The Royal Grecian, "desirous of going with the times," produced another version, on October 25th. Then the Surrey offered the best of the five, a week later.

Worse! it even became a bit confusing for all theatregoers. When one Londoner met another, in a pea-soup fog, inevitably, upon questioning his friend's destination, the answer would be, "To see *Uncle Tom's Cabin*, of course."

"Be specific, old boy!" the other would cut in. "*Which* one?"

They distinguished the various adaptations by the subtitles. The Standard had, *The Slave's Life in America;* the Olympic, *Negro Life in America;* the Vic, *The Fugitive Slave;* still another playhouse gave *Life among the Lowly....*

When the Adelphi—somewhat late in the day—participated on November 29th, the title was reversed, *Slave Life; or, Uncle Tom's Cabin,* which obviated forgetting the original title. This drama was the collaboration of the editors of *Punch*, Mark Lemon and Tom Taylor. As the Adelphi was small, with an intimate atmosphere, and came closest to being a London folk theatre, unusual interest centered around the new production. The playbill carried a "notice," which explained the liberties taken with the novel, for the adaptors felt that Mrs. Stowe had not designed it with the stage in mind. In their "interweaving of threads," as they called it, Messrs. Lemon and Taylor invented new situations. Uncle Tom was not the hero, and Legree, instead of whipping him to death, made short work of it — with a bowie-knife! There was really next to nothing of Tom, and neither an Eva, nor an Aunt Ophelia, and comparatively little of Mr. Shelby, and when George Harris ran away, he took along Topsy.

All in all, the adaptors had much in common with Mr. Vincent Crummles, as to the propriety of preserving the "unities" of the stage. To lend further authenticity, Madame

Celeste, who directed the play, was advertised flamboyantly as one "who has recently visited all the localities in which the action is supposed to take place."

However, a greater experiment was in store. The proprietor of Astley's Royal Amphitheatre, Mr. W. Batty, entered the lists with a production that Londoners felt was true to his name. The effect of *Uncle Tom* on horseback, with Eliza escaping across the ice on a Mazeppa steed, was a startling prospect! A runaway horse, in the early action of the two-act drama, typified the animal "that loves liberty," and in the course of its flight there sped by a bewildering succession of scenery, rocks, chasms, etc., while the pursuit itself blended directly into equestrian feats. It ended in the style typical of the Amphitheatre, a revolt and a conflagration.

The equestrian novelty caught the fancy of the provincial towns, and most notable was Nelson Lee's at the Royal Pavilion Circus in December, in which a Mrs. Alfred Cook as Eliza, in her fearless riding in "the escape," attempted dexterous feats on bareback. The City of London theatre, too, on January 17th, gave John Wilkins' new version, with Mrs. B. Barnett starring as Topsy, and with a trick donkey known as Tom Tit. Then the spectacle, *Eliza and the Fugitive Slaves; or, Uncle Tom's Cabin,* opened at Francon's Cirque in February.

But something even more fanciful now began, on November 8th, in Leicester Square, at the Royal Living Marionette Theatre. Heard at this time were the sounds of preparation for the Christmas pantomimes, which enjoyed then a vogue comparable to the Walt Disney pictorial animations of our day.

The Drury Lane's opening feature, that Christmas of 1852, was E. Fitzball's *Uncle Tom's Cabin; or, the Horrors of Slavery.* And it signalled a departure from tradition, for no one expected a plot in a pantomime — that, indeed, would have been too distracting. As the world-famous Drury Lane had undergone such a deterioration and loss of patronage, during the years, the lessee, the Duke of Bedford, was determined on its demolition. But now the unwashed inhabitants of the transpontine districts flocked to its doors to see *Uncle Tom's Cabin!*

Another Christmas pantomime, at Sadler's Wells, contained the novelty of a multitude of Uncle Toms. The Standard Theatre's pantomime satirized the times, and, of course, Uncle Tom came in for his share: With clever mechanical changes, Andover Union was altered into an old soldier's asylum, and Uncle Tom's cabin transformed into the proposed Wellington Arcade; in the scenic street from Whitechapel to Houndsditch, there was introduced artfully the cabin of another Uncle Tom — a pawnbroker; and the avuncular Tom joined a highly-polished ebony lady, Aunt Sally, and Uncle Graby, in a comic *Pas de Trois!* The Pavilion Theatre brought out Frederick Neale's grand pantomime, *Uncle Tom and Lucy Neal; or Harlequin Liberty and Slavery.*

Pantomimes were, indeed, not confined to London alone. The most noteworthy was by Mr. Harrington at Bilston, where the Uncle Tom material proved a trump card. Another beneficiary, Mr. Leigh, became such an enthusiastic admirer of Mrs Stowe that at his benefit at the Adelphi, in Liverpool, late that February, he passed out free copies of her novel.

As to the authoress herself. When Mrs. Stowe made her first visit to England, in 1853, the docks of Liverpool, as she landed, were thronged with eager crowds. All tried to catch a glimpse of her. At Stafford House, the Duchess of Southerland presented her with a gold bracelet, and Mrs. Stowe was hailed everywhere as the deliverer of the American Negro. She was lionized not only by statesmen and duchesses, but by colliers and factory girls, law clerks, ploughboys.

The English women drew up what Thackeray denominated a "Womanifesto against Slavery," the list comprising twenty-six folio volumes, with over half a million signatures

DIOGENES, ON HIS SEARCH FOR AN HONEST MAN, HAVING FOUND AN HONEST WOMAN, HAS PUT OUT HIS LIGHT IN HONOUR OF MRS. STOWE.

Diogenes Weekly, 1853

Diogenes, on His Search for an Honest Man, Having Found an Honest Woman, Has Put Out His Light in Honour of Mrs. Stowe

of British women from all walks of life. Conspicuous by its absence, however, was the name of Fanny Kemble.

The novel was on display at every railroad bookstall, and in every third traveler's hand. The purchaser was guided by the various illustrators: Cruikshank, Gilbert, Leech, Nicholson, Sear, Thomas; and the subtitles, too, distinguished one edition from another. It stimulated a greater interest in England than across the Atlantic. By the end of 1852 the American sale was one hundred and fifty thousand copies, while the English exceeded a million, and another half million was sold in the colonies.

Outside of London swarmed other rivalries. In Manchester, for instance, F. B. Egan produced the play at the Queen's Theatre as early as October, and found it a gold mine. A popular competitor was Thomas Hailes Lacy's three-act work, subtitled, *A Drama of Real Life,* which opened at the Theatre Royal, on February 1st. For purposes of realism Little Eva was left out — not even mentioned, and St. Clair became metamorphosed into Mr. Yahoo, described on the bill as "a Young American Exquisite" — something doubtlessly borrowed from Dickens' *American Notes.* This is the description of Eliza's escape in the acting script:

HALEY. I'll see (*peeps thru keyhole*). By heavens, 'tis she! Huzza! huzza! I've got her! Open that door! Open I say! (*knocks again*) Spifflicate me, but she's trying to get out of the window! Don't stand grinning there, ye infernal niggers. Come and help me! She'll be off! No, no, the door gives way! I have her! (*breaks open the door*) Hell and furies! she's thru the window, and broke the child's neck. Quick! quick! round and catch her!
(*Exit hurriedly, R. I. E. — front of Theatre very dark.*)
SCENE VI. *The whole stage; the Ohio frozen over in part; dangerous rocks and currents; precipitous banks. Winter.*

ELIZA *rushes on to a high bank, exclaims,*
"Heaven protect me!" *then leaps from the bank
to a raft of ice; and springing from one block to
another, reaches, with her child, the opposite
shore; here a stranger helps her (a girl, attired
to represent* ELIZA *in the distance; and a* CHILD
*to personate the man who received her, will add
much to the effect of the scene).* HALEY *and*
SLAVES *rush on; in vain he urged them to follow.*

TABLEAU *of Vengeance and Disappointment
on the one bank — Gratitude to Providence on the
other.*

Lacy's adaptation had a curious dramatic unity, rounded out with Legree shot by his mistress, Cassy, the quadroon; and Tom, while dying, added glory to his martyrdom
by taking the blame.

Striking to the American visitor must have been the
overstatement of American society in the various dramatizations. One tourist maintained that the English actors had
no more idea of Negro delineation than a real Virginia
plantation darky of the Court language of France. Uncle
Tom, as well as Eva, spoke in most pronounced cockney
accents; George Harris enjoyed an Oxford education, while
no archbishop of Canterbury could approach Uncle Tom's
piety. The Yankees were portrayed as coarse and noisy,
their peculiarities shown in expressions like, "Waal, I
calc'late," and other supposed Yankeeisms of an obsolete
humor dear to British hearts. Legree was full of "tarn-
ations," and if Phineas Fletcher became Phineas Van Trompe
of low Yankee comedy, it was for a good reason, as England
knew a Phineas Fletcher, famous poet of the Virgin Queen's
reign. As for the depiction of a black child, English audiences had seen but one type, the little page from India who
officiates as train-bearer to Lady Teazle — and that was

exactly the way the Adelphi, the Theatre Royal in Manchester, a n d other playhouses, presented Topsy. When severe Aunt Ophelia took her in hand, Topsy r u m m a g e d t h r o u g h h e r bureau drawers f o r a h u g e Moorish turban, and d r e s s i n g fantastically before the mirror said, "La—me— if I ain't quite bootiful!" Topsy was an extraordinary piece o f wild, r a u c o u s

An English Conception of Haley Victoria Theatre, London (1853)

nature as played by Mrs. G. C. Howard in America, but English actresses endowed her with all the astute villainies of the Artful Dodger.

Those were, indeed, the days of "the Uncle Tom mania." One critic, writing to the *British Army Despatch*, complained of the new social phenomenon: "On the stage, this work, aided by the morbid talent of its adaptors, and the exquisite cleverness of such actors and actresses as are now electrifying an Adelphi audience, is doing a mischief which a century cannot repair. Let the Lord Chamberlain look at *this*. We are playing the part of the despot and the priest, by insulting the United States of America. What have we to do with the internal affairs of the American Republic!...

Every American in London is disgusted with the Uncle Tom mania here. If he goes to a theatre, he is insulted and shocked. The English people, on the other hand, are deluded into the falsest notions of America. When the slave in the drama

Courtesy of Harvard Theatre Collection

The English Topsy

escapes into British India, there is a cheer. That cheer may cost us some day our best alliance... Yes, we are cutting our own throats with this hypocritical, lying sympathy. Let British ladies, if they want a safety-valve for their hysterical emotions, as well as a means of notoriety, form a committee for the emancipation of the monkeys which afford them so much amusement on Sundays in the Zoological Gardens. A most touching and a more truthful work than *Uncle Tom's Cabin* might be written on the ₊sufferings of these; while, politically, it would be harmless..."

Another reiterated, but to deaf ears, that English ladies had as little to do with slavery in the Carolinas as with polygamy in Algeria, and that they knew even less about it. An English poet, emerging from the dim classical past in which he cloistered himself, called Mrs. Stowe "the rampant Maenad of Massachusetts."

Of the many presentations now seen, *Punch* observed that from the good old claptraps of the British Drama, "the slave need only set his foot on British soil to be free." The humorous weekly emphasized the dissimilarity in point of fact between the London City mud and the British soil, which deprived the former of its emancipating influence, "until a quantity of filthy lucre is extracted from the pocket of the freedman." It hoped to see someone bring out a cockney *Uncle Tom* to shame the London corporation into relinquishing its commerce in freedom, and suggested that Mrs. Stowe be provided with the requisite facts for a successful rival to her own wonderful work on American slavery, a sort of companion volume to be entitled, *Uncle Cog's Crib* — a key to Temple Bar and the City's mysteries.

Oddly enough, that almost came to pass. The only place in London where the so-called "Nigger peculiarities" could be observed, aside from the numerous adaptations in the theatres, was Major Dumolton's, at the Strand. The novelty there was a company called The African Troupe, but actually consisting entirely of American whites. Conspicuous in that company was the celebrated "Bones" of a Mr. Pell, who, besides performing on the bones in a superlatively masterful manner, was one of the earliest adherents of the "dead pan." The public heard the usual fare, some new songs, funny, and plaintive, supposedly characteristic of "the Nigger style;" the programme ordinarily was divided into "Imitations of the Fashionable Darkies of the Northern States" and "Imitations of the Darkies of the Southern States."

This Troupe produced, on October 25, 1852, a new burlesque, in three scenes, by William Brough, *Uncle Tom's Crib; or Negro Life in London.* The sketch was built around Uncle Tom, the landlord of a "public," whose sign, the Negro's Nob, advertises a house of call for all darkies. The first scene represented some of the dusky fraternity of crossing sweepers, beggars, etc., singing and boozing over their beer. Tom has a daughter, Dinah, who is about to marry Mr. Caesar Augustus Squashtop, who professes to have 50 pounds, a good crossing connection, and a furnished house. Dinah's affections are, however, fixed on Dandy Jim, an Ethiopian serenader of exquisite hue. Jim deplores his poverty, and recounts how he was hocussed and despoiled of 50 pounds by a brother "nigger." Dinah resolutely rejects Squashtop for Dandy Jim, and, as may be guessed, the skit ended with the detection of the former as the culprit, and his ejection from the premises.

This bagatelle afforded burlesque, but the insinuating reference to the prevailing craze about "niggers" was by no means relished by the public. The *Crib* soon went into receivership.

Another farce, *Those Dear Blacks*, at the Lyceum in November, pictured the embarrassment of affairs when the darkey's social position is raised. The opening scene was the Chair Pier, at Brighton, where the tourists were all engrossed in the novel. Among them is a Mr. Bulwinkle and his daughter, Amelia, the latter infatuated with "those dear blacks" that she read so much about in *Uncle Tom's Cabin.* She is to be married to a Mr. Featheredge, who arrives on the cheap excursion train from London; he passes for a man of fortune, although really a clerk earning a pound a week, his entire wealth consisting of a penny roll, a return third-class ticket, and sevenpence halfpenny in change. A solicitor friend of Bulwinkle holds a writ against him for twenty pounds, and our adventurer is exposed. About to throw himself over the pier, there comes to his aid Adonnis Lilywhite, an emancipated Negro, who has just inherited his master's fortune. The broken-down gallant accepts a position as Lilywhite's servant in the most magnificent apartments of the West End. When he begins his duties, he is discovered asleep on the couch, wearing his colored patron's satin morning gown. His master bustles in, and following the servant's suggestion, decides to buy a new gown. The master initiates him in his new tasks, dons an apron, and proceeds not only to black his own boots but the servant's as well! Lilywhite also shows his servant how to wait at table, Featheredge acting as gentleman. The plot ended with Massa, who has to do all the work himself, taken into service of Featheredge, who had managed to do nothing!

Hardly a playhouse in the United Kingdom did not, at some time or another, succumb to a dramatization of the popular story. In Dublin, we find the most successful run at the Queen's Theatre early in October, 1852, where, without the least diminution, it continued on to Easter, followed by a sequel, *The Slave Hunt; or the Fate of St. Clair.*

In Scotland, the public conception of the Negro had to be altered radically. In the Spring of 1844, citizens of Glasgow arose and rubbed their eyes, one day, at the most incomprehensible posters and advertisements ever seen in their fair city: "Mr. R. W. Pelham, the neatest and best dancer living, will, on this occasion, appear in several of his new songs and dances. Mr. D. D. Emmitt, the celebrated banjoist and composer of negro music, will also sing a number of his original songs, with banjo variations in conjunction with dat fascinating hero ob de fantastic toe, Mr. R. W. Pelham, who will show de science ob de heel to de music ob de old banjo, making a grand display ob de heel-and-toe caperbilities, surprising to de white folks and sartin deth to all fresh-water niggers. Den kums de neber-to-be-forgotten and unkonkerable jig, by R. W. Pelham, which has exterminated, laid on de shelf, and driven into retirement all the oder heelologists in de East, West, Norf and Souf. Sich a set ob double-shuffles, Long Island troubles, heel-and-toe tormenters, and dandy-nigger flourishes, you nebber did see! verifying de truth ob Massa Charley Dickens, when he sez: 'De right leg, de leff leg, de hind leg, and all de odder legs will be brought to bear on dat 'ticular 'casion.' Music on de banjo by D. D. Emmit. So clare de track and let genus perspire."

When the Virginia Minstrels further *enlightened* the Glasgow public about slaves in the United States, the sable genus of humanity lingered long afterwards in their minds as a bundle of half-barbaric oddities, peculiarities, eccentricities, whimsicalities, and comicalities.

When the anti-slavery drama came to Scotland, almost simultaneously with the early London adaptations, the eight-year-old conception of the Negro had to be expurged. In Edinburgh, the play unfolded for the first time at the Theatre Royal on September 24, 1852, and the author, J. B. Johnstone, left out Eva and Topsy. In Glasgow, the Theatre Royal (where the Virginia Minstrels had played) produced on February 15th Edmund Glover's revue of the best scenes then current in London, wherein St. Clair lived on to the last, Legree was apprehended as a felon, and Cassy's companion was not Madeline's daughter, but Eliza.

The invitation of the Anti-Slavery Society of Glasgow, in 1853, was the real incentive for Mrs. Stowe's first visit to Great Britain, and the Scots raised a thousand pounds among their poorest citizens, through penny offerings, to help free the Negro slaves.

Managers everywhere found a gold harvest. A Mr. Pye, traveling about in the outlying district with a Moving Panorama, exhibited to the world all the frightful features of that slave exposition, and enlightened matters further with his lucid lecture. Even the celebrated Madame Wharton's troupe of Poses Plastiques lucratively added several scenes from *Uncle Tom's Cabin* to its pictures from the Antique, rendered to soft strains of a dulcimer. The dramatizations on the provincial stage, whose striking points were too numerous to be particularized here, could fill a fair-sized catalogue.

Many struggling managers attempted the play when all else had failed, and reaped a windfall. Typical of this group was John Coleman, of the Theatre Royal, Sheffield, who, in desperate straits, concocted an adaptation, *Slavery*, and afterwards claimed that it was the precursor of all the big dramas at Drury Lane and elsewhere in Great Britain. Charles Moorhouse, "a genuine American," depicted Legree, with Fanny Wallack as Cassy, and the distinguished little vocalist, Clara St. Casse, as Eva.

Coleman opened to a wretched attendance, but the following night a mob clamored to get in. The superstitious manager thought it best to order a thousand free passes and have them distributed for the following performance, because he felt it was too good to last.

Coleman was absent from the theatre the next night, attending an important banquet, when dire news reached him in the midst of a toast to the eminent guest, John Bright, who was rising at that moment to accept the honor. Suddenly Coleman felt someone tugging at his sleeve, and heard the whisper: "Mr. Johnson says you are to come at once, sir, or there'll be a riot, and the house pulled down about his ears!" Reaching the theatre with the messenger, Coleman was besieged by a milling crowd. Some had free passes, others strove to refund their tickets, while within, every seat was taken — the aisles packed!

Playbill of Theatre Royal, Oldham (1856)

The drama, *Slavery*, eclipsed all others, running for six consecutive weeks, and was revived, again and again. In the first revival the Eva was little Henrietta Watson, the prompter's daughter; at its second, Louisa Angel; at the third, Margaret Robertson. These three Evas began very promising careers here: Miss Angel retired upon marrying a millionaire, Miss Watson married a popular novelist, while Miss Robertson became a leading actress at the Haymarket.

The Coleman adventure was not an isolated instance. James Chute, of Bristol, whenever sorely pressed, would knock together his own adaptations, which tided him over. Edmund Glover, sharing confidences with Coleman, confessed that the play saved him from foreclosure in Glasgow.

Uncle Tom and his much-lived-in cabin were still in the public eye, in 1856, when *Dred* arrived. Queen Victoria preferred it to Mrs. Stowe's earlier novel, and now the new work temporarily usurped the place of the former favorite. W. E. Suter performed it in October at the Queen's Theatre, and Glasgow saw it for the first time on October 24th, with Glover in the title part. Later, in December, Astley's Amphitheatre converted it into an equestrian novelty. A new adaptation of *Uncle Tom's Cabin*, with a Mr. Wells, an American, was playing that summer at the Royal Park, Liverpool; while on May 5th, *The Slave Hunt* opened at the Theatre Royal, Oldham.

The older drama had evidently seen its day by the time 1857 rolled around. But that year the London public experienced a new treat, for the Howard family arrived on January 26th at the Marylebone Theatre.

Mr. G. C. Howard had the tour in mind as early as the Winter of 1854, while playing for Garry Hough in Syracuse, New York. "How would you like to go to England?" he asked Hough at the time. "Barnum has made me an offer to take an *Uncle Tom* troupe to that country. He wanted me to talk to you about salaries, and I told him I would let you know."

Hough then answered, "I will go with Barnum for a year at seventy-five dollars per week, and my cabin passage paid out and back."

The 1854 deal fell through, however. Mr. Howard declined to make a contract with Barnum, for the Great Showman would not agree to pay salaries while the company was idle.

Later, Barnum changed his mind, and under his sponsorship the Howard company sailed for England. The players who crossed the Atlantic included the famous midget, General Tom Thumb, and Barnum intended to conquer England with at least one of his Toms.

The 1857 American dramatization of the familiar old work was compressed within the limits of a three-act drama, ending with Eva's death. Omitted were the episodes of Cassy, Legree, and all that follows, the interest solely centering in the St. Clair family and Topsy.

London was naturally curious to see the American interpretation, for here was opportunity, indeed, to get the genuine tang of that country. As St. Clair's was a trifling part, the critics thought it required no great dramatic talent, but they found Mr. Howard investing it with a considerable amount of business: it was mild, reflective, sedate — all in all, quite natural. Topsy amazed everyone. The critic of *Era* described her: "Mrs. Howard's Topsy strikes us as an admirable performance — indeed, as such a perfect embodiment of Mrs. Beecher Stowe's Topsy that one would imagine both ladies had studied from one model. Yet it is not the Topsy we have been familiar with on the stage — it is not merely the droll, half idiot, wholly ignorant Topsy of the English stage, but the shrewd, cunning, naturally wicked, almost impish Topsy of reality — the child for whom nobody cared, that in a figurative sense may be said with perfect truth 'never to have been born,' that 'never had no fader, nor moder, nor broder, nor sister, nor aunt — no, none on em—that never had nothin' nor nobody.' At one moment she is stubborn, insensate, and unimpressionable — anon, she flies into an ungovernable, almost demoniac rage, and her cunning and revenge exhibit in a wonderful degree the effects of bad passions, allowed to grow up unchecked, like weeds in the fair garden of the breast. Her elf-like figure, and the strange, wild, screaming chant in which she sang the song, 'I'se So Wicked,' was something quite *sui generis* unlike anything we have before seen; but it seemed to us to realize the picture of the authoress, and we believe that it is a truthful representation of the original."

English audiences knew Eva as a grown-up young lady — not a little child. The impression Cordelia Howard made was that although she had been carefully coached, she gave a natural, unstudied performance. They found no fault with her, save, it may be, her French accent on the word "papa," which, of course, irritated English ears. Yet, her enunciation was remarkably correct, and they marvelled at the ease with which the child's voice carried to the most distant corners of the theatre.

In the ensuing weeks at the Marylebone, the Howards, to vary the bill and to suit every possible phase of dramatic predilection, switched to such plays as *Ida May, the Kidnapped Child,* and *Dred,* in addition to *Tom.*

The Strand Theatre next beheld them, on February 23rd, advertising *The Death of Eva* as played by them "one thousand times in America." Also given were *Fashion and Famine; or the Strawberry Girl* and *The Lamplighter; or, the Blind Girl and the Orphan.* When Little Cordelia took her Benefit on March 16th, General Tom Thumb appeared in the Grecian Statues act, and a hornpipe by sixteen, dressed in the blue jackets of Her Majesty's Service, concluded the programme.

The Howard family had the honor of inaugurating Sadler's Wells' opening on Easter Monday for the summer season. Then they left for the capital cities of Scotland and Ireland, and their starring tour was advertised: "The critics of London, Edinburough, and Dublin, were unanimous in their praise of The Gifted American Child." In June they sailed for home.

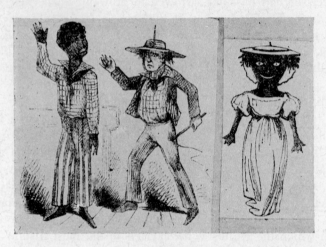

The English Marionettes

But the drum-beats across the Atlantic grew louder. The London bookstalls displayed, under the anonymity of a Neutral, *Uncle John's Cabin* (*next door to Uncle Tom's Cabin*), showing that the great question of "Cabins" had not as yet been fully answered. And *The Mud Cabin*, by Warren Isham, attempted to duplicate Mrs. Stowe's feat by revealing British social abuses.

When the blockade set up by the Union became effective, British sentiment was tested. The supply of cotton to the mills was cut off, and hungry Lancashire workers knew why they were jobless. Then a few Southern adherents felt it ripe to hold a proslavery meeting in Rochdale, where a skilful orator used his persuasive powers to show that their interests tied up with the Confederacy. When he finished the listeners took a vote among themselves, and passed a resolution censuring him for daring to make such a speech!

Surprisingly, not a few of the English remained entirely ignorant of events abroad. To them Old Tom was merely a variety of English gin. To that class belonged the young gentleman whose fatigued articulation and quiddities *Punch* often satirized, and in a poem in Gallignan's *Messenger*, he complained: "A must wead Uncle Tom," because "people one meets begin to talk of Mrs. Harwietbeechastowe.... A countess would pasist, last night, in asking me about haw book.... Bai Jove! A was completely flaw'd; a wish'd myself, or haw, at Fwance."

Had his wish been granted, he would have found himself there, alas, in an equally vexatious position. France was having her own *Uncle Tom* furor.

Chapter VIII

ON THE CONTINENTAL STAGE

Puisque c'est fête aujourd'hui,
Régalons-nous, hi! hi! hi!
Nous mangerons, pudding, gâteau,
Bravo, yo! yo! yo!
Oui, maîtresse l'a permis,
Ah! c'est un jour de fête,
Vous aurez tous, mes chers amis,
Pudding et galette!
—Opening Air of *Élisa*

FRANCE, TOO, WAS CARRIED AWAY by the excitement. In a neck-and-neck race, five newspapers in Paris serialized the novel in feuilleton shape, as fast as it left the hands of the translators. George Sand helped introduce it to the literary world, and the *Revue des Deux Mondes* discovered that a review of thirty-two pages left a great deal unsaid. As an instance of the prodigious frenzy, it is related that, one day, a Quaker, homeward-bound with the volume under his arm, was stopped by two respectably dressed men, who, each clapping a pistol to the good Brother's head, shouted, "Your *Uncle Tom's Cabin* or your life!"

The Negro had been depicted in the French theatre years before Uncle Tom came shuffling along. The Théâtre Français in 1830 offered *Le Nègre*, by Ozanneaux, picturing the separations of slave families, and the arduous labor on plantations, and one of the Negroes (a forerunner of Uncle Tom) worshipped his master's daughter. The Ambigu, two years later, presented *Atar Gull*, fashioned by Bourgeois and Masson from Eugene Sue's novel. In 1835 the Cirque Olympique produced another melodrama, Desnoyers and Alboize's *La Traite des Noirs*. A comic opera, *Le Code noir*, libretto by Scribe, followed in 1842, dealing with slavery in Martinique: A young man, who believes himself of a noble family, returns from France and is recognized as a slave, and sold by the government. Another, *Le Docteur noir*, by Bourgeois and Dumanoir, at the Saint-Martin, in 1846, centered around a white woman who became interested in a block doctor. Two years after the emancipation of Negroes in the French colonies, Lamartine wrote *Toussaini Louverture* for the same theatre, but despite the poet's praiseworthy sentiments, the African chief expressed himself in classic poetic imagery. The logical French rejected the play, and many parodies soon appeared.

La Case de l'Oncle Tom first saw the light of the lamps in January, 1853, at the Théâtre de L'Ambigu-Comique. MM. Dumanoir and D'Ennery did not scruple to take all sorts of liberty with the original text; desiring to be thoroughly American, they changed Eva to — Dolly, and stressed most of the interest on Élisa and her child, Henry. Uncle Tom was a man of about fifty-five, a departure from the type hitherto seen, for in those early days Tom was depicted as a young, strongly built fellow; here, he got off with a bastinado, and lived on to pray by his master's dead body! The hero of this eight-act dramatization was Le Sénateur Bird (pronounced *Beard*), in white cravat and drab leggings. When Haley came along with his dog — this adaptation was one of the first actually to introduce the animal — le Sénateur diverted the slave hunter with two "nigger" comics, Bengali and Philémon, then plied Haley with liqueurs, and put him under lock and key, repeating mechanically, "Very illegal what I am doing!" Haley was portrayed by a short, pudgy, odd-looking actor, who wore a coarse fur

LA CASE DE L'ONCLE TOM (1853)
Drama by MM. Dumanoir and D'Ennery

coat; then — as one critic pointed out — came his reform-
ation, and he exchanged it for the white coat of innocence!

The villain was not Legree (left out entirely) but
George's master, Harris, a former quadroon slave made
affluent through his father's will, who had himself become
a brutal master of slaves. It was a character inspired by Mrs.
Stowe's description of Legree's overseers, Sambo and
Quimbo.

The adaptors had their own ideas of staging. During
the ice scene, Élisa's son fell into the water (down a trap),
and she fished him up by the hair. George drew a bead on
Harris with his rifle — but Tom placed himself between
them! When le Sénateur Bird failed to persuade Harris's
men "in the name of humanity" to desist, he forgot about
his vote in the Senate Chambers, and aimed a ball at Haley,
who fell moaning. With a true Christian spirit Élisa nursed
him, whereon he declared that, *being sufficiently rich*, he
would retire from the slave business. "There's a fellow,"

observed le Sénateur, "who is going to be honest, when he has no more need to be a scoundrel!"

Haley set George at liberty by a trick deal, purchasing him from Harris: "I will give you five thousand dollars and you let me choose four of your negroes." Saint Clair bought Éliza and her child, but his sudden bankruptcy afforded Harris the opportunity of once more exulting over Élisa: "Ah-ha, my beauty! You're going to be sold at auction for your master's debts, and I'll be *there!*" To be sure, he was bidding in the following act, with Haley, Bird, and George. Harris was called away by Bengali's false alarm of fire on his plantation, and off he ran, enabling George to buy back his wife. How George acquired a fortune so quickly in Canada remained a mystery. The happy reunited family, about to depart, was abruptly stopped by a constable — *the child had yet to be sold!* Here it became evident that Harris would turn up in time to outbid the husband and his well-wishers, and the scene closed with a grand tableau embodying a *nature mort* of despair and victory.

Drawn to Harris's house by the cries of the little one, Élisa almost fell victim to the slaveholder but for Tom, who had indeed a habit of acting the *deus ex machina,* and the dark slave was committed to the overseers for a beating. Le Sénateur arrived on the spot, and — to lend an extra American tinge to the affair — challenged Harris to one of those terrible duels in the Southern fashion (where two adversaries meet in a wood armed with shotguns). George intercepted them, replacing the challenger, and shot Harris; Le Sénateur, in the meantime, freed the child, but killed the guard, *the rifle having gone off accidentally.* Then Tom tottered in, with a horse blanket over his lacerated shoulders, and beholding his dead master, cried, "The Lord have mercy on him!" Final curtain.

From the accounts, one would judge that the Parisian playwrights were pretty free with the novel, which all went

La Charivari, 1853

Uncle Tom Begins To Worry about His Great Popularity

to prove the validity of, "They order these things better in France."

The humorous periodical, *Charivari*, depicted Uncle Tom pursued from theatre to theatre in the most relentless manner; first one limb was bitten off, and then another, until finally Madame Stowe's martyr was so tortured and mangled, that even she would not have recognized her poor slave.

When Mrs. Stowe made her first visit to Paris, in 1853, the numerous French translators of her famous novel paid tribute to her. According to *Charivari*, the report of her presence in the city caused the translators to flock to the American hotel in the Rue de Verneuil. The authoress politely acknowledged that the French often improved upon the original style, and that they had a finer appreciation of the subtle shades of meaning than the English. She ordered ten copies of this note, and sent one to each of the ten translators who had left their cards. Ten joyous exclamations followed the receipt of these notes, and soon afterwards ten men hastened towards the Rue de Verneuil.

"Where are those ten men going?" asked the promenaders.

"They are going," someone answered, "to pay a visit to the author of *Uncle Tom's Cabin*, who has just arrived in the City."

They reached the entrance of the hotel together; they went upstairs together; they stopped together at the antechamber. There, each of the ten cast a triumphant look on the nine others, for each remembered that his pocket contained a precious note declaring his translation to be the best of all.

They were ushered into Mrs. Stowe's parlor. The celebrated *bas-bleu* courtesied gracefully, and said in English: "How do you do, gentlemen?"

They replied in French: "*Bonjour, madame.*"

A general movement of surprise. Mrs. Stowe thought that her translators would speak to her in English, and they expected that the conversation would be carried on in French, as the flattering notes were written in that language. They were unaware that Mrs. Stowe had her circular translated by the interpreter attached to the hotel.

She resumed the conversation: "I am very happy to see you."

The ten translators looked at each other with anxious and troubled faces. Not one understood a word of English. A pause followed, during which each hoped that among his brethren one would be found capable of sustaining a conversation with Mrs. Stowe. At length, one of the ten, bolder than the others, hit on this idea: "She wrote *Uncle Tom's Cabin*: she must know how to speak négre-French." Thereupon he addressed Mrs. Stowe: "*Nous petit blancs, mamzelle: nous aimer bon petit noir a li, bon papa Tom, bonne petite Topsy, bon mulatre George,*" (We little whites, miss: we love good little blacks, good papa Tom, good little Topsy, good mulatto George.") The idea of addressing Mrs. Stowe in this Congo French jargon was a happy inspiration of the moment.

The nine other translators adopted the expedient, and

exclaimed in chorus: *"Oh, papa Tom! oh, papa Tom!"* And they all began dancing the *Bamboula!*

Mrs. Stowe was puzzled. She thought that persons who translated English should certainly understand it. They must be French thieves. Frightened, she went to the window and called loudly for the police!

The gendarmes arrived and carried off the ten translators to the guard house, notwithstanding ten vehement protestations!

The crowd asked, seeing them pass, this time escorted by two ranks of gendarmes: "Who are those ten men?"

"They are the translators of *Uncle Tom's Cabin*. They do not understand English, and for that reason are being led to prison."

Also dramatized after the peculiar French fashion, was *L'Oncle Tom,* by Edmond Texier and L. De Wailly, opening on January 23rd at the Gaîté, which professed to stick closer to the original story than the L'Ambigu-Comique's, with how much truth we may judge from these excerpts.

Évangeline, neglected at the Ambigu-Comique, emerged most prominently here — the critics found her "délicieux!" The rôle was entrusted to Dinah Félix, fifteen years old, youngest sister of the famous actress, Rachel. And Topsy, fitted out with a crude black mask, was introduced as Shelby's crazy slave. Hélas! her mental state was a thing assumed, for, like Hamlet, she meant to avenge her murdered parent. Tom, *père noble,* was here the father of Élisa, and George rid himself of the damning brand on his palm by *burning it out!* When Loker (pronounced *Low care*) hove into view in the tavern, he bore a whip sticking out of his fur coat belt and a large knife in his boot, *à l'Espagnole.* His associate, Marks, dressed entirely in black, left no doubt as to his calling. The hit of the drama was one Le Capitaine Kentucki, on the paddle-box of a steamboat. The bluff get-up, in its unconventionality, seemed more American than any of the others; from the moment he shouted, "Stop!" the Parisians were enchanted. The Mississippi passengers sported every conceivable sort of outlandish dress — one of them a red uniform.

It is amusing to see how the play went astray. The curtain rose on the cabin of Uncle Tom in the midst of a

L'ONCLE TOM (1853)
Drama by MM. Edmond Texier and L. De Wailly

snowstorm! A further incongruity intruded when Mrs. Shelby came to warn Tom, and wore a morning costume, a rather light dress and lace veil. Out of penitence perhaps for mauling her mother to death, Loker bought Topsy, and on the steamboat a bout ensued between him and Capitaine Kentucki. Loker spied Tom, and shouted, "There you old hypocrite! put your hand on the Bible, and swear that this woman is not your daughter, and that her name is not Élisa!" As Tom could never perjure himself, Élisa tried to leap overboard, but sank back in a faint — ending the scene in a tableau.

The second act revealed the Saint Clair plantation, where a doctor informed the parents that only a miracle could save Évangeline. Tom fell on his knees, and urged the hesitating planter to do likewise, and immediately the physician proclaimed that she was out of danger! The joyful parent emancipated all his slaves on the spot. Then a mysterious visitor called on Saint Clair, in the guise of a white philanthropist; Adolphe, the valet, entering, recognized the visitor as the fugitive George, and was about to reveal his identity, when Monsieur Saint Clair interrupted: "You are not George, because I call you Delaunay; you are not a fugitive slave because I receive you in my house; you are not a mulatto, because I, who am a white man, give you my hand!" What vociferous applause!

Now occurred one of the wonders of nature. The adaptors thought that the Ohio River flowed straightway to Canada, and when the fugitives rowed *down* the river, a luxuriant panorama unrolled. Perhaps the whole machinery of this river of gauze was reversed; for with pulses beating faster, the fugitives escaped to Canada by going down the Ohio, although nature's arrangement was somewhat different. They struggled in a mad race with Loker's boat; almost overtaken, they approached the phenomenon of the greatest cataract in the world. *"La morte ou la Liberte!"* they cried. The pursuer's boat gained on them, but Topsy leaned out and (Indian fashion) stunned Loker with her pasteboard hatchet. His barque upset, and broke into pieces in the middle of the dangerous eddies and whirlpools; while George's canoe, conducted by a firm hand and stout heart, rode safely over the cataract. Loker went headlong down the roaring cauldron, and to give a vivid idea of the impetuosity with which he was dashed on his downward course — his head and arm rose several times, then vanished suddenly, to sound effects. A drop-curtain, descending meanwhile, created the illusion of a great waterfall — implying that the boats had *shot* Niagara! This drew up in a few minutes, disclosing a region too tropical even for Florida, but a placard notified the audience that it was "Canada — *Terre*

Libre." Stretching along the Canadian shore in a rather obvious fashion was the Horseshoe Falls — symbolizing their good luck. Here the fugitives fell on their knees, and the final curtain came down to thundering applause.

Of the two plays MM. Dumanoir and D'Ennery's achieved greater popularity. It chalked up seventy-five performances, not counting matinees, from March 5th to the 26th in the theatre of Batignolles, and at the Montmarte from March 26th to April 13th. (Those were the days when long runs were unknown). That Spring it was played at Havre, in Bordeaux, in Nantes, Lyons, Dijon, Marseille, Strasbourg, Toulouse, and in Amiens. The drama was translated into Spanish by Don Ramon de Valladares and Saavedra in 1864, and performed at the theatre of Instituto Espagñol, under the title of *La Cabana de Tom, ó La Esclavitud de los Negros.* Le Sénateur Bird was the hero everywhere!

The De Wailly and Texier drama lasted thirty-three days, and would have run longer if Dinah Félix had not left the cast. It was difficult to replace this popular actress, whose followers were legion. The play was never seen in the provinces.

The Théâtre du Gymnase brought out *Élisa, ou un Chapitre de L'Oncle Tom,* by Arthur de Beauplan, on February 21st. The Emperor and Empress attended the first night. This thinner conception, a comedy, was reduced to two acts, and Tom was unrecognizable. The critics agreed that he looked ridiculous, for he was made a foil of that foppish, coxcomical Negro, gourmand and thief, Adolph, who furnished all the comedy. A dissenting critic, Théophile Gautier, found nothing to laugh at when he saw it, and said he hoped to see the day when the characters in at least one play would all be white, in the midst of this sudden avalanche of black dramas in Paris.

It wasn't long before other Parisian playhouses set a

full pack of hounds on the scent of poor L'Oncle Tom. He was tracked down in the Revue at the Vaudeville, which satirized all during the year; the Théâtre du Palais Royal performed *Casine de l'Oncle Thomas*, a parody by Dormeuil; and another parody was the *Cave de l'Oncle Pomme*, attributed to Paul Michel, at the theatre known as the Batignolles. The Théâtre Lyrique entered the chase, with the drama set to music.

In a suburban playhouse, the Beaumarchais, audiences were misled by a drama, *Lebao le Négre*, but Labao resembled l'Oncle Tom in color only. Another, *Infortunes d'un Marchand de Cirage*, appeared at the Folies-Dramatiques, wherein a Negro servant was called Tom. Such was the rage for everything and everybody black during the early months of 1853, that all one had to do to assure success was to attach "noire" to an article, a play, or a name. The theatre Impérial Italien announced the songstress, Mlle. Marie Martinex, as a Malibran black, and because of her advertised color, flowers rained upon her at every performance.

The year's *Boeuf Gras* was named after the devoted Uncle Tom — a triumph indeed! During the carnival, the fat ox, bedecked with fluttering ribbons and other gaudy decorations, was customarily led through the principal streets of Paris, to the admiration of thousands. Now the other two fat aspirants were named Shelby and St. Clair! This recalled the scene wherein Little Eva fills Tom's button-holes with flowers, hangs a wreath around his neck, as he says, "Look yer, I'm like the ox, mentioned in the good book, dressed for the sacrifice." Thus, in no sense, did the excitable Parisians show any desecration in the cortege of the fête.

In shop windows of the boulevards everything went *à l'Oncle Tom*. Restaurants named American dishes and served them up in the most orthodox French *maître de cuisine* manner. Children bought liquorice advertised as "l'Oncle Tom candi," and read *Un Coup d'oeil dans la Case de l'Oncle Tom.* A reputable member of the Paris Bōurse predicted that if the popular excitement continued the black wax used by shoemakers would fetch an enormous sum.

Their ears caught a Schottisch, "Uncle Tom," by Musard, and their feet danced to a popular quadrille by M a r x. Even the writer, M. Michelet, announced a "Pensèe Fugitive," entitled *E v a.* Everyone sang "Élisa la Quarterone," "T o m ou le Chant des Noirs," "E v a, souvenir de l'Oncle Tom." And how the grisettes danced to the music!

La Charivari, 1853

Endowed with Too Much Sensibility, Uncle Tom Abandons His Dramatic Career

In the country of Voltaire no folly could long survive its traditional sense of ridicule. The Palais Royal, at that very time, was undergoing repairs for the reception of the Emperor's uncle, Jerome, and his son, Napoleon Bonaparte. The witty Parisians, unable to light on a name suitable for the edifice so long known as the Palais Royal (which changed under each Government) were inspired at last to call it *Uncle Thomas's Shed,* in a sense a double-jointed parody.

At the same time, Uncle Tom and his cabin happily

withstood the caustic observers, for he was being enacted simultaneously in five theatres.

A performer in one of these productions, at the Vaudeville, later became a *cause célèbre*. The reason for his engagement is somewhat obscure, since the actor was a trained monkey, but he made a brilliant success, and his death after the close of the engagement aroused an editorial battle of wits. The *Courier de la Gironde* informed the eager public that the late artist had put an end to his existence by swallowing laudanum, unable to bear the banishment from the scene of his triumphs. This was seized upon with Gallic glee by another faction, who insisted that the rash act was due to the unhappy animal's mistaking laudanum for whiskey, a habit undoubtedly acquired from his fellow thespians.

The Parisians, practiced observers, and especially adroit in their perception of the ludicrous, were not lacking in discernment of the more vital qualities, and George Harris became a national hero. Even Figaro, from whom they had absorbed their democratic sentiments, could not compete with him for an instant. The American novel was compared to Rousseau's *Nouvelle Héloïse*, which spoke for the peasant, and which had played its part in the social revolution of 1789; its rousing vindication of popular rights had then been attested by such words as — "I would rather be the wife of a charcoal-burner than the mistress of a king." Mrs. Stowe's novel now whetted the popular taste, with such imitations as *Noir et Blanc, ou le Nègre fugitive*, and Jules Rostaing's *Voyage dans les deux Amériques ou Les neveux de l'Oncle Tom*; the *Revue Britannique* serialized *Une Nièce de l'Oncle Tom ou l'Afrique Blanche*.

The vogue of anti-slavery plays continued for years. Toward the close of 1854 Jars' *Zamire ou la belle esclave* was seen. Plouvier's *Sang Mêle*, an operetta, came to the Port Saint-Martin in the Spring of 1856, and Lordereau's *Le Bon Négre*, another operetta, appeared two years later

La Charivari, 1853

Manager— *Come, hurry, hurry... the curtain is up!*

at the Folies-Dramatiques. The Gaîté, in 1859, gave Bou-
chardy's *Micaël l'esclave*. *Le Negrophile*, by Cauwet, was
given in 1864. After emancipation in the United States the
subject no longer intrigued the French public, but l'Oncle
Tom remained a conspicuous figure. When the War came,
France, thus influenced, proved more constant than England;
a cartoon of the period reflected the popular French sentiment, "John Bull Steps on His Former Protege, Uncle Tom,
to Seize a Bale of Cotton."

Every large city on the Continent had its own version,
and Madame Stowe's Negroes were usually shown as a coa-
lesced type, that of the Mohican of Cooper and the Friday
of *Robinson Crusoe*. In Germany more than half a million

copies of *Onkel Tom's Hütte* were sold, and new ballads caught the ear in the many Lieder-kranz, or vocal clubs. A composer, F. L. Shubert, became famous for three polkas, "Topsy, I Came from Alabama," "Elisa, When I libd in Tennesse," and "Chloe, Now Niggers Listen to Me." In Leipzig a Weber advertised the translations of George Linley's songs, but the less said about the German attempt to ieproduce the Negro dialect the better!

Berlin's earliest view of the play occurred during December, 1852, with *Negersleben in Nord-Amerika*, at the Königstadisches Theatre, by G. Dankwardt and W. Kahleis, music by Hauptner. Another adaptation, *Barbier und Neger, oder Onkel Tom in Deutschland*, in two acts, by Ernest Nonne, music also by Hauptner, dovetailed it almost immediately. The Vorstadisches Theatre served up *Onkel Tom's Hütte* by Therese von Megerle. Vying with these was a "Puppen-Komödie," in three acts, *Onkel Tom, der Berliner Negersklave!*

Advertised as a "Schauspiel," wherever given, the drama captured such towns as Leipzig, Frankfort-on-the-Main, Laibach, Freiburg, Funfkirchen, Troppau, Rostock, Lemberg, Linz, Mainz. Other popular dramatizations were seen in cities like Augsburg, Baden-Baden, Coblenz, and Hermannstadt. . . .

The demand for slave life remained unsatiated, calling more and more for "Shrecklichkeit" in the civilized States. The "Zeitgeist" produced imitations of Mrs. Stowe's work; over a dozen novels by German writers — who had never been in the United States — carried on the "Weltschmerz" of Mrs. Stowe's characters. One novel, Ferdinand Kürnberger's *Der Amerika-Müde*, 1856, is of interest, for it describes just such a dramatization of *Uncle Tom's Cabin*, and undoubtedly he had Mrs. Stowe in mind when he named one of his principal characters Mrs. Drake Harriet Store.

In allen Buchhandlungen ist zu haben:

Harriet Beecher Stowe.

Onkel Tom's Hütte;

oder

Negerleben in den Sklavenstaaten von Nordamerika.

Die Menschenwaare wird vor dem Verkauf besehen.

The Play Captures the German Stage

The "cabin" raced into every language on the Continent, reaching down into Africa. Florence Nightingale came upon soldiers reading the novel with absorbed interest while on fatigue duty during the rigors of an Eastern campaign. Uncle Tom, with marvelous rapidity, learned to express his woeful lot in more than twenty different tongues. He was known in Danish as *Onkel Tomas*, and as *Onkel Tom's Hytte*; in Dutch, *De Negerhut*; in Finnish, *Setä Tumon Tupa*; in Flemish, *De Hut van Onkel Tom*; in Bohemian, *Strýc Tomá's*; in Hungarian, *Tamás Bátya*; in Illyrian, *Stric Tomova Koca*; in Polish, *Chata Wuja Tomasza*; in Portuguese, *A Cabana do Pai Thomaz*; in Spanish, *La Cabaña del tio Tomás*; in Swedish, *Onkel Tom's Stuga*; in

Servian, *Chica-Tomina Koliba;* in Wallachian, *Bordeiulu Unkiului Tom...* The necessary type of the printer's font is lacking to reproduce the Armenian title, the Romaic or modern Greek, and the Arabian.

The simple play stung the world's conscience. The flaming torch reached out to Russian serfdom, where many of the aristocracy, moved by the appeal of *Khizhina dyadi Toma,* liberated the Slavs — a little above slaves — who were bound to the soil, and subject to the master's will. Emancipation became the fashion not only in Russia, but also in Siam.

In Italy, however, *La Capanna dello Zio Tommaso* ran into difficulty because of the impassioned eagerness with which readers received it. Two editions were published in Turin and in Genoa, and one newspaper printed the translation by chapters — day by day — following the example of the Paris press. Most likely, the Papal authorities became apprehensive of the spirit manifested in Paris: there, many, particularly the *ouvriers,* would ask anxiously at the bookstalls for the "real Bible — Uncle Tom's Bible." Moreover, someone had said that Uncle Tom was a better man than Enoch of Biblical memory; since Uncle Tom had been "translated" over twenty times, while Enoch was translated only once! Whatever the reason, the novel was placed on the Index Expurgatorious, but a nonevangelical edition soon appeared in England, and on the Continent editions were adapted to the tenets of the Romish creed.

Most of the vehement attacks, however, came from across the Atlantic. A Baltimore pamphlet, A. M. Hart's *Uncle Tom in Paris, or Views Outside the Cabin,* censured the French for admiring the novel and play. The *New York Monthly,* commenting on the fact that the English were naming dramas, songs, and dinner sets after Uncle Tom, suggested Uncle Tom doughnuts — "They are made of rye flour, varnished with stove-blacking."

The *Irish American* carried an inflammatory article,
"Mrs. Stowe in Cork," with this masterpiece of exaggeration:
"Skull and Skibbereen, Blarney lane and Blackpool have
invited the female Barnum, the princess of humbugs to 'that
beautiful city called Cork,' to an abolition ovation. Uncle
Tom's Cabin! Father Pat's Hut! Uncle Tom well fed, well
clothed, well housed, well doctored, and, in many instances,
well educated! Father Pat dying in a ditch after being
thrown out of his birth-spot — raging in a spotted fever —
without a drop of water to cool his burning tongue — without
food, raiment, or medicine—without sympathy or aid—save
from his penniless peers—rotting, rotting, rotting away out
of existence! Uncle Tom decently coffined and interred!
Father Pat thrown, like a piece of carrion, into the red earth,
a shriveled remnant of skin hanging about his bones, without
a shroud, a coffin, a sigh, or a tear—the hungry dog howl-
ing after and tearing him from the earth at night, and holding a carnival over his putrid body! Aye, inhabitants of
Cork city, your white brothers lying upon your waysides,
the steps of your hall doors, in your streets, covered with
vermin, fever maniacs, with parched lips and cancerous
stomachs, how dare *you* interfere with American institutions
— institutions fostered, fed and supported by the cotton,
rice and tobacco lords — selfish and knavish hypocrites
that they are — of England. Aye, take Mrs. Barnum Stowe
to Skibbereen and Skull. Show her the spot where the bones
of your kindred lie bleaching—women and men homester,
better and purer than you — where the 'mere Irish' have
melted into the earth, 'having been told, (according to the
eminent and philanthropic Everett,) in the frightful language of political economy that at the daily table which
nature spreads for the human family there is no cover laid
for them in Ireland,' and that 'they have crossed the ocean
to find occupation, shelter and bread on a foreign soil!' Aye,
take Uncle Tom's historian to Father Pat's grave — that
spot of red damnation — remind her of the blood-hood

banquet, the festering corpse, the howls of the famine-stricken, the blasphemous ravings of the insane — and ask her should *you* intermeddle for the black, while you have white slaves by the millions, whose condition you have done nothing — you do nothing — to alleviate! Father Pat starves in a hut not fit for an aristocratic h o g ; give him a human dwelling. Poor Father Pat is without food; give him to eat from 'the daily table which nature spreads!' Father Pat is ignorant, unenlightened; educate him, and you will be blessed of God. Do this —perform t h e s e duties — contribute to free your own white slave (called, by a mockery, a delusion and snare, a free man) — a n d then you may fête Mrs. Stowe, Lucy Stone, or Abby Folson, and sympathize with American bondsmen, whom you propagate by purchasing that cotton which they, and they only, can produce."

Transatlantische Skizzen.

Schwarze Courtoisie.

Kladderadatch, 1852

During the summer of 1853, when an actor was mortally wounded by a pistol shot during the scene of Legree's attack at the papier-mâché rocks, the New York *Herald*, on September 18th, placed the crime at Mrs. Stowe's door: "Thus, Mrs. Stowe, the philanthropist, has caused the death of a man! Horrible, indeed! The accident took place on the stage in Bade, Switzerland." Considering the great number of performances given from one end of Europe to the other, it was inevitable that this should happen. But the shots sounded strangely like those of Concord Bridge seventy-eight years before — they, too, were heard round the world!

CHAPTER IX

THE GATHERING OF THE FORCES

Legree's big house was white and green.
His cotton-fields were the best to be seen.
He had strong horses and opulent cattle,
And bloodhounds bold, with chains that would rattle.
His garret was full of curious things:
Books of magic, bags of gold,
And rabbits' feet on long twine strings.
But he went down to the Devil.
      —Vachel Lindsay's "Simon Legree"

THE DARK CLOUD OF ELIJAH rolled over the country. It started in the East the size of a hand, a black man's hand, then rapidly grew and extended as far west as California. The San Francisco settlers decided firmly against slavery.

To reach the mining camps was so arduous a trip, however, that hardly a troupe attempted it. On March 8, 1854, encouraged by influential citizens in San Francisco, Charles R. Thorne staged the Conway version at the Adelphi Theatre. He himself undertook Tom, his wife Topsy, and his young namesake began a distinguished career as George Shelby. Although pared down to three acts, the drama excited everyone; Thorne played the Coast for two years, taking it afterward to Sydney, Australia.

Itinerant exhibitors ventured to the outlying districts in those days, their wagons rigged up with panoramas. The earliest had the great drama painted by Leslie, which was seen at Cincinnati during the Summer of 1853. Another soon appeared in Buffalo, with additional curiosities such as "a woman weighing seven hundred and sixty-four pounds, and a little fairy thirty-two inches high and thirty-two years old." A talented artist, Mr. Hayes, spent over a year in Covington, in the Hoosier State, on a panorama of slavery — "the entire history of Uncle Tom's adventures." It contained some fifty scenes, with the characters large as life.

These dissolving views enjoyed a vogue in the West. If the health of the journeyman showman of *Uncle Tom's Cabin* remained unimpaired, he usually cleared upward of two thousand dollars a month. His associate might bring a working "nut" of about five hundred dollars as a share in the investment; later, the panorama views were sold either separately or together, or exchanged for other property. A perfect example of their business technique was J. N. Still's Grand Diorama of *Uncle Tom's Cabin*, exhibited publicly for the first time in June, 1855, before going West. Its mammoth yards of canvas — to the accompaniment of pianoforte and lecture — unwound at church socials, where half the proceeds went to charity.

That the historical Purdy run had stimulated curiosity in the West, became evident in the opposition of a local press. As late as 1856 we still find the anti-theatre moral emphasis, when the Ohio *Statesman*, October 7th, complained, "To see *Uncle Tom* performed, the most pious rushed to the most disreputable holes, nicknamed theatres, and led their families where but for the negro fanaticism, it would have been considered a very vile sin to have entered."

Among the early itinerant managers, who toured Illinois, was Joseph Jefferson (the second), cousin of the Howards, and father of the actor famous later for his Rip Van Winkle. He was the first to take a company into the limits of Springfield, where the elders of the town, in their deep and determined indignation, placed his license so high as to be prohibitive. The actors were stranded, and to aid them in their distress came a young lawyer, a lanky figure in ill-fitting clothes, who offered to go to the City Council and have the license fee reduced. His name was "Abe" Lincoln.

While the outlying territory opened gradually to the play, the so-called enlightened East was not without its theatrical abuse. In Boston, despite great abolition sentiment, a leading playhouse gave the antislavery drama — but restricted Negroes! It incensed at least one citizen, who wrote to *The Liberator,* on September 2, 1853: "I wish to say a few words to theatre-goers, and particularly to colored people, about the Howard Athenaeum of Boston. Mr. Willard, notwithstanding the severe rebuke lately administered to him in the Police Court, has issued his customary notice, 'Colored persons only admitted to the Gallery.' Now, why *only* to the gallery? I am a working man, sir; work ten hours a day daily at my trade; have a wife and family; and the gallery fits my purse better than any other part of the house. What I want to know is, if the colored population are a nuisance in the boxes, why Mr. Willard should thrust them upon me? His announcement is as gross an insult to the *white* frequenters of the gallery as to the *colored* ones. The real truth seems to be, Boston people have aristocracy. They are not republicans, however much they may mouth it so in after-dinner speeches at Faneuil Hall; and Mr. Willard bows the knee to that class. So be it, say I. Then let him be supported by that class, *and none other.* Drivelling, flunkeyish imitators of an effete European aristocracy, who make color a caste, instead of poverty or want of rank, might fill his house nightly, if he can only get them out, I doubt not. But, by all that is manly and republican, let no *man* or *woman* enter the Howard Athenaeum till the obnoxious restriction is removed; and, in particular, none of our colored friends should so degrade themselves. The Boston Museum is open to them, on equal terms with white people. I am not aware that the National Theatre imposes any restriction. Let Mr. Willard have the house to himself; and, as in the case of the *White Slave of England* (performed to one hundred people nightly,) he will soon find it unprofitable, as well as ungentlemanly, to insult any class of the community, however poor or despised by humbugs."

Having stayed the hand of one ambitious playwright, Mrs. Stowe never resented the dramatizations which appeared constantly — without her permission, and in a letter to a friend in 1853, her husband said: "The drama of *Uncle Tom* has been going on in the National Theatre of New York all summer with most unparalleled success. Everybody goes night after night, and nothing can stop it. The enthusiasm beats that of the run in the Boston Museum out and out. The *Tribune* is full of it. The *Observor*, the *Journal of Commerce*, and all that sort of fellows, are astonished and nonplussed. They do not know what to say or do about it." Perhaps his wife, who believed the stage a trap set by Old Nick, also didn't know what to say or do about it.

Mrs. Stowe received nothing from the "longest theatrical run in history." The play spread like wildfire across the country, but neither she nor her family received as much as a penny. She did not think of dramatic rights, and could not have protected them if she had. In those days plagiarism was one of the inalienable rights of the country's aspiring playwrights. No fees were paid for borrowed material until the first copyright law in 1856, and authors had to wait until 1870, when — at last — they could reserve the dramatization rights.

The only tangible profit Mrs. Stowe ever made was a free box in a Hartford theatre, when an *Uncle Tom* road show came to town. It was a perennial joke with Charles Dudley Warner, who accompanied her, that she never understood the script of the play. Lithograph portraits of Mrs. Stowe, twenty times larger than life, were customarily pasted up on dead walls as an adjunct to performances.

That Hartford event, in her old age, was not Mrs.

Stowe's only presence at the play, for there is extant a description of her first attendance at a theatre: Then a woman of forty-three, she sat heavily veiled, hidden in the shadow of a box, and deeply moved by the acting of the Howard family. The eye-witness, Francis R. Underwood, one of the founders and managing editor of the *Atlantic Monthly*, gives an account of the unique experience:

In the winter of 1852 or 1853 a dramatization of *Uncle Tom's Cabin* was performed at the National Theatre, Boston, — a fine, large theatre, in the wrong place — that is to say, in one of the worst districts of Boston. It was burned a few years later, and never rebuilt. The dramatization was not very artistic, and the scenes introduced were generally the most ghastly ones of the painful story. Of the lightness and gayety of the book there was no sign. The actors were fairly good, but none of them remarkable, except the child who personated *Eva*, and the woman (Mrs. Howard) who played *Topsy*. Mrs. Howard was beyond comparison the best representative of the dark race I ever saw. She was a genius whose method no one could describe. In every look, gesture, and tone there was an intuitive revelation of the strange, capricious, and fascinating creature which Mrs. Stowe had conceived.

I asked Mrs. Stowe to go with me to see the play. She had some natural reluctance, considering the position her father had taken against the theatre, and considering the position of her husband as a preacher; but she also had some curiosity as a woman and as an author to see in flesh and blood the creations of her imagination. I think she told me she had never been in a theatre in her life. I procured the manager's box, and we entered privately, she being well muffled. She sat in the shade of the curtains of our box, and watched the play attentively. I never saw such delight upon a

human face as she displayed when she first compre-
hended the full power of Mrs. Howard's *Topsy*. She
scarcely spoke during the evening; but her expression
was eloquent, — smiles and tears succeeding each other
through the whole.

It must have been for her a thrilling experience to
see her thoughts bodied upon the stage, at a time when
any dramatic representation must have been to her so
vivid. Drawn along by the threads of her own romance,
and inexperienced in the deceptions of the theatre, she
could not have been keenly sensible of the faults of the
piece or the shortcomings of the actors.

I remember that in one scene *Topsy* came quite close
to our box, with her speaking eyes full upon Mrs.
Stowe. Mrs. Stowe's face showed all her vivid and
changing emotions, and the actress must surely have
divined them. The glances when they met and crossed
reminded me of the supreme look of Rachel when she
repeated that indescribable *Hélas!* There was but one
slight wooden barrier between the novelist and the
actress — but it was enough! I think it a matter of
regret that they never met.

The *Eliza* of the evening was a reasonably good
actress, and skipped over the floating ice of the Ohio
River with frantic agility.

The Uncle Tom was rather stolid — such a man as
I have seen preaching among the negroes, when I lived
in Kentucky.

The Hon. F. Underwood went surely amiss in the date.
That it was during the winter apparently lingered in his
memory because of the forceful ice-floe scene, for the
Howards' engagement at the Boston National began on
June 19, 1854.

Mrs. Stowe, on one occasion, expressed it as her opinion
that none of the actors had ever read the novel. She could

never be reconciled to the conventional stage idea of Legree. "I dressed him like a Southerner and made him blonde," the authoress insisted. "I had a certain similar man in my mind as I wrote of him, but the actors all dress him like a Western borderman, with sombrero, red shirt and high boots, and make him of dark complexion." There was this to be said of Mrs. Stowe's discontent in regard to his complexion, that among so many black faces a blonde Legree would surely hold the picture better. She felt a similar dissatisfaction with the greater part of her creations when she saw them through the flesh and blood of real actors.

In 1855, Mrs. Stowe tried her hand on a dramatic construction, *The Christian Slave,* and Mrs. Mary E. Webb, daughter of a Spanish father and a Negro mother, read it at antislavery meetings. Her striking appearance was described, "A Cleopatra come to life, with a white wreath of flowers in her raven hair!" Among those who heard her melodious voice, on December 6th, was the poet Longfellow. The large but apathetic audience found few elements of the theatre in the script, especially in Act III, where Cassy sang in Latin, and delivered speeches 170 lines long. It was never staged.

Mrs. Stowe, however, became the flashing fountainhead of many other plays. Her novel, *Dred,* saw many adaptations, the earliest by C. W. Taylor, in which the Howard family appeared. The famous Cordelia Howard removed all trace of Little Eva by blacking up, covering her golden curls with a horse-hair wig, and donning a pair of ragged breeches. She was called Tom Tit, in a Topsy-like character.

When feeling over the slave question ran perilously high, seven days after John Brown's execution, *The Octoroon; or, Life in Louisiana,* opened. It was the work of Dionysius Lardner Bourcicault, better known in the New World as Dion Boucicault, who had a reputation for ransacking the plays of others, and who once claimed, "I am an emperor and take what I think best for Art, whether it be a story from a book, a play from the French, an actor from a rival company!" In that way, he had about one hundred and twenty-five plays to his credit. His bald head and magnificent goatee, no doubt, inclined some of his simpler-minded followers to accept him as a reincarnation of Shakespeare.

With a flair for despoiling genius to make the crowd worship it (as he put it), he now transmuted dross into gold by borrowing *The Octoroon* from the French versions of *Uncle Tom's Cabin,* then available in printed scripts. De Wailly and Texier's featured Capitaine Kentucki in the Mississippi steamer paddle-box, a sight captivating, indeed, to

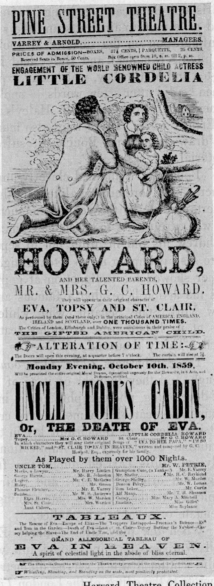

Harvard Theatre Collection

Last Appearances of Little Cordelia

Parisians; Boucicault, gauging its effect abroad, went further, and gave us Captain Ratts and the sure-fire claptrap of the conflagration on the steamer Magnolia. The duel between Capitaine Kentucki and Haley had its counterpart in Wahno-tee and McCloskey, which may explain why the Indian — when he did utter a few words — spoke in French! Scudder's repentance rang similar to Haley's in the Dumanoir and D'Ennery work. There were also many adaptations of *Dred* to draw from, and Boucicault suffered from no lack of material.

Boucicault remained cleverly unpartisan, so that Southerners and Northerners alike left the theatre praising the entertainment. In the repugnant auction sale, for instance, he was careful not to offend anyone: A Southern character withdrew his bid in order not to separate a family; slaves were seen primping up to fetch a higher price, and old Pete rather showed his indignation at going cheap. So realistic was the action here, that a famous anecdote is related of a New York State Senator, who, while the bidding for Zoe was at its height, rose from his seat in the audience, and cried, "Thirty thousand, by G—!"

To Southerners, *The Octoroon* sounded reasonable enough, and they thought of it as of Scudder's invention, a self-developing photographic plate ingeniously exposed in a camera — catching a momentary crime! But the magnificent impudence of Boucicault lay in that he condemned the institution of slavery by implication, all the time. Tactfully, playbills carried quotations from Shakespeare and Virgil (in original Latin), and their literary weight communicated to theatregoers that nothing in the *Octoroon* was extenuate or set down in malice.

When the play first came to England, in 1861, the Civil War was on, and Boucicault was bewildered at the public sentiment which veered diametrically, as if overnight. He wrote to the editor of the London *Times*: "Since the Uncle Tom mania, the sentiments of the English public on the subject of slavery have seemed to be undergoing a great change; but I confess I was not prepared to find that change so radical as it appeared to be when the experiment was tried upon the feelings of a miscellaneous audience." He further claimed that a long residence in the Southern states had convinced him that the delineations in *Uncle Tom's Cabin* were not faithful; that, with every facility for observation, he had found the slaves kindly treated, and that they were warmly attached to their masters. "But, behind all this there are features in slavery far more objectionable than any of those hitherto held up to human execration," he went on, "by the side of which physical suffering appears as a vulgar detail. Some of these features are, for the first time, boldly exhibited in *The Octoroon*.... But when the Octoroon girl was purchased by the ruffianly overseer to become his paramour, her suicide to preserve her purity provoked no sympathy whatever. Yet, a few years ago, the same public, in the same theatre, witnessed with deep emotion the death of Uncle Tom under the lash, and accepted the tableau of the poor old negro, his shirt stained with blood from his lacerated back, crawling across the stage, and dying in slow torture. In the death of the Octoroon lies the moral and teaching of the whole work. Had this girl been saved, and the drama brought to a happy end, the horrors of her position, irremediable from the very institution of slavery, would subside into the condition on annoyance."

Despite his plea, Londoners insisted that Boucicault change the ending. He obliged them, the revised drama thereafter carrying a program note: "A New Last Act of the Drama, composed by the Public, and edited by the Author, will be represented on Monday night. He trusts the Audience will accept it as a very grateful tribute to their judgment and taste, which he should be the last to dispute." Now Zoe was saved from an unhappy end!

One unfortunate association with the Boucicault drama came about through its leading player, George W. Jamieson.

While adding to his reputation considerably by impersonating the "old uncle," Pete, Jamieson suddenly became convinced that the New York adaptation favored the abolitionists. What alarmed him, moreover, were the heroic qualities of John Brown in a drama at the old Bowery, toward the close of 1859, *The Insurrection, or Kansas and Harper's Ferry*. Worse! the same theatre soon after showed *A Colored President...* Jamieson meant to deal a desperate blow at their patronage, and midst the surge of political feeling, he scare-headed the town with *The Old Plantation, or the Real Uncle Tom*.

The Bowery Theatre, on the morning of March 1st, beheld bill-posters industrially plastering the front with battle cries, "UNION! UNION! UNION!" and "DISUNION HUMBLED!" One, larger than the rest, announced: "Those who wish to see a truthful representation of SOUTHERN LIFE AS IT REALLY IS, and witness a picture of Southern servitude as drawn by Mr. G. Jamieson, which is free from eating fanaticism as it is antagonistical to the representations of ABOLITION ENEMIES OF THE GLORIOUS UNION, will be delighted with the Drama of THE OLD PLANTATION." All over town flamboyant signs caught the eye: "Mr. Jamieson will give the Only Truthful Stage Type of the Southern Plantation Negro."

The Jamieson play centered about a rascal Yankee abolitionist, who forced the abduction of a quadroon slave. There were such characters as a New York dandy Negro, another slave who wanted to go North to pick up gold in the streets, a free "bloomer" Negress, and so on. Uncle Tom, listed in the playbill as *the real*, was undertaken by Mr. Jamieson. Despite its scarehead advertising, the drama was exceptionally dull, and as public interest waned, Jamieson, in desperation, added another of his own, *Cheating in Play Never Prospers*, unintentionally an apt title.

As the heavy suspense hung over the fate of the nation, both North and South weighed the issue dramatically. In New Orleans, *The Old Plantation*, with Jamieson in the lead, held the boards of the St. Charles Theatre two months before the firing on Fort Sumter. Up to the outbreak, a wearied, much-traveled agent attracted crowds with *Union-Dioramic Views against Dissolution*. Another series of tableaux, *Extracts from Uncle Sam's Magic Lantern*, on the question of Secession, became the sole entertainment at Laura Keene's, the only regular theatre open in New York in those alarming days. *Distant Relations, or, a Southerner in New York*, at the same theatre, advertised the slogan, "No North, no South, but Justice and Fraternity!" *The Octoroon*, of course, came to mean many things to many audiences. The inflammable *Uncle Tom's Cabin*, and its companion piece, *Dred*, were seen everywhere.

When the storm broke, two versions competed in Philadelphia. Mrs. Harry Chapman enacted Topsy at the Continental, with Mrs. G. C. Howard at the opposition theatre. Mrs. Chapman said later of her rival, "She played it as a Northern woman would play it, but I, having been brought up in the South and having seen just such characters, patterned my portrayal after nature."

One of the critics declared he never had seen two actresses play the same part so differently and yet so well. And Madame de Marguerittes, an authority on her own, once having enacted Eva, answered him, "True, both are great. Mrs. Howard is more like a minstrel wench, thoroughly Northern. Mrs. Chapman is the *bona fide* little nigger, and, I fancy, has seen a great deal of plantation life."

Many Northern and Southern managers, ever cautious, dropped *Uncle Tom's Cabin* like live coals. The all-permeating slave drama was too much for them, yet it now created an excitement unparalleled in the annals of the stage.

Within a week the play burst upon no less than four theatres in New York. The Winter Garden took the lead in those hectic days of 1862. Then other managers set out to beat the originators of the revival, in their excited imaginations beholding a harvest of halves and quarters. At the Winter Garden the play opened on February 25th, and suffered from hurried production. The new scenery failed to arrive on time, and a critic beheld:

"In place of rural Vermont there was classical Italy or something very like it — a mediaeval fountain, surmounted by statues of fawns or other mythological barenesses, such as I never heard of among the Green Mountains— but that is no matter; *Uncle Tom* is not a piece for show scenery, and if the proprieties do get a little mixed and the unities a little bothered, why need I make a time about it?"

The old Bowery, where S. P. Stickney's National Circus had its stamping grounds, whipped it into suitable form that identical day. There the manager relied upon his gelded horses to pull crowds, and the good people of Brooklyn, Williamsburg and Jersey City were exhorted to see "the Equestrian Moral Drama."

Two days later the new Bowery leaped into the fray, starring the popular Fox brothers.

The Howards, ever in the forefront, were caught up by the Athenaeum in a fourth dramatization, described as the work of an eminent member of the Pennsylvania judiciary. This playhouse had been Wallack's old theatre, at the southwest corner of Broadway and Broome Street, which the new managers, Lewis Baker and George Ryer, took over solely for "the moral and religious drama." Aside from the musical nature of this adaptation, which ended appropriately enough with "Poor Old Slave Has Gone to Rest," it did not vary much from the well known Aiken drama. Baker and Ryer had taken some pains to prepare this great work "in all its Grandeur and Purity," but it closed within a week.

They all had rushed out without proper rehearsals.

Many parts were cut down to but a single speech, and others required constant prompting. As was pointed out later, a single theatre might have flourished, but four were too many. The rival managers emerged from the cut-throat business, each with a particularly large flea in his ear, and nothing in his pocket.

Prepared to satirize the passing follies of those days, the Gaities soon advertised, "The Great Anti-Hypondrical Spectacular Burlesque!" It was arranged expressly for the establishment by "one of the first writers of the age!"

The Gaities was two doors below Laura Keene's, between Houston and Bleecker Streets, the entrance upstairs. No boys admitted.

The proprietor of the Gaities nursed one pet grievance. He insisted that though other places might advertise Female Minstrels, his was the "only original, the others being poor copies — mere plagiarisms!" He prided upon the TWENTY-FIVE FAIRY-LIKE SYLPHS, whose repartee rendered them unapproachable! Audiences were said to be CHARMED by these laughter-provoking fairies, and nightly attested their appreciation by unanimous shouts of laughter. Each talented lady artist shone with undiminished lustre, every one a star of bright radiance in the profession!

"Fearless of the shoals and breakers cast in its path by opposing cliques," this favorite amusement place now defied the whole Concert Room world to equal it. "To merit the encomiums nightly bestowed by a discriminating public," the proprietor surpassed himself by advertising a programme which eclipsed all.

About a week later, the proprietor announced in the City's newspapers that he wished to thank his faithful patrons and the public in general, but — here the mystery began — he begged to submit a copy of a placard, which "has been secretly circulated" throughout the City during the past week:

NOTICE TO THE PUBLIC

Being a perfect stranger in this city, I was induced by the glaring advertisements in different newspapers to visit

A CONCERT SALOON IN BROADWAY,

No. 616, *upstairs, called*

THE GAITIES,

and see their wonderfully talented and beautiful Danseuses and Vocalists, Wire Walker, Vaulters, Ethiopian Delineators, and at least one thousand other celebrated performers, not forgetting the Female Minstrels and Pretty Waiter Girls. I have no occasion to find fault with any of the above mentioned acts or actors, as everything went off smoothly and gave great satisfaction to a very large audience; but when Concert Saloons begin burlesquing strictly religious and moral works I think it high time to

PUT A STOP TO THEIR EXISTENCE.

On the occasion of my first and only visit they concluded their performances with a shameful attack on Mrs. H. B. Stowe's beautiful story, entitled

UNCLE TOM'S CABIN;

or

LIFE AMONG THE LOWLY.

Read the manner in which the characters are arranged, copied from their bills:—

Uncle Tom, *a sassy nigger* .... Mr. Pony Smith
Gumption, *a live Yankee* .... Mr. Harry Hartley
Legree, *the great I am* .... Mr. Billy Coleman
The Auctioneer .... Prof. Nicholls
George Harris .... Prof. Daniel
Gentle Eva, *the pet of the public (only seven months old)* .... Miss Jenny Johnson

— 200 —

Topsy, *in which character she stands without*
a rival .... Miss Davis
Eliza Harris, *a beautiful Octoroon* ...... Miss Nelly Gray
Other characters .... By the full strength of the company
 If the citizens of New York will allow performances
of such a nature to take place in their principal thorough-
fares, and at such a time, I am sorry for their morals.
 Not wishing to sign my own name to this at present, but
in case I am wanted to testify to the above, I will be on hand.
 Yours, respectfully,

A STRANGER.

The proprietor insisted, "The peculiar malignity of
the NOTICE emanated from the brain of some aspiring
disciple of Garrison and Beecher!"

As regarded burlesquing Mrs. Stowe's great work, he
had certainly done so — not to bring the work itself (which
is a gem!) into ridicule, but to hit off the mania of the
simultaneous performances of the past few weeks.

"In spite of the venomous attack of the nameless
STRANGER," the proprietor reiterated, "I will keep on
presenting for the public pleasures the great tragi-comical,
anti-abolitional and side-splitical burlesque, *Uncle Tom's*
Log Shanty; or, Life among the Nigger Heads."

These altercations excited great curiosity, and many
rushed to see the controversial hit. When the NOTICES
appeared in shop windows and on fences in large number,
the public dismissed it as a publicity stunt.

New Yorkers who wanted to see the great American
play — in unadulterated form — now took the ferry to
either New Jersey or Brooklyn.

Farther west, in Pittsburgh, a new star was rising. The
soubrette of the local company had been injured accidentally during the Rocky Pass gun fight scene, and Mrs. Lillie
Wilkinson happened to arrive in town just then, on a rainy,

miserable day. In Pittsburgh were 20,000 soldiers, awaiting orders from General Grant, and as she stepped from her hotel to cross the street to the theatre, she saw them by the hundreds leaning upon their muskets or lying on their knapsacks upon the sodden street, drenched to the skin. She hesitated, wondering how to cross the street, when up sprang a soldier, who, without more ado, tucked her under his arm and landed her safe and dry on the opposite side. "Come to the theatre tonight!" she cried, spontaneously. "Come and see me play Topsy!" And they came, not the whole 20,000, but enough to jam the theatre to the doors. Her appearance was the signal for a great demonstration, the poor soldiers showering her with their few bits of loose change. When the curtain went down, $18.75 was picked up.

Mrs. Wilkinson contributed to the Topsy role some of its best lines, which survived down a school of later-day Topsies. She made stage history the first night. When a roar from the house indicated that something was amiss, she discovered that her black tights and stockings had separated, the parting of the ways clearly apparent to the audience by generous strips of white skin. In a twinkling, Mrs. Wilkinson summoned her native ingenuity to the rescue. "Golly, Marse St. Claire," she ejaculated, "guess I must be mortifyin!" This line, inserted by Topsy to save the day, has been used effectively ever since.

The great moral drama now inundated playhouses all over the country. George Harris's sensational speeches on freedom inflamed audiences, and were applauded to the echo.

What really excited the people were the torchlight processions through the streets. Many grabbed up placards and brass torches with wicks soaked in kerosene, and march-ed until they dropped. They did their "wack" for freedom! Others would stand before the picket-fences of their houses all along the line of march, or sit on the porches, yelling and singing as the procession passed by to the local theatre.

Uncle Tom's Cabin had precipitated the war between the States. That was the opinion of Lincoln, who, when he met Mrs. Stowe, said, "So you're the little woman who wrote the book that made this great war!"

When the War ended with the fall of Richmond, a shocking tragedy occurred amid the rejoicing — the most lamentable that had ever befallen the nation. The place was Ford's Theatre, in Washington, D. C. The proprietor, earlier in his career, had been associated with George Kunkel's Nightingale Minstrels, and now his only competitor in the Capitol was this same Kunkel giving matinees of *Uncle Tom and His Cabin* at the New National Theatre. The last play of the season at that rival theatre was *Mazeppa*, starring an educated horse, Don Juan, and it is said that the President had been offered a box for this show. Had he accepted, it might have altered the course of history.

Lincoln liked to go to Ford's Theatre, and his fondness for the stage made popular the saying that it was as easy for an actor as for a diplomat to obtain a hearing at the White House. The tired President found relaxation from the strain and worries of the day by coming into the playhouse, softly, unannounced; his customary box seat was a rocking chair drawn back of a curtain, shutting off the audience's view. When something amused him he would rest his head against the wall and chuckle, and few ever suspected the presence of the tall, gaunt figure.

On the night of the fateful 14th, however, the flag was draped on the upper right-hand box, and although it was Good Friday, everyone knew that the President would be there. The house was in gala mood; the North was celebrating the recent surrender at Appomattox Court House. Laura Keene, the first actress-manager in this country, was making the final appearance of her all-season stock engagement in Washington, in *Our American Cousin,* by Tom Taylor, and this was the comedy the President had chosen to see.

The play was on. There was a sudden ripple of applause, and one of the actors said to Miss Keene, "That line went well."

"Yes," she replied. "Mr. Lincoln has just entered the box."

The applause was short, a simple friendly greeting. The President bowed modestly once, then took his usual place in the outer corner of the box with his back to the audience, his face half-obscured by the drooping fold of the lace curtain. Mrs. Lincoln sat in the opposite corner, and her guests, a young major and his fiancee, occupied a sofa in the rear of the box; General Grant and his wife had been unexpectedly detained. There was no bodyguard.

It was nearly ten o'clock, and the second scene of the third act was on. Mrs. Muzzy (as Mrs. Mount Chesington) discovers that Mr. Harry Hawk (in the title part) while lighting his cigar, has destroyed a will which bequeathed to him a large fortune, and in anger she now cried: "Sir, it is plain to be seen that you are not accustomed to the manners of polite society!" She then disappeared into the wings, and the stage was clear except for Hawk; it was a shallow interior, the rear wall about a dozen feet from the footlights. He proceded with his lines: "Not accustomed to the manners of society?" Pretending to be a bit rattled here, he called after her: "Well, I know enough to turn you inside out, woman —" A sharp pistol report rang through the theatre. Hawk hesitated. He inferred quickly that this might have come from the property man, who had the habit of discharging old firearms in an alley in the rear in order to reload them. As he turned to go on with his lines, he was attracted by a scuffle going on above him. The chandelier of gas lamps surmounting Lincoln's box made it all too clear: the President's head drooped forward slightly on his breast but otherwise his attitude remained unchanged, while a curl of smoke suspended ominously above him. Smoke now floated out over the auditorium. Almost instantly, someone mounted the balustrade rail, and jumped twelve feet to the stage below; one of the spurs of his riding boots caught in the flag decorating the box, throwing him into kneeling position. He was up in a second. Immediately, Hawk recognized him as a fellow-actor, John Wilkes Booth; indeed, he had lunched with him that very day. Booth was apparantly unhurt from his fall, although it afterward developed that he had sustained a fractured ankle. It seemed as if he had carefully rehearsed a part, thinking of himself as a Brutus, for he shouted melodramatically, "Sic Semper Tyrannis!" Brandishing a dagger to cut himself loose from those who might intercept him, he scampered across the stage to the rear of the theatre, through passages evidently well-known to him. Brushing past Miss Keene and a call boy, he turned the angle of the side wall — and continued on. He cleared the back door, and felled a boy who held his horse's bridle. He swiftly mounted, and the beat of horse's hoofs on the cobblestones of the alley were heard distinctly — in the tense hush — until they died away in the distance.

All this transpired in a few seconds — a minute at the most — but seemed an eternity. Hawk, fearing that Booth was going to attack him in a sudden fit of insanity, backed away, and found himself in the greenroom without knowing how he reached it.

The audience sat stupified, uncomprehending, and none had as yet realized or understood what had happened. On that mimic stage — with gas lights — it looked so unreal. At last the spell broke, followed by indescribable wild disorder; by this time they clearly realized what had occurred, although no one seemed certain of the assassin. Then men began swarming up over the footlights on to the stage. Soldiers, the gleam of steel in their hands, appeared from nowhere, and in that pandemonium there were cries of "Where did he go?" "Who was it?" Someone said, "Booth," and others cried louder, "Booth!" . . . Many shouted, "Kill him!" Then came loud outcries of "Burn the theatre!" "Burn the theatre!"

The curtain rang down for the last time, and the playhouse of the never-to-be-forgotten tragedy is today a storage house for Government archives.

John T. Ford, the proprietor, was at once suspected of complicity with Booth, but the citizens of Baltimore believed in his innocence to such an extent that they offered a million dollars bail. After forty days detention in Carroll Prison, he was released, there being no proof whatever against his loyalty.

John S. Clarke, comedian and brother-in-law of Booth, was also arrested, but his innocence was likewise proven. Hawk was held as a witness, and cross-examined in a theatrical boarding house across the street, where Lincoln had been carried unconscious; the actor gave his testimony in the front room, while the President lay dying in a first floor rear room. Released, Hawk was appprehended again and again, and for a time afterward he had to assume another name so as not to fall victim to over-zealous officials.

Twelve days after the President had been struck down, the fanatical John Wilkes Booth was overtaken by Union soldiers, surrounded, and shot. Legends still persist about his escape from the burning barn, but these are all based on sensational rumors which catch-penny journalists found rather lucrative during the tremendous excitement of that period.

The South was plainly distressed, realizing that the compassion and temperateness of a Lincoln were needed grievously to solve their problems.

Lincoln's death suspended dramatic performances during the nation's mourning, and among these was *Uncle Tom's Cabin*. The original version was then playing at the Old

Bowery Theatre, where the Fox brothers and their sister, Mrs. G. C. Howard, were the attraction. The formidable effect of the play had been really felt by now. An historian summed it up, "The stage possibilities of the story appealed first to the theatrical managers, and then to the political managers, and presently thousands of men and boys who never read a book were thrilled and swayed by the dramatized version. Mrs. Stowe's interpretation of the slavery system was of immeasurable influence in shaping the thinking of the Northern youths who came of voting age in the years from 1852 to 1860."

An army chaplain, Henry Clay Trumbull, described in his war memoirs how many Southerners, coming North after the War, went to see the play out of deeply ingrained curiosity. Two of his acquaintances, one from Missouri, the other from South Carolina, saw a performance in New York. Leaving the theatre, they walked for some time in silence, until the South Carolinian, profoundly moved, burst forth, "Well, *that's* what licked us!"

Bowery Theatre, where the Fox brothers and their sister, Mrs. G. C. Howard, were the attraction. The formidable effect of the play had been really felt by now. An historian summed it up. "The stage possibilities of the story appealed first to the theatrical managers, and then to the political managers, and presently thousands of men and boys who never read a book were thrilled and swayed by the dramatized version. Mrs. Stowe's interpretation of the slavery system was of immeasurable influence in shaping the thinking of the Northern youths who came of voting age in the years from 1852 to 1860."

An army chaplain, Henry Clay Trumbull, described in his war memoirs how many Southerners, coming North after the War, went to see the play out of deeply ingrained curiosity. Two of his acquaintances, one from Missouri, the other from South Carolina, saw a performance in New York. Leaving the theatre, they walked for some time in silence, until the South Carolinian, profoundly moved, burst forth, "Well, that's what licked us."

PART II

ALL ABOUT THE TOMMERS, WHO THEY WERE, AND WHAT THEY DID

When your show cum's we'll all turn out,
An' see what the play is all about;
I see the bills upon yonder fence
Which put the price at fifteen cents.

By Gosh! I'm a gowin' to see the fun,
An' I don't keer a durn if it cost's more mon',
I once saw a play, called Uncle Tom's Cabin,
An' more gosh dinged fun I di'nt sp'ose there wuz havin'.

Now, I rather kinder have an idear
That your show is like the one I saw prior,
For they called thet Uncle Tom's Cabin *when't cum,*
While the name o' this seem's to be Uncle Tom.

Bill Sikes an' I, we both went in,
An' you'de oughter see Bill 'gin to grin
When Marks an' his donkey buth cum' out;
Well, Lor! I roared, but Bill did shout!

Wal, yas, I live in this small jay town,
Whar ther' don't a great many shows cum' roun',
Except Uncle Tom, *an' then I dont' keer*
If it costs a dollar; I'm always there!

Am I goin'? Wal, now, by gravy; you bet!
I'll miss all the rest, but never miss thet,
For that's the show that'll always last —
But I say, my fren', cin yer spare a pass?

F. Buoman's "Uncle Hiram and the *Uncle Tom* Agent"

SEE OTHER SIDE.

TOPSY!

UNCLE TOM'S CABIN.

CHAPTER X

WILD TURKEY TOMMERS AND SWEET JUBILEE SINGERS

Scenery, prop's and lights — heigho!
The selfsame fortune must befall,
Except for Uncle Tom, *they go*
Into the storehouse, one and all!
—Berton Braley's "Limbo"

POST-WAR CONDITIONS HAD a deleterious effect on the theatre. Daily, seedy-looking actors gathered in Union Square to discuss their ups and downs, old conquests and recent defeats; they assumed a lordly stride and noble pose to awe ordinary mortals, but the merciless realism of the noon-day sun — alas! revealed the moth-eaten fur on their overcoats. Haunting the Square's barrooms, they sought "touches," expecting something to turn up any minute; meanwile they negotiated, hoping that some day the ghost would walk. Now, the professional jargon was unintelligible to an outsider: Shakespeare first made the ghost walk, via *Hamlet*, and the expression, "The ghost walks," meant that salaries were paid, but of late years he had not been any too regular in his spiritous tramps to the Square, and they now complained, "The ghost is dead!"

However, there was one compensation. Every holiday found them conspiring for a raid on the rural districts for "one consecutive night." They were called "turkey actors," that first lean Thanksgiving season after the War, though usually it was too hopeful an appelation, since really sub-

— 213 —

stantial people had scarcely enough money to pay for turkeys, to say nothing of actors. Those who carried to the rural towns the so-called standard dramas came back disappointed — "thrown over," while the players who had prepared *Uncle Tom's Cabin* returned with a head of lettuce in the shape of greenbacks — "a bumper." Without delay, the "turkey actors" hit upon a schedule of four combinations during the season, selecting the holidays as follows: Thanksgiving, *Uncle Tom's Cabin, or Life among the Lowly;* Christmas, *Uncle Tom's Cabin;* Washington's Birthday, *Uncle Tom;* Lincoln's Birthday, *U.T.C.;* and the Fourth of July, *Uncle Tom and His Cabin.*

The "turkey actors" took into account the farmers, who, arriving in dusty surreys from outlying districts, were unable to obtain standing room, and turned away with "Shucks!" Why not prolong the holiday season there? Consequently, the players covered the hot, dusty territory on foot, with only their clothes on their backs plus an extra collar in the pocket. They washed in creeks, and their progress was slower than the Second Coming. Then they got the habit of venturing out with a one-horse rickety wagon, its sides decorated with Lincoln offering the nation the Emancipation Proclamation. In each little village a Tommer dickered with the local butcher, trading "comps" for hog fat, which was poured later into molds; the crude footlight torches were made by combining pine sticks with the available fat. It fell to Eliza's lot to find a likely housewife from whom to borrow enough furniture to dress the stage.

"Yankee" Robinson was probably the pioneer barnstormer. He straddled a show wagon as far back as the Spring of 1854, when he gave the play in a billowy tent. The tour sprouted in Dayton, Ohio, and closed its prosperous season at Indianapolis. G. A. Hough, famous for his Gumption Cute, whittled out his own axletrees in the Spring of 1869, and travelled sixty-five days in the West, during which time he cleared the nice little sum of $4,000; in the '80s, at

— 214 —

the age of seventy, he was still bouncing around with the play. Another 'way-backer was the sorghum show of "Yankee" Locke, who, enacting both Gumption Cute and Phineas Fletcher, proclaimed during the summer of 1879, "As played before the American public over 3000 times."

Penetrating the backwoods, the "turkey actors" of post-war days drew the natives like flies around a molasses barrel. The critics said that it was worse than the cinch on the green bugs in Kansas or the grasshoppers in Oklahoma. Hinterlanders flocked to the weather-beaten canvas of the Tommers' wagons, lured by the daubs of symbolical characters in a nineteenth century morality play. They agreed that Eva's voice tinkled like a golden harp, and that it was as good as a camp meeting to hear Uncle Tom sing!

The Tommers now had the advantage over the rest of the profession, for preachers even then were inveighing against "adjuncts of the devil's backyard." The Caroline Hayes troupe, touring Ohio two years after the War, discovered the immunity of the anti-slavery drama when, with Little Katie Ballard as Eva, they came to Urbana. They found a religious revival on. The minister of the Second Methodist Church had announced, before the troupe arrived, that he would preach about it at the Weaver House. They decided to go down in a body to the Church. They were the focus of all eyes, what with Uncle Tom in his clerical-looking coat, carrying his Bible, and ethereal Little Eva with her nimbus fastened on her golden locks. The minister, in the light of this visitation, assailed minstrels instead.

The early "turkey actors" brought the play to the American cross-roads, slogging along with a gilly wagon piled high with scenery. They carried the flimsiest, second-hand canvas; the sets often collapsed, prematurely smothering Little Eva and Uncle Tom. The historic drama was given in livery stables, on a shaky stage of rough

lumber, with bobbing kerosene lamps as footlights. Some
times, more fortunate, they put it on in places like the
Tunkhannock Court House, or the W.C.T.U. hall, or the
Odd Fellows' Hall, or in a railroad station. Mary Austin,
the novelist, describes those days: "I am not sure Mary got
any further that winter of '79 than *The Lamplighter* and
Harriet Beecher Stowe. It was played in the County Court
Room, and everybody went, even — or especially — Method-
ists. Children were brought in wagons; you saw them going
out later, rolled in bedquilts and tucked under the seats,
sound asleep within twenty minutes of the play's ending."
Indeed, in its antediluvian surroundings, the old stand-by
always drew like a mustard plaster, and Uncle Tom went
out each night in a blaze of glory!

Playbills were cheaply printed, full of slapdash errors.
A typesetting conspiracy lent added proportions to the slim
troupe, and an actress would undertake both Eva and Topsy:
As Eva she passed through the pearly gates, was lowered
down on the stepladder, hurriedly smudged her face with
burnt cork — and for three acts thereafter was Topsy.
The others, when not doubling, played in the orchestra, or
joined the celestial choir in the wings in swelling crescendo.
To such a degree did they double, that an eloquent quatrain
survives:

> *Act I, I was a cake of ice;*
> *Act II, I was another;*
> *Act III, I was the mob outside*
> *And Little Eva's mother!*

Those were the pioneering days, when the over-worked
manager came out in front — if the drama called for a dark
scene — and noisily puffed out the row of reeking oil lamps.
It would never do to have an audience sit in total darkness,
but the farmers were prepared, having brought along their
wagon lanterns. The cold outer air whistled through the

rough-board partitions of the makeshift theatre. They found it more comfortable to keep the lanterns under their benches. The dogs of the rural spectators were there, too, and the place became an uproar, for they all ran barking at the strange dog chasing poor Eliza across the pine-board stage.

The isolated little towns were out of reach of splendid legitimate theatres, and this one crude play held them spell-bound. They found it as wholesome as a New England primer. Its influence became so strong that when the time came for choosing a profession, many youngsters headed for the stage. Amy Leslie recalled: "I had at one time beheld the loveliest and saddest performance of *Uncle Tom's Cabin* at a Council Bluffs theatre, built over a robust and profitable livery stable. It was a blow for me to learn that the winged little Eva of Council Bluffs was a diverting back number in Chicago, for the vision of Eva and her silver-star wand wiggling against pink and blue tarleton clouds stricken with tin foil, had been the twilight dream of my childhood's occasional moments of intense reflection. I plead for Eva against the war play with some vigor, for that special de-livery of *Uncle Tom's Cabin* was certainly 'the saddest play I ever saw for fifty cents.' In fact, even as I think of it now it makes me feel very badly. I doubt whether I could ever again hear 'Lily Dale' without wilting into moods; for while my Council Bluffs Eva ascended mysteriously from the livery stable thru the stage floor up toward a celestial, juju paste firmament, the entire company in subdued tremolo accompanied by the melodeon rendered that harrowing ballad with words subjected to poetic transfiguration so that they came out appropriately:

Oh Eva, dear Eva, sweet Eva St. Clair,
Now the wild flowers blossom o'er your heavenly shore
'Neath the trees of the flow'ry air!

"I have cause to remember the words vividly for they were demanded with sobs over again and again, and General Grenville Dodge, who had taken me to see the show, was rudely awakened out of a sound sleep by my pitching my small head upon his breast and weeping as if my heart would break, much to that distinguished soldier's helpless consternation. With my mind still in this primitive state of undisturbed blankness regarding the drama, Rosina (Hooley) all aglow, led me into Hooley's Theatre, where I drank in the splendours of a real, magnificent, thrilling play, after which my Missouri-slope Eva took a tumble in her tarletans which, with deepest gratitude, I shall regret as long as I live."

The trail-blazing Tommers journeyed as far as the Alleghenies, in the beginning, and when cold weather set in they returned to the East. They repainted their wagons with cumulous clouds on the blue sides, refurbishing the scenery for the coming Spring, when all a-glitter, they would be off again. Then the trips became longer, they ventured farther and farther—ever westward. Now permanent "turkey actors," the profession dubbed them "prairie actors," or "the wild turkey Tommers." They played against great natural opposition — swollen rivers, impassable roads, rainstorms, blinding heat. Struggling wagons sank deep in the mud, to the hubs. They forded the fast streams; and there — opening up before them, a glimpse of the Eldorado in the rip snortin' territory farther on. *There* were the silver dollars — "noble Susquehannas!" "cartwheels!" "buzzards!" (called so because of the queer eagle adorning one side of the dollar); and, of course, the small silver pieces — "pegs!" Then they reached the mining sections of the Rockies, and the Tommers came in for their share of the nuggets which industrious gold seekers, using primitive methods of cradle and rocker, washed up in their flashing pans.

In the newly-settled country they rode mule-back from one mining camp to another. They gave the drama in shanties

and sheds, packing 'em in and turning 'em away. The [
pards acclaimed them with the pay dirt in their bag
rarely fell to their lot to see a woman at the diggin's,
especially an actress, prospectors welcomed with open arms
Eliza, Topsy and Eva — a veritable horn of plenty. Strong
men were not expected to stuff dirty red neckerchiefs down
their larynxes when Little Eva tells old Tom that she is
"going there," but at the end of every performance the
atmosphere was suspiciously damp. Nor was it Eva or Eliza
that excited them so greatly, as Topsy! — burnt-cork Topsy,
in her ragged calico dress, who set the camps in an uproar
with her drollery. The only music they knew was an orchestra of fiddle and guitar, which squealed and thrummed but
three pieces, "Zip Coon," "Hail Columbia," and "Oh
Susannah!" Topsy's torch-singing set them on their ears.
With her raucous voice, like that of a cricket with
laryngitis, the wild waif of Mrs. Stowe's imagination became
the living embodiment of the "wickedest nigger on earth."
That mischievous "I'se So Wicked!" reaped a golden harvest, as Topsy sang:

> Oh! white folks, I wuz nebber born:
>> Aunt Sue she raise me on de corn,
> Sen' me errands night an' morn',
>> Ching-a-ring-a ring-a ricked!
> She used to knock me on de floor,
>> Den bang ma head again de door,
> An' tear ma wool out by de core:
>> Oh! 'cause I wuz so wicked!
> Black folks can do naught, dey say;
>> O guess I'll teach some how to play,
> An' dance about dis time ob day,
>> Ching-a-ring-a bang goes de break-down!

> Oh! Massa Clare, he bring me here,
>> Put me in Miss Feeley's care;

Don't I make dat lady stare —
Ching-a-ring-ring-a ricked!
She hab me taken clothed an' fed,
Den sends me up to make her bed.
When I buts de foot into de head:
Oh! I'se so awful wicked!
I'se dark Topsy, as you see,
None ob your half-an'-half for me:
Black or white it's best to be:
Ching-a-ring-a hop goes de break-down!

Oh! dere is one will come an' say:
Be good, Topsy, learn to pray;
An' raise her buful hands dat way —
Ching-a-ring-a ricked!
'Tis Little Eva, kind an' fair,
Says: If I'se so good, I'll go dere;
But den I tells her: I don't care!
Oh! ain't I very wicked?
Eat de cake, an' hoe de corn,
I'se de gal dat ne'er wuz born,
But 'spects I grow'd up one dark morn:
Ching-a-ringa smash goes de break-down!

The rest was subordinated to allow irrepressible Topsy her full measure of specialties — a variety of songs, dances, and banjo solos. The highest praise for an actress undertaking Topsy during that decade was, "She is a genuine wench, and has quite a reputation in California!"

In the dramatic firmament of San Francisco, Alice Kingsbury, shining with all the brilliancy of a star of the first magnitude, packed Maguire's Opera House during the Fall of 1866. Her Topsy, eyes rolling and teeth flashing in contrast to the counterfeited black face — like "pearls in order placed" — enticed the prospectors away from their claims at the diggin's.

Lotta as Topsy
She Staked a Claim in the Role, and the California
Miners Threw Nuggets at Every Performance

David Belasco as Uncle Tom

*The Twenty-Year-Old Actor as He Appeared at Sheil's
Opera House, San Francisco, 1873*

The Coast also had a soft spot in its heart for Helen Dauvray, who made her stage debut in San Francisco as Eva at the age of five. The cast at Maguire's must have been a wonderful one, for almost all became celebrities: Ben Cotton (Uncle Tom), Agnes Booth (Eliza), Frank Mayo (George Harris), Charles Thorne (St. Claire), Louis Aldrich (Legree), Mrs. Saunders (Ophelia), and Mrs. Leighton (Topsy). The success of the little girl as Eva laid the foundation of her fame and fortune. Helen, afterward, played Topsy to John E. McCullough's Uncle Tom. She was known wherever she went as "Little Nell, the California Diamond."

Her immediate rival on the Coast was Charlotte Crabtree, better known as Lotta. While traveling with the Mart Taylor troupe they stopped at Placerville, and put on *Uncle Tom's Cabin*, with Lotta, who accompanied herself on the banjo in this song, "Bekase My Name Am Topsey:"

I can play de banjo, yah, 'deed I can!
I can play a tune 'pon de fryin' pan,
I hollo like a steamboat 'fore she's gwine to stop,
I can sweep a chimbley an' sing out at de top —

She did a lusty breakdown, and the frenzied miners showered her with gold nuggets. Spontaneously, she kicked off a shoe, and still in character, filled it with the precious metal. Hoydenish, squealing and grimacing, she ran about, exulting at the find in the smoky kerosene lamps of the rough pine stage. Thus began the fortune of America's richest actress.

Later, John Brougham adapted for her talents *Little Nell and the Marchioness*, but the swift and grotesque gestures of Lotta's Marchioness, the antics of breakdowns, the "Unrivaled Clog Dance," and banjo solos, all smacked of Topsy. In truth, the combination of the angelic Little Nell and the soot-covered "slavey," the Marchioness, reminded audiences that Mrs. Stowe had borrowed from the *Old Curiosity Shop*. Little Nell, like Eva, too, had a premonition of early death; her old protector was like Uncle Tom; and the ragged little Marchioness was animated by a rebellious spirit, like Topsy's, which expressed itself in comic pranks. The play ended with an apotheosis of Little Nell.

Lotta's two plays enlivened the country. Even the Mormons admired her romping, for in July, 1869, "The City of the Saints" turned out en masse to see her.

Nor was it the first time the faithful had witnessed *Uncle Tom's Cabin.* Back in 1852, a Social Hall had been erected for community purposes, as well as for the Deseret Dramatic Association. David McKensie had the honor of being the first Uncle Tom on the Salt Lake stage. In that first production, Heber J. Grant, President of the Mormons, made his first and only appearance on the boards — as a pickaninny! The Mormons gave the play again in January, 1872, with Eliza Couldock enacting Eliza in such an ambitious manner that the strain resulted in her death. David McKenzie, again as Tom, was directed by George Pauncefort (the George Harris), who was a purist even in crude folk drama, for he made Uncle Tom speak *without* the dialect. When Brigham Young heard about it, he hurried to the Hall, and with indignation requisite to a "Moses of the West," commanded that Uncle Tom's accent be restored immediately! Further, he was dissatisfied with Uncle Tom's coat. The actor entreated that he be given until morning to recover his Negro dialect, but he was at a loss just how to get another garment. "Here it is," Brigham said emphatically, taking off his old "Prince Albert," and trying it on McKenzie. They both were of equal height, so it fitted quite well. And for the remainder of the engagement Uncle Tom not only spoke with the dialect, but also wore Brigham's own coat.

But to return to the fortunes of the play on the Coast. In 1878, a revival at the old California Theatre starred Maude Adams as Eva. David Belasco was struggling forward into prominence, having that same year adapted at least two dramatizations of the anti-slavery play; in the Fall of 1873 he had portrayed Uncle Tom at Shiel's Opera House, and for six weeks he enacted Lawyer Marks, Legree, Topsy, George, Sambo. Hobart Bosworth was starting his career. in the small part of Tom Loker in another company, with Annie Adams, mother of little Maude. Then Belasco "re-touched and arranged" Bouciault's *Octoroon*, which was revived at the Baldwin Theatre under the management of Gustave Frohman.

When Frohman's lease expired on the first of July, Jay Rial moved in two days later with *Uncle Tom's Cabin*. The news of its success reached Frohman, who had gone on an unprofitable tour with the Stoddart Comedy Company. When he reached Kentucky all the baggage was gone, for it had been left behind at the hotels as security for unpaid bills. At Richmond, he hit upon what other harrassed troupes, time and again, had found to be a life-saver — *Uncle Tom's Cabin. Why not have a real Negro play Uncle Tom?* he said to himself. Immediately, Frohman wired his brother Charles:

GET ME AN EVA AND SEND HER DOWN WITH SAM LUCAS STOP BE SURE TO TELL SAM TO BRING HIS DIAMONDS

Lucas, the dapper-looking colored performer, previously a member of the Callender Minstrel troupe, was fond of sporting sparklers. He had the very means with which to back the Frohman enterprise, as well as the talent. In return he was promised the part of Uncle Tom. In the innocence of his simple soul, Lucas felt he had now attained the culminating point of his career.

The first performance crammed the theatre at Richmond. But Lucas, on edge with his heavy responsibility, became rattled, and made the queerest breaks in his lines. The worst, that night, occurred when Eva asked: "Uncle

Tom, when you die, where are you going?" He rolled the whites of his eyes upward, gravely responding: "Up in de *flies*, Miss Eba, up in de *flies*." As a minstrel he was familiar with the *flies*, and so confused it with skies.

With sufficent returns to get the company out of Kentucky, Gustave now booked the adjacent towns, envisioning overflowing houses in Ohio, and particularly at Wilmington, the home town of Sam Lucas. He ran into difficulty. As is often the case of home talent, attendance at Wilmington was negligible. To complicate matters, Sallie Cohen (later Mrs. John C. Rice) tired of the hardships, and left the company. Little Eva had to be enacted by Polly Stoddard, a large, well-developed woman. On this night, ensconced in the arboreal lap of Wesley Sisson, she not only concealed from view her papa St.Clair but almost prostrated him. The tour ended at Wilmington, where Lucas, poor soul, pawned more of his precious stones. The stranded troupe managed to get back to Cincinnati.

Later, Lucas again attempted the part for Nixon & North's revival, but all he got out of the engagement was his fare from Boston. Managers hired him for his specialties in the plantation scenes.

In 1876, when everyone was discussing the coming Centennial Exposition in Philadelphia, comparisons were made with fairs of the past. In particular, it reminded Mr. and Mrs. G. C. Howard of the Crystal Palace exhibition, when their drama first came to Purdy's. They had been appearing in their old roles for almost a quarter of a century. As the holidays usually found them in Brooklyn, they were now celebrating Washington's Birthday there. About a week later they began an experiment at the Brooklyn Theatre that opened up a new era in the history of the play.

Introduced at this time were the colored Georgia Jubilee singers. The crudely made sheepskin banjo vied with the home-made fiddle in old-time plantation melodies, and the wild flings to the accompaniment of a tin horn band! This started the rage for genuine plantation music in the play.

During the Centennial week, the Howards secured an engagement at the Park Theatre, where, reenforced by Slavin's Original Georgia Jubilee Singers, they cast a spell on the public.

That Spring, jubilee singing came to the fore. The Centennialities, "thirty colored ladies and gentlemen from Fisk University," impelled crowds to the concerts at Tammany Hall. And the Slave Troupe Jubilee, with the prominent Horace Weston, packed 'em in at Steinway Hall.

The Howards, at the time, had intended to remain in New York two weeks, but stayed twenty-seven!

Everywhere, the perennial flower was shooting into full bloom. On May 13, 1878, the Boston Museum opened with William Warren in his famous part, with this added emphasis: "40 - - JUBILEE SINGERS - - 40." "We're the high-flavored *Uncle Tom* companies," boasted managers. "From the bayous, the canebrakes, the tobaccer regions an' cotton plantations!" Bobby Newcomb and Rollin Howard, enacting Topsy in that halcyon period, found the "genuine Negroes" indispensible. When Laura Alberta promised her Topsy for Woods, during the summer of 1877, she brought along Sawyer's Original Jubilee Singers, one hundred colored folks.

Now in its glory days, two New England managers, J. V. Farrar and C. H. Clarke, introduced in their grand street parade not only a bull-whacker with guide rope and long whip leading Tom, but a thundering juggernaut, a southern log cabin, "The only one exhibited in New England — Copyright Secured." This planted the theme, lock, stock and barrel, details and all.

The Jubilee craze spread to Cincinnati, where Colonel Robert E. J. Miles enlivened the drama, in 1877, with the

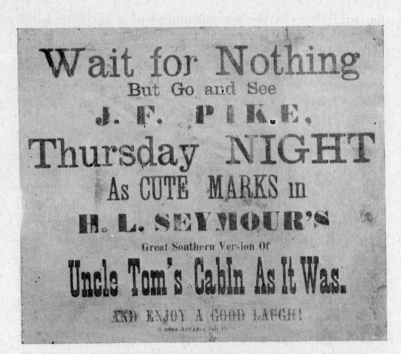

How the South Enjoyed the Play

New Orleans Jubilee Singers. The same year, David Bidwell secured the Tennessee Jubilee Singers for the Academy of Music in New Orleans. Liberal to a fault, this Southern manager was also uncommonly shrewd. He knew the natural reaction with the war wounds still raw, and therefore emphasized Lawyer Marks (J. F. Pike). Everyone wanted to see the much heralded and nostalgic "Morsels of Ethiopian Mirth, Fun and Frolic descriptive of the different phases of SLAVE LIFE ON THE OLD PLANTATION!"

A greater deluge of jubilee singers flooded the land the following year. Already the market price for "Jubilee Singers" of Negro extraction had jumped up several notches. Early in 1878, an advertisement in the New York newspapers called for "100 octoroons, 100 quadroons, 100 mulattoes, and 100 decidedly black men, women, and children capable of singing slave choruses." The candidates were directed to apply at a curiosity shop, of the deepest dye, at Twenty-second Street and Broadway. A sign was hoisted up so high that the lettering was barely discernible; at the foot of the stairs, however, in full view from the Broadway sidewalk, a large black and white placard announced that so many "Sweet-voiced mulattoes, quadroons, &c., are wanted for the approaching reproduction by Jarrett & Palmer of the unique, ornate, magnificent, and triumphant work of genius, *Uncle Tom's Cabin*, the colossus of the stage, and the wonder of the wonders of the nineteenth century."

On that day, a *Times* reporter, sauntering down Broadway, saw the sign. He was struck, moreover, by the peculiar behavior of the darkies: Some of them studied the placard for as long as five or ten minutes, threw frequent glances up at the third story of the warehouse, scratched their heads, but seemed to lack courage to enter. One young colored gentleman paused on the corner, and peered suspiciously up and down the street. Seeing none of his friends in sight, he stepped cautiously up to the sign, stood before it a minute or two, again looked up and down the street, and bounded up the steps. But, alas, someone happened to be coming down the stairs at that same moment — the potential singer of sweet jubilees heard the footfalls, and sprang to the sidewalk again, darted around the corner, and did not reappear for more than three-quarters of an hour.

The curious reporter decided to investigate. The agent in charge of hiring "darkies," he found, was a small, sharp-looking man, who not only resembled the Secretary of State, but coincidentally also bore his name — Mr. Evarts. The agent attributed the absence of colored sweet singers to the fact that it was yet rather early in the morning, but he expected them to show up at about eleven o'clock.

"We never have any trouble getting all the colored singers we want," he said. "In Philadelphia we didn't advertise at all, but just sent word among them, and we had such a crowd the police had to clear the sidewalk. You never saw anything like it. They can all sing. When the orchestra gets to going they can't help themselves, but either stand perfectly still and bewildered or go to dancing and shouting to the music. I've seen them get down and bump the stage with their heads. We don't try each particular voice. I can tell about what each of them can do by the cut of his jib."

"How much do you pay them?" asked the reporter.

"Not much," answered Evarts. "Of course, some Uncle Toms — maybe a dozen or so — get from $50 to $150 a week, and they are the very best in the business." He mentioned an actress: "We have a Topsy that is a Topsy. Now, there's Mrs. —; she's a very good Topsy, but she's too refined for the part. Our Topsy can sing plantation songs like a born slave. Her nose lays right flat down on her face, too. She was made for the part. Why, she stands on the stage and turns a somersault without touching the floor. That's the kind of a Topsy we have."

While Mr. Evarts was expatiating on the beauties of his Topsy, the first of the would-be singers arrived. He peeped in furtively through the glass door, and came in swiftly lest he lose courage. He was not an octoroon, nor a quadroon, nor a mulatto, nor decidedly black; Evarts was puzzled. The journalist suggested that his color was a cross between New Orleans molasses and New England rum, although the exact shade could be found only near Thompson and Sullivan Streets.

"Is dis de place fur to sing fur Jarrett & Palmer?" asked the object of their study. "I'm a jubilee singer. I was in *Uncle Tom* in de Gran' Op'a-house."

"Then you know pretty well what to do, without being told about it again."

"Well, I 'specs I does, boss. I knows all 'bout 'hearsin', and them things."

He was instructed to appear the following Wednesday morning.

"The pay won't be very big," warned Mr. Evarts, "but, of course, we'll pay you more than we would a greenhorn who don't know anything about the business."

Next, an intelligent-looking young mulatto, with black side whiskers, entered. "Don't you have anything but singing to do in the piece?"

"Yes, plenty of things," said Mr. Evarts. "What can you do?"

"Mos' anything. I never acted any of the parts, but I've studied 'em all. I could play George Harris."

"Why, bless your heart, man! We have a man at $100 a week to take the part of George Harris. That's one of the biggest parts in the play."

"Well, I could do mos' any of 'em," insisted the would-be actor.

"You'd make a good Eva, I think," observed Evarts dryly. "But, unfortunately, we have an Eva engaged. You come round next Wednesday, and we'll see what we can do for you."

Two more were examined, a tall "decidedly black" man, whose neck was tied up suggestive of the mumps, and a very short roly-poly man with a beaming face, that would have been the fortune of a minstrel. Asked what he could do. the tall fellow answered, "I was in de Gran' Op'ra."

"That's all right then." Evarts addressed the black dwarf, "What can you do, my little man?"

"I dunno."

"Can you sing?"

"Dunno. Guess mebbe I might, ef I sh'ld try."

"Can you dance?"

"Dunno. Mebbe."

"Do you want to sing in the chorus?"

"Wat's dat?"

"That's to sing plantation songs and jubilee songs. You can do that, can't you?"

"I jes can, boss. I'se yer man."

Within an hour enough jubilee singers gathered to start a small Liberia on Broadway. But the observant reporter noticed that they were all young men. Although the industrious agent had advertised for women and children, not a one showed up. "This is going to be one of the biggest things ever brought out in New York," Evarts warned them, "and I want you all to be here next Wedneday morning at 10 o'clock sharp, and bring your friends. Above all, bring your mothers and sisters."

They scampered off, vowing that the whole family would be there. One of the singers, smarter than the rest, was heard to confess that this would be the fourth time "the most magnificent spectacle ever produced in New York" had been brought out during the month.

With the incursion of the colored inhabitants of Thompson Street, Jarrett & Palmer hired a corps of specialty artists to head the choruses. The famous Louisiana Troubadour Quartet of liberated slaves, as well as the Jolly Colored Four, "real slave minstrels," figured as units, with Horace Weston (now called the greatest banjo strummer in the world) making his entrance propped up on a moving scow with a cargo of cotton bales. Miss Sarah Washington, the Richmond camp-meeting leader, was later added. However, a weird-looking, ugly young Negress vied for honors, although in a secular way, and her exuberance gained her the soubriquet of "The Mustang." Her violent kicks, discordant screams, and extraordinary arm-swinging, set her apart; she was acknowledged the leader of the jubilee singers. She had prospered in Uncle Tom revivals at the Park Theatre and at the Grand Opera House, by reason of her wild and peculiar calisthenics, and her awesome wardrobe — a sulphur-colored handkerchief, a bright bandana turban, and an apron scalloped with devil's points!

Niblo's Garden, New York, 1876

Jubilee Furor of the '70s

Old Climaxes of the Play Were Submerged by the Songs, Dances, and Incidental Specialties

The problem of grouping such masses of freedmen, women and children, was assigned to three celebrated artists, Joseph S. Schell, Matt Morgan and Russell Smith, who worked industriously at tableau pictures, evolving some realistic effects: Romantic Mountain Scenery, A Cascade of Real Water, The Ohio in Midwinter, Moving and Crunching Ice Floes, Orange Grove of Real Fruit, Old Time Slave Market, Great Plantation Festival, Scenes of the Mississippi,

Realistic Steamboat Race, Apotheosis of Gentle Eva, all advertised as masterpieces of stage painting.

The spectacular revival, ablaze with African light, opened at Booth's Theatre on the historical February 18, 1878. The first night the lengthy drama reached midnight, with a full act more to go.

The dark invasion engulfed another first-class theatre, when the Fifth Avenue Theatre opened to John Pemberton Smith's company, on April 1st, with the Howards in their celebrated parts. Mrs. Howard had played Topsy 3,500 times, and the dramatic critic of the *Herald* found it "just as spontaneous and crisp as it was twenty years ago."

Smith, as a Southerner, knew exactly where to get the best material. His Great Southern Specialty Troupe included: Primrose Kelly of South Carolina, and the best grotesque dancer (Juba patter) in the world; Jasper Green, the famous camp-meeting shout singer, from Lynchburgh, Virginia; Henry Duncan, the well-known cottonfield "coon," from Danville, Virginia; Little Sawney, the unrivaled boy dancer from Clinton, North Carolina; George Washington Slaughter, the only jaw-bone player, from Petersburg, Virginia; and Warren Griffin, reputed the champion of all banjo players, from Milledgeville, Georgia. The Old Dominion Quartet, selected from colored choirs of Richmond, rendered weird cabin songs of the South; the bass, a stalwart Virginian, had a voice as deep as a church organ.

In Smith's play were seen a cotton field in full bloom, the historic steamboat race between the Lee and the Natchez, and the Mississippi flatboat carrying the Congo Melodists. One critic remarked that it would have required a Jubilee Christopher Columbus to discover its equal. The play was advertised as, "Dramatized by J. Pemberton Smith and G. C. Howard, who have originally and specially introduced THE VIRGINIA JUBILEE SINGERS, in Sacred Songs of the Sunny South."

The same day, the Olympic swung into action, promising more satisfaction to its clientele — for ten and twenty-five cents, and a dime admitted one to the gallery. Here the plantation scenes suffered a meagre supply of jubilee singers when compared to rival theatres. However, the young "gods" of the gallery joined in the airs that particularly pleased them, as "Whoa, Emma!" "Get on Board," and "Carve dat Possum," which invariably produced the full chorus of six hundred juvenile voices.

The middle of the month, Wood's Theatre was drawn into the jubilee fray. The W. S. Higgins family headed the cast, with Louisa Higgins as Topsy, and the five-year-old daughter Lulu, as Eva, ("as played by her over 500 times"). Hosts of liberated slaves overflowed the stage, high-lighting Miss Georgia Allen, the colored Southern nightingale, and Weston's Mississippi Cabin Jubilee Singers.

The Bowery Theatre drained further the colored race, on July 19th, with Millie Sackett as Topsy. Then the Grand Opera House, on September 9th, advertised in all the City's newspapers as "The home of *Uncle Tom's Cabin*," with Sallie Partington as Topsy and Grace Wade as Eva, in a company including the Bohee Brothers, the Original Jubilee Singers, and all the novel features as first introduced to the world at this theatre by Messrs. Poole & Donnelly, "the originators of the genuine Slave Plantation Scene."

The perennial play burgeoned forth as profusely as the cotton pods in the plantations of the sunny South. Poor old Uncle Tom didn't get much of a chance to rest in his grave. A contemporary critic suggested that a theatre be devoted to a perpetual performance, to be known as the Topsy Theatre, Eva Hall, or the Plantation Comedie. Another insisted that someone write a sequel, *Uncle Tom and Little Eva in Heaven!*

It now became almost fatal to stage the play without colored singers, and a story in connection with this may bear retelling. An actor, after frightening not only poor Tom but numerous audiences for years, was convinced that he was indisputably the best Legree. He knew that the play was destined to run a very long time, and that Legrees would flog Uncle Toms for countless aeons. With this conceit in mind, he grew lax in his work, administered less vigor into his whip strokes, and slurred the nuances of his Red River dialect. Soon he was alienated from his manager, nor would others hire him for the rôle. He joined the ranks of the down-at-the-heels actors of Union Square, and found himself "up against it" for some time, until he fortunately came into some money. But it rankled him, as it would any other player, that he could not get his old part back. Then he hit upon an idea. He had been associated with the *Uncle Tom* shows so long that he knew all the jubilee singers. He now spent days hunting them up, and forthwith signed them to contracts, paying them advance salaries. When his old manager, who exercised a directing influence over most of the *Uncle Tom* shows in the country, came to hire jubilee singers — lo! there were none. Desperately, he hurried to the outcast actor to plead for terms. The other held out until the season was dangerously close; then, and only then, did he yield. The contracts were exchanged in consideration of a handsome bonus, and a five-year agreement for himself, at a much increased salary. It is the only instance on record where a "corner" was made on actors.

In the shrill days, Thompson Street experienced an exodus, as African hordes were recruited by the hundreds at fifty cents a performance, to sing, dance, cakewalk, or pluck banjos. Carrying on their hunched shoulders second-hand peach crates, or baskets, stuffed with twigs, leaves, or paper, with a layer of cotton batting on top, they sang at the rise of the curtain the old slave refrain, "Cotton Pickin', Cotton Pickin', Down on de Ole Hi-O." In the auction scene they had everything their own way for about fifteen minutes,

when Skeggs interrupted them with the authoritative thump
of his mallet, sternly reproaching them, "Here, I want you
folks t' behave yourselves. We're going t' have an auction
here, and I expect some of my best bidders."

"Hi — yah!" they chorused.

"So-o-ld!" banged away Skeggs' mallet.

When Jarrett & Palmer erected the cabin at the Academy
of Music in Brooklyn, in March, 800 old-time "cotton field
han' " participated in the festival scene. In a season of
fourteen weeks the company cleared $45,000, giving the
piece to $27,000 in a single fortnight in Philadelphia. Dur-
ing the farewell representations, before the departure of the
troupe for London, a genuine shortage of colored jubilee
singers existed in New York. H. C. Jarrett and his representative, Commodore Joseph H. Tooker, had to go to Florida
to secure colored talent. And one wag said that they, without
a doubt, took a lariat along.

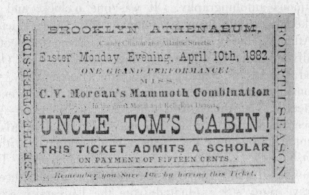

Chapter XI

FURTHER ADVENTURES ABROAD

> Uncle Tom — *Mahster, do you know*
> *where such courses h'end?*
> St. Clair — *No.*
> Uncle Tom — *Then let me tell you,*
> *mahster. They h'end in 'ELL!*
> —Heard in Liverpool, 1897

On a Spring day in 1877, an eighty-eight-year-old Negro, who, from his appearance, could be taken for a Methodist preacher, was walking up the steps of Windsor Castle. His arms hung queerly at his sides: they were crippled. With him were his wife, and his friend, the editor of his famous autobiography. It was one o'clock, and they were keeping a luncheon appointment with Queen Victoria.

Attended by Prince Leopold and Princess Beatrice, with divers ladies-in-waiting in the corridor, the Queen greeted Mr. Josiah Henson, calling him affectionately, "Uncle Tom!" She could not restrain her delight at his remarkable health. The Queen said that for many years his story had been well known to her. She may have recalled, also, at the moment, the interview Henson had previously with the Archbishop of Canterbury, who, on asking "Uncle Tom" what university had prepared him for the ministry, received the grave reply, "I graduated from the University of Adversity."

Now Victoria conducted him through the state apartments, insisting that he inscribe the date of his birth in her private album. The old Negro felt ill at ease, for all around him he heard, "Uncle Tom!" "Uncle Tom!" He thanked the Queen not only for the honor conferred upon him, but for the protection of the fugitive slaves during the critical times, especially for the haven in Her Majesty's dominion of Canada. At four o'clock, the royal reception was over. And everyone in Windsor Castle, from footboy to high dignitary, had been thrilled at the sight of "Uncle Tom."

The Prototype of
Uncle Tom

Josiah Henson, the guest, was the reputed original of Mrs. Stowe's creation. He had worked for an easygoing master, whose little daughter read to him from the Bible; but like most slaves, he was not so fortunate in his other masters. When a boy, his arms were crippled (like Uncle Tom's in the novel) by a brutal Maryland overseer. He paid $450 to one of his masters to buy back his freedom, only to be victimized. Suspicious and unscrupulous as his masters were, he was frequen'ly allowed to leave the State, even to venture North on business. Once, entrusted with a number of slaves, he took them to his master's relative in Kentucky, in this way preventing their passing into creditors' hands. The master who cheated Henson out of his manumission rights later shipped him to New Orleans to be sold by his son; before the sale was consummated the latter was stricken with yellow fever, and Henson nursed him back to health. Subsequently, the Negro escaped, was pursued by bloodhounds, and hiding in the swamps, threw them off his track. The generous captain of a schooner then took him to Canada. Henson became the pastor of a church. At the age of fifty-five he first learned to read and write. When he had mastered this difficult task, he wrote an account of his struggles, a seventy-six page pamphlet, published in 1849.

While passing through Andover, Massachusetts, he met Mrs. Stowe, and from his own lips she became acquainted with the characters of George Harris and wife, Eliza, whom Henson knew intimately. There were others, too, like Aunt Chloe, Henson's first wife, whose real name was Charlotte. When Henson rewrote his autobiography, in 1858, Mrs. Stowe contributed a preface. She also acknowledged her debt in the *Key*, and Josiah Henson, thereafter, became popularly identified with her chief character.

Josiah Henson's reception by Queen Victoria had its repercussions across the pond. Ambitious managers felt the time ripe for a revival in England. Although the Tomitudes craze which struck her twenty-five years previously was long forgotten, still, there were all the pretty babies that had gone down in the Registrar-General's long list of Evas in 1852, while every comical-looking ragamuffin in the dirty streets of London — for some reason or other — continued to be nicknamed Topsy. The possessors of these two names alone could fill the most capacious playhouse. English performances of *Tom* were now few and far between. One of some merit occupied the Adelphi, in 1875, with Miss Hudspeth as Topsy, while Mr. M'Intyre modelled his Legree after Bill Sikes — terminating his existence in a sensational scene, where he was thrown from a high rock after securing himself to a swinging rope for his escape. No dramatization had as yet been given with colored specialty artists and jubilee singers.

The new conquest of England was systematically planned by those competent New York producers, Jarrett and Palmer, who, after their triumph at Booth's Theatre, decided to send across their genuine "freed slaves." When Thompson and Sullivan Streets got wind of it, the ebony inhabitants left home like the Israelites from Egypt under Moses. They descended on the Germania Assembly Rooms for rehearsals. There talent was encouraged to abandon itself to their rhythms and intonations, under the direction of J. H. Slavin and A. A. Lucas, the latter a colored man. Every darky who could "catch" an air or coax his feet into the pattern of a jig was ready, nay eager, to contribute his bit to the forthcoming sensation abroad. Mr. Jarrett preferred the true Southern type, but realized the wisdom of the statement, "Dese rebel niggers ain't nuffin, nohow. We New Yorkers kin sing and dance dere legs off!"

Jarrett and Palmer, in their subjugation of Great Britain, beheld her as Caesar did Gaul — divided into three parts. On August 3, 1878, one party of sixty left New York; another, of an equal number, followed two weeks later; a third was dispatched to liquidate the smaller cities of England, Ireland and Scotland. The first opened in Manchester, about the 19th, and the second in London, where it played simultaneously at two theatres — the Princess Royal in the afternoon, and the Royal Aquarium, evenings. London audiences had the choice of scenic conceptions by Julian Hicks, at matinees, or the equally realistic settings by William Perkins, at evening performances.

The opening performance in London, on August 31st, found the boxes and galleries jammed in the best tradition of Boxing Night at the Drury Lane. The promise of "crowds of real American freed slaves" enticed patrons away from all other London theatres, including the Haymarket, where E. A. Sothern was starring.

Jarrett and Palmer's adaptor relied less upon the intrinsic merits of the drama than upon the spectacular effects, for George Fawcett Rowe's play was a weak-jointed composition, running over four hours, with many unconnected tableaux scenes. The fourth act was almost entirely devoted to a Negro concert. But such was the eagerness to see the "freed slaves," that the utmost impatience manifested itself until the overture; even when the curtain went up, and revealed the cabin, with Tom and Aunt Chloe enjoying the sweets of their simple home, the audience was restless. Nor were they appeased when Mr. Charles Warner came on as George Harris. But when the entrance cue finally announced the real "darkies," frenzied excitement ran through the house. The first jubilee chorus took the English audience by storm.

Then the two managers, mindful of the public pulse, cut the drama unmercifully. The old climaxes were submerged by the incidental specialties, songs and dances, and the plot was no longer recognizable. Too, all the sentimental roles, except Uncle Tom, were assigned to English actors, although the comic ones were played to the hilt by the Americans; to further flatter London crowds, the part of Harris was embellished with high-flown allusions to the British flag, "under which men of all color are free." But in spite of the patriotic appeal, it was the Americans who hit 'em hard. Mrs. W. A. Rouse, using her maiden and her married names, doubled Ophelia and Chloe, to the double delight of unsuspecting London playgoers.

Jarrett and Palmer amassed a fortune. What contributed considerably to their success were the posters, the like of which was unknown to the astonished eyes of Londoners. The Yankee practice of lavish lithographic advertising in matters theatrical had not as yet crossed the Atlantic; canny Captain Purdy, if you remember, first discovered their appeal. Even the scholarly John Ruskin was carried away by these singular posters, and later appraised their popularity in *Modern Painters*: "Let it be considered, for instance, exactly how far in the commonest lithographs of some utterly popular subject — for instance, the teaching of Uncl Tom by Eva — the sentiment which is supposed to be excited by the exhibition of Christianity in youth, is complicated by Eva's having a dainty foot and a well-made slipper."

The new art introduced in the drab-looking London streets overwhelmed the untrained eye with colorful promise:

Chocolate slaves on verdant plantations, ultramarine blue Uncle Toms, red Satanic Legrees, and great steamboat races in all their aurora borealis glory! The verbal lyricism burst out in no small le ters, and described the magnificence of the company: "Together with a host of genuine freed slaves from the Southern States of America, who will make their first appearance in Europe in their original Plantation Festival scenes."

The American "darkies" were lionized in London. A pretty little mulatto was particularly popular at London dinner tables. She approached the Topsy of the company, Marie Bates, one day, "Say, Mis' Bates, doan yo' know dey all 'specks I's Topsy?" So Miss Bates did the work, and the little girl ate the dinners. Another, old Aunt Sally, a very stout Negress from Philadelphia, began putting on airs. She had never worn shoes in her life, but now bought a pair, and with the greatest difficulty struggled into the boots. Someone in the company suggested that she should have tried out their size before buying them, and she answered, "Silly, min' yo' own business. Dem's mah feet an' dems mah shoes!" She stuck to them bravely, until the voyage home, when she threw the shoes overboard, vowing she'd go barefoot on the Philadelphia streets until she died.

The greatest pet of all was Horace Weston, a free-born Yankee, whom the London public fondly believed an ex-slave. His father, Jube Weston, had been a gifted performer before him, and found the little Horace an apt pupil. At seven the boy knew the accordion; at ten he mastered the second violin, the violincello, the double-bass slide trombone, and the guitar. He even had a smattering of dancing. But his interest in the new art of the banjo started in 1855, when, accidentally breaking his guitar, he had to borrow a crude "tub banjo." In a cheap little room in a New York lodging house, he learned how to pick out a couple of tunes. While down on his luck, he struck Hartford, the home town of Mrs. Stowe, where he drove a hack for a Mr. Litchfield, perfecting himself in his spare time on the instrument that was to bring him world acclaim. He made a banjo out of a peck measure, attaining such mastery in a month that he left his employer. Weston was knocking out tunes in the streets for a livelihood when the War began. He made his way to Harrisburg, where a large group of Negroes were trying to enlist in the Union Army, but found that no colored volunteers were wanted. He proceeded to Boston, and shipped in the United States Navy, taking his banjo along. He practiced off watch hours, and added to his worldly reserves by entertaining the crew at fifty cents a month each. Then he threw his banjo overboard, enlisted in the Fifty-fourth Massachusetts Volunteers, saw action, and was wounded. Jarrett & Palmer discovered their rising star entertaining with his banjo on the boat Plymouth Rock, and took him abroad.

The banjo as a musical instrument was practically unknown in European capitals. Although heard in the minstrel companies that went across, it was seldom associated with a soloist, but merely as a part of the band. Now Horace Weston filled two London theatres for three months, and leading music critics were awed by the large and powerful man who could coax such tonal combinations from a little box. One old critic said, "Positivly reminds me of nothing so much as Paganini!" Royalty occupied the boxes, and Weston's skill earned him fourteen medals in the European capitals. When he went to Berlin with Jarrett & Palmer, he received an ovation. They opened at the Italia Theatre, in Breslau, Germany, and stayed six weeks. The same sensational reception greeted him at Strauss' Theatre, Vienna, and from there he went to Hamburg, then to France, and returned to America a year later.

While the fever was on in London, publishers flooded the market with new editions, and no less than nine were

announced within a week. Five productions ran simultaneously! Augustin Daly was so impressed that he wrote home:
"I went to the Standard after the dinner Saturday.... at
the east end, and found it to be one of the finest theatres in
the metropolis. It is fully as large a place as our Academy;
has four tiers and an acre of space called the pit. They were
playing an English adaptation of the French version of the
American *Uncle Tom*, in which Eva is restored to life and
Tom does not die. The inventive Frenchman has also created a mate for Topsy in the character of a fancy darkey
named Julius — and the two dance breakdowns together,
and sing comic duets and talk comic trash in a mixture of
cockney Irish and Scotch, which the innocent (or rather
guilty) actors imagine is a good imitation of the genuine
canebrake lingo. Five of the London theatres are playing
Uncle Tom now, but no one place is hurting the other. I
remarked to the manager of the Princess' Theatre the other
evening that the opposition must affect him. He said that
there was no such thing as opposition in London; that each
place had its own special attendance; and it seems so."

After three months, the Jarrett & Palmer company left
for the Continental cities. In Germany, Marie Bates gave
Topsy in the native tongue, supported by German players.
Harold Fosburg, the Legree, would stroll through the streets,
in costume, attended by two of the Negro jubilee singers, at
whom he cracked his blacksnake whip, overwhelming the
amazed Berliners.

Touring for about nineteen months, the company visited
Austria, Hungary, Switzerland, Holland, and Bavaria. They
would have sojourned abroad longer, but Henry C. Palmer,
in charge of the European venture, suddenly became ill.
Negotiations for France had to be stopped because Jarrett
was in America, and Palmer's death in London completely
changed all plans. Most of the actors returned to America,
but Marie Bates carried on her Topsy in the principal Ger-

man cities for two more years. Alfy Chippendale and her husband also found Europe profitable, and toured the provinces with their own *Tom* show.

The Jarrett & Palmer influence remained. One of their agents, George Dolby, had made arrangements to bring the entire troupe to John Coleman's theatre in Glasgow, and the manager was dismayed when the engagement was cancelled abruptly, as he was meeting with heavy losses in a pantomime. Desperate, he dispatched by the next boat a representative who carried to Liverpool a *carte blanche*, and within forty-eight hours the whole black contingent arrived in Glasgow. In the meantime, Coleman dug up from his trunk an old script of *Slavery*, the adaptation he had made a quarter of a century ago; he revised it, brought it up to date, allowing proper gaps for Negro specialties. In less than a week his company produced the emotional crumpet. The last night of the pantomime was for the benefit of a great local favorite, and grossed twenty-five pounds, but the following night *Slavery* opened — and took in two hundred pounds.

The drama jammed them in for a whole month, but had to be taken off, unfortunately, to permit an opera company a previous engagement. Then Coleman's company, together with the darkies, transferred its activities to the Theatre Royal, Edinburgh, where its triumphal reception lasted another month. It proceeded on to Dundee and Aberdeen; a return visit to Glasgow; then to Newcastle-on-Tyne, Leeds, and Hull, where the contract with the Negro jubilee singers ended. So grateful was Coleman that he, for one, acknowledged his debt to Mrs. Stowe by sending her a basket of fruit, flowers, a copy of Mrs. Browning's poems, and a half-dozen photographs, which Mrs. Stowe graciously accepted.

Among the managers who organized provincial touring companies was Horace Lewis, and his unusual version required fifteen characters, but only five actors. Another traveling manager, John Carter, claimed that he alone was the original portrayer of Uncle Tom in England.

When Jarrett & Palmer left the field, London theatre-goers still clamored for more "darky" entertainment. Haverly's Minstrels lost little time in coming over, but the white men in burnt cork gave "the imitation nigger" — a burlesque on jubilee singers. The Ministrels did numerous takeoffs, stressing virtuoso effects: A banjoist strummed a solo with his left hand, while he swung the instrument backwards and forwards! The Jarrett & Palmer Negroes were crude, instinctive, all singing by ear; but the professional Minstrels, presenting the "comic nigger," were calculating — too smooth and precise.

However, on August 5, 1882, Jay Rial transported to Her Majesty's Theatre an elaborate *Uncle Tom,* comparable in splendor to Jarrett & Palmer's. The Magnolia Jubilee band rendered their songs, and among them was an earnest member, rather prominently active in singing, marching, arm-waving, and in all the hand-clapping business — a miniature "darky," age three years, who captured the house. "Clever little tike!" roared the Londoners.

Later, as "Mrs. Harriet Beecher Stowe's ever-memorable American drama," the Standard Theatre, in July, 1886, opened with Harry Dickeson's production, its plantation scene an integral part, and with real Negro talent.

One of the favorite and probably apocryphal tales is about Alfred Denville, who, during a performance, gave the usual number of songs, concluding with great effect "Pity Poor Uncle Tom." He was about to lay down and escape his earthly persecutions when a voice from the prompter's box whispered, "Spin out the dying, Alf — give us a little more time to set the next piece."

Denville "gagged" with the heart-rending picture of his secular trials and tribulations, then prepared once more to die. But an anxious voice from the wings exhorted:

"Keep it up a bit longer!"

Deferred again, he was at his wits' end how to stave off dying. Then he rose to his feet, and said to those about him, "But now, white an' black folks, befoh I pass away, I will sing yuh de deah ol' song, 'Good Ol' Jeff Hab Gwine t' Rest', an' den I shall die happy!"

When the moribund Uncle Tom was through with this favorite of Christy Minstrel ballads, he discovered that even then he was ahead of time. He augmented with, "An' I feel that I could even do de good ol' plantation dance, which yuh kind folks always lubbed so." He fulfilled this wish, then being tipped off that all was well backstage, he languished quickly, after the manner of his long line of predecessors, and to appropriate music!

The play now began to suffer with the years. Victorian managers conceived a contempt for anything from across the water, and paid little regard to accuracy in either American stage setting or dialogue. H. T. Peck came across this announcement in Liverpool, in 1897: "All parts being filled by Americans, this presentation affords a vivid, realistic picture of contemporary American life, as delineated in that most famous of all American plays, entitled UNCLE TOM'S CABIN." Seized by nostalgia, he entered. When the curtain rose, it disclosed Shelby's white marble mansion: it had Italian pillars, a heavy tropical growth around the Negro quarters (in close proximity to the mansion), and in the background gondolas sailed on the blue waters of an inland sea. The Shelbys then appeared, the husband in white duck trousers and jack-boots, his wife in a low-necked dress with a queenly diamond tiara. Uncle Tom came in fresh from the fields, after hoeing corn and digging sweet potatoes, wearing white cotton gloves. His deep, bass voice had the richest Whitechapel accent, and upon learning that he had been traded in to Shelby, he observed with some emotion that it was very 'ard. He then rendered a hymn;

indeed, all the field hands there had a habit of breaking into hymns at the slightest provocation.

The second act depicted the tavern, with a large poster on one of the walls offering: "One Hundred Pounds Reward for a Runaway Slave—" The Kentuckians evidently preferred the English monetary system. Phineas Fletcher wore the makeup of a Jesse James; when Haley, with his hounds, called for Eliza, the Quaker, reaching for the pistols in his boots, held him at bay. Haley's myrmidons came to the rescue, disarmed Phineas, but the Quaker reached down the back of his neck — and pulled out two more pistols!

St. Clare's New Orleans mansion was seen with a garden in a dense thicket of fir-trees, and in the distance appeared mountains peaked with snow. Aunt Ophelia, instead of repeating, "How shiftless!" varied the form to, "Now, that's really very shiftless, you know!" and "Drat it, you're really quite too shiftless!" She was much concerned with what she termed the 'ouse. St. Clare was portrayed as a gay blade, hair parted in the centre, continually lighting cigarettes, and calling for cocktails. His later stabbing was mentioned as having occurred at "a drinking bar."

The last scene found the fugitives safe on Canadian soil, George raising a paeon with heartfelt emotion: That at last he had reached a land over which the flag of Hengland floated, where 'ealth and 'ope were possible to hevery one, and where, as hall men know, Britons never, never could be slaves! Meanwhile, he reached into one of his coattails, pulling out what seemed at first a large cotton handkerchief, but when spread out under his chin, proved to be the British emblem. The orchestra struck up "God Save the Queen," upon which the audience, rising as one, joined in, applauding with patriotic might.

On the French stage, *La Case de L'Oncle Tom* continued to be a kind of "cause célèbre" down through the years. Dumanoir and D'Ennery's adaptation was revived on December 29, 1877, for a month, at the Ambigu, with Mlle. Tallandiera as Eliza. Paris viewed it again in 1888. Mary Austin saw it in rather strange surroundings: "And once more in all its melodramatic glory, the original play, in a French provincial town, with an audience composed chiefly of Senegalese soldiery, fairly pop-eyed over the authentic presentation of the behavior of Whites to Blacks in the great and wealthy *Étates Unis,* and still one of the most absorbing dramas ever written there."

Its early years in France were traditional enough in a dramatic sense, but by 1896 the play had become an extraordinary affair. There was no Eva, no Topsy — no one seemed to miss them — while the chief interest was built around George Harris, his wife and child. The first act of the drama, seen that year, revealed two low-comedy "darkies" seated on the floor, before the cabin of Uncle Tom, picking over and over again the same cotton wadding from a basket; a sufficiently cruel overseer encouraged their industry by cracking his whip. The two "darkies" combined French with a soft Southern intonation, in a laugh-provoking nasal yammering. Uncle Tom, however, spoke in formal French, in the heroic, classical style, so that the critics called it a palpable imitation of Mounet-Sully's *Aedipus.*

One of the important scenes showed the Southern home of Senator Marks, where at breakfast time he partook of toast and tea; a realistic Southern touch was added, much to the audience's amusement, when the comical Senator poured rum into his tea. The fugitive slaves came in, and caught the sympathetic ear of the wonderful Senator, and his spouse, who embraced Eliza and called her sister. Then Marks sallied forth with the runaways, armed to the teeth, and bravely held off the slaveholders, first with speeches, then with pistols. The pursuers were eliminated in a style typical of American frontier days, and the play ended happily.

As we leave the Continent, we find the veteran drama rather more faithful to the original script. Its first glimpse of Australia came by way of San Francisco. The Thorne family, in the early '50s, had played it up and down the California Coast for a couple of years; then Charles R. Thorne, Sr., decided to experiment further, and thus became the pioneer American manager to visit Australia. He took along his two boys, Charlie and Edwin, both gawky lads, the former having made his debut as Master George Shelby. The daughter, Emily, barely sixteen, enacted Eliza, and the mother, Topsy.

En route to Australia, the company stopped off at the Sandwich Islands for a command performance before His Majesty and Her Royal Highness, who came in their bare feet to the playhouse, hardly more than a shed with board seats. They made another stay at Navigator's Island, at that time believed to be inhabited by cannibals. The fame of the novel had preceded them, extending to the remotest places. We hear of the Emperor Soulouque, then sovereign of the French end of Hayti, having it read to him twice, and expressing his gratitude for that pleasure in a letter to Mrs. Stowe. The fortunes of the Thornes rode in with the tide.

On their arrival in Sydney, the Thornes leased the Lyceum Theatre. The local citizens were all interest, for this was the first American troupe to visit their land. Notices were posted that the enterprise was under the patronage of His Excellency, Sir Charles Fitzroy, and as they aimed to draw fashionable audiences, they opened with a polite drawing room drama. However, the opening was not cordial, and Thorne soon realized that the bushmen expected a sample of real American stuff, not the old standard numbers. He therefore prepared the Conway dramatization, with J. J. McCloskey as the lively Yankee, Penetrate Partyside, who wandered through the piece somewhat extraneously, but with comic effect. For eight weeks they crammed 'em in!

From Sydney the players went to Melbourne, where again excited spectators welcomed them. Then they did the play in the mining districts, under a tent. When they left on a prosperous tour of the other British colonies, one player, Rolfe, stayed behind to become the editor of an Australian newspaper; McCloskey remained in Geolong, where there was a Scotch colony numerous enough to support permanent stock. After performing in Ballarat and New Zealand, the troupe returned to New York by way of Callao and other South American cities.

The Thorne venture helped make theatrical history. Some twenty years later, in 1876, Theodore Hamilton tried his luck with a stock company in Melbourne, where he pleased audiences with *Ten Nights in a Barroom* because they erroneously believed Henry Ward Beecher to be the playwright. Since they had heard so much of the noted preacher, naturally, they were curious to see his play. The Melbourne *Argus*, reviewing it, commented: "If the Rev. Henry Ward Beecher preaches as badly as he writes dialogue, we sincerely hope that he will never visit Australia."

The same misconception prevailed at Sydney. There, the manager of the Gaiety Theatre asked his patrons to select the Shakespearean play they next wished to see, and *Uncle Tom's Cabin* led all the rest! If the Bard of Avon was credited in Sydney with more than his due share, it may have been because they had seen *Othello* the week before, and they associated one black with the other.

When the Gaiety Theatre attracted the public with Sheridan and Dampier's *Uncle Tom*, in February, 1886, it competed against the Academy of Music, where another Uncle Tom company was in full stride, under F. E. Hiscocks, proprietor of the Federal Minstrels. That September, Her Majesty's Theatre offered a slightly altered version, with some startling stage effects, and the introduction — for the first time — of real blocks of ice for Eliza's escape. Eliza was played by a man, Roland Watt Philipps.

On the farthest point north on the Australian coast was a settlement named after Captain Cook, which the discoverer had reached on his first voyage. It was a coal-mining section, numbering less than a thousand inhabitants, many of them Chinese, and known as the town that hadn't seen a play in years. Separated by an expanse of desolate, torrid country, and connected with the roughest kind of roads, it lay isolated some four hundred miles from the nearest community. The vagabond actor, Jefferson De Angelis, was having a hard time of it then, and, in desperation, decided to try his luck in this God-forsaken spot.

When his little troupe reached the town, to their dismay, there was not even a structure resembling a playhouse, but the miners, long starved for entertainment, joyfully welcomed the itinerant actors. Hardly had the players wiped the dust from their shoes, when solicitations poured in for the American success, *Uncle Tom's Cabin*, whose fame had reached out even to Cooktown. The troupe avoided putting it on, for the good reason that they lacked a script. So persistent were the miners, however, that the players decided to piece the drama together from memory; each had at one time or another appeared in it, so they remembered a few lines. The members hunted out the indispensable "props" — soap boxes, covered with painted muslin, for Eliza's hop over the rectangular cakes of ice; they also recruited two listless bird dogs, who, insufficiently trained, ignored the "ice" and walked on the "water." Native raw singers supplied the chorus of, "Nearer, My God, to Thee," offstage, when Legree whipped Tom to death, and fortunately, there was red fire for the final tableau — "The Gates Ajar."

The small troupe doubled the parts, and local talent filled in the bits. The *Natal Mercury* (South Africa) said later, when De Angelis took the drama there: "These assumptions of dual parts by the same members of the company caused some little confusion to those of the auditors who were not well up in the plot and perhaps had not perused through the story beforehand." De Angelis was Lawyer Marks, and afterward he described the St. Clair of Mr. Frost as "introducing more up-to-date slang and bad grammar into the part than was ever heard, I am sure, in that distinguished planter's mansion thruout its entire history." Sallie, sister of De Angelis, was Topsy, who entranced the Capetowners, and a little local girl stepped into the shoes of dear Eva. The postmaster, also, attempted a small part, while a young captain, whose schooner was anchored in the harbor, was cast as Salem Scudder — a part from *The Octoroon*, but which none suspected at the time, not even the actors.

Despite its drawbacks, the drama caught the natives, who demanded another performance. Sure enough, those who had attended the first time came again.

This memory version was then carried by the De Angelis troupe to Hong Kong, where Virginia Loftus performed Topsy to Sallie's Aunt Ophelia. They stayed there over a month, playing to far more sophisticated audiences than in the mining towns left behind. English was limited there, of course, and the actors learned pidgin English, which helped in drawing capacity houses.

When they came to Grahamstown, the drama that most foreign newspapers labeled, "Mrs. Stowe's masterpiece," met with further success. The daily *Eastern Star* published an extra supplement, three columns wide and eleven inches long, entirely devoted to a review of it. The company left by train for Cape Town, where they leased the Theatre Royal, only available playhouse, and would have had matters all their own way except for the arrival of another troupe headed by Charles E. Vernon. It was thought best to combine the two groups. Then they discovered that Vernon carried in his trunk a genuine script of *Uncle Tom's Cabin*. As the De

Angelis forces exulted in almost continous success with their gag form, they anticipated even greater heights with the straight dramatization. They tried it out, and were stupefied by its flat failure! They tried again — once more it flopped. So they threw away the script, reverted to the memory version, and played to phenomenal houses thereafter.

Troupes that visited Australia usually came by way of San Francisco, but frequently were diverted by the neighboring islands, where the natives were just as eager to see the antislavery drama. Many a company found the business close to home quite lucrative.

In 1878, the old California had a promising Eva in Little Maude Adams, and a traveling company was formed to support her, with Alice Kingsbury as Topsy. An account book left behind by Charles B. Wells reveals how few were the members of such troupes. They comprised a half-dozen at the most, relying on local amateurs to fill out the cast. During the summer of 1879 they sailed for Honolulu, playing repertoire, where they attracted King Kalakawa, who came as a curious spectator. At which performance he sat in we do not know, but his name is down in Wells' notebook on the leaf listing the receipts of *Uncle Tom's Cabin*, and we can guess safely at the popularity of the plays from the gross receipts taken in: "*East Lynne*, $168.25; *The Two Orphans*, $321.25; *Hamlet*, $160.50; *Othello*, $80.75; *The Octoroon*, $219.00; *Uncle Tom's Cabin*, $470.00."

During the early '80s, the drama popped up in Africa. An Irish comedian, T. B. Butler, making an eight-year tour of the world, stopped off in the city of Bloemfontein, capital of The Orange Free State, South Africa. A dramatic club was organized to dedicate a new hall, and the actor was asked to suggest an opening piece. He had the script, and offered not only to direct the play, but also to do Tom himself. The Topsy was a problem. None of the ladies had ever seen the play, and as for blacking up — they couldn't imagine it! One staid gentleman was of the opinion that his servant girl, a "tottie" (Hottentot) was full of life. When they brought her in, the attempt to break her into the part resulted in panic, and sudden flight. They finally prevailed on the daughter of the Landwert, or Judge, to try it, but she made one reservation — that she be permitted to speak the lines in Dutch, the language used throughout the country. Eva was singled out from the family of the editor of the tri-weekly, *Express*, and a bright boy he was. Legree and Fletcher were doubled by a gentleman formerly a missionary in Zululand.

After a fortnight of rehearsals, the play opened under the patronage and in the presence of President Brand, father and first President of the Colony. They thronged the hall for five nights. The dialect used by Butler struck them with wonder, for the Negro they knew spoke either Kaffir or Dutch. The Irish comedian, upon returning from his trip, observed: "From my experience I should say that if twenty companies, including one *Uncle Tom's Cabin*, were to start on a tour around the world, the last would get back while the others would stop on the way and grow up with the people."

Chapter XII

CAVALCADE OF TOM SHOWS

There was a colored person, and his name was Uncle Tom,
*   Who was foaled long ago, long ago;*
And where'er this pious person was announ-ced to perform,
*   There the populace would crowd the show.*
Then lay down the pen and pencil, oh,
*   And hang up the dramatist, also;*
For we've no more need for any new plays
*   Till we' laid this colored person low.*
                                    — Anon., "Poor Old Tom"

ON THE THRESHOLD of the '80s began the rage —
Tomming, which lasted over the decades, and broke all
records. In 1879, the New York *Dramatic Mirror* listed the
routes of forty-nine traveling companies, and twenty years
later the list was nearly ten times that number. Tom troupes
sprang up like mushrooms overnight. Their managers scoured
the country, giving the sturdy play in the backyards of the
nation. Like beacons on the countryside, scores of Uncle
Toms ascended to Heaven nightly, each in a flaming red
shirt.

The play was the bread and butter of the profession.
When other means of subsistence failed, actors metamorphosed themselves into Tom troupes. No longer did they
loiter all year in the Rialto, strutting pompously before the
sidewalk worshippers of Union Square. A few did remain,
indulging in illusions of grandeur, calling themselves the
legitimate — a term invented to cover an invidious class

distinction, and they thought they had a proud advantage over the hard-working, nomadic Tommers. These idle histrions, with their mangy fur collars, and phony air of importance, rejected one-night stands; they would grace only the stages in the big cities. The threadbare brotherhood mocked the Tommers with scornful looks, and mimicked sarcastically: "How I have suffered in some of those barns in the rural 'deestricts' — and out West!" The *legitimate* classed the Tommers as "lunkheads," "chumps," and "lugs," while one sweeping term of "jays" covered all our country cousins.

An actor had to be quite "rotten" to go there, and the profession added to its argot the derisive term — "Tomming the tanks." It was true that in their wayfaring the Tommers went off the beaten track, penetrating the remotest regions, to the water-tank towns, to the places that had never enjoyed a play. The idle hangers-on of the Union Square saloons jibed that a Tom show caused the most excitement in Kalamazoo since the day the sheriff's horse ran away, that the unaccustomed ablutions of the yokels caused the water tax rate in Albuquerque to rise the day the Tommers arrived, and that the mayor of Tuscaloosa had never been on singing terms with a bathtub. Of a piquant flavor, too, were the names of the cities visited by the Tommers: Beaver Falls, Pa., Bogalusa, La., Chicopee, Mass., Grand Forks, N. Dak., Kankakee, Ill., Woonsocket, R. I., Muskogee, Okla., North Tonawanda, N. Y., Keokuk, Ill., Eureka, Calif., Evansville, Ind., Meadville, Pa., Lynchburg, Va., Muskegon, Mich., Oshkosh, Wis., Paducah, Ky., Sheboygan, Wis., Torrington, Conn., Aurora, Ill. Ohio, especially, provided material for the flippant with such succinct names as Ashtabula, Shaker Heights, Chillicothe, Steubenville, Zanesville. But what a thriving circuit for the Tommers!

If the *legitimate* was spared further the humilating custom of dealing with agencies, it was because there weren't any in those gus y days. Jimmy Connor, a little, consumptive Irish comedian, conceived the idea of a dramatic agency when he was no longer able to barnstorm. He opened a dingy office which became a rendezvous where many actors spent their days, looking for "angels," waiting for something to turn up. Connor, also, was the first to hang up handbills of country fairs. Managers would write to him, requesting: "*Send on a chirping heavy, able to sling 'em a nasty Uncle Tom, Wednesday night, in Willimantic, $15 sal. No beaders wanted.*" Whereupon Connor would turn to a gang of heavies seated on an old, over-stuffed settee known as the mourner's bench, and interrupted their tie-wig parables, "How many of you's up in Uncle Tom?" They all spoke up at once, while a stout old man, probably Charley Salisbury, would pipe in a childish treble, "I play Eva this season." Connor practiced a sympathetic system in his business: he would pick out the most wretched-looking actor to fill the role. His choice would rise, stuff an Uncle Tom wig in his pocket, and hurry off to meet the engagement.

With the Tomming fracas of the early '80s, various raffish troupes were formed on the curb of Union Square.

"Don't miff the chance," the entrepreneur would size up those within earshot, producing the vest-pocket investment of ten dollars.

"Uncle Tommyrot!" jibed the seedy-looking sceptic.

"Travesty cannot wither," answered back the prospective manager, "nor custom stale the infinite variety of *Uncle Tom.*"

"Down among the cabbage patches!" the die-hard defender of the standard classics would retort, one arm behind his back, the other stuck in his bosom.

"All that you'll attract are the boll weevils. Now, you don't pull for hands out there with *Uncle Tom*. The applause — it's a hurricane!"

A manager, his offices in his battered high hat, would stroll into a barroom, and call out, "Beer for the house!" And the Tom troupe was assembled right there and then. In another Union Square resort an excessively self-important manager boasted about his "discovery." He had taken a girl right off the boat at Castle Garden, given her the part of Eliza, and she had made a huge hit!

"The girl played it for all it was worth," he related blusteringly. "She wasn't afraid of the hounds and made her escape without missin' a step. She's goin' to the front as an emotional actress, and don't you forget it." He would try her out in *East Lynne* on his next barnstorming trip. "I think there's the stuff in 'er to hook 'em to her in Lady Isabel," he beamed proudly. "I'm goin' to try to pull 'er to the top, enyhow."

Another manager, Charles Forbes, engaged leading actors at the rate of a dollar a day, and discharged them at a moment's notice. He could do so with impunity. Good Evas were quoted on the curb at six dollars a week; their mothers, who doubled all the female parts, besides doing the cooking, weren't offered much more. A Marks, who would take care of the horses, could be had for seven dollars. The salary was "low but sure." Usually, the manager's partner had the capital, and he acted as treasurer of the venture, but generally all operated on a shoestring. The party traveled in light marching order, their baggage consisting of one trunk and about three carpetbags — woe to the hotel proprietor who levied on it, for he was stuck!

In close proximity to the lowly "Curb" of Union Square was the "Stock Market," at 29 Beekman Street, where one T. R. Dawley constituted the Board of Directors. Here the excited Tom managers got their supply of flamboyant "stock" posters, and the transactions sounded like the real thing further downtown. Quantity orders poured in for: "A 3-sheet Topsy!" "More Markses!" "A 6-sheet Slave Auction!"

"12-sheet Plantation Jubilee!" "3-sheet Legree Thrashing Uncle Tom!" "12-sheet Escape of Eliza!" "A 12-sheet Steamer!" "Some Ophelias!" "A 6-sheet Wench head..." Boom days, indeed!

Jarrett & Palmer were the innovators of the large pictorial show-bills, and during their tour abroad created a sensation in all the European cities. Although the French theatres had done something similar, their lithographs were very small, and really meant for home decoration. Even when Captain Purdy first introduced them here, despite his munificence, the size was still restricted; they were printed on hand presses, colored by hand. The old wood block process, with its limited size, persisted until Jarrett & Palmer startled the country. But the real inception of lithographic posters dated from 1880, when the Courier Company, in Buffalo, produced a nine-sheet lithographed poster, in four colors, showing Eliza crossing the ice pursued by the hounds. The same year, the Strobridge Lithographic Company, in Cincinnati, entered the field, and acquired Matt Morgan, tableaux arranger of the spectacular revival at Booth's Theatre in '78. Another that ran off lurid Tom show posters was the Forbes Lithograph Company, in Boston. And the "Stock Market," at Beekman Street, housed the Great American Engraving and Printing Company. With bolder experiments, the single sheet was enlarged and now required several strips for one complete picture. The "Stock Market" offered, in the later '80s, a 48-sheet stand which eclipsed them all: the mammoth American play was put on a sumptuous pictorial show-bill large enough for a drop curtain in the smaller theatres. Any single part could be left off, without destroying the unity; it could also be divided, and pasted separately to fit any billboard. It was like the old play itself.

With paste pot and rolls of gaudy paper, the Tommers plastered the chicken coops along the countryside, and adorned barns, rocks, and ugly fences, till they all glowed with color. The lithographs, so beguiling, so flattering, made Topsy seem more sportive than her prototype; Eva was younger, and far more sublime; Simon Legree was tremendous, incredibly fiercer than in his natural state. They threw all the small boys and girls into ecstasies, even disturbing the equanimity of older heads, most of whom found an excuse for going to the Tom show, if only to take the children. The American public literally "ate them up."

Unsound financially, with unmistakable marks of haste upon them, scores of troupes during those brawling days went out on blind chance alone. Cocksurely, they called themselves, "The Original Uncle Tom's Cabin Company," or "The Real Uncle Tom Troupe," or "The Standard Uncle Tom's Cabin." From their lithographs they all looked alike. The term, "the original Uncle Tom's Cabin," was vigorously contested; for like stage ingénues up to the age of fifty they tried to be as young as possible, but after sixty they tried to be centenarians. Each proclaimed itself the largest and best troupe in the world.

They promised the rural sections a great deal, that, alas! never materialized. The much-heralded floating fields of ice, spectacular steamboat blow-up, hosts of jubilee singers, fee-rrr-o-cious hounds, and trick donkeys were *invisible*. True, there was a mangy, flea-beset ass, which had to be hauled about the stage. The dogs were accounted for as being detained at the last town, sick with distemper; in their place two very innocent and humble-looking coach-dogs mildly trotted after Eliza, who had to encourage them to her side. The play was given against an old rag to the accompaniment of a squeaky fiddle — no gorgeous scenery, not even pasteboard ice! The whole business was a snare and delusion. Cheap prices and a hasty departure frequently saved the Tommers from a grim fate.

In the wide, haystack circuit there must have been true patrons of the dramatic art, who did not especially like the Tommers — as instanced in the story of the happenings at Pike County. A summer sojourner at Dingman's Ferry, Pa., once asked the local barber about amusements in the neighborhood. Well, there were pictures of the Passion Play at the Reform Church, and although the barber didn't know what they were, he insisted, between shaves, that *they had better be good!* This rather surprised the stranger, whereupon the barber, loquacious in the tradition of his trade, spilled the beans:

"Last year, when I was down to Bath, we done up an Uncle Tom troupe that showed there under a tent. The bills said it was to be great, with fine scenery, two Topsies, two Marks, real ice and a pack of Siberian bloodhounds. They had picters showin' just what it was goin' to be like, and everybody in the village went. Well, sir, I've seen a lot of bum shows, but that was the gol durndest. There was about five people in the troupe, includin' the manager, who played Marks and Legree both. The little Eva, I guess, was really Uncle Tom's grandmother, and the Topsy was old enough to be her sister. The only scenery they had was a house that fell apart every few minutes and a curtain with the Brooklyn Bridge by moonlight on it. The 'real ice' was a couple of soap boxes white-washed, an' the skinny purps they call Siberian bloodhounds forgot to chase Eliza and fought over a bone that somebody chucked at 'em."

"How long did all this last?" asked the vacationist.

"It only lasted about an hour — an' before the play was over, some of us boys agreed to get square on the troupe for buncoin' us. After the manager made his speech about the grand concert that would be given after the performance, in which all the artists would appear, the crowd got out without givin' up the extra ten cents. Then us fellers sneaked around to the different ropes that held the tent. We counted three and then each man cut a rope. Down came the tent kerflop, with all the troupe under it. By gosh, sir, you never hearn sech swearin' as came from under that tent. There was a string of cuss words that would reach from here to Port Jervis. We stood around an' watched the fun as the 'Colossal Collection of Eminent Artists' came crawlin' out. They was madder than John Drake was when he fought Bill Hubbard, but they didn't dare try any 'hey, rube,' game on us. There was too many strappin' big boys itchin' for a chance to lick 'em. We told 'em if they didn't want more trouble, to git right out of taown as fast as their bonesack nags could trot."

"And did they leave?" the other asked.

"Oh, yes. They seen we meant business, an' didn't waste no time in perlite farewells. The tent and the gorgeous scenery was hustled into the waggin', and the troupe, still in their costumes, jumped in, an' daown the road they went, lickin' the horses like all creation, with the Siberian bloodhounds yelpin' after 'em. Just so they wouldn't go hungry, we give 'em a parting shower of apples an' eggs an' garden truck."

"Didn't they loiter awhile?"

"I reckon they didn't stop till they got to Stroudsburg. They had bills up in several teawns araound here, but nobody seen 'em again. They don't want any more of Pike County, I'll bet."

If a dissatisfied audience didn't bust up the Tommers, other contingent dangers did. Should the troupe be delayed by storms, the local theatre attached the scenery, including the hounds, to cover loss incurred by the cancelled date. The Tommers capitulated to the local constable, with the canine member the only fortunate one to escape, for the outraged hotel proprietors were hot on their heels; they missed odds and ends in furniture, which the destitute Tommers converted into props. The Tommers often disbanded under a spell of hot weather, rain, floods. . . . Stranded, perhaps at daybreak, they waited disconsolately at a prairie way-station, with the lone hound fretfully scratching.

A Tom troupe might be doing fair business, when unceremoniously the manager would skip off. His histrionic creditors had little hope of ever seeing him again, and they counted the railroad ties to far-off Union Square. They vowed bitterly never to go out with a Tom troupe; however, the next season they were back, eager and hopeful as ever.

The early Tom manager was a grass-root biting, rugged individualist, and a hustler. Wearing a battered high silk hat and a long overcoat, he blew into town and rented the court house hall. He got a lot of carpenters and built a stage and put in planks for seats. Then he billed the town with a lot of red pictures showing bloodhounds and death scenes and Eliza crossing the river. He sold tickets at the door, and when he caught his cue, he would go onstage, "to sell a few slaves." Most of his lines were not delivered to the spectators, but to the actor relieving him at the door, whom he admonished, "Keep your hands in sight," "Take anything if they haven't got the price," "Jack-knives go..." Then he would rush behind, double several parts, and play the piano between acts. Meanwhile, he advised the actor who tended the door, "Don't hold out more than the price of two drinks, and count me in on one..." He was equal to every emergency.

Unscrupulous managers with their shoddy, cheapjack shows mushroomed in those raucous barn-storming days. *Uncle Tom* appealed to the more crafty because it was an almost certain money-maker, and it also relieved them of the monstrous task of reading new scripts. Should the unforeseen occur, and the tour "flop," the producer slyly quoted the unfriendly dramatic critics, or blamed the incompetent cast.

However, many managers who took the road did stay, not leaving it for a whole decade; some played *Uncle Tom's Cabin* for two, or even three decades. The eve of the sprawling '80s was the toe-mark for many Tom managers, and with the turn of the century they were still going strong. They contributed genuinely to the growth of our one American folk play. Such a one was J. Pemberton Smith, originator of the jubilee version. His idea was immediately taken over by Jarrett & Palmer, who not only competed against him, but bought off his specialty singers in the bargain. It was popularly said that Smith initiated Pullman car vaudeville through his earlier play, *The Tourists*, while Jarrett & Palmer imitated him via steamboat cabin, conscripting Horace Weston from the excursion boat, "Mayflower."

Smith was in on the ground floor when the jubilee furor started in '78, and had the advantage over his rivals, in so far as Mr. and Mrs. G. C. Howard were in his company. Smith himself played the auctioneer, Skeggs, and a critic, alluding to the applause he won nightly, claimed that from the manner in which he handled the hammer, Smith must have had considerable experience in the "knock-down" business. Officiating as auctioneer, he introduced lively gags in the famous slave mart scene, where the "darkies" proved their worth with specialties. Among them, of course, was Horace Weston with his banjo, the Magnolia Quartette, whose price was skyrocketed at each performance, Jasper Grew, who executed a hoe-cake reel, and Amy Washington with her banjo.

In the summer of 1888, Smith announced a "grand revival of a new version of Mrs. Stowe's great work." To *revive* a new version was rather unusual, but the manager meant that his was a radical departure. Previously, a fair measure of plantation features was judiciously interspersed, but now the sombre parts were relieved by a "variety" show. Uncle Tom was made insignificant so that a certain Dan Hart could do some minstrel business, and a funny duet with his sagacious dog, "Yaller." Gone entirely was the antique savor.

Gone, also, were Mr. and Mrs. Howard. They had been playing with the old-time richness, and the Topsy that was *the* Topsy was as sprightly as ever — until the year before, 1887, when Mr. Howard suddenly passed away. On January

21st, Mrs. Howard went to live in retirement in Cambridge, Massachusetts, after having enacted Topsy for thirty-five years.

Anthony & Ellis, early in the field, added novelties which seemed to take well, or at least to eliminate the monotony of its regular performance. They altered the script considerably, excluded the Deacon and Gumption Cute parts, and a cabinet organ was installed, torturing many a critic. Another innovation was a real waterfall, with gallons of water dashing and sparkling in St. Clair's garden. The Memphis University Students, six imported Siberian hounds, and the donkeys, "Tony" and "Bruno," made the company very popular in the provinces.

During their fifth season, 1881-1882, Anthony & Ellis had two troupes, clearing forty-two weeks through the year. They traveled in style, with new palace and dining hotel cars. The company's headquarters were in New Bedford, Massachusetts, home town of both whaling ships and mammoth Tom shows. Two other Tom troupe proprietors in that city were C. H. Smith and Simeon Folsom. When H. M Ellis died in '83, his partner, Arthur F. Anthony, speculated in skating rinks, a fad of the hour, and lost the fortune made in Tom shows. He joined his brother in publishing the *Evening Standard* of New Bedford, but Mr. Anthony soon resumed Tomming. He was going strong at the end of the decade.

The deluge of Tommers resulted in keen rivalry. It brought to the fore new inducements to attract the public. The jade-green leaflets of Stedman & Gouge's, typically, promised: "Saturday Night — A BARREL OF FLOUR AND A TON OF COAL GIVEN AWAY!!! — All Have an Opportunity." Charles Draper initiated very low admission prices, twenty-five and fifty cents, on the principle that the antebellum drama ought to conform to ante-bellum rates. During the summer he showed in a tent, the rest of the year indoors. He featured the Partington sisters, Kate and Sallie, as Topsies, to Marcia Putnam's Eva. Closing his season at Chicago, in the summer of 1885, after a tour of forty-six weeks, he began his seventh season with a colored man, Sam Crisman, as Tom, and advertised: "No 'Jim Crow' actors or 'Dinky Dido Jubilee shouters' carried along to swell out the house programme. Everything bright, new and clean. Endorsed by managers, people and press as the only legitimate *Uncle Tom's Cabin* now traveling."

Draper drew the largest houses, as well as the noisiest, for his audiences consisted mostly of school children. His agent, W. W. Kelly, an advertising wizard, issued free passes to public school teachers, and distributed checks redeemable for a seat on payment of ten cents at the box office. But a requisite was that the small theatregoers must be "students," and as American scholarship was never found wanting, Draper prospered. This experiment was first tried at the Chicago Museum, on July 4, 1884, where over 8,000 packed the doors; the average thereafter was 5,000 a performance. Ten-cent shows were seized upon by rivals, many admitting children under twelve to free matinees. In the competition Tom managers beat the admission price down, lower and lower — to the popular ten, twent' and thirt'.

While managers boasted that theirs alone was the leader of the vast army of Tom troupes, W. A. Rusco & W. L. Swift's claimed they had "No Opposition Strong Enough To Down the Gold Mine!" They opened their fourth season, in '88, with special notices: That despite "Moody and Sankey" (the performer's name for revivalists) at three different churches in Ottumwa, Iowa, against them, their troupe played to standing-room! Their assets were: The Standard Quartette, Six Mammoth Hounds ("the Finest and Best Acting Bloodhounds in America"), The Only Trick Alligator Ever Introduced on Any Stage ("Erastus — 15 ft. in length"),

Jerry ("the Funniest Donkey in Existence"), and a Company of Sixteen Acting People. The star of them all, however, was a colored man, Lewis G. Clark, proclaimed as the original of George Harris.

Edward O. Rogers was among the very first to set the pavilion fashion so prevalent during the '90s. He had begun by making annual summer tours on wheels, playing in halls, not under canvas. In the Spring of '83, in old-time circus style, he transported the ladies of his company in a separate carriage, preceded by a band wagon, a baggage wagon for the pack of hounds, and two advance wagons. His musicians doubled in brass and string, and were also the actors; as an example, the Blackman Brothers did their song-and-dance, and assumed the characters of St. Clair and Haley. In 1885, he began his eighth season as E. O. Roger's Mammoth Uncle Tom's Cabin, an improvement over the old title of The Standard Uncle Tom's Cabin, and now advertised as "The largest dramatic organization in the world." In its twelfth season, but the sixth under canvas, the company was called Roger's Pavilion Uncle Tom's Cabin.

Also covering great distances was the Boston Ideal U.T.C. company, whose proprietor, John McFadden, had formerly been manager of the Boston Museum. He toured mostly in the far West, with particular success around Salt Lake City. After ten years of hard constant travel, his health broke, at Denver, in '86. His brothers, Johnson and George, carried on, opening three years later new territory in the West: California, Oregon, Washington, Idaho, British Columbia, Manitoba, Dakota and Winnipeg. Nor did they suffer any accident during all that time, except the loss of probably the oldest Tom show donkey on the road, which they had bought nine years before at St. John, N. B., for the sole purpose of supplying "gags" for Lawyer Marks. And when its tired soul went winging above the tall tree tops of Portland, Oregon, the distressed members turned out en masse to the burial, with drum corps beating taps.

Any number of troupes listed the play under the title of "Ideal," but the first to use it was the former manager of the Boston Museum. His incredible title of "The McFadden Famous Original Boston Ideal Uncle Tom's Cabin Company" should have sealed the doom of the enterprise. However, other troupes soon incorporated it into their billing, glorifying other cities, and most prominent was the Chicago Ideal U.T.C. Combination, which in the Spring of '81 closed a prosperous season at Macon, Georgia. Matters were further confused by several troupes infringing directly on McFadden's inspiration, such as: the Abercrombie Boston Ideal Uncle Tom's Cabin Company; Waterman's Boston Ideal in the Canadian provinces; a third, a consolidation of a Boston Ideal and Charles Kirk's, toured the Northwest by rail in '88 in its third successful season. Another Boston Ideal was managed by Frank L. Spanogle and Lillian Peck; however, the last year of the decade saw a change in the title to Greene & Spanogle's. But Edward L. Brannon's Boston Double Uncle Tom's Cabin Combination outstripped them all.

There were many Ideals without "Boston." Anthony & Ellis inserted Ideal in their advertising, and H. P. Lewis was the owner of another, The Ideal U.T.C. The most unusual of them all was formed in Boston, in '80, the Hyers Sisters' Ideal Uncle Tom's Cabin Company, featuring the colored parts by colored people, the others by whites. When their play opened at the Howard Theatre, on March 8th, Sam Lucas, who portrayed Tom, read a new prologue by Mrs. Stowe.

And many a company bore the name of a city without "Ideal." Far back in the Spring of 1878, the Park Theatre Troupe of New York's Uncle Tom's Cabin traveled through

Illinois. In the closing years of the '80s there was Vreeland & Middaugh's New Orleans' Uncle Tom's Cabin. Successful, too, was W. H. Davidson & Lane's Union Square Uncle Tom's Cabin, two companies of which toured the West, and an idea of their affluence is given in a contemporary account of the exchange of gifts among members of the cast, in the *Clipper* of January 19, 1889: "Mrs. W. H. Davidson, of the Union Square Uncle Tom's Cabin Company, was recently presented by her husband with a five stone diamond ring and a gold handled umbrella. The husband received a gold watch in return. Edna Adams, of the same troupe, came in for a gold locket and chain and cameo ring from Mr. and Mrs. Davidson. Eva Adams received an opal ring from the same source, and a brooch from O. Q. Setchell."

Nor was this an isolated instance of a Tom troupe's opulence. The same newspaper had carried a week before: "After the performance of *Uncle Tom's Cabin* by the Rusco & Swift Company, at Rock Island, Ill., the company gathered, by invitation of the managers, in the dining room of the hotel, and, after the distribution of nearly a dray load of presents, they seated themselves at a banquet. Among the most valuable presents were a gold watch, received by Mr. Rusco, an elegant monogram charm and diamond cuff buttons by Mr. Swift, diamond ear rings and ring by Mrs. Swift and gold watch with diamond set by Mattie Lewis. Phil Phillips, stage manager, was remembered by the managers with a gold watch chain and with an Oddfellow's charm attached by the boys of the company. Everybody was remembered in a most substantial way."

Thus the riches piled up from the play about the lowly. Sometimes they came to light in unusual stories. C. D. W. Wilkinson, at the beginning of the decade, made one of the most prosperous tours through New York State and Canada at twenty-five and thirty-five cent admissions, and in Michigan, in the Spring of '80, the same streak of good fortune

Between Performances

The Uncle Tommers' Christmas Dinner on the Road

was with them. Lillie Wilkinson cast aside an old corset in a hotel in Holly, and a week later recollected that $250 in greenbacks was sewed into it. A member of the troupe was dispatched post haste to the town, and was lucky enough, after digging through a lot of rubbish, to recover the corset and cash. That incident made gossip in Union Square, where many referred to it as "the staying power of the play."

The country was overrun with Tom shows. Sometimes the public was attracted by a stunt — the play as Europe had seen it. *Onkel Tom's Hütte* could be said to be cousin germain to the *Uncle Tom* as seen by native Americans. Further, German-speaking citizens avidly read a novel published shortly after the War, Bernard Hesslein's *Jefferson Davis,* in which Mrs. Stowe's characters were thinly disguised.

The furor abroad interested Americans. "The European *Uncle Tom's Cabin,*" at the People's Theatre, in St. Louis, during the season of '81, attracted many on the strength of its title. Another, called "The London Illusion in *Uncle Tom,*" consisted of variety specialties and pantomimic views of the familiar scenes.

Tommers were looked upon as gypsies in those days, and people feared that their children might be carried off; hence, local talent could usually supply whatever support was needed, but seldom an Eva. Therefore, managers were compelled to stage the "English version" without an Eva.

With Eva missing, the wonderful production underwent a slight revision. Uncle Tom would hobble out, in the garden scene, and in a voice choked with sobs, say: "Po' Miss Eba — she's so sick she cain't come out t'night." His master asked anxiously: "Do you think she is much worse, Tom?" The old Negro would bow low: "Yas, Massa St. Clair. Ah's afeerd she'll go befo' long." Then St. Clair, rising from his chair and applying a handkerchief to his forehead, recited

these famous lines to the accompaniment of weeping fiddles:
"Has there ever been a child like Eva? Yes, there has been;
but their names are always on gravestones... Their singular
words and ways are among the buried treasures of yearning
hearts... When you see that deep, spiritual light in the eye
when the little soul reveals itself in words sweeter and wiser
than those of ordinary children, hope not to retain that child;
for the seal of heaven is on her brow and the light of immortality shines out from her eyes. Oh, Tom, my boy, this
is killing me. Take me into her room —" Slowly, to plaintive
music, the slave led his forlorn master into the wings; then
the stage darkened rapidly, and became the bedroom. In
front of a makeshift couch were gathered all the St. Clair
slaves, who, bunching, hid the fact that Little Eva was only
a pillow on a couple of pine boards placed across two kitchen
chairs and covered with sheets borrowed from the hotel.
Over this deathbed St. Clair was wont to shed bitter tears,
with Uncle Tom kneeling devoutly near the foot, while the
slaves (keenly desirous to obtain the fifty cents a performance) chanted: "Then she fell in slumber deep, leavin' us
alone t' weep...."

Many outlandish stories survive of how some of the
Tom troupes were constituted during that hectic period. In
one company in the West the manager's wife took the reins
in her own hands, and the actors had to submit to petticoat
rule. Whenever a Tommer was lippy, she invited him into
a room, locked the door, and horsewhipped him until his
knees hugged the floor, and he blubbered, "Peccavi!" She
paid salaries regularly, however, so that she found many
debased souls who tolerated the lash. This was the only
known case of a female Legree.

Some managers found the long "jumps" too risky for
large companies. Since they carried twenty-five players or
more, with additional jubilee singers, band, and accessory

menagerie, the distances ate up their surpluses. Colorado proved the graveyard of many an over-ambitious aggregation. But the itinerant troupes, usually a single family, got along quite well on one-night stands in out of the way places. With few theatrical props, strengthened often by an additional donkey loaned by a farmer, they were able to "skin" a few dollars. They held forth in village dining rooms, livery stables, skating rinks, storerooms, warehouses, or on lawns. They possessed no advance agent, but billed the day they arrived. While the mammoth competitors featured pedigreed hounds, theirs in the "grand" parade were nondescript talent picked up in the village streets. One little band in the West consisted of eight members, and their parade through the town during the noon hour was a sight for sore eyes: A wan, elderly Little Eva rode in a baby carriage, out of which stuck gawky, long legs, as she was pulled forward by the "ferocious blood-hounds;" Lawyer Marks, riding a spavined ass, escorted her as an outrider. Often the rickety wagon shows came to grief, unable to withstand the vicissitudes of the American cross-roads, and many a meagre 7x10 tent show dissolved and faded away in the far neck o'woods. Although quiescent for a while during the winter months, the vagabond Tom troupes cropped up afresh each Spring.

There were, also, brigands who reaped what others had sown. They victimized Western hotel keepers, claiming that they were the agents of the arriving Tom show, and borrowed on orders which they left for Tom managers to pay. They booked dates with local managers by representing that the other Tom company had exchanged territory with them for the season. Many a citizen mourned the loss of an umbrella which the Tommers (perhaps Marks) mistook for a prop. The scenery of the local opera house was carted off in the same manner. The carpetbag pirates bought up the odds and ends discarded by rivals and traveled on the "paper" of their richer competitors, and advertised players they couldn't possibly engage. If Alice Harrison was promised as Topsy,

they could run in most any one blacked up for her. One
beheld a full-length picture of the late John T. Raymond as
Col. Sellers, seemingly engaged in reading a reward for a
runaway "nigger." They planted pictures of Sarah Jewett,
thereby leading the simple Northwest yokels to believe that
the lady was with them. They announced that the play was
for charitable purposes, and offered ten-cent Bibles to those
who came to their "strictly moral show."

The Tom looters thrived because a certain class always
went to the play no matter how often or how badly it was
done. The managers with principles were forced to offer
tangible assets to the public gaze. Stetson rented the leading
store window in town, and displayed $5,000.00 in green
backs and gold as a guarantee of financial standing. Other
managers carried the usual glassware, a small fortune in
diamonds, exhibiting their chattels to awe the multitudes
into paying for their entertainment. They kept pace with the
hustlers of the profession.

The wild-catting carpetbaggers did well nothwithstand-
ing. Often the leader of the conspiratorial group skipped
town, leaving them destitute, but there were always some
citizens fully alive to the principles of humanity who relieved
them of their pecuniary embarrassments.

The broken troupes had to resort to make-shift changes.
The remaining members doubled and tripled their parts to
such an extent that often an actor found himself talking to
himself. At one time, Frank Losee was asked to play three
parts. At the rehearsal all went well, until he discovered
that the third character was to meet the first at centre stage.
This was the straw that broke the camel's back — and he
rebelled. "But at that," he said afterward, "I *did* play three
parts — indeed, even more, for between my scenes it was
my duty and pleasure to stand in the wings and portray the
bloodhounds, several of them, by baying and barking in

different tones. In those days every actor engaged in a stock company knew that sooner or later he would be asked to 'bark.' "

Frequently a Tommer was compelled to perform white and black characters, in turn, which necessitated washing off and putting on burnt cork during the "waits" backstage. As Tom in the Chloe scene, he made his exit to appear later as the white George Harris; the last act found him back again in a new coat of blacking, ready for Legree's whip.

Soap was an indispensable asset to doubling. Maude Howe would double lively as Topsy and Eliza, and on one occasion Simon Legree had inflicted the finishing stroke with the butt end of his bullwhip, and the black martyr was in his death throes, when Maude looked in from one of the wings, and asked in a voice audible throughout the house: "Tom, O Tom, where in the devil is the soap!"

Tom rolled over, propped himself up on one elbow, and answered in a clear and natural manner: "It was on the window sill the last time I saw it." Then he got back into position, and died without further delay.

Such was the dearth of members in the average Tom company that if they could have gotten away with it, they would have doubled Uncle Tom and Little Eva. At one time, in 1885, the drama was given with only three players. All that remained of a disorganized troupe were the manager, T. F. Stratton, his wife, the property man (who could not be entrusted with a speaking part), and an actor, H. Blanchard. As they were billed in Amherst, New Hampshire, for September 15th, they were resolved to give the performance, playing to a $75 house, and giving satisfaction, although Uncle Tom never uttered a word. The cast was made up in this manner: Act I — Chloe and Eliza Harris (Mrs. Stratton), Marks (T. F. Stratton), Fletcher (H. Blanchard). Act II — Haley (the property man), George Harris (Mrs. Stratton), Little Harry (a rag baby), Marks (T. F. Stratton).

Acts III and IV — Topsy (Mrs. Stratton), St. Clair (T. F. Stratton), Uncle Tom (the property man), Aunt Ophelia (H. Blanchard). Acts V and VI — Marks (T. F. Stratton), Legree (H. Blanchard), Emeline (Mrs. Stratton), Uncle Tom (the property man). They also supplied such offstage effects as the barking of hounds, jubilee singing, etc.

Under a different handicap "Old Uncle Jimmy" Nixon slapped together an equally unusual show. What made the performance more remarkable was the fact that it took place south of the Ohio River, a risky game in the post-war years. His company was in an Alabama town, one evening, about to begin the experiment, when he missed Lawyer Marks. That unhappy actor was soon discovered in a nearby saloon, drowning his sorrows in the cup. Nixon tried to explain the state of affairs to the manager of the theatre, and proposed that the performance begin a half hour later, as that would allow time for Marks to regain his faculties.

"Never, never!" objected the local manager. "The last show that was here tried that. They cut one whole act out of the play, and the people did not like it a bit. And if you wait so late you might have to leave out something, and our people won't stand for it. Is the drunken fellow in the first act?"

"Oh, yes," replied Nixon. "That is his best act, too."

"Is there any act he is not in?"

"He is not in the third act," said Nixon.

"Then begin with the third act," advised the local manager, "and play it through, and by that time he may be sober, and you can begin then and act the first and second acts, and the people won't know the difference."

The curtain rose on the third act, and by the time it descended, Marks was himself again — and now the play proceeded with the first act. The spectators had never witnessed the drama before, and never suspected anything wrong.

Peculiar variations of Nixon's adventure cropped up in the South through the years. Once "Uncle Dick" Sutton, pursuing the hazardous business, ran into a snag in one town.

"The world is not ours, but, my gentle friend," he tried to persuade the local manager, "you will not find any other Tom show like this on earth! — and you will not have any other in your town this season."

"If you play here, you will play on my reduced terms, Mr. Sutton," the manager held firmly.

"Two special cars of our own, measuring nearly 150 feet in length, both cars jammed with the property of this, the largest and grandest Tom show ever on earth!"

"I've made up my mind."

"The parade of this monster show is better and really worth more to see than the Donnybrook Fair."

The town did look profitable, and Sutton had to accept the conditions. When he was leaving the office, Sutton caught the parting shot: "Now, see here, I want all of this *Uncle Tom* show. You have six acts. Mind you don't leave any of them out!"

"All right," answered Sutton, swallowing his reluctance as best he could, "you shall have them."

The opening night brought the townspeople out in great numbers. Most of them had never seen *Uncle Tom's Cabin* before, and certainly *not* as it was performed that evening. Sutton kept to the stipulations of his contract, but he exacted a malicious satisfaction by overhauling the drama a bit: He played the first act, then the last one, the fourth act, then the second. It was *Uncle Tom's Cabin* upside down, but neither the local manager nor the audience discovered the difference.

The play's overhauling to a set of circumstances was heralded as, "The Newest Edition of the Oldest Favorite." Most managers, further, had their own conception where to put the emphasis. Jay Rial, for example, divided the play into "3 Epochs," instead of acts. When George Lowery, after enacting Marks with various companies, joined with Leon Washburn, he was given the additional task of directing. He asked what script he would use, and Washburn answered, "What's the difference, as long as it leads up to the pictures on our advertising — Eliza's Flight, The Slave Market, and Eva's Ascent."

So the play's body, like old Tom's, was kicked around considerably, but its soul still belonged to showdom. Rigged up for tears and laughs, bits of "business" stuck to it like a handful of cockleburrs, and the cast got the maximum out of their parts, which remained a tradition with the Tommers. They knew the old play backward, and went on at a moment's notice for any part.

There was no written script.

The general attitude of the players toward one was reflected in the instance of a Tom troupe stopping at the town of Altamount, N. Y., years back. One of the members took cognizance of April Fool's Day, and rushed into the hotel room of a sleeping actor, Charles Drake. He roused him with,

"Charlie! Charlie! Wake up — quick! Come and help save something. The theatre's on fire and will burn to the ground!"

Drake was startled for a moment — then remembered the prankish day of the calendar. He rolled over:

"Oh, damn the theatre!" he yawned. "Let it burn. But save the manuscript."

Sectional feeling was still strong in the border states along the Mason-Dixon line, where few Tom troupes dared take the risk. Almost immediately after Lincoln's death, the chance recollection of a poker game saved Sam Sanford's life. He had booked the play in Ohio that winter, and made arrangements for a week in Louisville. He received letters, mostly anonymous, warning him that if he tried *Uncle Tom's Cabin* there he would never leave the town alive.

Apparently the citizens boycotted the show, for Sanford opened on a Monday night in the face of a frost—to a $6.00 house, playing to the gas. On Wednesday he went to the manager of the theatre. "Look here," he said. "I've contracted to pay you $75 a night for the theatre, and I'd like to have you let me out."

"Well, well, Sanford, I thought you had more nerve than that," chided the other. "I didn't think you were a quitter."

"I've got nerve enough under certain circumstances," fired back the other. "But both of us are throwing away our money. What's the use of going on with the show when it's clear the people don't want us?"

"Don't worry about the pay for the theatre," advised the manager. "If you'll go on and show these rebs you've got nerve, I won't charge you a cent for the use of the house."

Sanford decided to stay. His troupe worked late into the night, mailing several hundred envelopes — with two reserved tickets in each to the best people in town — for the Saturday night performance. All through the week they played to empty seats, but either out of curiosity or some other reason, the theatre was thronged on Saturday night.

Some of the lines were hissed, but no one went further than that. The play reached the point where Uncle Tom comes in with a candle in his hand. The dressing room was down below the wings of the stage, and Sanford, as Tom, was on his way up the stairs with the aforesaid candle, when, "Hold on there, Sanford!" a rough-looking townsman accosted him. "You don't go on the stage till you have paid your posting bill." The actor explained that the scene would be ruined if he was held back. Came the retort: "Why, don't you know that if I say the word, I can get the whole troupe mobbed?"

Sanford, still holding the candle, could not help observing the man closely, particularly the notches on his gun handle. He was certain he had met him before. "Look here, Mr.......," he said, "do you remember one night when you played poker with Tony Pastor and Tony Hart and another chap, and in the morning we had a round of brandy at seventy-five cents a throw, only I took beer?"

The man paused a minute, then exclaimed, "Are you that Sanford that used to be with the old gang — now I see that you are! Well, I'll right up. The bill-posting won't cost you a cent."

Later, Sanford described his experience: "Well, sir, after the performance we had a great old time, and he turned out to be a first-class chap. Most of these Southerners were when you got them away from their bitter sectional feeling, and after all you couldn't blame them...."

That was not the only time the South saw the play. Scarcely seven years after the War, the petitions of a few patrons and the colossal nerve of the Academy of Music company inspired its production in New Orleans. The fact that Mrs. Jefferson De Angelis had been born in New Orleans was given special significance. Her husband played Marks, her daughter Sallie was the flower of the South — Eva, and Alice Harrison had the Topsy role. The cautious director curtailed many of the anti-slavery lines, but the toned-down version still happily retained some of the elements of the drama's grand fire, passionate action, tragedy and retribution, sentimentality, and low comedy relief. During the run the hostility carried into the theatre was dissipated by the time the final curtain came down.

More frequently, Tom troupes tried the hostile territory, led there by either one of two reasons: The cold weather or the prestige involved in the hazardous venture. Sometimes a wandering troupe forgot its geography, finding itself below the Mason-Dixon line to its regret. In '81, the Chicago Ideal Tom Company was greeted with a shower of stale eggs at Griffin, Georgia. The scenery was cut and torn, and it was harassed all along the route. In Atlanta the audience consisted of two small boys. The meagre receipts resulted in a reduction of salaries. One night, the manager, who doubled the parts of George Harris and St. Clair, took exception to the manner in which Uncle Tom interpreted his death scene.

"Why," he reproached the actor, "you actually smiled in that scene."

"Yes," replied the rebuked Uncle Tom. "In view of the salary that you now pay me, death seems a pleasant relief."

In Savannah they made only enough to pay for the theatre. Then they were stranded, and their baggage surrendered to the railroad company to get home. Thereafter, the troupe's agent, Harry M. Clark, advertised proudly in the North, "We are the first company ever thru the South with *Uncle Tom's Cabin!*"

Abbey's troupe, the following year, attempted to win the title by striking boldly into Virginia. That December the Southern newspapers protested against the Tommers; the Norfolk and Richmond papers waged a war against them, with particularly hard blasts from the Norfolk *Landmark*. The towns along the route were lithographed days ahead, but these posters were ripped off. The troupe got only as far as Lynchburg (foreboding name), then cancelled all dates and returned North.

The prejudice lasted through the years. The Mississippi River tank towns and allied territory became known as the "Death Trail." And if any Southern youth were asked what he thought of it, his answer was similar to the reply given on one occasion: "No sir; my sympathies are not with the play, sir." Articles were still written refuting Mrs. Stowe. The *Century* Magazine carried a few, such as Walter B. Hill's "Uncle Tom without a Cabin" (April, 1884), and James L. Allen's "Mrs. Stowe's 'Uncle Tom' at Home and in Kentucky" (October, 1887). A play, Alice W. Rollins' *Uncle Tom's Tenement*, in 1888, described the well-known characters in a slum of a modern city, brutalized by a rapacious landlord. The "cabin" writers still carried on — Adah M. Holland's *Uncle Ned's Cabin* (1884), Samuel A. Echols' *Uncle Ben's Cabin* (1886), etc., etc. About that time a rumor spread that Mrs. Stowe had recanted, that she had discovered how irresponsible and worthless Negroes were, but she denied this emphatically in a letter to a friend, in 1887, "It is a vile slander to say that I ever in any shape or form took back the things I said in *Uncle Tom's Cabin.* I did not find the Southern Negroes 'degraded, ignorant and shiftless,' but considering their advantages far better than many white people. Please assert these things boldly on my authority." This kept the issue very much alive, with many Tom troupes taking full advantage of it.

Most of the criticism thrust at the Tommers came from local correspondents in the North, who set themselves up as important dramatic critics. A petulant facetiousness was evident in their reviews:

Items: Seeing we are to be tortured with an invasion of Uncle Toms, it seems that kind fortune has sent them both at once. The air already seems pregnant with odors of Africa, and after the two parties depart from their respective abodes, Managers Whitney and Brooks are to have their theatres thoroughly disinfected.
Detroit —   Jan. 1, 1881.

Professional Doings: A Griffin (Ga.) audience last week pelted the performers in Uncle Tom's Cabin with a lot of debased eggs. This is about the only way to get the drama off the stage, and the example of the Griffin people should be religiously followed by other communities.
New York —   April 23, 1881.

Pike's Opera House: Draper's Uncle Tom's Cabin c. has held the boards during the past week to fair business, the gallery element predominating. The troupe, on the whole, will compare favorably with similar organizations; but speaking from a Cincinnati standpoint, the highly-colored moral drama is rapidly outliving its popularity, and there is every probability that within the ensuing years a long-suffering public may arise in its might and extinguish the meekly, prayerful Uncle Toms, the talkative Markses and the angelic Evas. They *do* say that the interior inhabitants of Ohio, upon the announcement of a party performing this drama, immediately betook themselves to the woods.
Cincinnati —   April 30, 1881.

Abercrombie's Uncle Tom's Cabin 27th to better business than they deserved.
Columbia, Penna.   May 14, 1881.

Academy of Music: Slavin's Uncle Tom's Cabin 24th to big business; a show unworthy of notice.
Fort Wayne, Ind.   Nov. 5, 1881.

Opera House: This week, an entirely new play called Uncle Tom's Cabin, with bloodhound and nigger attachments, will hold the boards. George E. Stevens is responsible for this outrage.
Detroit —   Jan. 21, 1882.

Masonic Opera House: Draper's Uncle Tom's Cabin will catch the coons and Quakers 11th.
Oskaloosa, Iowa —   Dec. 16, 1882.

Fulton's Opera House: Minnie Foster's Uncle Tom Cabin co. to fair house, 17th. This is about the tenth Uncle Tom co. that has visited us this season, and no more are wanted.
Lancaster, Pa. —   Feb. 24, 1883.

Schultz's Opera House: Rial's Uncle Tom, 3rd. All the town except regular theatre-goers, who generally held their noses in disgust. The performance of Uncle Tom was given "hind end befo" and the dogs were disposed to be unruly.
Zanesville, Ohio —   April 14, 1883.

Schultz's Opera House: The Wellesly and Sterling U. T. co. gave two performances, 11th and 12th .... None of our regular theatre-goers would be even caught dead at an U. T. performance, consequently Manager John Hoge only provides the worn-out attraction for the rustics and Sunday school children .... There was nothing else to notice besides the dogs, which "did themselves great credit."
Zanesville, Ohio —   Sept. 20, 1884.

Academy of Music: Draper's Uncle Tom's Cabin co. 20th, 21st, succeeded in drawing the usual full house. Of all the troupes that have visited us for a long time this one should have the pancake. A worse co. and a still worse performance I have never seen on the stage of this house. The play, if presented by anything but a pack of barnstormers, is endurable, but as presented by the half dozen people who comprise this co. it is worse than a farce. A few more ten-cent shows like this one, I think, will bring theatre-goers to their senses, and drive dime shows where the woodbine turneth.
Allentown, Pa. —   March 28, 1885.

Pavilion: What a sane man is thinking of when he attempts doing that moth-eaten chestnut, Uncle Tom's Cabin, at a Summer resort beats me. I admire courage though, and Mack is entitled to the cake.
Portland, Maine —   Aug. 14, 1886.

Items: It is a standing joke with variety cos. about having played at Steep Brook, the northern part of the City, but it remained for Storer's Uncle Tommers to have that honor, last Tuesday night.
Fall River, Mass.   Nov. 13, 1886.

Items: An Uncle Tom's Cabin gang are pillaging the small towns of the State.
Portland, Maine —   May 14, 1887.

Academy of Music: The biggest business of the season was done by Abbey's Uncle Tom's Cabin co. Standing room only was the rule — There is considerable rankness about the Uncle Tom show, but it did the business. J. Barry, a former clown, is managing the concern. Though once a fool for the public, he is now presumably engaged in making fools of them.
Halifax, Canada —   June 4, 1887.

G.A.R. Opera House: A party of barnstorming amateurs, three "dorgs" and a donkey meandering about the country under the name of Abbey's Uncle Tom's Cabin co., slaughtered that time-worn play to standing-room only 12th. Thruout it was the worst show we have had this season, and that means a great deal.
Shamokin, Pa. —   Jan. 21, 1888.

Music Hall: Stetson's U.T.C. gave a mediocre performance of that ancient drama 13. As usual the attendance was good. We have not had a good presentation of this play for a number of years, and why our people go into ecstasies on an announcement of an Uncle Tom play and so continually allow themselves to be imposed upon, while cos., and plays of merit receive light patronage, is an enigma to your correspondent.
Bethlehem, Pa. —   Nov. 23, 1889.

What really antagonized the critics was the play's longevity. What a bore to hunt through the amusement columns only to discover that *Uncle Tom's Cabin* would be given again tomorrow — for the nth time that season! They complained that the Ancient Thomas had passed away to Green Pastures long ago. Yet judging by the popular Saturday matinees, audiences still loved it. Of course, the spectators were mostly school children, who laughed and cried as their parents before them, and as their offspring would after them, unless, as one critic prayed, "Unless a benign and merciful Providence deposes some of our statesmen to amend the Constitution and prevent it from being inflicted on 'the children of a third and fourth generation.' "

In the Spring of 1878, with the resurgence of the Tomming fad, the *Spirit of the Times* observed: "Why, look you! This is a moment of Uncle Tomitudes. Three theatres staggering back to Topsy-turvey variety and religious cork. Behold Uncle Tom, how it waxes! It has been revived at the same moment with Maggie. But it is a drivelling old melodrama in the sear and yellow leaf of time. We look at it as we look at the bones of the pterodactyl, and wonder how so cumbrance a frame ever flew."

Dramatic criticism was enlivened with shafts at what became known as "the Great Tom (Fools)!"

One manager, Jay Rial, took issue, and answered his dramatic critics: "*Uncle Tom* is by no means played out, no matter how much it may be abused and made fun of by you newspaper chaps. I am quite as tired of the piece itself as you are, or as anybody else can possibly be, and there is nothing I should like better than to shelve it. But while the piece continues making money, as it has done of late years, I should be rather silly, in a commercial sense, to part company with it. I suppose dry goods men must get rather tired of selling calico, but so long as the public wants calico, they are obliged to give it to them or shut up shop." At that time he was sending out a new Tom company, the sixth under his management.

After they had acquired fortunes from the play, many Tom managers felt that something should be done for the *legitimate*. They were actuated by accounts of the down-at-the-heel actors in the comic weeklies, especially Tom P. Morgan's, in the pages of *Puck*. He had a Mr. Walker Ham explain to the Ruralville hotel owner: "It happened in this wise, sir," replied the thespian, thrusting his right hand into the bosom of his antiquated frock coat. "The average Uncle Tom's Cabin actor is, paradoxical as it may sound, a person who cannot act, and, barring myself, the members of the organization of which we are speaking were no exceptions to the rule. But in my palmy days, sir, I was with Booth and Barrett, and 'twas said that I supported them becomingly. After joining this grand aggregation of 7 — count them — 7 genuine Siberian man-eating blood-hounds,

I kept the fact that I could act carefully concealed for a time, and all went well. But, last night, in a moment of abstraction, I forgot myself and acted. The manager caught me in the act and discharged me. He asserted that such conduct as mine was not entirely unprecedented and unprofessional, but also positively dangerous to the prosperity of his organization. If I was permitted to remain, other members of the company might be inspired by my example to try to become actors, too, and the public, missing the familiar methods, would, he declared, be likely to turn from the dear old drama, and business would be ruined. Accordingly, he fired me. 'Tis thus that genius gets it in the neck!"

The veteran Garry Hough, after a most prosperous season under canvas, was in Detroit with nothing in his hands but idleness and a great deal of money. He dismissed his Tommers and hired a company of *real* actors — every one of them savagely *legitimate*. The opening night came with great fanfare, but the play fell flat as a pancake! He discharged the actors, hunted up the Tommers in town, and every stray dog and every old ragged umbrella he could pick up were pressed into use. He put on the play again, with dramatic mutton — and crowded the theatre until the walls bulged! From then on, whenever an actor applied for a position, Hough would always have the same reply: "I don't want any but reliant Tommers."

The average play exploited a leading man or woman who hogged the fat parts, while the rest of the cast merely served as local color or background. A Tommer, on the other hand, could do pretty well as he wished with his lines, as long as he got a laugh or a tear. No other play was such a free-for-all, with so much "gagging" and gusty horseplay. Once Col. F. J. Owens, chaplain of the Showman's League, came across Davis & Martin's troupe in Chicago, and was invited in. "Drop in and see the show," Martin urged. "I've got a great company. If you find an actor among 'em, I'll kill you."

And any number of instances substantiated that attitude of Tom managers. On one occasion, the veteran Gotthold was stopped on the street by a friend, who said, "Milt, I'd like to see *Uncle Tom's Cabin* played damned bad."

"Here's a ticket," said Gotthold, soberly. "Come to my show tonight, and see it played just that way!"

Once a Tom troupe in its peregrinations off the beaten path entered a town where the natives knew little about plays. In the audience there happened to be a citizen of Cincinnati, who kept objecting throughout. When the show was over, he sought out the manager, and insisted that he had seen better in Cincinnati. "It may be pretty good," he went on, "but I don't like the fellow who plays Marks."

"You ought to see him in the street parade," swore the Tom manager. "He's hell on the cornet!"

Charlie Forbes, with a reputation in the far West during the early '80s, first began to style Tommers as "hands." He would turn up in Chicago once or twice a year, and whenever he was asked what he was doing in town, replied, jingling his pockets, "Oh, just looking for a few hands." He paid low salaries, six dollars a week or so, and "keep." The recruits were won over by the honorarium promised with the matinees. Forbes would exclaim, "A matinee every day and travel the rest of the time — no chance to fritter away your money, my boy!" His Uncle Tom, an elderly man named Archer, never washed the burnt cork off his face the entire season.

Another case in point is A. B. Stover's experience with the haughty manager of a repertoire company. "You can take Tom actors and they will make good in repertoire," Stover was fond of saying, "but you can't take *rep* actors and make good in *Tom*." Once chance threw Stover and "Jap" Rockwell together at a little railroad junction in Maine. It was the noon hour. When the manager of the legitimate troupe caught sight of the despised Tommers, he flounced off, and hurriedly shooed his proud ones into the dingy depot lunchroom. There, seated on hard stools, they appeased their hunger with very thin sandwiches and watery coffee. Stover, on the other hand, paraded his seven Tommers to the little country hotel across the street, where they were waited on at tables, and ate a regular, substantial meal. The jaunty Tom manager dug down in his jeans for the last cent and supplied his players with cigars. They then marched back to the station, where they took their constitutionals on the platform, ostentatiously puffing away on their "segars." The *legitimate* actors had the vain satisfaction of the grand manner, but no lunch. Devastatingly, Stover lifted his high hat, and directed the gold head of his cane (every Tom manager sported a gold-headed cane) toward a snobbish player peeping out of the window, "What do you think of Tom actors now? If you'd been with us, you'd have got something to eat."

Dame Fortune smiled on the thriving Tommers. Critics hoped that Uncle Tom had died and reached his Heavenly reward, only to be disappointed by his resurrection each Spring, his time for getting around. The play magnetized audiences as if it had been sprung on them for the first time, and set the pulse dancing. The hinterlanders fixed the date of any particular local happening as "about the time the last Tom show came here," and in the big cities the play was called "the Lenten sensation." Its true popularity was just beginning.

Chapter XIII

THE PLAY THAT WENT TO THE DOGS

And so, subsequently, we hung them up gently,
And only once more were they e'er taken down—
When they served as a fetter, in lieu of a better,
To tie up the bloodhounds we put on in Tom.
—B. E. Golden's "Ms. on Dressing Room Floor"

WHAT JARRETT & PALMER DID for jubilee singers, Jay Rial, later, did for animal talent. Fearless insurgent, he loosened the leash holding back the free movement of the play. For some obscure reason American drama slavishly followed the laws of Greek dramaturgy, and the iron-clad rule Rial broke had alleged that the action must be exiled somewhere in the wings—out of sight of those who paid their hard-earned drachmae. Our famous transfluvial epic never had a dog in it until Rial came along. Hitherto, the only tangibility evident was the designation for Simon Legree, bracketed in the playbills, as "The human bloodhound."

Dogs were heard, but their cries came offstage. A story is told in this connection of a couple of thespians who tried to settle the question as to who was the best actor in the world; as a matter of fact, only the Union Square championship was involved. Ever since their first meeting, when in rival companies, they crossed verbal swords. "I'm a better actor than you ever dreamed of being," one insisted boastfully. "You an actor?" sneered the other, and with polished sarcasm, he asked, "How did you start in the business? Barking in a barrel for an imitation of the bloodhounds in *Uncle Tom's Cabin* fifteen times a day in a Bowery museum!"

At this, the two histrionic half-portions hammered each other all over the sidewalk, one sustaining a cut lip, tragedy indeed to an actor. A policeman interfered and arrested them both, and the public was never enlightened further on the important question.

Visible quadrupeds in the Eliza flight scene had been overlooked by Aiken, and none of the scripts of later adapters gave directions for their use. Aiken's play, however, suggested the layout so famous later on, but it was done in this fashion: Eliza with her baby jumped out of a window as the tavern door was forced; the scene changed with pantomimic suddenness to a moonless sky and an icy river where the fugitive stumbled along the loose cakes, till she floated off with the current just as her pursuers stopped in terror at the shore. The young playwright was faithful to Mrs. Stowe's story, which mentioned no bloodhounds. Haley, who chased Eliza, did not have them. Witness the dialogue in the novel on this point:

" 'Your master, I s'pose, don't keep no dogs, said Haley, thoughtfully, as he prepared to mount.

" 'Heaps on 'em,' said Sam, triumphantly: 'thar's Bruno — he's a roarer; and, besides that, 'bout every nigger of us keeps a pup of some nature or uther.'

" 'Poh!' said Haley — and he said something else, too, with regard to the said dogs, at which Sam muttered:

" 'I don't see no use of cussin' on 'em, no way.'

" 'But your master don't keep no dogs (I pretty much know he don't) for trackin' out niggers.'

"Sam knew exactly what Haley meant, but he kept on a look of earnest and desperate simplicity.

" 'Our dogs all smells around considerable sharp. I 'spect they's the right kind, though they han't never had no practice. Here, Bruno,' he called, whistling to the lumbering Newfoundland, who came pitching tumultuously toward them.

*Eliza Crosses the Ice-Clogged Ohio with Human Bloodhounds
at Her Slipper-Shod Heels*

" 'You go hang,' said Haley, getting up. 'Come, tumble up now.' "

That disposed of the matter of dogs for the time being. When Eliza arrived at the tavern and was spied by Haley, those following at her slipper-shod heels were human bloodhounds. Frustrated, Haley returned to the tavern, where he agreed with Loker and Marks to trail her, and once more the dog question arose:

" 'I 'spose you've got good dogs,' said Haley.

" 'First rate,' said Marks, 'But what's the use? . . . . Dogs is no 'count in these yer up states where these critters get carried; of course, ye can't get on their track. They only does down in plantations, where Niggers, when they runs, had to do their own runnin' and don't get no help.' "

So much for the dogs, for there was no further talk of them in the novel. Had the dogs been used, it would have rather complicated matters, for the frozen water broke the scent. Whereas Mrs. Stowe abided by logic and the forces of nature, the Tommers were concerned only with dramatic effect.

In 1879, when the Tom show excitement struck the country anew, Jay Rial left the Grand Theatre, in New York, which he was managing, and assembled his second Tom troupe, Rial & Draper's. In Delaware, Ohio, Rial bought a very young hound, and began to break him in. During the ice scene, he would hold on to the dog until the cue, then let him loose, but the canine had no more spirit in him than a cocker spaniel. A little discouraged, Rial got a mate for the dog. In five weeks he had them so well trained that they understood what was expected of them. On their opening performance, the actress who skipped blithely from ice cake to ice cake over the frozen "Ohio," carried a choice hunk of raw meat in her shawl as a lure for the dogs. She gained the opposite shore of papier-maché, and safety, but the hounds were left in a precarious position in the middle

They Introduced Dogs into the Play

of the "stream." Later, some dog biscuit was substituted, for economy.

Eliza's great scene was thus intensified — and became indescribably thrilling.

Mrs. Rial enacted Eliza, and the Legree was Charles Krone, who belonged to the bellowing school of acting. He howled dreadfully, and several critics suggested that Rial could economize and reduce his live-stock by having him do an invisible bloodhound.

The new company drew topheavy houses. The attraction consisted, firstly, of low prices — twenty-five cents, thirty-five for spendthrifts; and, secondly, the actual introduction of two hounds and a donkey *upon the stage*. There was also a quartette of genuine "darkies" for the plantation songs, but the hounds were the drawing card. When Rial & Draper came to Pittsburgh, that summer of 1880, the Opera House was fearfully jammed. The local proprietor decided on the spot to organize his own company, which he styled "Manager

Ellsler's Uncle Tom Party." He secured a trick donkey for Lawyer Marks, and defied critics who prophesied that he would ruin himself if he kept the Opera House open during the hot summer months. He made a fortune.

Rial & Draper, in 1881, introduced "the only genuine trained Siberian Bloodhounds" — ten real, ferocious animals. They had a trick donkey, "Jerry," and also "Marks in the Dog's Mouth," a sketch that set audiences screaming. When the company played in Lynn, Massachusetts, the New York *Dramatic Mirror* correspondent made history with his pithy criticism of June 25th: "L. Stockwell as Lawyer Marks was well supported by an intelligent mule and two bloodhounds."

Rial disassociated himself from Draper after their fourth year together, and struck out with a sensational vigor. He advertised as having given the play over 1600 times. Now the Bloodhound Chase, the Trick Donkey, the Spectacular Transformation, the Beautiful Gates Ajar, and a reserved seat in the parquette were among the moral perquisites. Rial claimed that he had the Ideal Uncle Tommers.

Indeed, managers everywhere credited Rial for filling the parts with the "genuine article." Thus when Tom show agents tried to arrange booking at theatres, the proprietor invariably replied: "Yes, I can book you, but I won't have any of the actors standing in the wings barking like dogs. Have you got real hounds?" All actors who once bayed hoarsely in imitation of a pursuing pack were discharged. Each manager tracked down the most fierce-looking dogs in the country, which grew in number with each passing season, and were proudly referred to as the "entire strength of the company."

Then Little Eva was given a Shetland pony, Legree a mule cart, and Marks a mouse-colored donkey. The latter was in all probability a carry-over from G. W. L. Fox, who excelled as Phineas Fletcher and Lawyer Marks; the comedian had appeared in January, 1870, as Ferguson Trotter, in

The Writing on the Wall, at the Olympic Theatre, where he brought a donkey on the stage as comic relief. Afterwards, Lawyer Marks and his donkey became traditionally as well-known as Yankee Doodle and his pony.

Of course, the open barouche of the St. Clares was introduced, but disaster met this innovation, for the white horses pulling it often became excited, jumped the footlights, and panicked audiences. However, it remained a feature in the street parade.

Season after season, Eliza and her baby were chased across the Ohio River by more ravenous hounds, more moonlight, and more realism. The dogs grew larger and more hungry-eyed, the celebrated trick donkey more diminutive. Folks were thrilled by the news that Simon Legree had been bitten by a dog, or that one of the four-footed thespians ate a part of Lawyer Marks the week before.

Troupes were reinforced with alligators and other novelties, and soon many spirited gentlemen in the audience saw snakes without going out between the acts. And, of course, we must not forget the angels, the cherubim and seraphim, flying nightly upward with Eva during the Apocalypse.

The Tom troupes soon resembled circuses. In 1880 Lehnen's carried fifty actors, twelve dogs, a mule, and an elephant. On the playbills of Wellesley & Sterling's a notation, below the cast list, flaunted: "The wonderful dogs, Sultan, Caesar and Monarch, for which Buffalo Bill makes a standing offer of $5000.00, or $3000.00 for Sultan alone, take part in the play. To see these wonderful dogs is worth the price of admission." Booth and Collier's Mammoth proclaimed, in 1887, that theirs was "Positively the largest in existence under canvas," — the stage was 60 feet square. The close of the decade beheld James P. Stenson's out for the long green under an eighty-foot round top, with a fifty-foot middle piece; a flashy outfit with lots of "paper," it traveled by wagon, with eighteen head of horses, hounds, and donkeys, and had a parade band in addition to the orchestra. Other managers under canvas in the '80s were C. W. Park & Ballard, C. G. Phillips & F. E. Griswold, with two companies, and Charles Kirk, with two more.

There were thirty head of stock in Charles Ogden's, a wagon show with headquarters in Waupaca, Wis., covering that State and Minnesota for a decade. His horses were never shod, Ogden claiming that Nature had never intended them to be. He further excited public interest by arriving ahead in each town, and hitching his odd-looking horse and buggy at the local post office or in any conspicuous spot. The animal had two humps on its back, like a camel, and its hind feet were cloven. This freak was the result of a mare in foal being frightened at the sight of a camel in the parade— the haughty owner explained. Ogden featured the horse in the concert, walking it around the Tom tent.

The pursuit scene was worked up, year by year. One manager hit upon the happy thought of having the dogs fight upon the side of virtue in the Rocky Pass scene. He advertised: *"Terrific Struggle between Haley, the Trader, and Dog Sultan!!!"* In companies strong in invincible hounds, with large, brass-spiked collars, the dramatic ability was subordinated to such a point that the animals were the only good actors in the show; they knew their cues better than did Eliza, which militated decidedly against the effectiveness of the acting. Here is a terse and devastating dramatic criticism of a Minnesota paper in the early '90s: "Thompson's Uncle Tom's Cabin company appeared at the Opera House last night. The dogs were poorly supported."

The exploitation of dogs for the Tom business demanded an emphasis on wild barking and lusty smelling. As tyros, they needed a seven-mule power behind them to propel them across the stage; when they squatted on their haunches to scratch broodingly, a few blasts of buckshot from the wings spurred them on. The matter of timing was also important. Artistic restraint required that they arrive at the finish line *not* several yards ahead of Eliza, but once the rudiments were mastered, they leaped nimbly across the cakes of ice after her with almost incredible facility.

Without a slacker in the pack, they often got beyond control. While enacting Tom Loker in San Francisco, in 1887, in a company that included Maude Adams' mother as Ophelia, Hobart Bosworth recalls the amusing check on the dogs. L. R. Stockwell, as Marks, running out on the swollen ice-choked Ohio, customarily yelled, "Go back! Go back!" as the slack wire measured the length the great Danes should reach across the ice. On this nightly excursion, instead of snapping at Marks' cue and taking up the sensational pursuit of Ethel Brandon's Eliza, they did not stir more than a half-dog length from the wings. "Go back!" Stockwell yelled again, to hold the audience, at the same time stimulating the dogs via sotto voce: "Come on! Come on!" Then, rattled, he kept whispering, "Go back!" and yelling, "Come on!" Through a blunder of the new property man, the dogs had been tied short, and when they were permitted at last to run the length of their tethers, the audience set up a roar of laughter. Instead of being tied with the almost invisible wire, the dogs were leashed with a new white clothes-line!

To stimulate the hounds, the early Tom managers talked of rubbing Eliza with a strong essense of fox, so that the mere passage across the stage would leave a good line. This was abandoned, however, in favor of aniseed and fox-litters, both popular substances for making the scent in drag hunting. Later, a foxy odor was induced by stringing very foxy-smelling cords across the stage just before curtain time. And as audiences expected some savagery, too, with the dogs bounding at Eliza's throat, a solution to that realism had to be found. The actress in the role was assigned the task of feeding the animals, and carried the meat in the same bundle that constituted the "prop child." Through long association, the dogs leaped at their "dinner" every time Little Harry was hugged to Eliza's bosom. One manager,

A. B. Stover, of Boston, had three Great Danes that were perfect in the "business," thrilling audiences beyond measure. Anticipating Prof. Pavlov's studies of conditioned reflexes, the Tom show magnate made it a practice to feed his dogs in one way only. A butcher supplied him with a healthy portion of minced meat each day, which he divided into three equal portions; these he tied in three red bandanna handkerchiefs. Then he hung each bandanna, in turn, about his neck. The eager, hungry dogs, one at a time, were made to leap — again and again — before they were given the meat. The association of red bandannas and meat was thus built up, and, thereafter, when Eliza shuttled across the ice she was careful to wear a red 'kerchief.

If the dogs aroused astonishment with their size, ferocious aspect and general intractability, the same qualities could at times be a source of embarrassment or even danger. When the pack of destroyers did not seem to be making mincemeat out of the fair fugitive, the excited spectators cried, "Sic 'em! Sic 'em!" How the men and boys helped persecute poor Eliza on the ice from Ole Kaintuck' over tew O-hi-oo! Both she and her child were often thrown bodily to the floor, so badly hurt at times that she was unable to appear in the following scene. And for many decades Haleys and Markses were bitten by dogs; but their wounds were cauterized, and they lived on, for actors are notoriously hard to kill. Sometimes audiences were treated to a scene not down on the bills. The dogs would engage in a desperate fight, rolling over into the orchestra pit, which was sufficient to start a panic. More than one public-spirited theatregoer remarked that he "wished the brute had chewed up some of the Tommers!"

Besides the "heavy" business at night and at matinees, the dogs were paraded through the principal thoroughfares during the day, on weighty chains off the anchor of some battleship, strongly muzzled, and guarded by a retinue of uniformed, ebony-hued American citizens. But the bloodthirsty canine adjuncts had a habit of slipping their muzzles, fighting furiously among themselves, or biting the most conspicuous spectators, and they chose, with admirable presence of mind, the mayors of the small towns. Dogs frequently were run down by the heavy Tom wagons.

Many smaller troupes found that their canine actors ate up the receipts; for as "stars," they were entitled to more than ordinary consideration. When business was very light, with hardly enough taken in to feed them, the dogs supplemented their meagre meals by an occasional mouthful of a Tommer's hide.

Sometimes a small company could muster out in force but a single dog, and at that a pipsqueak puppy, a fraction of a foot long from the tip of its tail to its moist nose, and incapable of a single noteworthy bark — but it was dog! Tom shows that started out on a shoestring had often a local dog attached to it, and the undersized mongrels — hastily conscripted from the street — had to be booted and pinched to resentful barking. The stage hands began the baying to start them off, during the overture, before their entrance. Curiously, Tom shows were at the mercy of the brutes, and it was not an unusual thing for the sorrowful manager to throw himself on the kind indulgence of his audience with the explanation that the chief bloodhound had the colic, or — as may have been the case — that the star dog had been badly chewed up in a street fight.

Once an itinerant Tom company, in its rounds of the sparsely-settled and isolated communities, succeeded in borrowing a real thoroughbred from a farmer. Chained up with the rest of the "mutts," the pedigreed dog attempted to slip his collar, and unfortunately choked to death. It was explained afterward as a clear case of suicide — the result of keeping bad company!

Whenever a troupe encountered adverse circumstances, Lawyer Marks would depart clandestinely with the dog. Then the manager would scurry off for a search warrant.

and head for the nearest saloon. On the street pavement he found the mainstay of the show bearing a placard, the lettering touched off with many curlicues: *Dog For Sale — Inquire Within*, while the long leash and Lawyer Marks' legs were visible through the swinging doors.

One such Marks, blessed with some ventriloquial ability, once stalked into an unpretentious saloon. He set the canine on the bar, and made the hungry maw *work* by feeding it a pretzel. "Give me another pretzel," came the *basso profondo* from the dog, whereon the bartender stared. Then the seedy actor, striking that Dr. Munyon pose familiar in the cautioning advertisements of the Philadelphia patent-medicine man of a generation ago, apostrophized, "Ah!" and carried it off further: "A mere matter of correct, scientific methods in adapting the animal to these unwonted tasks," he elucidated, and went on confidently: "This dog is not as bright as we had expected and our Tom' company is considering his disposal." The bartender was glad enough to trade a couple of bottles of whiskey for such a *talking* dog. The poor animal kept protesting in the whining manner of Uncle Tom: "Don't sell me, mas'r, don't sell me!" But the actor waved a grandiloquent negative. "Ef yuh does," came then the solemn vow from the dog, "I'll neber — neber speak ag'in!" When the actor departed, the bartender's first command was, "Speak!" But the faithful dog stuck to his promise. That story is ever popping up; somewhere in the first decade of the twentieth century it was credited to the vaudevillian Jim Thornton, and when the movies came along, W. C. Fields used it in *Poppy*.

In an age of jealousy between rival Tom managers, many a prize hound fell victim to poisoned meat, or was lost, strayed, or stolen. Once an imposter, passing himself off as a member of Stetson's troupe, convinced Major Kibble's wife that he had rented the large Siberian dog, "Leo." When the parade leader heard about it, he fumed, "I am indignant that a man should take advantage of my absence on tour and rent my dog. *The villain has not sent me one cent of rent due!* If the dog is not returned at once, the party who stole it will be dealt with according to the full extent of the law." And the Major's ire may have been justifiable, for the crime fell under one of two heads: a clear case of dognapping, or the refusal to pay dog rent.

Indeed, the breeding and renting of hounds to Tom shows was a lucrative business. The ones in the "Skip" Kibble parades were from the famous Red Onion Kennels, owned by "Doc" H. H. Null, who crossed mastiffs to a real bloodhound. Siberian bloodhounds and Great Danes were most in demand. One Philadelphia raiser hired out ugly mastiffs, and his throughbred Danish hound, "Koloss," was reputed to be the largest in the world. Sired by a renowned Ulmer dog, "Faust," winner of the first prize at Vienna in 1885, and a prize bitch, "Minka," it was well trained for fording the swollen "Ohio River." At three years of age, its height to the shoulder was 3 feet less 2 inches; to the head, 3 feet and 8 inches; and the length from the nose to the tip of the tail was 7 feet.

The average Siberian hounds used by the Tommers weighed 150 to 170 pounds when aged 11 to 13 months. Anthony & Ellis, in the Spring of 1881, imported six Siberian hounds, the heaviest weighing 230 pounds and the lightest 170. During the Fall of 1885, E. O. Rogers advertised that he had "the only $5,000 pack of trained man-hunting Cuban bloodhounds, including the dog 'Emperor,' the largest Cuban bloodhound in America." F. E. Griswold, in 1889, had as the star of his kennel, "Tip," so called because it measured 7 feet, 4 inches from tip to tip, and weighed 246 pounds. One of the dog's accomplishments was to stand with all fours on the floor, and drink from a pail placed on a table of the usual height.

The Tom managers had their eyes cocked at the larger and more ferocious species, those with insatiate maws — heavy, undershot, and red. Provided the dogs were large enough, audiences felt they were getting their money's worth. Rare, indeed, were the occasions when even the oldest Tom show frequenters could remember ever seeing a *genuine* bloodhound, for it was really a small, inoffensive-looking creature, its deep-throated baying impressive, but little given to biting. Managers rationalized that real bloodhounds are manhunters, but other large dogs are woman-hunters — quite suitable for Eliza.

The dogs became so famous that they received complimentary press notices. A Russian poodle, "Andy," the main feature in E. O. Rogers' company at the Detroit Opera House in 1881, was called before the curtain — an honor seldom extended to canines. There were wonderful stories told about them, too: how they discovered fires backstage, spreading the alarm; how they saved Tommers from robbery. On one occasion marauders stole the watch, clothes, and cash of Fred R. Wren, who started after 'em with a gun. A week later, he recollected to his sorrow that he could have used his Tom show hounds in tracking down the thieves.

Once a Tom manager felt that a glorious tradition was ruthlessly violated by his rivals, and he decided to get the real thing — authentic bloodhounds. When he exhibited them, in the street parade, the mournful expression characteristic of the breed struck all spectators to the soul. The hounds bore an ineffable melancholia in their large, pouchy eyes, and each shed a lugubrious tear; their baggy, drooping jowls seemed to hold twin quids of cut plug, and their long ears hung down as from exhaustion. Never had they seen such dejected-looking animals, and it was hard to believe that these timid dogs could pursue Eliza. Word soon passed around that the show was a fake.

CHAPTER XIV

THE DOUBLE MAMMOTH

*Mr. Haley and Tom jogged onward in their wagon,
each, for a time, absorbed in his own reflections. Now,
the reflections of two men sitting side by side are a
curious thing — seated on the same seat, having the
same eyes, ears, hands and organs of all sorts, and having
passing before their eyes the same objects — it is wonderful what a variety we shall find in these same reflections!*
— from the Novel

SOMETIMES PERFORMANCES of the old perennial verged
on absurdity, and the wonder was that it still survived. Once
the sudden illness of the leading actress made it impossible
for her to appear, and the stage manager enacted Topsy,
although he wore a heavy, walrus moustache. Again, when
Maud Temple could not go on, Topsy's lines were effectively
rendered *offstage* by the other actors when not otherwise
occupied before the footlights, which undoubtedly must have
created as eerie an effect as the voice of Hamlet's father.

Out of many awkward situations, glaringly inconsistent
at the time, one was later incorporated into the drama, to
the delight of thousands of Tom show spectators. There are
many claimants to the honor of first conceiving a double
Lawyer Marks. Thomas F. English insisted that he had
popularized the idea in C. H. Smith's Mammoth Double
Tom's Cabin Combination, portraying *one* of the Markses
for nine whole years. "Once one Marks was regarded as
sufficient," he said later, "but an extra Marks appeared to
me as a sort of novelty, and it was only tried as an experi-

ment, and it seemed to make a hit at once. Now you very rarely see an *Uncle Tom's Cabin* company without two Markses. One seems to be necessary to the other, and the double presentation of the quaint character has caused a lot of fun about the country."

So much for Mr. English. Others maintained that they were the true originators, among them Edward R. Salter and Charles Fisher, the latter contending, "I have always that distinction, or rather have that sin to answer for." During the season of 1875-76, three simultaneous revivals of *Uncle Tom's Cabin* were playing at three Philadelphia theatres — at the Chestnut, Roland Reed was the Marks; at Woods' Museum, William Davidge had the part; while at the Arch Street Opera House, Fisher attempted it. Fisher had a dispute with his manager, C. W. Bolton, over salary — the "ghost" failing to walk. Although fully made up, he refused to go on. The manager sent at once for Will Kensil, who assumed the character, and neither actor was aware of the other's presence until both stepped from their dressing rooms, and met in the passage-way, much like the two Dromios in *A Comedy of Errors*. Fisher explained to Kensil, who then declined the part until the former's claim was settled satisfactorily. Sarcastically, the manager told the altruistic Kensil, "For all I care, both of you can go on and play Marks."

Which they did, much to the amusement of the patrons! They played the double Marks for the balance of the engagement. Fisher, in backing his claim, refers to the New York *Clipper* of that year, insisting that its Philadelphia critic, Doc Wade, had commented on this unusual proceeding. But when we verify this, we find that the amusing incident occurred not in 1876 but in 1882; its actual inception was on April 12th. The review appeared ten days later, with a slightly different story, to the effect that only during a portion of the play was the audience regaled by the sight of two Markses, for Kensil soon stepped out, leaving the field to Fisher.

In the Days of the Doubling Fever

It was all due, however, to events elsewhere in the amusement field. In the past there had been a little "Jim Crow" to a big "Jim Crow," as in the case of the four-year-old Joseph Jefferson and T. D. Rice; also, a "Little Mose" to the "Big Mose" of F. S. Chanfrau. These were really intended for the introduction of burbling prodigies, and limited to a few performances. The novelty was emphasized in the Fall of 1879, when the Siege of Paris Music Hall, in Boston, was converted into a theatre, and John Pemberton Smith presented the historic play with a Lilliputian cast.

Then when the two circus magnates, P. T. Barnum and J. A. Bailey, combined shows in 1881, offering two circuses for the price of one, with twice as many clowns, twice as many performers, twice as many animals, the consolidation intrigued their closest competitors, the Tom show managers. Each Tom manager had been zealous in proving his company worthy of the title "Ideal," but when Barnum began to feature the elephant Jumbo, the rival term "Mammoth" was at once adopted. Probably, Barnum's "Carolina Twins," two colored girls linked together Siamese-twins fashion, may have suggested the idea of double Topsies. Furthemore, the average Tom show manager owned more than one company on the road, and frequently these made a junction that enabled them to combine forces to vanquish an immediate rival. The double Tom show was inevitable after the admission prices reached the lowest level of ten, twent', and thirt', which now became, "Everything double but the prices!"

The new style in Tom shows was hit upon by C. H. Smith, in Boston, who exposed it to the public for the first time in April, 1881, under the resounding name of C. H. Smith's Ideal Double Mammoth Uncle Tom's Cabin Company. It brought many a headache to sundry typesetters, particularly in the tour through Pennsylvania where Smith visited such towns as Manayunk and Conshohocken. His innovation included two Topsies, two Markses — Marks, Sr., and Marks, Jr., — three donkeys and ten Mammoth Siberian hounds. The wayward Topsies were No. 1, "with Songs and

Dances," and No. 2, "the Sunflower of the South, who introduced Cuckoo Song and Reel Dance." The critics nicknamed the enterprise, "C. H. Smith's Boston Alphabetical Quadrilateral Mammoth Double All-Star Uncle Tom's Cabin Combination." They complained that there were two Markses, two Topsies — but only one C. H. Smith!

The uniqueness of twin Topsies and a brace of knockabout Markses appealed to audiences, and other managers seized upon C. H. Smith's idea. The "barn scrubbers," too, had many bitter experiences in the past of booking a one-night stand, eagerly anticipating "the rhubarb engagement," only to find the town covered with a rival's still-wet posters; now they could combine troupes into an elaborate affair, treating the town to two Evas, two Topsies, twin Elizas, and a duplex whipping by bloodthirsty Simon Legrees to a couple of clogging Uncle Toms! One Topsy accompanied with banjo the other's song and dance, amicably dividing the lines. They chased each other in a game of tag, and played practical jokes on each other or on someone else. The firm of Marks & Marks, Lawyers, found one of them devoted to pantomime as his partner did all the talking; often they dispensed with this specialization, and as is the case of most law firms, both partners spoke simultaneously. They would announce, in the same breath: "Our names are Marks, Sr. and Jr; we are lawyers — and good ones; here are our cards. . . ." Marks, Jr., got a very cold bath in "the River," and Marks, Sr., disconsolate, sang the "Where Has My Darling Gone?" parody. Tableau.

Later, other characters acquired schizoid personalities, and alter egos followed closely on their heels.

The double conception afforded a Roman holiday for the critics, who found it a double dose. Some saw it as a game of cards, where the dealer held two Topsies, two Markses, two Jacks, and six hounds; others contended the stars were dual and sextette, with the support fractional.

However, the managers did not worry much about it, for they drew crowds sufficiently at each double mammoth performance for *two* "S. R. O." signs.

Each Tom troupe called itself the only legitimate mammoth on the road, nor did it spare the billboards. The interminable titles reached halfway across the country, as for example, Peck & Fursman's Mammoth Spectacular Double Uncle Tom's Cabin Combination. Another, which awed the natives, was Anthony & Ellis' World Famous Double Mammoth Ideal Uncle Tom's Cabin Company. The local editors, to conserve space, abbreviated their titles, and the following enigma is gleaned from one newspaper: "B.I.D.M.U.T.C.CO. TO S.R.O. AT 1,2,3." Unraveled, it meant that the Boston Ideal Double Mammoth Uncle Tom's Cabin Company played to Standing Room Only at 10, 20 and 30 cents. As most troupes called themselves "The Mammoth Ideal Uncle Tom's Cabin Company," there was great confusion, but one manager in Pittsburgh was more definite, for during the Spring of 1888 he offered the world, "Harris' Own Mammoth —"

The complexity grew, for with further consolidation of Tom companies and with the typical Yankee fetish for bigness, they became "Alphabetical Quadruplical." The Topsies, Markses and Toms were tripled — then quadrupled! They were four-ring circuses. Anachronistically, the full title was no longer used, and succinctly it was called a "Tom show."

"The Barnum of them all!" Stetson advertised his double-headed troupe of bipeds and quadrupeds. His noon parade was a triumphal procession. At the head were two expert drum majors leading a line each of richly uniformed brass bands, one white, one colored; the first executed lightning and intricate movements with a musket, while the other deftly handled the baton. The star was the ponderous dog "Carlos," who chilled potential theatregoers to the marrow. The players appeared in character, the two Topsies and two Markses inseparable in the line of march; there were two Toms, one white, one a Negro. The street specialties introduced the Lone Star Quartette, the African Mandolin Students, the trick donkey, Eva's pony, and also the only colored Glockenspiel player in the world. There was an allegorical wagon, upon whose gold-leafed sides cherubim were elaborately carved; Eva and her father rode in the costliest carriage, hard-wood with heavy silver mountings, a shimmering thing of beauty. A calliope tooted the rest of the day, piping Foster melodies from the steam piano, an infectious reminder of the performance in the evening. The canvas on the grounds seated four thousand people. The tenting season would usually end in Indiana, where the horses were sold, the wagons stored away, and the company immediately reorganized for the winter, proceeding to play opera houses without the loss of a day.

"The Very Largest Tom Show Ever on Earth!" boasted Sutton's Grand Double Company. The owner, Dick P. Sutton, introduced a vast number of specialties between the acts, promising: *"2—Entire and Complete Shows—2."* The troupe numbered thirty-five, besides the pack of hounds, four Shetland ponies, and a couple of donkeys. When they traveled through the Middle West, a sixty-foot sleeping car held them all: In front were the upper and lower berths for the actors, with the ponies just beyond; the donkeys were stalled in the back, close to the dining room and the kitchen; most of the dogs were in the "basement" of the car, and the remainder near the ponies.

In 1888, when Fred Stone was about fifteen, he and his brother Eddie, two years younger, played the two Topsies in this supercolossal road show. Their father was along, bearing the unctuous title, "Master of Transportation." The two boys would march in the noon parades, topped with plug hats. Fred had so many fist fights with village children during the parades that the manager thought it best to dress him as Simon Legree, with a villainous-looking moustache and bull whip. Between the acts, the Stone boys did a back somersault over a donkey and bloodhound, keeping time with the music all the while. As Topsies they wore stuffed black union suits that fitted very badly.

This same Sutton used a bit of strategy in his overnight cross-country "jumps." When the show car was hooked to the end of the train, the conductor would begin to count noses, but was reluctant to venture into the sleeping quarters to check up because the sly manager would purposely provoke his dogs.

"Keep away!" Sutton warned. "Those ferocious dogs take a nip at a Tommer's posterity on every occasion. And you're no exception!"

However, a long hop over Sunday made it more difficult to keep out that railroad functionary. An actor would stand guard at the door, and when the zealous conductor appeared, he at once heralded the news to the other players. Thereupon ten of the smallest members found themselves precipitated into upper berths; Fred and his brother, both diminutive, were always of that number. They remained concealed until the conductor departed, and if he happened to be a garrulous type the shut-ins had an uncomfortable time of it. Thus, the manager paid only twenty-five fares and carried thirty-five people.

Yet none would ever suspect "Uncle Dick" Sutton's strong sense of economy from his personal appearance. He weighed well over two hundred pounds, poised on stumpy legs, and encased in a voluminous chinchilla overcoat, with large fur collar. A high silk hat and an ebony cane, with a massive gold head, gleamed through a rift of the smoke of his quickly-consumed little cigars.

Working for him was not profitable, as many of his troupe discovered. The highest paid was the advance agent, fifteen dollars a week. Once Sutton hired a new actress for Aunt Ophelia, who arrived bringing her young son along. Although fifteen years old or so, the boy was so undersized for his age that Sutton fitted him out with a wig of golden curls. "You will be our Little Eva," Sutton said to the boy in a breezy fashion.

One day the mother approached Sutton with a request for fifteen cents. The wary manager retorted in a hurt voice: "What for?"

"Well, to tell the truth," confessed the parent, "Willie has got to be shaved or he cannot play Eva tonight."

"Can't help it," was the admonition. "No money in sight today."

"Very well," countered the mother, with strong maternal passion, "you will either have Willie shaved—or change the bill to *Ingomar the Barbarian!*"

Another time, the parsimonious manager of the much-vaunted "largest Tom show ever on earth," discovered on arrival in a little, backwoods town that his lithograph posters were strangely missing He immediately started looking for the owner of the local opera house. At last he found him, busily engaged in a nearby saw-mill: "Yes, sir," he said, "I built that house out of boards I sawed right here in this mill." Sutton testily told him to keep his opera house and his mill, that he wouldn't play there that night, that he was going to the next town.

"What's the matter?" asked the carpenter.

"Matter!" snorted Sutton. "What did you do with all those lithographs I sent you to put up?"

"Them what?" asked the mill owner, squinting in perplexity.

"Lithographs! Lithographs!" shrieked the Tom manager.

"Oh, you mean them colored pictures?"

"Yes, them colored pictures," mocked Sutton.

"Well," recalled the other, with a patronizing smile, "I sent them around to all the houses and had 'em hung up in the parlors. Mighty nice pictures they were!"

This knocked the wind completely out of Sutton's avoirdupois, his jaw sagged, and he garumphed a vague promise to think it over. But as he left, he saw an odd sight in the street: Many of the citizens were armed with chairs, and he inquired what was up.

"Why," answered one, "we are carrying them over to the opera house. You see, we need a lot of extra seats as the house has all been sold for the next three days."

Now a pair of short legs frenetically propelled their possessor back to the saw-mill. He tore up the stairs, burst into the room, and with double-voiced vigor proclaimed that everything was all right. He would play that night!

While Tom managers were doubling all efforts in casting, trundling out an untold number of specialities, nothing was overlooked by them. The spectacular fever infected the rival managers all at once, and they made the Apotheosis of the Gentle Eva (as it was called in the playbills) an attraction beyond description. The closing tableau became the epitome of the drama. It was not to be wondered at, for could anything surpass "the Pearly Portals of the Golden City," as given in the Hebraic description of Paradise in the Book of Revelations of St. John? Tom audiences caught a glimpse of Heaven nightly, and all for a dime!

This gorgeous illuminated pageant was first given by G. C. Howard in 1852 to meet the devout attitude of New England audiences, but Mrs. Stowe's own description suggested its use to him: "Over the head of the bed was an alabaster bracket, on which a beautiful sculptured angel stood with drooping wings, holding out a crown of myrtle-leaves. From this depended, over the bed, light curtains of rose-colored gauze, striped with silver..." This was effected by lifting Eva from the death bed with invisible piano wire; she floated in the midst of a hovering celestial choir, enclosed in an intermixture of gauze drops, which were raised in turn, and enhanced with calcium lighting.

The experience of Izola Forrestor, as Eva, in Minneapolis, reveals typically how some itinerant Tom companies handled the Ascension. The death scene was always exciting to her "because of the acrobatic dexterity it required for one to die with 'Love, joy, peace' on one's lips, be covered decently with a sheet, and then wriggle out from under it while the group around the bed concealed one's movements from the audience and sang a loving dirge...Just here I would slip on the floor and creep offstage to where a ladder was set on a table close to the backdrop. On top of the ladder Eva had to stand with a wreath of roses in her hand to hold over Uncle Tom's head as he knelt on some sort of scaffolding. Suddenly the great circle of light would flash on for the transformation scene and the violins begin their agitated tremolo. Mr. Sterling played Uncle Tom and would mutter at me under his breath, 'Don't wabble, Zola! For God's sake, don't wabble!' "

Thus the earliest conscious experience of many other young actresses was of a trip to heaven nightly, according to schedule, up the backdrop. They recollected, likewise, an iron footrest and bands of iron around the waist, covered by a long white shroud, while they clasped their hands and assumed an angelic expression as, slowly and creakingly, they were hoisted into the beautiful blue. They were dimly conscious, too, of sobs and sighs in the audience below, and remembered hazily that Uncle Tom lay on the floor....

But the final scene, the Apocalypse, put audiences into the seventh Heaven of delight. Scenic artists, to bring out its innate grandeur, were guided by Mrs. Stowe's description of Eva and Tom in the garden, watching an intensely golden sunset which the novelist compared to a blaze of glory, with the water another sky, and the white-winged vessels like so many spirits. Eva reads in her Bible—" 'And I saw a sea of glass, mingled with fire,' " and asks Tom where the new Jerusalem is, to which he answers, "O, up in the clouds, Miss Eva." "Look in those clouds!" she exclaims, "they look like great gates of pearl; and you can see beyond them — far, far off — it's all gold. Tom, sing about 'spirits bright.' "

When Jarrett & Palmer's "European Uncle Tom's Cabin Combination" was brought to this country in 1880, George Fawcett Rowe had rewritten the drama in nine acts, which surpassed all others scenically. The spectacle opened at

Booth's Theatre for the Christmas holidays, with playbills ringing in this new note: *"The audience will kindly remain seated until after the curtain descends upon the allegorical tableau representing Mansions in the Skies."* The Apocalypse was painted in dead gold, while an electric light — used for the first time on the stage — afforded the necessary glow of celestial effulgence. Each evening, as the last intermission ended, with the promised Gates Ajar about to open wide, there were heard calls for those lagging in the lounge, "Everybody down for the Sweet Bye-and-Bye!"

De Wolf Hopper fondly recalled an Apotheosis which he beheld in 1897. Rehearsing in Pittsburgh, one day, his company was dismissed earlier than usual. He and Herbert Cripps left for their hotel, but in passing the Grand Opera House were attracted by the promising lithographs, and decided to drop in on the old stand-by. The manager, George Edeson, father of Robert Edeson, recognized them as they were about to buy tickets. He insisted that his guests sit way down front, stressing with a foray of adjectives that the Apotheosis of the Gentle Eva was the greatest of its kind. Hopper described the Legree of Harry W. A. Whitecar as a hirsute wonder, for Whitecar had difficulty, that night, with his horsehair moustache, which was tethered with a metal clip to his own brush lip growth. In the Cassy scene he adjusted it repeatedly, but the horsetail escaped from its corral, falling before the footlights, and Legree kept his back turned to the audience for the rest of the scene.

At last the Apotheosis finale! Three tiers of profile pink and white clouds, edged with gold and silver spangles, were planted on the stage floor. The voices of a celestial choir issued from behind the gauze-covered perforations of the canvas drop, then the floodlights backstage were turned on, and the holes became little golden stars twinkling through the glow — revealing a winged Eva — with a covey of attendant angels suspended in midair with piano wire, all swaying as if in a gentle Spring breeze. And in the foremost rank of the profile clouds, Uncle Tom knelt with uplifted arms. Then a golden shower drenched Uncle Tom, a scenic effect startlingly new to Hopper. Before he could turn to utter his professional admiration to Cripps, the shower of gold underwent a sudden transmutation: a rain of pebbles rattled like hail on Uncle Tom's shellacked wig! One of the sandbag counterweights that supported the attendant angels had sprung a leak. Hopper's admiration now was directed toward Uncle Tom. "Walter Edwards, like a good trouper," he commented afterwards, "rose with a sprightliness unexpected in a dying man, moved very cautiously over the first row of nimbus clouds, hands still upraised to Eva's paradise, then fell on his knees again and proceeded with his part." When the performance was over, George Edeson's head protruded from a wing with a look of expectancy as he addressed Hopper and Cripps gravely: "What did you think of our spectacular performance?"

The shining gates of the New Jerusalem, with their blaze of colored light, were ever imaginative triumphs. Once their very realism stampeded a Pennsylvania audience with fatal results. Stetson's company was playing in Johnstown, on December 10, 1889, when during the last act a spectator shouted, "Fire!" Panic-stricken at the cry, there was a wild rush for the doors. Many leaped from the top gallery to the parquette thirty feet below, resulting in the death of ten and the serious injury of forty.

In later years the final tableau underwent a change, which won immediate favor. Barbour and Harkins, in 1897, introduced a different transformation scene: Lincoln reading the Emancipation Proclamation. Often men in blue, carrying the American flag, came out and sang in the grand finale. During the Spanish-American War the uniforms were modernized with the spirit of the times.

Spectacular effects were not confined to the ending alone. The force and sweep of the Mississippi panorama, in the middle of the play, became a glorious sight. The early wandering troupes were sadly limited, with but a few

When Tom Shows Outrivaled the Circus

set-pieces which went around over and over again; so that
the Mississippi scenery consisted, apparently, of the same
flatboat in the same bay, chased by the same hills and trees
at two minute intervals. As for the ice on the Ohio River,
there wasn't enough to fill a family refrigerator. The wealth-
ier Tom show managers, on the other hand, used the mechanical agitation of realistically painted waves, and Tom jumped
boldly from a practical end-wheel steamboat to rescue Eva.

— 319 —

Once Leon Washburn decided to have genuine ice for the Ohio scene. The colored characters in this production were the synthetic kind, whose burnt cork came off when exposed to the damp, and spectators saw Simon Legree whip a "darky" who turned white under the ordeal. Washburn returned to ice painted on scenery.

With everything double in the first-class productions, a race between two steamboats, likewise, magnetized audiences. Peck & Fursman's, in 1888, introduced the historical regatta between the Robert E. Lee and Natchez. The mechanical models were prepared from plans reputedly authentic: steam whistles, bells, lights, etc., with the collision and explosion of the Natchez the most complete piece of stagecraft hitherto accomplished. Other Tom companies depicted either the race between the Baltic and the Eclipse, or the battle of the Monitor and the Merrimac.

The use of gunpowder became double-barreled. The lavish expenditure of saltpeter, charcoal and sulphur stepped up the play so that the gallery yelled and cheered as if they were celebrating the very signing of the Declaration of Independence.

The average Tom show, moreover, advertised as heavily as two combined circuses. When the play arrived, the lobby was draped in old rose velvet, with pastel portraits of the principals in oval frames, lending a quaint atmosphere. Walls were dressed up with cotton boils, smilax or Spanish moss, to suggest a Southern setting. The box office was often built like a miniature log cabin, with strings of leeks, bunches of tobacco, red peppers and corn hanging from the ceiling, coonskins nailed on the door, and the ticket seller in character; or it resembled an auction block, with Topsy a most unruly and laugh-provoking human chattel; or again, it had a simple trellis, painted white and draped with artificial magnolias, screening its business-like facade. A small museum of slavery relics was on display: Civil War uniforms, pistols, slave shackles, original slave whips (blood-stained in the seams), old posters offering rewards for runaways.

branding irons, spiked dog collars, the "original" Bible read
by Uncle Tom... Two-fold was the treat when Eva appeared
at the curb with her Shetland pony, making it bow right and
left to the crowd's delight. *That* doubled the size of the
potential audiences!

Tom actors kept doubling until bathed in perspiration,
and it took over five hours to do justice to the full play,
"making it coherent," as many managers insisted. The
drama's chief drawback was its extreme length, while new
mechanical devices became so spectacular that by contrast
the well-worn dialogue sounded shoddy. It looked now as
if the rich promoters had mortgaged not only the cabin of
Uncle Tom but also the St. Claire and Legree plantations.
Augmented by jubilee and bloodhound trimmings, such a
showpiece was perhaps too copiously freighted, but how animated nevertheless!

Often the double-header was cut down to regulation
size. If two Topsies were promised, only one showed up,
who overplayed the character sufficiently for two. Or an
old stickler would advertise that he was offering no double-
jointed, back-action snap, but a straight, legitimate company,
with *U. T. C.* as it should be — "correct in every detail." Such a manager relied on the old Chatham Square
days. But always the double-mammoth managers carried
the day, vigorously defending their duplicate versions on the
grounds that Shakespeare had used the very same technique,
with three witches instead of one in *Macbeth.* Further, *Uncle
Tom's Cabin,* in its three distinct plots, was comparable to a
triptych, and doubling certainly made everything twice as
intriguing! The billboards of the nation compelled attention
for several decades with the reiteration that *Uncle Tom's
Cabin* was to the hall show what Barnum's was to the tent
— the Greatest on Earth!

The pattern of our American folk play was determined
always by the resources of the particular troupe. At the

same time that the ancient was put on in fine style, the sable hero was frequently given a natural outdoor setting for his woes, a practice dating back to the salad days of the '50s, when it was seen on boats or barges plying along New Philadelphia, Canal Dover, Ohio, and around Cincinnati and Portsmouth. The spectators brought their own cushions and blankets, and sat on the banks, and the stages on the canal boats were lit up with whale oil torches.

When C. H. Smith's company came to the Park Garden in Providence, Rhode Island, during the summer of 1882, they transformed one side of the lake into a Southern plantation, complete with cotton fields, Negro quarters, St. Clair's mansion, etc. Poor Eliza escaped across the park lake on a raft, with a pack of nineteen hounds swimming after her!

A half-dozen years later, Sam Lucas and Kate Partington projected Tom and Topsy in a company that booked its route according to the public parks of the cities. In Boston, a portion of the Oakland Garden lawn was utilized as a cotton field, plants set out, and the lake so arranged as to do double duty for the Ohio River.

The "special natural" setting for Eliza's flight became an obsession with Tom managers, and sometimes it led to serious consequences. In the Spring of 1890, L. W. Washburn, manager of Stetson's company in Chicago, boarded a steamer for St. Ignace, Michigan. As it was foggy, with the ice running in the straits, the captain refused to sail until the following morning. This greatly irritated Washburn, who called him a coward. The enraged captain struck Washburn, whereupon the Tom manager returned the blow with his gold-headed cane, incapacitating him. And when the burly second mate interfered, he, too, was knocked insensible. Washburn was arrested, and his fame spread as "the hero of St. Ignace." At the trial, the captain admitted striking the first blow, but the Tom manager insisted in court, "Over a period of years everyone of my Elizas ventured out on more dangerous crossings!"

In 1882, the play saw still another phase. H. Wayne Ellis believed that the novel had appropriate material for an opera. He sought out the composer, Caryl Florio, and the result of their joint labors opened at the Chestnut Street Opera House in Philadelphia. "Florio at first didn't tackle kindly to my libretto," said Ellis before that dismal opening of May 22nd. "He said he's been an actor, had played every male part in *Uncle Tom,* and was sick of it." This was immediately borne out in his music; but for the laughing quartette in the third act, it caught all the spirit of funeral dirges. To provide a part for the prima donna soprano, a St. Louis girl, Letitia Louise Fritch (never before on any stage) a new character—Rosa, an octoroon—was made most prominent. The novel barely alluded to her as one of St. Clair's servants.

With the exception of one humorous act — Topsy in her time-worn antics — the whole composition was lugubrious and dreary. One critic held some hope for Uncle Tom if only Mr. Florio could compose the music all over again, with Topsy as the prima donna and Phineas Fletcher in the tenor role. On May 27th the first attempt of the famous play in opera form petered out.

The Holman Opera Company, on June 26th of the following year, offered another arrangement, by Harrison Millard, at the Zoological Gardens in Toronto. The libretto adhered more closely to the well-known play than did Ellis's, but the opera was withdrawn shortly. Later it was better mounted, yet proved far from successful. Detroit had an opportunity to see it in August, 1886.

The Gilbert Opera Company produced a third version at the Music Hall, Lynn (Mass.), on October 5th of the same year. The music was by George Lowell Tracy, to Dexter Smith's libretto, which had enough of Mrs. Stowe's old-time story to merit its title. The usual severity of grand opera was relieved here by an entertaining duet by the two lawyers, D. Webster Marks and C. Cushing Marks.

In fact, not a single attempt at the formal opera style

The Next Thing in American Grand Opera.

Uncle Tom's Cabin.

appealed to the American audiences. One manager went as far as to promise, "Two Uncle Toms and a ballet of Little Evas," but nobody was willing to take him up.

It was really paradoxical, for the average Tom show comprised a series of songs, with audiences applauding what might be called "operatic parts." Nor did it seem at all incongruous for a child (as the very breath left her frail body) to sing her parting words to her sweet papa, who in turn chorused back his anguish. Her last bell note still vibrant in the air, Little Eva was then wont to swing upward in a golden nimbus of glory, and a score or more of husky darkies would fall on their knees en masse in two rows across the stage, the very walls of the St. Clair estate quivering as they lifted their powerfully deep voices. American audiences could accept all that in a whacker of a Tom show, yet strange to say, they wouldn't tolerate it in the operatic form.

Furthermore, the dignified operas had none of the camp-meeting airs indissolubly associated with the crude Tom shows; there, perhaps, lay the crux of it all. It should not

Frau *Butz as Little Eva.*

Monsieur *Rumbleround as Uncle Tom :* Herr
Andreas Pimple as Simon Legree.

Puck

be forgotten that with the Tomming furor of the '70s came
the popularization of jubilee singers, and the phrase, "with
all the sacred music," was rather conspicuous in the playbills. As there were two deathbed scenes in the drama, some
sort of light entertainment had to relieve the tension, and
the indigenous song and breakdown fitted in here to advantage. The stage directions of the average Tom show were
of such an elastic nature that the drama could be halted at
the most auspicious moments for solos, choruses, breakdowns, etc., for the necessary atmosphere. Topsy and
Marks made their every entrance to music, and Legree struck
poor Tom to crashing chords. Music was such an integral
part of the play that troupes, before starting out, devoted
one day to the dramatic rehearsal and one day to the music
rehearsal; the second was called "the long day," for *Uncle
Tom's Cabin* held the record for music cues.

What a wealth of songs was built up around the talents
found in the Tom shows! Carrie Swain, especially, popu-

larized Alfred Singer's "Topsy Whopsy" from San Francisco to Australia. Carrie had a remarkable voice, executing the verses in double mammoth fashion, in what playbills set forth as "Two distinct voices, beginning in low E flat and running to G, thus proving that she has a complete register of two and three-quarter octaves, from low E flat to high C."

About 1894, an operetta appeared in England, with lyrics by George R. Sims and delightful airs by Ivan Caryll. Then the old-time favorite cropped up in a new guise of music in Kansas City, at the Willis Wood Theatre, in February, 1903. Curiously, not a single song here was composed by the author of the opera, but was done entirely with the cumulative prop tunes of the older Tom shows. The curtain rose on a cottonfield background, the hands giving the opening chorus, "With Joy Again We're Meeting." Uncle Tom, in the centre, when informed that he was sold, sang very touchingly, "What Have I Done, Oh, Massa Dear, That I Must Now Be Sold?" Eliza came in with her child, announcing that she was going to run away because she had been sold, but not before she had sung, "They Shall Not Take My Child Away." On her parting from Uncle Tom and Aunt Chloe, an invisible chorus struck up "My Old Kentucky Home." Little Eva died to the tune of "Nearer, My God To Thee," sung by twenty kneeling slaves, and St. Clair admonished to the music of the old Methodist hymn, "The Doxology." This, with other well-known tunes, comprised the first half. At that point, the author of the opera, either tired of the novelty or wishing to serve up the proper proportion of comic relief, capitulated, and the remainder of the opera was devoted to vaudeville turns by the company. Lawyer Marks sang to Topsy the old-fashioned, "Has Your Mother Any More Like You?" to which the dark minx answered with her "Calico Wrapper" song and dance. And so on, until the last act, when Uncle Tom died as in thousands of past Tom shows, with the stage darkening and his vision of Little Eva in a halo of brilliant light, while the orchestra struck up "The Holy City."

When Uncle Tom Married Little Eva

*Perkins D. Fisher Added Years to His Makeup,
and May Hillman as Eva Tried To Be as Young
as Possible. They Were Really Man and Wife.*

Schoolhoused, church-socialed, and townhalled through the years, the drama underwent every conceivable variation. Often actual experiences in the Tommers' lives suggested new possibilities. During the summer of 1890, the newspapers carried the account of a Mr. H. G. St. Clair, an actor, who drowned at Toronto, after his rowboat was capsized by a steamer. The public was convinced that this was a new adaptation ballyhooed by an advance agent. Not only was there similarity in names, but the audiences remembered vividly Eva's fall overboard from the La Belle Riviere; further, the drowned actor left a widow, Maude De Orville, traveling just then with W. N. Adams' Pavilion U. T. C. company.

Earlier the same year, the press publicized the matrimonial knot between Lawyer Marks and Little Eva, at Oregon, Mo. This referred to the marriage of M. B. Haws and Kittie Gibson, who interpreted the respective roles in Gibson's company.

Then there was a time when Uncle Tom married Little Eva! Perkins D. Fisher, who added years to his Tom make-up, while May Hillman as Eva tried to appear as young as possible, were husband and wife in private life. What a variation for the play, the one possibility remaining: Uncle Tom kills Simon Legree, and marries Little Eva! But this is not as fantastic as one may imagine, for the great Victor Hugo actually used that situation in the *Hunchback of Notre Dame*, where the little heroine commingles her ashes, many years later, with the loyal hunchback's. It was a spiritual union of the two, in the grave, similar to what Tom audiences saw in the Apocalypse scene.

CHAPTER XV

GRAND PAVILIONS OF THE NINETIES

> *Don't see no donkey or dogs in sight,*
> *Oh, thought 'twas Uncle Tom tonight...*
> *But a feller as alus does well here,*
> *An' comes about three times, a year,*
> *Is Uncle Tom. By Jove! it's funny*
> *T' see that feller rake in money!*
> — Ezra P. Kendall's "Effort"

THE WORLD'S COLUMBIA EXPOSITION, the high mark of the Nineties, was a year late in getting under way in Chicago. When it opened in 1893, visitors had an opportunity to gaze at the original cabin of Uncle Tom! However, they soon became rather sceptical about it, for so many run-down Southern habitations purported to be Tom's. After the Exposition, the historical cabin was left standing for a half-dozen years at the north end of the Libby Prison grounds; then the prison site was cleared for the location of a large auditorium, and the "original" cabin demolished.

The Fair appealed to the artistic impulses of the nation, but the greater portion of spectators were captivated by the "Oriental" insinuations of Little Egypt and her dance, which saved the Exposition from bankruptcy. Soon, in Tom companies all over the country, innumerable Topsies executed a take-off of Little Egypt, in lieu of the wild breakdown. Lawyer Marks, too, offered his usual spoofing in the auction scene, but each time departed for the wings with his arms in that classic Serpentine pose. A legion of brisk Lawyer Markses now made their exits that way, for it heightened every "gag," and convulsed audiences.

During the year of the Exposition, L. R. Stockwell, a famous Marks, evolved a combination of colored pugilism and the drama. The crowd that turned out at his San Francisco theatre, on February 27th, signalled its new approaching vogue. The colored Peter Jackson, heavyweight boxing

Puck

As It Will Have To Be Played If Johnson Wins

Uncle Tom (to Simon Legree)—*Did ah heah yo' say, white man, dat yo' done own Me, body an' soul? Huh?*

champion of Australia, enacted Uncle Tom. After he had moved all with, "May de Lawd ha' mercy on my soul!" he was sold to Legree, but there the drama would halt, and Charles D. ("Parsons") Davies, the well-known sporting figure, would step before the footlights, and announce: "Now, ladies and gentlemen, Peter Jackson will box three friendly and scientific rounds to show how he will wrest the pugilistic crown from 'Gentleman Jim' Corbett!" Then the curtain went up on a stage set with a roped arena: Uncle Tom stepped out of character, having shed his white wig, and now dancing gingerly about in fighting trunks, he turned boxer long enough to whale the living daylights out of his sparring partner, Joe Choynski, who had enacted Shelby. Thereupon Jackson went back to Legree's plantation and the whip. The lively bout drew particularly the sports addicts who admired Uncle Tom's manly art of self-defense, but the fashionable element also turned out, especially in Boston, where the overflowing houses consisted largely of ladies.

Many contended that it was a dramatic mistake not to engage a boxer for the part of Legree and let Uncle Tom knock him out between prayers. One manager, Joseph W. Goodrich, for a number of years identified with a wagon show covering Connecticut and New York, acted on this inspiration. One Fall he organized a Tom show known as Downing & Goodrich's, acquired as his big attraction John L. Sullivan, and toured the Eastern cities. As Legree, the famous champion's efforts were tempestuous. He played hard with his fist, and used up a half-dozen Toms in the course of a few weeks. The Tom lasting the longest was Ern G. Estey, for he artfully wore under his red flannel shirt a vest lined an inch thick with cotton padding; but even this protection proved at times inadequate against the "punch" lines which Sullivan put across. The idol had a habit of entertaining admirers in his dressing room, where many a heated discussion took place regarding the relative merits of the two fistic thespians, and if someone dared hint that Peter Jackson was the better actor, Sullivan vindicated himself by descending on his hapless Tom of the moment. The rough diamond, at any rate, was not lacking in finish, and he left nothing to the imagination. John L. remained with the Goodrich show as long as it was on the road, then it ran short of Toms.

In those days, indeed, if you wanted to succeed as an actor, you had to be a champion pugilist. Even the world of letters could not compete, as James Whitcomb Riley and Bill Nye learned to their chagrin. They were lecturing in a small town, and one night found themselves competing against the Stockwell company. The town was attracted to the antislavery play and the boxing match, so the Riley-Nye house was thinly populated. The two lecturers hurried up proceedings, got through early, and went to see the other show. They arrived just as the exhibition bout began. At the end of the drama, Mr. Stockwell met Bill Nye, and asked, "Well, how did you like Jackson?"

Thereupon Nye summed up the actor's powers: "I like him very well anatomically, but not Uncle Tom-ically."

In spite of criticism, Jackson worked hard at acting, and even wished to attempt Othello, inspired, no doubt, by that other notable colored Othello, Ira Aldridge, who won fame on the English stage. Jackson's ambition was a source of fun to his colleague, "Parson" Davies, who quipped that since many actors went abroad to acquire an Oxford accent, Jackson might "go to England to study the Negro dialect, and by mistake come back a cockney!" The "Parson" himself was rarely worried by the need of self-improvement. He enacted both the auctioneer and the fugitive Harris with the nonchalance expected of a man long in the public eye, but sometimes he was lax in his duties. In Baltimore they missed him at a performance, to discover later that he had slipped away to see the Corbett-Mitchell fight in Jacksonville.

Interrupting a performance for fight announcements was rather in high favor with Tom shows of those days. In the Spring of 1900, the Bailey Company, in Cincinnati, had Uncle Tom read from the stage the returns from the Jeffries-Corbett fight! Manager Bill Emmet, while holding forth at the Academy in Chicago, had a positive genius for this sort of intimate contact with audiences. He would stride right out on the stage during the play, regardless of what was transpiring at the moment. Once, while George Thompson was about to die, Bill breezed along and counselled, "Hold on, George, don't die yet — I want to make a few remarks to the audience." He delivered a short address, ending it as was his habit with, "Yours truly, Bill Emmet." Then he turned to the reprieved Uncle Tom, and waving his arm, said, "You can go on and die now, Thompson," and bowed himself out.

Chicago was the focal point of the country because of the Exposition, and also became recognized as the market for Tom actors. Many a Tom manager with an office on Halsted Street, whenever he needed an extra, would hang the part out on a fish-line; the first Tommer that chanced along nibbled at the bait, and was pulled in. At that time, one William T. Hall humorously suggested: "A movement is on foot, headed by Tony Denier, Jr., son of the old clown, to establish here a regularly organized Uncle Tom exchange to handle the Uncle Tom market, which is pretty active just now. For instance, an Uncle Tom manager bought a Simon Legree for $35 and sold him again the same afternoon for $40. At present the quotations are as follows: Uncle Toms, prime, $60; fair, $50; culls, $40; Little Evas, prime, $50; fair, $45; culls, $40; Legree, prime, $50; fair, $40; culls, $35; Marks, prime, $45; fair, $40; culls, $35. By prime are meant those who can double in brass and take care of live stock; fair are those who only double in brass, while culls are merely actors." Denier received letters from ever so many Evas and Uncle Toms asking to be listed in the proposed new exchange!

To be a true Tommer, however, one really had to master brass. Unfortunate was the troupe with only three mouthpieces in the band, for it had to watch out carefully and parade when the fewest people were on the street. Marks was required to blow a tuba, do the cooking, and understand the proper care of horses. A first-class Cute had to be a "snare drumatic virtuoso," and sell reserved seats as well as drive stakes, and, at times, was given the barber shop privilege to complement his income. The lady for Eliza was expected to have a little girl to play Eva. Often the little one was a slack-rope performer, and the night's entertainment culminated with Little Eva going to Heaven by walking the slack-wire. During the intermissions original specialties enlivened proceedings, including the Great Mocking Bird Imitator, lightning crayon sketches, a serpentine dancer, a colored drum major or drum drillist. The pure musicians, hired for "B. & O.", doubled in the

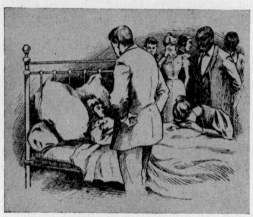

The Back Stage Tragedy

parade band and orchestra, and also bobbed up in small bits in the drama.

All engagements were arranged through correspondence; the Tommers were required to state "the lowest and honest" salary in their very first letters. As for qualifications, actors had to be gentlemen, sober and reliable; boozers and soreheads were warned to save their stamps. In return, the manager acknowledged that his Tom troupe was one of the largest outfits on the road — in fact, the greatest on earth! "Pecking and padding" (eating and sleeping) were provided if it was a "car show," that did not stop at hotels. The successful candidates were warned not to expect fancy salaries, but were assured that the "ghost" walked regularly every Sunday morning, that the shade was an old acquaintance of the show, that the gent in the white robe never failed to perambulate with the money satchel — in other words, everybody in the troupe was well and happy.

The average Tom troupe consisted of a family. They formed a kind of guild, tomming all their lives; they worked forty-eight weeks a year, and lived in a large wagon or a Pullman car far superior to a cheap theatrical boarding house. They were born in the wagon, grew up in the traditions set by Tommers for decades, married within that circle, lived full careers, then shuffled off as the grim Messenger came along — without attempting a part in any other play. Tom's progeny carried on the customs in an unbroken line.

The Tom show was ever a vagabond affair — a happy family, whose home and furniture consisted of: A 90-ft. top tent, a 60-ft. middle piece, a dozen lengths of high blue seats (cheap) and red (expensive) seats, as many stringers, one centre pole, three dozen side poles, two score stakes, a couple of bale rings, a half-dozen lamps; a stage with a 14-ft. opening, with at least four drops; one property trunk for such items as a plug hat for Marks, a wig for Tom, red fire, a whip; one rope box, with pieces of making, 1 bill trunk with "paper;" 1 ticket box, 1 bass drum, a donkey, a mastiff dog, a cookstove and a set of dishes, and often a mortgage on top of this nomadic homestead.

Sometimes a partnership was formed with another family who might invest three hundred dollars in a half interest. If they squabbled, the partnership split up, and they divided the show by ripping the top in half and actually sawing down the centre pole in the middle — in two! On the other hand, if they prospered, with a favorable balance on the right side of the ledger, two canvas shows were rigged out — No. 1 and No. 2, and each partner headed for a different route, taking along his own family.

The average Tom show ran the year round; it was the first to go out and the last to come in. With the cold weather, the hall season began, and the canvas was stowed away in the winter quarters. Many troupes took the road on April first, playing the theatres until June, then went under canvas; others disregarded the cold rains usual just before this time, and opened the tenting season early in May.

With the approach of early tent show weather, the "trouping" fever gripped every man and beast, and the Tommers worked late into the night to clear the "decks" for action, for the summer campaign held out golden promises. Wagons were repaired, the Sunny South scenery scrubbed and sloshed down, patched up, retouched, and the horse clippers bestowed the most patient care on the rolling stock. Each season beheld the Tom show enlarged, two or three more vehicles added — a new band wagon, another ticket wagon, or a third advance wagon. Last, the hardwood frames of the reserved camp chairs were painted blue, with everything gilt-edged from stake to bale ring. Then the large bill wagon was loaded, and a day later, the second brigade of bill posters started out. Everything in apple-pie order for the overland dash, the Tom show looked as bright as a new Columbian half dollar.

The early Tom vans found it tough. They weathered the deep thrumming April rains, pulling through heavy mud, and fording streams swollen by Spring thaws. In the words of a veteran Tom canvasman, April was the "most undryest" month of the year. Members were laid low with severe colds. Occasionally a Tommer lurched off the wagon while drousing a bit, for the word "sleep" was forbidden around a Tom show tent, much less practiced. In bad weather a "blow down" might result in the stage catching fire from the footlights. A rough idea of what they endured is set forth in a letter by a member of Andrew McPhee's troupe in '94: "Notwithstanding the continued downpour of rain during the past two weeks, business has been fair. The co. was in the midst of the flooded district, and dogs were lost May 22, 23 on account of bridges being washed out between Sunbury and Williamsport, Pa., but business since has been such as to make up for the lost time. At Elmira, N. Y., June 2, we turned people away at both performances. Geo. B. Howard was bitten on the hand by one of the bloodhounds last week while playing Marks. During the perf., 2nd, Robert A. Fisk received a telegram stating that his eight-year-old daughter had died of typhoid fever at Burlington, Vt., Mr. Fisk's home, and he at once left for that place. The co. now numbers twenty-five people, and will go under canvas, 11th at Canada..."

Tom shows and Spring rains became associated in the minds of the inhabitants of rural towns. One manager, George E. Witherell, visited Harmon, New York, in '95, and had no sooner struck the town when an old settler hobbled up to him, and said, "George, I'm glad you have come, 'cause I known it will rain 'fore night." For the past twenty years it had never failed to rain on the annual visit of the show. Nor was the settler disappointed this time, for rain it did, with a vengeance!

Buffeted about though they were, the troupers had their lighter moments. This is by a Tommer traveling with Swift & Carroll's in '96: "We experienced a touch of high life during the Illinois cyclone of May 27; it struck us at dinner time, but, luckily, everybody was on the lot to lend a helping hand, and no great damage was done. We thought we had lost one of our most valuable men, 'Deacon Graham,' but after the dust of the terrible battle had cleared away we found the lost deacon in an old dry cistern, quietly munching away on his piece of roast beef. By Mr. Swift's good management and cool head everything was in shape for the evening show. Mr. Carroll is in the South buying a few more horses; every horse in the show is coal black..."

After roughing the early blows, which tore the dramatic end to shreds, the Tom tents, all askew, finally sailed into smooth water. But hot days and long drives were the go now. The scorching heat and dusty roads made them long for a few raindrops. The indestructible moral play, served up piping hot with all the fixin's, clutched at the rustics' affections. "Proclaim it in no uncertain terms!" the manager waxed into rhapsody before the entrance. "The cynosure of all attractions! The kind o' show grandpa and grandmaw used t'see, yep! redolent with the ozone of old southern plantation

Photographic Drawing by L. L. Roush

At a One-Night Town

days! It rules without a rival..." Then as it took a deep
breath, the calliope evoked a thirst not to be slaked with
one draught yearly.

"The old rag opery" did a thumping business, for it
still had a bit of ginger in it. Many Tom troupes charged
not one, but three admissions: First, the general admission;
then, inside, a reserved seat upon payment of an additional
fee; and after the performance, a third payment entitled
one to stay on for the "concert." The players assisted the
"front" of the house, straightening out the queue of eager
school children. The manager, picturesquely flourishing his
gold-headed cane, manipulated the pasteboards in what he
boastfully called "the jam of humanity eagerly pushing its
way to the door!" Between acts, the pivotal players in makeup vended song books, photographs, prize packages, pink
lemonade, peanuts and confectionary.

The farther West, the more remunerative the tour. The Buckeye and the Hoosier States panned out well, as did the "strip" towns of Oklahoma. Here is an excerpt from a letter of a Tommer with Shea's in '93: "Since we struck Illinois our business has been big. We now have the long green laid aside, whereas when we were at Cairo the silver was easily counted. Bessie and Lulu are doing splendid work in brass, and Mrs. Shea is becoming a good tuba player... Barney, the donkey, is the big attraction on parade; his bucking, kicking and chasing Marks make the crowd shout every day. We close at Marshalltown, Ia. Oct. 15, making just one year, four months and nine days without closing the show, and having traveled eight thousand miles by wagon and boat without accident."

They traveled long distances and covered many states. Sutton's, during '93, opened its tour at Aurora, Illinois, in November, and embraced the Northwest, California, and went back through Arizona, closing the season at Monmouth in April, after having trekked 10,942 miles. Other troupes reversed the season: with the beginning of cold weather, they headed for the orange groves of Lower California. Up among the Lakes in the North the Tommers caught fish, which the ladies of the company cooked. In the lumber country of the West their double-barrel shotguns (the same used in the Eliza pursuit scene) kept the table supplied with wild geese and ducks. The members of Charles York's, one summer, doubled in berry-picking until the weather cleared. Frequently a baseball match was held between the Tommers and the town boys for the benefit of the local Library Fund.

High adventure beckoned on every route. In the South, of course, Tom troupes still ran into hostile territory. Many experienced the reception that met Ed. F. Davis', in Charlottesville, Virginia, early in '94: the morning after billing the town, most of the "paper" was smeared over with S. C. V. in large letters, which stood for "Sons of Confederate Veterans." The lithographic three-sheets bearing Lincoln's picture were entirely blotted out with blacking, and over the big stand of Eliza's pursuit the portentous initials appeared again, this time followed by "Lie." When the play opened in Culpepper Court House, the whipping of Tom was judiciously left out; but a mob stormed the doors, prepared to bombard the actors with stale vegetables. The players were aware of the conspicuous absence of women in the audience. Yet, despite the pronounced feeling against "that damyankee show," the troupe was applauded, and requested to come again the following year. Davis gave the play in Alexandria for five days running, and in the Spring of 1897 he took it to Louisville, Kentucky, for three weeks.

Texas was rather a tough spot for Tommers, for even the ordinary "rep" companies carrying the play on their schedule ran into difficulty there. One such group, a quarter of a century after the War, did not fully realize the local situation at Bonham, and unfortunately announced the drama at Russell's Opera House on the very night preceding Jeff Davis' burial. The town was mustered out, and paraded to the theatre, where it commenced to play "Dixie." Someone turned in the fire alarm, and in about ten minutes over two thousand men and boys crowded before the Opera House. They popped cannon crackers, rang bells, shouted, while the band blasted away at "Dixie" without a letup. The manager summoned the mayor, but that local official was helpless in quelling the uprising. The jittery actors put out the lights and huddled together in a secluded part of the building, quiet as a Quaker meeting. At last the mob was dispersed, but such spirit had not been seen since the War.

During the season of 1895-96, Will H. Locke, of the Lyceum Comedy Company, attempted a performance in Texas, and was warned, "There'll be an epidemic of lead-poisoning in town!" The whipping scene was retained on the principle that it was better to be run out of town than stranded there. That week-end, the Texan hostility was as varied as the company's own repertoire. Although they hurled

stale eggs, and flourished revolvers, more patrons attended
than during the rest of the week.

Another time, Locke offered the drama in a town of
German settlers, and engaged a local, fair-haired infant prodigy for Eva. Her accent was modified during rehearsals,
but the little girl reverted to type under duress of the actual
performance. The audience was moved by her beatitudes,
although the supporting members were startled by the mu-
sical-comedy aspect of her lines. As she led the wreathed
Uncle Tom into the arbor setting, her treble sounded off,
"Ach, Onkel Dom, how funneh you look yat!" And while
ensconced in the lap of the devout darky, the flower of the
South exclaimed, "Onkel Dom, vere is dot Neu Yahroos-
laum?"

The Tom controversy was still on. There appeared, in
1892, Annie Jefferson Holland's *The Refugees, a Sequel to
Uncle Tom's Cabin;* in 1894, *The Landlord's Revenge, or
Uncle Tom Up to Date;* in 1895, Benjamin R. Davenport's
Uncle Sam's Cabin; in 1897, *Uncle Tom of the Old South*
by Mrs. M. F. Surghnor; later, Mrs. W. L. Bruce's *Uncle
Tom's Cabin of Today...* These tried to arouse sympathy
for the Southern cause, and at least one, Mrs. Holland's,
saw production. Lee Peeler, the adaptor, undertook Uncle
Tom at Austin, Texas, in the Spring of 1893, and the cotton scene, where they actually ginned cotton on the stage,
created a sensation.

Two managers, Waller and Martell, were inspired to
glorify further ante-bellum times. They tried a reversal of
Uncles Tom's Cabin in *The South Before the War,* which
pictured darky happiness in bondage, with such characters
as Aunt Chloe, George Harris, etc. Much was made of the
leading Negro character, who returns from the North after
great suffering there, and is consoled by his former master.
It featured such novelties as a cotton plantation scene, the
explosion of the Robert E. Lee, a camp meeting at Frog's

Hollow, the drawing of razors, and a "Great Prize Cake Walk," and was advertised as the greatest production of the Century, "not excepting *Uncle Tom's Cabin.*"

Perhaps it wasn't honorable, but such was the fierce competition of the times that Stetson's company secured the patronage of the other party with *Uncle Tom's Cabin, or the South Before the War.* The subtitle was billed in very large type. Stetson's was a jump of six or eight weeks ahead of his rival, and when Waller & Martell came along later they wondered why local managers cancelled their engagements. Another time, in Middletown, New York, difficulty arose over a contract which Stetson's troupe alleged had not been kept regarding the local orchestra. One of the Tommers stepped before the footlights, and explained to the audience why there was no music, which so enraged the theatre manager that he had a warrant issued for the offender's arrest. But the actor was made up as one of the Negro characters when he addressed the spectators, and at the first sign of trouble washed off his burnt-cork. When the sheriff fluffed in, the actor was more zealous than anyone else in trying to find the guilty party.

Overshadowing everything else at the close of the Nineties was the Cuban question, and a tidal wave of sympathy swept the nation. In the great excitement it was noticed that *Uncle Tom's Cabin* made a slighting reference to the Cuban cause. In a scene at the end of the play, Gumption Cute appeared in an old, faded uniform, and was asked by Lawyer Marks what he was doing in "that soldier rig." He answered, "You see, I'm engaged just at present in an all-fired good speculation, I'm a Filibusterow! Don't you know what that is? It's Spanish for Cuban Volunteer; and means a chap that goes the whole porker for all that ere sort of thing." Matters grew worse as Cute continued: "You see, I bought this uniform at a second-hand clothing store, I puts it on and goes to a benevolent individual and I says to him, — appealing to his feelings, — I'm one of the fellows that went to Cuba and got massacred by the bloody Spaniards.

Off Stage Amenities

Manager (Uncle Tom's Cabin Troupe).—*What's the trouble now, cuss it all?*

Simon Legree—*Little Eva refuses to go to heaven unless she gets what's coming to her.*

Manager—*Say, if she should get what's coming to her, our Little Eva would never go to heaven.*

I'm in a destitute condition — give me a trifle to pay my passage back, so I can whop the tyrannical cusses and avenge my brave fellow sogers what got slewed there ... I tell you it works up the feelings of benevolent individuals dreadfully. It draws tears from their eyes and money from their pockets. By chowder! ..."

The lines had first been written into Aiken's script some forty-six years previously, and in the present crisis their significance was completely overlooked by the bustling Tom managers. Immediately the satirical lines were deleted, disappearing forever.

The advertising dodgers and handbills began to carry: "Take the Children and Give Them an Ideal and Lasting Lesson in American History!" One company, Ed. F. Davis', would open the show with a crack band and big fireworks. The overture was invariably "Fall of Santiago," which finished with six trombones blasting forth "The Stars and Stripes Forever;" then followed a big explosion — a globe was lowered over the band, and the flag of the United States floated over the stage!

The play met the exigencies of the times. James Oliver Arnold converted it into an historical pageant, *Uncle Tom's Freedom*, dedicating it to the Grand Army of the Republic. In the tableaux were seen such figures as Abe Lincoln, John Brown, Jefferson Davis, General Sherman, Henry Ward Beecher, President Hayes, Robert E. Lee, Lincoln's assassinator, fire-eaters, soldiers and marines of both sides.

In the New England States, Tom managers were now cautioned against admitting children under thirteen years unless accompanied by adults, a misdemeanor carrying a penalty of $100. The Parental Home Association sent out agents to round up boys at Tom matinees. When the attendance sloughed off, John P. Smith snared the parents with his famous slave auction; as the auctioneer, he distributed gold watches, sewing machines, Britannia ware, leather goods, plush albums, a box of gumdrops or a five dollar gold piece, and other prizes by calling out numbers held by the audience. To the accusation that he was violating the lottery laws by this sort of gift enterprise, Smith retorted, "The policy is to give away as much as possible!" One critic predicted that the time would come when Tom managers would give a free dinner and cab fare to anyone who came to the play. But the souvenir presents did attract pat-

The "Uncle Tom's Cabin" Season

Manager—*Look here, Mrs. Jimpson, if you don't stop bringing that grandson of yours here, we'll have to get someone else to play "Little Eva";—the rules of this theatre must and shall be observed!*

rons; better, it helped counteract the anti-juvenile laws passed about 1892. When Smith gave the play in Brooklyn that Fall, the Garry Society would not allow Ada Venden Gilbert, the Eva, to sing, "I See a Band of Spirits Bright," because they feared the child's health might be affected.

During their heyday, a cycle of humorous stories spread about the "Uncle Tomasses," ever disreputable in the eyes of the *legitimate*. One was at the expense of a Tom manager forced to leave a certain town "on account of my belief," and when asked to explain said he believed that they would kill him if he remained ... When a Chicago woman posted a prize for the best name for a shelter for destitute cats, a critic suggested Uncle Tomcat's Cabin... When "Punch" Wheeler telegraphed Billy Keogh, manager at Charleston. S. C., to book Irving's *Uncle Tom*, the answer Billy gave was the worst shot ever fired at an agent: "Would be pleased to play you, but we expect the yellow fever that week, and don't want them both."

No play withstood more spoofing.

But most significant, the Tom shows achieved their crest of popularity during the lush Nineties. Tom troupes sprang up then — well, like Tom troupes. Some played a half-dozen years, others through the decade, and well into the new century.

A cursory glance at the Tom troupes of that profligate period discloses some of their perambulating architecture. Defying flooded lots, blowdowns and heavy mud roads, H. B. Marshall's took off in high gear with an 80-ft. round top, and two 30-ft. middle pieces, and required fourteen head of stock to transport the complete show. Wentworth, Hobbs & Company toted along an 80-ft. round top, wending its way with six wagons and thirty horses, and fractured a number of house records along the route. E. F. Gorton's gave the sky-rockety play in a 70-ft. tent, with a 30-ft. middle piece, augmented by a 30-ft. round top dressing room, and a horse tent; thirty people trundled by wagon. The Union Square troupe, harbingers in Ohio, did not whip Tom under canvas at the beginning of the decade, but its owners, W. H. Davidson and Lane, soon turned it into the pavilion idea with an 80-ft. hooligan. Howard's Pavilion was a 90-ft. big rag and two 30-ft. middle pieces, with three cars — one for

troupers, another for stock, a third for baggage. Owen's
Pavilion, operated by R. A. Barker and M. O. Harkness,
was a 95-ft. oblong canvas, with two 30-ft. middle pieces,
transporting twenty-eight head of stock. Glenford's disport-
ed under a 100-ft. big top, with a 50-ft. middle piece, and
the troupe of twenty-one traveled by wagon. Andrew Mc-
Phee's lugged a 110-ft. top, with 50-ft. middle piece, three
cars, all 60 ft. long — a combination dining and sleeping
car, one flat and one stock car, for thirty-five people; each
town was enlivened with a parade featuring the Brothers
Ronans in gun drills, Prof. Meach's Military Band, the Alabama Pickaninnies, a calliope, and eight head of stock, including a goat. George Burtch's, beginning in the later
Eighties as Burtch & Parnip's Pavilion, toured Canada for
years with a 120-ft. top and 30-ft. middle piece. . .

Each Tom company had a reputation for some particular feature. Cumming & Alexander's two troupes doubled
in brass and presented excellent specialities between the
acts; they stopped at hotels. S. F. Darling's troupe trotted
horses on parade. Wakefield's emphasized the ice scene
with twenty-four hounds. The Eva of Russo & Holland's
rode in a coach advertised as once owned by the famous
Mr. and Mrs. Tom Thumb. Davis & Busby's concentrated
on scenic effects, such as the Ohio River by moonlight, the
race between the steamers R. E. Lee and Natchez, and Little Eva's Ascension. The Hatch Brothers' exhibited an electric plant made expressly for them — unusual for the
early Nineties — and also hauled a steam calliope, twenty
wagons, and a band of fifteen. The two Daisy Markoe companies flaunted the "World's Greatest Topsy," with Daisy
herself in one contingent, and Kate Partington in the other.
Although not strictly a canvas show, T. S. Gilmore's was
among the first to begin the decade with special props for
several scenes hitherto neglected, plus Major Kibble's lightning drill which zipped up the parade. During his tenting
season, Pete Conklin's carried 100 colored performers, buck
and wing dancers, cake walkers, quartette singers, and a

pickaninny band to match the white; at the close of the decade he signed up the Crandall-Randall family, and the ten played all the parts, besides comprising one of the parade bands.

Each town was treated to a spectacular display. In the parade the leading unit was the famous log cabin on wheels, motivated by its own steam power escaping through the chimney, and at its first glimpse the whole town knew what play was on. Once an advance agent for something called *Hooligan's Troubles* asked a diminutive native of Valparaiso, Indiana, what band show had appeared there last. "Stetson's," said the little lad.

"Did they have a very big house?" inquired the agent.

"Naw!" drawled the boy, "it was jes a little dinky house — they hauled it on a dray."

All of which lent individuality in a decade overrun with Tom shows. Burke's, owned by C. E. Beyerle, heralded more blazing-away musicians than any two rivals, and bragged that the players, as they swung down the Main Stem, were "All White and Dressed Up!" Lincoln's Triple included in the parade twelve ponies, six mules, six donkeys, ten dogs, an aluminum chariot, five floats, a cabin wagon, two big bands (black and white), Creole drum corps, calliope, and forty-four players; specialties were crammed in between the acts. With the latest mechanical and electrical devices, all were transported by a special train of three decorated coaches, baggage and stock cars. John Shea's marked a departure from the usual, for he gave the drama in a 60-ft. stern wheel boat, with a 30-ft. barge for tent, and sometimes the old storm-beaten tent was stretched to the limit, the audience packed to the side walls. The end of the decade found Hobson's a matter to contend with: the parade had Prof. Carrette's Red Hussar Band of 14 pieces, a colored fife and drum corps, the Charleston Glee Club, the New Orleans University Students, the famous "Cottonville Whangdoodle" Band, gigantic Dane dogs, two big mules, a herd of Shetland ponies, and a force of cooks, waiters and porters, plus thirty actors.

George Witherell & Clarence Doud's, a mud-scow outfit pulling out of Chatequay, N. Y., awed the yokels of Northern New York, Maine and Vermont with the only Harvard College graduate in the profession; Charles Brickwood (real name, Brickett) after studying law, forsook his practice to do Lawyer Marks. A competitor, Mason B. Morgan's, boasted a titled Englishman, Sir Ralph Christy, its property man. These two companies met the opposition of Dr. James P. Morgan's, from Lyden, N. Y., a Tomming medicine show; it sent out a sparkling advance wagon, a cluster of heavy bas-relief carvings, mirrors and gold leaf, which the agent would leave standing in the town hall square, where it was sure to catch the eyes of the citizens. Whenever it ran into Witherell & Doud's, or other rivals, the "Doc's" agents erected special billboards to "paper" against the opposition. During intermissions the "Doc" pulled teeth and sold Alfalfa Physic Tea.

When Boyer Brothers' and Kiser's united in the Spring of 1899, the aggregation numbered seventy people, making it possible to use two Ohio Rivers, and for Eliza to double-cross the iceman. They opened their hall season in the Fall, traveling in a sleeper 65 ft. long, and carried along forty-two kinds of special printing, two cars, sixteen Siberian hounds, eight prettily spotted ponies, and two bands of eighteen pieces.

They soon met the formidable rivalry of James W. Shipman, who for several years had been with Sig. Sautelle's wagon show in New York and Maine. Securing the backing of a wealthy Syracuse furniture dealer, A. A. Graff, who later financed the Shuberts, he organized, in Syracuse, his own company. He toured the East as the largest Tom show. George A. Eades, the prominent executive for the Shubert forces, was the manager for Shipman's, and another young fellow, Frank H. Stowell, who left the Sig. Sautelle show, was in charge of the bill wagons, and later headed his own Tom company.

Shipman's pageant tied up traffic, with six beautifully carved tableaux wagons glistening like wedd.ng cakes, a gorgeous chariot, floats, a cotton wagon, a log cabin, fourteen panel-box baggage wagons, supplemented by the largest horse and the smallest pony in America, two bands, a female fife and drum corps, a troupe of cake walkers, dogs, oxen, donkeys, six mules, eleven ponies, and forty horses. His "papering" that summer in Ticonderoga, Vermont, covered a board four and a half sheets high and forty long, without duplicating a sheet.

At the close of the first season, Shipman broke all records. His large tent packed in 2,000 at each performance, to see Tom whipped in first-class style. The owner completely overlooked the winter quartering of the seventy odd-head of stock. When he began his second season, at Syracuse, he headed eastward through the Empire State, but the long jumps began to tell on the livestock, and by the time it reached Brattleboro, Vermont, the mastodon was unrecognizable. It drifted then on to Winchester, N. H., where Shipman salvaged a baggage wagon, a passenger wagon, a cabin wagon, and a pair of rather discouraged-looking dogs, and ventured North, plugging through New Hampshire, but at Livermore Falls, Maine, the outfit became snowbound, and the company broke up. The following Spring, when the buds popped, farmers were peddling milk in sparkling tableaux wagons that had cost them little or nothing.

Mack's Pavilion Spectacular outdistanced its rivals in June, '94, when it pulled out of Guelph, Ontario, for upper Canada. The overland train comprised twelve conveyances, with a propelling power of thirty-four handsomely dappled gray horses. A waterproof canvas enclosure, seating 1,190, was a model of construction: attached to the main supports of the top were cooling and ventilating fans, "impregnating the atmosphere with choice perfume," while all was effectively lighted by double-acting bench lights, stage reflectors and illuminators. W. J. McGolphin, the proprietor, knew the psychology of juvenile Tom audiences, and advertised the smallest donkey in the world, "Pat Thumb," which he had purchased the previous St. Patrick's Day while visiting his home in Ireland. The animal joined the laughing and singing jackass, "Glory," in a double source of delight for the little ones. Children were treated to free rides on the ponies after the matinees.

The competing pavilions tried to surpass each other with their parade costumes. Lloyd's was an A-1 street flash, three blocks long, the band sporting three sets of uniforms: in the afternoon parade — white flannel, with white caps; in the evening concert — red coats, loping braid and epaulets, and "plug" hats of the same color; in the actual show — velvet and gold. Lloyd's, like Mack's, toured the cold country. Early in '95, it took the route along the Elk River, to Washington, then down the Palouse River as far as Moscow, Idaho, with a record of "canvas packed each night." It played a number of towns along the Northern Pacific Railroad with snow skirling about the canvas, every seat inside filled.

Most surprising about the Tom companies is their longevity. Many underwent a change in title, when one partner either dropped out or sold the "good will," but frequently they retained the same name throughout the years. During a fortnight at the Star Theatre, in Cleveland, F. E. Griswold combined forces with another Ohio Tom manager, Charles G. Phillips, and from then on their show involved a hundred head of ponies, a mile-long street parade, with wagons all gold and glitter, the full effulgence of the carvings and mirrors blinding all spectators. Phillips & Griswold's Mammoth Pavilion of 1886 was then re-formed, Phillips touring the East and South with one-half of the company, Griswold starting West with the other. In '90, the show changed to Phillips & Marney's, and three years later it was known as C. G. Phillips' Grand Colossal Pavilion U. T. C. Shows

— No. 1 and No. 2, with winter quarters at Windsor, Ohio. It started its tenth consecutive year in '95, and during all that time did not miss a single salary week. Thirty-five people were transported in a sleeping car, "The Cora Griswold," named after the manager's wife, who was the treasurer, and in his absence the manager as well. When illness forced Mr. Griswold to retire, William McGowen bought out his interest, and the show became Marney & McGowen's Mammoth Pavilion Uncle Tom's Cabin Company. A classic review, still preserved, from The Clay City (Ind.) *Weekly*, stated that "the show had been on the road so long that Topsy had growed up and the bark had slipped off of the dogs."

Rusco & Swift's of 1890 was owned five years later by the brothers E. L. and C. F. Powell. Perry & Gilger's Double began the decade and ended it as F. C. Perry's Pavilion. The proprietors of the old New Orleans' in '89 were Vreeland and Middaugh; it became Middaugh, Pfaff & Goodman's in '92, touring Western Canada; Middaugh soon left, but it reached the end of the decade as Theodore Darwin Middaugh's Original New Orleans'.

Many local managers in the West and Northwest confused the De Forrest Davis' and Ed. F. Davis' companies, the two having split early in '98. Ed Davis a few seasons later, staked by Ben Wallace, heralded his show as Cook Twin Sisters' Big Double U. T. C. "Monkey" Davis was well known in the environs of Michigan. He had made his start there as a crackerjack salesman of lightning rods and windmills. Whenever his Tom company hit the farming district, Davis' genius for selling induced many a prosperous farmer to put rods on the house, barn, chicken coops, and even in apple and shade trees; he promoted the windmill end of it by insisting that they would pump hot and cold water alternately! Leo Blondin, the assistant manager of the show, describes a typical Davis parade of 1897-98: "None ever finer or better. Ed. Davis on big white cake walk horse, big banner carried by man, four kids in uniform hold guy cord. Nickerson's Red Hussar Band— 16 pieces, banner dog, Eva Tableaux, four ponies, a dog banner. Marks and Topsy mounted on mules, Uncle Tom in old-time ox cart. Figures in mule wagon with log cabin on wagon. Quartet of Negro singers on wagon. Uncle Eph, Negro old man, doing cake walk with a possum behind. This parade would have to be seen to know the beauty of wardrobe, stock, trappings and finery. It covered four blocks and got plenty of press comment." Davis built a special combination car for the company, 80 feet long, and often the western mountain railroads refused to permit it on their rails for fear that its length would not make the curves.

"All other Stowe's U. T. C. companies are myths and infringements!" avowed John F. Stowe's playbills. His competitors accused him of adding that e to his name. Several troupes called themselves Stowe's, among them J. K. Stowe, who came honestly by it through birth. But the more prosperous, and oldest by far, was J. F. Stowe's, which reached the eleventh year of Tomming in '99. Each year he opened in Portland, Me., playing without a break to Portland, Oregon. He scrunched his rivals by proclaiming that his troupe was "Absolutely the Largest and the Grandest in the World! A Street Parade Surpassing Anything Ever Seen. Presenting More Novel Features Than Were Ever Conceived by the Mind of Man!" His lithographs carried Mrs. Stowe's name as authoress, with his own printed alongside as manager; the public naturally thought they were related. But the veteran Tom showmen knew better. They spun yarns about his uncle, Eley-Ikum, who pioneered with an overland show in the raw days, and who would plant himself barefooted on the top of the ticket wagon, and "speechify" before the natives: "Friends an' neighbors, ef yuh 'gin us a good house we 'gin yuh a good show!" The nephew prolonged the line with a troupe of forty, featuring Daisie Markoe as the world's greatest Topsy. He acclaimed that it was the only company with a genuine Cotton Gin and Press in full operation on the stage!

Harry L. Palmer's reached its tenth year in '99, and its parade was in fine fettle: two bands (white and colored), twelve giant cake walkers (in royal purple and gold, with expansive grins), the moving cabin of Uncle Tom, Little Eva and her wonderful pony, and the Kentucky Jubilee shouters. George E. Witherell & C. H. Doud's rounded out its tenth year in '98; with grace and skill, the ladies of the company trotted handsome grays, caparisoned with gilded trappings, and the riders' new uniforms gleamed in the sunlight.

Stetson's Original Big Double (not to be confused with Jim Stenson's, a canvas outfit of 1889, from Bath, New York) ended the decade in its eighteenth year, heralding its achievement, "Is Firmly Founded, and Lasting as Gibralter. Constantly Aims to Elevate!" The parade was three blocks of tinsel and glitter, including three golden chariots drawn by tiny Shetland ponies, tableaux cars, two bands, a Ladies' Drum Corps, six of the largest and ugliest dogs in creation, donkeys, etc. A close rival for the longevity title was E. O. Roger's, attesting on the billboards in '99: "The Oldest, the Largest, the Most Successful Organization in the World —Twentieth Year under the Same Title!"

However, E. A. Mason & H. B. Morgan's outstripped them all, blazoning as far back as '91, in 36 styles of elaborate special printing, "TWENTY-ONE YEARS ON THE ROAD!" With the exception of the many Evas who outgrew their parts, remarkably few changes took place in the old company's cast. "Aunt Annie" Jamison, at the age of 72, still Topsied on. And down through the decade of the Nineties new audiences were given what they desired most: the world's smallest donkey, as well as the largest hounds, Russian, Siberian, and English. Without even an orchestra or band, the outfit was a master production, nevertheless, because of its spectacular sets. Morgan was replaced by W. C. Downs, at the time of the Spanish-American War; but the street parade still retained the white and colored windjammers, with the colored band in Cuban uniforms.

The most gargantuan of all was a relatively young company, Al. W. Martin's, which adopted the shibboleth, "Too Big for Imitators — too Strong for Rivalry!" It was organized in 1895, at Peru, Ind., as Salter & Martin's. Two years later Martin bought out his partner, and began to eclipse his rivals. He billed with the most lavish assortment of "paper," and the scenic investiture was unsurpassed: 20 drops and 28 set pieces. Martin claimed the distinction of carrying bands and an orchestra whose members *did not* double on the stage. There were no waits between the acts, various specialties making it a continuous performance. The plantation scene had "A Senegambian-Contingent, Representing the Crème de la Crème of the Colored Profession in a most Sumptuously Dressed CAKE WALK, Buck and Wing Dancing, Jubilee Shouting and Plantation Pastimes." The steamboat race between the Natchez and Robert E. Lee, and the grand allegorical transformation were mechanical marvels. Martin forbade the objectionable customs prevalent in most Tom shows, abolished after-concerts, and prohibited the peddling of peanuts, song books, photographs, and like articles.

Martin's superiority was evidenced in his parade: Lady Zouave Drum and Bugle Corps, Mlle. Minerva's New Orleans Creole Girls' Fife and Drum Corps, 18 Real Georgia Plantation Shouters, the "Original Whangdoodle Pickaninny Band," Eva's $1,500 gold chariot, a log cabin, floats, phaetons, carts, ornate banners, dazzling harnesses and uniforms, 3 full concert bands, the drum major an 8-ft. colored boy ("Long Tom" Brockman, the Black Giant, seventeen years old), 10 Cuban and Russian ferocious, man-eating hounds, 25 ponies, donkeys, oxen, mules, horses, and burros, all trained as entertaining tricksters. Martin secured bookings in cities controlled by the Stair & Havlin Circuit, and often as many as 50,000 people gaped at the parade. When it came to New York, the spectacular procession stretched some eight blocks on Broadway. Martin paid his brokers three percent of the gross receipts, guaranteeing never less than $3,000 a season, which gives some idea of the earning power of his company in those days.

The Martin show required three 70-ft. magnificiently equipped palace cars to transport it. One was fitted with built-in grooves for set pieces. A 'possum-belly car, "Kitty," domiciled the players. In the dining car, "Cordelia," sumptuous dinners were served to the local press; the heavily-embossed menu cards offered them an elaborate choice prepared by the company chef, John W. Slater, who had formerly served McKinley on the presidential yacht. Martin kept his Tom show going well into the Twentieth Century, "papering" the entire country in letters tall as a man: "JUST AS IMMORTAL AS THE DECLARATION OF INDEPENDENCE!"

Chapter XVI

THE TWENTIETH CENTURY

But, even as he mused, he tried to picture
The South, that languorous land where Uncle Toms
Groaned Biblically underneath the lash,
And grinning Topsies mopped and mowed behind
Each honeysuckle vine.
— Benét's "John Brown's Body".

AT THE TURN OF THE CENTURY, Edward Terry, in England, proposed an annual congress to discuss various theatrical developments of the year. When the movement got under way, some wag commented that a conference be held here between the Royal Geographical Association of Great Britain and the Amalgamated Association of Uncle Tom Managers of the United States and Canada, to help the British lexicographers locate all the new towns discovered by Tommers during the last decade.

In its amazing vitality the play withstood a new generation of critics, who held up to ridicule its every performance. Here is the way the Dayton *Courier-Press*, for example, described Davis & Busby's company: "If four Indians and a yellow pup at a siwash pot-latch would give as bad a show as that, they would be shot on the spot and not even accorded a decent funeral. It was the essence of bumness, the ne plus ultra of rankness, and the acme of rottenness. Shades of Harriet Beecher Stowe, but what a mutilation of what was once *Uncle Tom's Cabin!* They had Uncle Tom, but he acted and looked like an iron hitching post. Topsy was there, but she had no more symptoms of the original

Harbinger of Spring

Topsy than a colicky cat has of an angel. Miss Ophelia was there, too, but her makeup, her acting and her voice reminded the audience of a horrible case of mistaken identity, while Marks — well, the less said about Marks the more praise he has. They had an ice scene, but the dogs came on, looked at the audience, got ashamed and went back. The death scene of Eva was thrown in, and she was permitted to die with her shoes on, with three chairs covered with a sheet for a bed. They did not overlook the auction scene, and the bass drum player and slide-trombone player vacated their seats, and with no thought of a different make-up went on the stage to bid for the slaves; the death scene of Tom was omitted, but he was killed off in a new and improved manner."

The play's influence with the public, nevertheless, was strong, sufficiently so as to sway a New York City election during the Fall of 1901. Seth Low, president of Columbia, had been derisively nicknamed "Little Eva" by his opponent Devery, and the popular reaction to the light use of the beloved little lady's name resulted in Devery's defeat for mayor. It precipitated the retirement of Tammany's Boss Croker.

The year 1901 was a memorable one. On March 4th, Al. W. Martin opened at the Star Theatre, in New York. On that same day a formidable rival, for once, excelled him in the magnitude of production. William Brady had conscripted 200 buck and wing dancers and singers, all from 'way down south of Thompson Street. In that delegation an admiring Negress sang his praises, "Dat's Mistah Brady, dat little white man in his shirt sleeves dat sweahehs so. He writ de play, 'deed he did — he freed de slaves!" Brady's show was mounted with eighteen complete sets, besides twenty-one scenes for the transformation; the latter fell in the valentine class, with Eva going to Heaven via the most approved electric-lighted route.

Wilton Lackaye, one of Brady's "All-Star" cast, had earlier suggested that he would like to play Othello, but Brady answered, "If you're interested in those black face things, why not try *Uncle Tom's Cabin?* I've got scenery for that."

"Now," chuckled the actor, "if I really go on as Tom, that will certainly surprise Israel Zangwill."

"How's that?" asked the manager.

"Well," said Lackaye, "before I enacted the old rabbi in *Children of the Ghetto*, Zangwill felt rather strongly that an actor should be in religious and racial sympathy with his part. He preferred a player of Jewish birth and background, and told me as much. I had to put up a stiff argument to the dear fellow, that these things are not a matter of ethnology, but of drama. To make my point I asked him, 'Should a Negro be preferred to me for, say, the role of Uncle Tom?' " Lackaye paused a moment, lit a cigar, and with a merry twinkle, added, "Zangwill said that he hoped some day to have the opportunity to see me as Uncle Tom."

"Well, well, that's all very interesting," said Brady. "But I want you for Legree. That's the part everyone would expect you to play."

"Exactly," answered the actor. "And why not let's surprise dear old everybody and let me play a part nobody would expect me to play? My ability to play Legree is not in question; but folks will wonder what sort of a mess I shall make out of Tom. Besides there's another reason."

"What's that?" asked Mr. Brady suspiciously.

"It will interest Zangwill so much, in case he hears of it."

"All right," said Brady. "I'll try Theodore Roberts for Legree."

Lackaye distinguished himself in the part. A half-dozen years or so later he was guest of honor at one of the Friars' weekly sessions. Lew Dockstader was chairman at the time, and it was suggested that Lackaye and Dockstader appear on the same bill as America's leading burnt-cork artists. But Jean Havez, representing Dockstader, drew the color line, and protested that it would be unbecoming for the "Minstrel King" to compete against a mere "Uncle Tom" player.

Brady's choice of Theodore Roberts as the sinister Legree was pure inspiration. No other actor devoted more time and careful consideration to the art of realistic make-up, and not a single harrowing detail — no matter how minute — escaped Roberts' covetous eyes. He invested the Red River planter with wild and gloomy qualities, a nightmare that lingered vividly in the memory for years. It was a sharp departure from the Legrees hitherto seen, and his creation was accepted as the ideal realization of the character. Other Legrees had long, black, snaky locks, with a jet chin piece and drooping moustaches, but Theodore Roberts' was red-headed and baldish, with a broken nose, and glowering, savage face. The flogging he gave poor Uncle Tom

Theodore Roberts
as
The Arch-Fiend with the Traditional Blacksnake Whip

(the final coupe administered on the head) froze the spectators in their seats. During rehearsals he suspected that the blow with a whiskey bottle might look like a palpable fake to the audience; he experimented, breaking every sort of vessel he could find, and finally hit upon a tar composition strong enough to hold, brittle enough to shatter, and which would contain the "blood mixture" that flowed when Tom was hit on the head. Throughout the long run Theodore Roberts spent his spare time modeling tar bottles, for he needed one a day, and often two.

Maud Raymond, as Topsy, benefited from Roberts' ingenuity. She was dead-set against the burnt-cork, to begin with. Now the vivacious soubrette discarded the makeup used since the birth of minstrelsy, and at the dress rehearsal presented herself with face and neck covered with her own brand of dark-brown grease paint. It made a distinct impression at first, but as the paint hardened like so much molasses candy, she realized that she would never succeed in revolutionizing the black-face line, and that she would just have to follow meekly in the footsteps of "Daddy" Rice and Lew Dockstader. Her costume called for a meal bag, or a scanty coffee-sack garment, so she went to the grocer and got a potato sack. This was too heavy, whereupon she thought of burlap, and got some from a furniture store; and thus another departure was achieved in the costuming of Topsy. One member of the company, Eliza's four-year-old son, had a habit of sidling into Miss Raymond's dressing-room, and edging up to her would plead, "Please, don't steal Aunt Ophelia's ribbon." The little fellow never spoke to the actress when she was in her street clothes, but the moment she was in character he would come running over.

Brady cut and strengthened the old play, and although he preserved its spirit throughout, certain anachronisms crept in nevertheless. Topsy, for example, sang, "Shoo Fly, Don't Bother Me," and "I'm a Methodist till I Die," and danced to the music of Offenbach. As Miss Raymond was a graduate from the vaudeville stage, she encored a "coon" song of that year of Grace, 1901, "I Won't Be Your Lady Friend No More," and pat ered about her bran'-new automobile and other modern contrivances. And the Ophelia of Mrs. Annie Yeamans, who had been talking Harrigan & Hart Irish for a quarter of a century, eliminated the brogue from her voice, but her gestures remained unmistakable.

While New York was flocking to the play, Brady telegraphed Jay Rial in Chicago to arrange for the summer opening at the Haymarket Theatre. Then wily Florenz Ziegfeld, Jr., proposed to Mr. Brady that the Auditorium would attract swell theatregoers, for the play would, indeed, be "something new" to them. The Haymarket deal was cancelled, and Rial, accepting the challenge, moved in his own company.

The Brady production struck the Windy City hard. Within a block of each other, Jay Rial's was resplendent at the Haymarket, and around the corner at the Academy of Music, Al. W. Martin's shone with effulgence. A nice little traffic problem faced the Chicago police, if the three companies decided on simultaneous street parades, with the many Evas, Uncle Toms, and hounds mixing at an intersection.

A Tom war of large proportions enthralled the Westsiders. When Brady brought his "All-Star" cast and 300 State Street Senegambians and Ethiopians, Mr. Rial countered with "genuine cotton-pickers from the South," and promised that Eliza and her baby would be pursued by "not less than thirty ravenous bloodhounds." Rial claimed his was the "only original," which was borne out later by the testimony of a friend, who cited, "If any of the oldest inhabitants can remember a predecessor of Mr. Rial, he can get a free pass to the show by sending in names and dates. Mr. Rial sent Little Eva to heaven with a Bible in her frail hands in the days when the Oxford edition cost $2.85 a copy. He chased Eliza across the Ohio River early in the present century, when bloodhounds were valued at the prohibitive price of $1.30 a bark. He was the first manager to send Lawyer Marks across the stage on a live donkey, and he claims to be the originator of all the cotton-field 'business' peculiar to a popular rendition of the old play." When the New York interloper exploited his "All-Star" production at rather high prices, Mr. Rial attempted "'a majestic revival" at 10, 15, 25, and 50 cents.

The Chicago competition was not unusual, except for the intense animosity that crept in at the beginning of the Century. During the famous "All-Star" run in New York, a benefit was held for the Actor's Fund, sponsored by Brady, and De Wolf Hopper and Dan Daly were billed in a travesty on *Uncle Tom's Cabin*. The evening's festivities began with Weber and Fields in costume, which no doubt encouraged Hopper and Daly to do likewise in their skit. Hopper, as Uncle Tom, stood in his stocking feet "five foot twenty inches" (as he expressed it), and like Mrs. Stowe's dusky soubrette, "just grow'd." The final curtain came down on Legree exclaiming: "I'll lash the piety outer yuh, —yuh! Yuh belong ter me!" whereupon Uncle Tom answered with deep feeling: "Mah body belongs t'yuh kaze yuh paid fer et, but mah soul belongs ter Weber an' Fields!" While he was dying—the curtain going up and down to the applause—a little man walked solemnly to the centre of the stage, and said, "Uncle Tom, you're mine now!" It was none other than Inspector Thompson, who made the most of the dramatic opportunity of his life. He wore his famous duck-hunting cap, always a storm signal in raids. He pounced upon his man, and a police captain, at his heels, placed his arm within Simon Legree's, while an ordinary policeman gathered in Brady.

Brady, after communicating with his stars by telephone, enlightened the sergeant, "They've got Daly all right, but Hopper skipped. He says he's no jailbird."

This had an electrical effect on Inspector Thompson, who at once clapped a hand into his famous side pocket,

bringing out his equally well-known and frequently described little billy, which he shook savagely in the direction
of the Academy of Music. He shouted, "I'll swear out a
bench warrant for him in the morning, and serve it on the
stage at Weber & Fields' tomorrow night!"

"He's a fighter and you had better look out," warned
Mr. Brady, "for he'll lick you, billy and all."

"I'm something of a fighter myself!" snapped the Inspector.

The three alleged malefactors were arraigned the next
day, and learned to their surprise that the Sunday law (dormant for years) had suddenly been enforced by Inspector
"Big Bill" Devery. All other theatres, dives and saloons were
permitted to stay open on Sunday, but the letter of the law
was invoked arbitrarily on this occasion. The whole case
hinged on Section 277 of the Penal Code, which prohibited
costumes in stage performances on Sunday, the shifting of
scenery, or the lowering and raising of a curtain.

According to the Inspector's testimony, Hopper had
worn an old dress-suit, with streaks of chocolate smeared
on his face — not near the mouth. Uncle Tom had not
been all black, but striped like a zebra, and Hopper claimed
it a concession to the Sunday law. He had worn evening
clothes of antiquated shape and ample proportions, swallow
tails which dragged on the floor, and, of course, the wig
that always concealed his lack of hair. That was the Inspector's strong point.

"He wore a dress coat which must have been at least
fifty years old," testified the chief raider, "and sang psalms
to Little Eva."

"Was it his own coat he wore?" asked the Magistrate,
quickly.

"I can't say positively, but if it wasn't it must have been
borrowed from either Joe Jefferson or Joe Murphy. It was
a costume, certainly. It was more than that — it was an
outrage!"

Dan Daly defended his accomplice, and insisted that

Hopper violated the law to a greater extent every day by appearing on the street with a toupee.

"And what about Hopper?" asked the Magistrate of another officer. "Did he have on any paint?"

"Not that I could notice," was the intelligent response. "Perhaps the light is a bit different here. He seemed a shade darker last night."

Dan Daly was entered in docket. He had worn the Legree clothes of Theodore Roberts, miles oversized for his thin frame, plus a ferocious gray moustache and an accessory English drawl.

"Perhaps he has shaved since then," suggested counsel.

"The latter was certainly costumed," the Inspector protested. "I know he was, because I could see his outlines without shading my eyes. He wore a wig from the Couldock Collection, and a false wig. His hair was sprinkled with saleratus and talcum powder to make him look over sixty. He carried a rawhide whip in one hand, and a great fierce dog was gnawing at his right leg."

The Inspector's last bit of evidence implied that even the bloodhound recognized the actor in Daly's makeup. Roberts' constant companion, "Dan," contributed his share to the Actor's Fund that night, and the animal detected the odor of the familiar suit as soon as he came on the stage — the dog leaped immediately at Legree's throat! The Inspector swore that Daly had to back rapidly away, and take refuge in the wings, and offered as Exhibit A Daly's hat that had fallen off and which the dog had chewed.

"Daly was playing the part of Simon Legree, the slave driver," the Inspector repeated.

"Did he look like a slave driver?" asked the Magistrate.

It was admitted that Daly's rawhide lash on Hopper's back lacked the usual cruelty.

"Did either Daly or Hopper *act*? Did they cause any outbreak on the part of the audience? Any unseemly demeanor?" asked the Magistrate.

"No," replied the Inspector. "I saw nothing unusual. The audience merely walked toward the door."

"And why did you arrest Brady?"

"Well, the hound began growling around Mr. Daly, and Mr. Brady tried to restrain him..."

"No theatrical costumes in the full meaning of the term," ruled the Magistrate. "The whole point to be weighed is: Were these men really *acting?* If they were, I will hold them."

Daly whispered to Hopper, "But if they prove that we *were acting?*"

"Oh, well, if that's all that's bothering you," Hopper replied, "have no fear. They couldn't prove that in a thousand years."

The cross-examination went on:

"And you didn't see any *acting?*"

"No."

"And Mr. Hopper wasn't really an Uncle Tom?"

"No."

"And Mr. Daly wasn't a real Legree?"

"No"

Whereupon the Magistrate declared that he was unsympathetic with the severe interpretation of the law, and would "temper injustice with mercy." The Yorkville Police Court was speedily cleared.

Dan Daly later lamented that here he had been doing songs and dances and cavorting about the stage generally, but the minute he began to *act* they arrested him.

An attempt was made to bar Mrs. Stowe's book from the New York school libraries. The reason was given that the book had served its purpose, and had no value whatsoever for the present generation. Faced with public indignation, the Board of Education rescinded the order. One newspaper pointed out that Simon Legree still lived in the persons of Theodore Roberts and in those who objected to President

Theodore Roosevelt's reception of Booker T. Washington at the White House.

While the controversy was on, F. Hopkinson Smith, author of *Colonel Carter of Cartersville*, argued that Mrs. Stowe's novel had precipitated the Civil War. Victor Virde offered a drama, *Uncle Sam's Cabin; or White Slaves*. On the other hand, although Colonel Henry Watterson of Kentucky did not agree that Mrs. Stowe's work was an untruthful picture of slavery days, he felt it was a spoke in an inexorable wheel, and that nothing could have delayed the ultimate trial of arms. In 1906, a novel by Mrs. William L. Bruce, *Uncle Tom's Cabin of Today*, carried on where Mrs. Stowe had left off over a half century ago, but Uncle Tom now mused, "Times is changed since den. Times is changed since den. Times is sho'ly changed since den!"

In Indiana, a manager, upon retiring after fourteen active years at South Bend, pronounced proudly, "In all that time an *Uncle Tom's Cabin* company has never graced the boards of Oliver's Opera House." When a committee of women of the United Daughters of the Confederacy (Lexington, Kentucky, chapter) petitioned the local opera house manager, Charles B. Scott, to refrain from booking any more Tom shows, he answered: "Ladies, a copy of your resolution in reference to *Uncle Tom's Cabin* has been received. Replying to the same, I have only to say, the war has been over about thirty-six years."

Then the Arkansas Legislature passed a law prohibiting Tom performances. To put an end to what it believed a gross libel on ante-bellum affairs, the Howard County Court in Missouri levied a tax of $200 a day on all Tom shows. Many towns in the State charged the Tom troupes a $500 license fee, which effectively kept them out. In Texas, Florida and Mississippi a large fee was exacted from itinerant shows, which became more prohibitive with the years. As recently as 1927, Alabama passed a bill raising the fee from $35 to $300 a week. Tommers evaded the laws by showing at the edge of the towns, but the new State Laws granted the incorporated towns the right to collect from any traveling show within reasonable distance of the city's limits, in Minnesota within a mile, and in Montana within three miles. This discouraged Tomming, and the new century saw a sharp decline in the number of troupes.

Traveling through the Canadian provinces during the Fall of 1906, H. H. Whittier, the advance agent for Al. W. Martin's, perpetrated a joke on the city of Guelph. The good city fathers met, one day, to discuss seriously a letter asking for a loan of $50,000 to a brick and sand plant that would establish a branch there. The firm was stated to be in Shelbyville, Ky., the letter was signed by Geo. Harris, and the name of the foreman was given as Mr. S. Legree. Anyone familiar with *Uncle Tom's Cabin* would have recognized immediately all three names, yet such was the diminuition of the once popular drawing card, that no one suspected the hoax.

Whittier also gauged the Tom sentiment in the far South. He sent out notices requesting bookings. He thought he would have a little fun, and addressed a Tom show letter to a certain opera house manager in Texas. An answer came promptly, scrawled across the bottom of Whittier's letter: "We have only one policeman in this town."

Chicago, on February 27th, 1901, served up the anti-slavery drama in Yiddish, at Glickman's Theatre, "Where One Persecuted Race Portrays the Hardships of Another." An exiled Russian Jew, Ellis F. Glickman, was the burnt-cork Uncle Tom in a Prince Albert coat, pleading for deliverance from the knout of the muzhik owner, Simon Legree. The patriarchal Tom took the Oriental-looking Little Eva on his knee, caressed her golden curls, and read sonorously of the New Jerusalem — from the Talmud. Eliza and Harris resembled new arrivals at Castle Garden, and recounted their sufferings in a curious mélange of Russian, German, Yiddish and English. Marks was a typical "shyster" lawyer of the police courts, and St. Claire's wife presented the startling apparition of a Levantine beauty in hoopskirts. Simon Legree, in red Russian boots, swaggered in, booming out Yiddish expletives in a deep bass voice. Topsy, blinking and rolling the whites of her eyes, her Israelitish countenance shining through the burnt-cork, intoned deeply, and lapsed into English, that she was never born — then sang "coon" songs in Yiddish, and executed a cakewalk.

Jewish audiences, in New York, were also stirred profoundly at the People's Theatre on the Bowery, where, on March 16, 1906, Boris Thomashevsky corked up as Uncle Tom, with his wife, Bessie, as the irrepressible Topsy. The players often reverted to English in emphasizing some comic climax. Phineas Fletcher, the Quaker, lifted his hands to his ears, palms upwards, rolled his eyes, and sighed: "Oi, oi, verilye!" When the good auctioneer misled Harris' pursuers to the cellar trap, he shouted with glee: "*Geht und ziecht* him — by golly! Look for him — dere is he not; yeah!" As the Kishineff massacre of Jews was quite recent, a villainous-looking pursuer dug up from a prop trunk a Cossack blouse used in the drama, *Darkest Russia,* which he now wore with great bluster, and won a storm of hisses each night. Lawyer Marks was projected in an essentially Yiddish manner, his name spelled Marx on the program; but this was rather fitting for local audiences, and may have recalled the ambition of Mr. Lawrence D'Orsay, who said he wanted to play "Marks the Barrister" in *Uncle Thomas' Residence.*

Nine years later, on February 8th, Hammerstein's Victoria Theatre put on *Uncle Thomashevsky's Cabin.* Originally written for the Vaudeville Comedy Club, Tommy Gray's skit became a headliner in variety, with Lillian Shaw as Little Evavitch; other characters were distorted to Lawyer Markstein, Simon Levy, Elizy, Topsyadie.

Indeed, vaudeville made a shambles of the old drama, perhaps because many of its performers had gained their early foothold in Tom shows. Gertrude Haynes, before ac-

quiring an enviable position on the marquee, portrayed Mrs.
St. Claire to her sister's Eva. Marilyn Miller was with the
play, one summer, under a tent in Indiana; she wanted to
be Little Eva, but was cast as one of the angels, while her
father sooted up as Uncle Tom. The Excelsior Uncle Tom
troupe broke up at Rushville when the treasurer absconded
with the funds. They set the bloodhounds after him, trail-
ing him to Crawfordsville, but the treasurer fed the dogs and
started a new Tom troupe with them. So the Millers went
back to vaudeville.

A former Eva was now unmatched in vaudeville —
Tanguay. Always called "Little Eva," her behavior, however, suggested Topsy, and her "I Don't Care" was so
much like the dark hoyden's "I'se So Wicked." With
her fuzzy-wuzzy hair, Eva Tanguay was indeed a personal-
ity in 1915. *The Variety Weekly*, of April 2nd, conjectured:
"If she played Topsy in a revival of *Uncle Tom's Cabin* —
and why not, in these days of prosperous revivals! — it
would not be Eva Tanguay as Topsy, but Topsy as Eva
Tanguay."

Vaudeville managers often gave what they called a
"double bill" — the everlasting drama plus the usual variety turns. In 1901, Miner's 125th Street Theatre first tried
this combination, and the "legitimate" part of the bill made
a hit—but as a farce! They used standardized sets, and when
Legree and Marks turned up their coat collars and talked of
"a river of ice," the drop behind them pictured an idyllic
summer afternoon in Central Park.

A variety performer in Chicago, at the turn of the century, appeared in a sketch, *Marks the Lawyer*. And Mary
Austin later recounted in her autobiography: "Twice after
that I saw it, once in a suburb of Boston, degenerated to
a farce, with Marks as the stage Jew, and Uncle Tom as a
comedy 'black face.'" Another, Jessie Couthoui's act,
tailored for her talents by Charles Horwitz, was entirely in
Irish dialect. After Belasco's *Zaza*, with Mrs. Carter, sure
enough, a skit followed during the Fall of 1907, *From Zaza*

to Uncle Tom, with the team of W. H. Murphy and Blanche
Nichols, and Georgena C. Leary as Simon Legree. Earlier
in 1903, Murphy and Nichols had regaled vaudeville patrons
with *Murdering Uncle Tom.* Elsewhere were A. L. Kaser's
The Filming of Uncle Tom's Cabin, and a song-monologue
by Walter Ben Hare, "Uncle Tom's Cabin at the Op'ry
House." In 1909, Harry Deaves and his Tom company of
Dramatic Manikens dished up a burlesque.

As for the corny quality of the vaudeville humor, here
is an excerpt from the Russell Brothers' act: "I love tragedy!
I love tragedy! I'll never forget the night I went to see *Uncle Tom's Cabin;* I thought I'd die laughing at Topsy, she
was so comical, but she was the dirty-looking thing: when
she opened her mouth, you could see her brains. There
was one scene that was awful sad; it was the saddest thing
I ever saw for half a dollar. It was where Eliza was crossing the ice and the bloodhounds were chasing her. You'd
pity the poor woman, she had no place to go—all the saloons
were closed!"

Do you wonder what a genius could have done with that
material? Well, here is a most delightful piece of non-
sense from one of Stephen Leacock's lectures: "A lot of my
earlier work was done with a touring company, one of a
chain of companies acting in that grand old drama, *Uncle
Tom's Cabin.* I am sure you know it so well that I needn't
describe the plot to you. In any case I couldn't; I wasn't
part of the plot. My work was in the great climax scene,
where the fugitive slave, Eliza, her unborn babe in her arms,
is fleeing across the Ohio — leaping from one ice floe to
another in the swollen flood of the river. That's where I
acted — I was a chunk of ice in the Ohio, the third one from
the Kentucky side, working under a blue curtain. I put my
heart into it. I said to myself: 'If I am to be ice, I'll be the
most dangerous ice in the river. If Eliza puts her foot on
me, up she goes!' Well, I worked away consciously night
after night until it happened one night the general manager
of our chain of companies was down front. And he saw my

work and he said: 'Who is that ice? The third from Kentucky?' And they told him, and he sent for me and he said: 'Look, I've seen your work. You're too good for ice. How would you like to be First Bloodhound?' That was my first big move up."

George Jean Nathan once described how a Tom troupe fell victim to the hazing of Princeton undergraduates. The college town had no theatre, so the students would go to Trenton, where they made it so uncomfortable for any dramatic company that the actors invariably referred to their recent engagement as the "Battle of Trenton." A Tom show was advertised and the scholars conspired for two whole weeks, and on the opening night descended in a body on the theatre. The performance had hardly started, when an undergraduate in a balcony box leaped to his feet, and in declamatory tones protested the appearance of a "colored" performer on the stage; his conspirators backed him to a man. Then another student, in the front row, rose, and exclaimed: "I protest, too, but I think we should give him a chance to prove his worth."

The Uncle Tom had never faced a college audience, and was completely taken in. With the utmost gravity, he approached the footlights, and reassured all that he was not really a Negro, but a white man in burnt-cork. "Oh, well," many in the audience shouted, "if that's the case, it's all right!" And the play proceeded. Then another interruption, as someone else loudly took up the issue: "He is deceiving us. I think he really is colored, and I object to a Negro acting in a company of white actors."

Once more Uncle Tom pressed his denial, but they refused to be reassured and insisted that not until he removed part of his makeup would they consider it tangible evidence. The actor obliged, and exposed a white swath where shellac wig and burnt-cork had met. The play was permitted to continue.

Now Eliza was about to make her exciting jaunt across

the ice, but fresh outcries persisted that it wasn't right for a lady to make the dangerous trip alone. They called for volunteers to escort her across, and two solemn upper term men jumped onto the stage, and assisted the helpless fugitive and her babe-in-arms across the "ice floes."

"Now, you boys, keep quiet or we'll bring down the curtain!" warned the Uncle Tom.

The students promised to behave, and the play went on, but this time a dead silence presaged something new in the offing. Sure enough, during Eva's solemn death scene, an overfat undergraduate, grinning mischievously, declared that he had fallen in love with Little Eva at first sight, and that he couldn't bear the thought of her dying. "If they let her die," he threatened, "they'll have to answer to me." The actors at last caught the implication, and quickly brought down the curtain!

Despite the many vaudeville take-offs, the ancient seemed good for at least fifty more years.

Tom companies were good, bad, and indifferent, but there was magic in the very title. "Doc" Dionne's wagon rekindled good business through New Hampshire and Maine, as did E. J. Preston's, of Oneida, New York, whose wheels sunk deep in the far north of that State. Cosgrove & Grant's, of Lowell, and Dow's, of Boston, breezed along to fairly good profits in the New England section. There were Bernard McGraw's, Martin Sullivan's, Billy Furlong's, Billy Reap's, Wilson & Co., Frank Walter's, Jim Silver's . . .

Andrew Downie's big two-car show percolated in railroad roundhouses. The company began when the Panama Exposition closed at Buffalo, where Downie purchased two cars which had run to the Exposition grounds over trackless streets — a great novelty then. The Tom manager converted the cars into sleepers as comfortable as Pullman berths, and four horses pulled them from town to town; they did not have to stop at hotels for lodging or meals. Another cabin-like affair on flat-tired wheels housed the band; it was topheavy, swayed at crazy angles, and during the night drive spilled the musicians from their bunks. The Downie show was a household word along the Great Northern and Canadian Pacific. The players dressed up in Royal Mounted uniforms for the 11:45 procession, led by a very clever little lady, Andy Downie's Wife, the Little Eva, who did wonderful tricks with her baton.

Not all troupes could emulate the topnotchers who entered a big town with acetylene flares, luring the crowds with balloon ascensions and other sideshow attractions. The smaller nomadic Tom wagons, whose wheels screamed for grease on the dusty roads, played the cross-road towns during the summer and the dime museums in the winter; nor did they ever overlook any dot on the map, covering every water tank in the East and every grain elevator in the West. They rented folding chairs from local undertakers. And once Una Pelham went to heaven standing on a beer keg! The auction block would sometimes be an empty box that formerly contained cans of the world's best known baked beans. Mary C. Crawford, describing the background of the American theatre, revealed the intimate aspect of the Tommers, "I myself remember seeing a production, about 1900, in a little New Hampshire village with so crude a setting that between the acts a borrowed best sofa, on which Little Eva was subsequently to die and go to heaven, was passed solemnly over the improvised footlights!"

In 1902 sixteen Tom troupes pitched tents, and any number of "rep" or "rave and tear" companies were hanging 'em from the chandeliers. Perhaps the latter enjoyed an advantage over the regular Tommers, for they avoided such mishaps as befell the wandering units. Witherell & Doud's, in its twenty-third season under canvas (in 1921), was completely destroyed by fire, and was compelled to consolidate with the J. Shipman company. That February, C. G. Phillips' was also wiped out by fire at its large winter quarters in Courtland, Ohio. Four members of Ed. F. Davis' lost their lives, in March, when the mammoth sleeping car ig-

A Tense Moment in the Folk Play

nited from a defective flue, and some leaped into the snow in their night clothes. That September, the noted Topsy, Kate Partington, of Stetson's troupe, was mortally injured in a railway accident in Illinois...

How were the large troupes faring? In its twenty-fifth year, in 1904, Stetson's Big Double Spectacular owned four companies. Leon Wells Washburn (or "L. W.") controlled the foursome, assisted by four very able managers: C. T. Brockway headed the Eastern contingent, Al Gould operated along the Pacific Coast and Northwest, William Kibble (for years featured as a lightning drum major in the street parade) now led the Northern and Western company, and Grant Luce carried on in the Middle States ("L. W." traveled with the latter). Each outfit included 56 ponies, 25 hounds, 20 chariots, 8 donkeys, and 8 carloads of scenery, the parade turning every town into a glorious holiday. Washburn kept a weather-eye open for such attractions as Gus Gaines, who led the procession juggling knives. Once, while watching the street show from a prominent corner on Main Street in Reading, Pa., the assiduous proprietor detected a flaw in the band. He hurried to the theatre, pacing nervously, until two trombone players drifted in, and he beckoned the two aside: "Say, boys, you play damned well. But can't you get together, and get those slides to go out and in together? It *would* look much better." Washburn realized his greatest triumph when Stair & Havlin offered him their city circuit. They stipulated, however, that his show must measure up to Martin's. He fitted out the No. 4 company (managed by Grant Luce) with a complete change in uniforms and scenic appurtenances, and pooled all the ponies, dogs and chariots of his other three Tom shows. When the splendid Washburn retinue streamed down Broadway, from the old Star Theatre in Harlem, the first impression was that Barnum's circus had struck town. Washburn refused to go on at terms of first money to theatres, then a 50-50 split, and insisted on straight sharing. So he returned to the small towns.

Quaint, rugged, and vividly self-confident were the

Stetson lithographs, which boasted during 1904: "It stands like a towering monument of all that is great. Its record is the beacon of success and stands the test of time. The Whale and the Minnow, the Rose and a Weed — Have been used so much, they are too old for us. We are up to date...It is now, and will be for all time, the invincible monarch of them all! We know nothing of Rivals. We are positively, undeniably, incontrovertibly the mightiest U. T. C. Company on all the green earth!"

This sublimity may have cast a pall over many a would-be imitator, but it failed to awe at least one company, a Tom show from Kalamazoo, Mich. When Ed. F. Davis' invaded the East, near Buffalo, during the same autumn, its large posters announced: "The only one that *squares* with every written and pictured promise. POSITIVELY THE GREATEST TOURING PRODUCTION OF THE PLAY EVER PROJECTED, Transported on its own Train of Palace Cars. OUTCLASSING ALL OTHERS. ALWAYS BEYOND ALL RIVALRY. THIS IS NO BLATANT BLAST OF UNCLE TOM 'HOT AIR' ORIGINATING FROM THE OVER HEATED FURNACE OF IMAGINATION, but a plain statement of a simple matter of fact. No Good Old 'Has Been' or 'Will Be,' but 'Is' IT RIGHT NOW."

The nation's billboards saw the greater incursions of Al. W. Martin's, which proclaimed: "Other so-called Tom shows follow us — and do a fair business on our reputation! We are THE ONLY ONES always fully abreast in the march of progress, while imitators, metaphorically speaking, continue swinging by their caudal appendages, from bough to bough, in the forest of mediocrity."

Martin's was now really too big for imitators. He was called "Minister Plenipotentiary of the Side Show," and he had two large units — one in the East, the other in the West. In each "Mastodonic" were 80 acting people, 20 in the (white) Silver Coronet Band and Orchestra, 12 in the Creole Girls' Drum and Bugle Corps, 14 in the African (male) Drum and Fife Corps, 30 ponies, horses, donkeys, mules and

oxen, cages, chariots, traps, and a tally-ho. There were "15
—Ferocious Man Eating Bloodhounds—15," an acquisition
hailed by the promoter as "the only specimens of this noted
breed that figured so conspicuously in the war between Spain
and Cuba that have ever been brought to this country for exhibition." From the kennels of a Havana fancier, Jose Sil-
varado, they were not as large as had been popularly imagined, but the size of ordinary bulldogs, and Mr. Martin appropriately named two of them "Maceo" and "Gomez."

About 1908, the man who had reached an all-high in
the street parade, suddenly decided to abandon it. Martin now
claimed that a street exhibition placed his players in the
light of freaks, rather than actors, and that it detracted much
from the real sentiment of the drama. His formal band of
twenty-five gave concerts, instead, at the noon hour and
in the evening. He abandoned his ingenious novelties, such
as the voodoo worship scene, and tried to restore the original
dramatization without the "cuts" (made for the induction of
specialties). Martin began to hire white actors exclusively,
maintaining that white men had proved their ability to depict
the Negro in a way far excelling the Negroes themselves. He
rehearsed from a book of the play, but found a rebellion on
his hands, for the actors threw away the scripts, and shaped
out the scenes as had been handed down to them.

In 1907, James W. Harkins and Edwin Barbour, repeating their experiment of ten years previous at the Star Theatre,
also stripped the play of its familiar adjuncts. They eliminated entirely the hounds, the ice scene, the slave mart, and
the ascension of Eva. No longer were Lawyer Marks and
Topsy mirth-provoking, but merely subordinate characters;
the Quaker, too, was gone. Without recourse to any of the sensational incidents, the playwrights felt there would unques-
tionably result a more dignified production. With all the ten-
twent'-thirt' thrills missing, it would seem that very little
was left of the original play, but when it opened at the New
York Majestic, on May 30th, it lasted all of four hours. The

playwrights introduced a few new dramatic slants: Mrs Shelby (Charlotte Lambert) snatched Legree's whip as he was about to shackle Uncle Tom (John Sutherland) and laid it upon his back with considerable vigor—much to the approbation of the audience. The fourth act showed Eva (Gretchen Hartman) dying in an upright position in a flower-draped red cart, wheeled about by Tom. The following act revealed the inebriated Legree (Herbert Bostwick) grappling with his former mistress, Cassy, on the bridge, and he fell into the awful abyss below. The concluding tableau embodied the realization of Uncle Tom's dream: the freeing of the slaves by Abraham Lincoln.

Other prominent players in this adaptation were Mary Hampton (Mrs. Bird) and Lucille La Verne (Chloe and Cassy). It meant a real sacrifice for Miss La Verne to appear in the drama. "While a source of personal gratification," she said, "it meant complete ostracization by my family, who are rabid rebels, even to this day. My grandfather fought and died in the field of Shiloh for the Southern cause, but I was bound to play the part in spite of family opposition. Here I am — behold me! — playing in a New York production of *Uncle Tom's Cabin* and wearing, as Cassy, the very muslin gown worn by my grandmother when they brought her news of what the war had cost her."

The Harkins and Barbour production was a tame affair. The *Sun*, in its review, commented: "The new edition would hardly enjoy greater vogue here than did the old south of the Mason & Dixon Line."

A year later, Charles E. Blaney projected the Harkins and Barbour play as an Easter attraction at the Lincoln Square Theatre in New York, with some few changes, like the restoration of the Apotheosis. It was thought best not to print the names of the two collaborators on the program. Frank Ward O'Malley, who covered the opening night for his newspaper, gave this glowing observation of Blaney: "He evidently has so much faith in his play that he was the only

manager with nerve enough to brave the theatrical terrors of
Holy Week by presenting a première. He had faith in his
play and confidence in his star, Miss Edna May Spooner,
perhaps the greatest emotional actress ever born in Bergen
Street, Brooklyn." Edna had the part of Ophelia. When
the critics gathered in the lobby to discuss the mysterious
authorship of the dramatization, O'Malley overheard someone say that *Uncle Tom's Cabin* had certainly contributed
much toward the outbreak of the war. This was not lost upon
two others, a "young Mr. Young Corbett and his brother,
younger Mr. Young Corbett." O'Malley's ear caught the
following:

"Do you think it had anything to do with the war?" the
younger brother asked young Mr. Young Corbett.

"That I cannot say," answered the older Mr. Young
Corbett. "But," he went on, "what's the difference? We
licked hell out of the Spaniards anyway."

It would be an injustice here not to reproduce the *Sun's*
headline which Selah Merrill Clarke composed, that day, for
O'Malley's article:

THE DRAMATIZED NOVEL AGAIN

SOMEONE HAS MADE A PLAY OUT
OF UNCLE TOM'S CABIN

*It Deals With Political Ethics and Has
Many Strong Points, but Seems to Lack
the Elements of Enduring Success
—Well Acted, and Lavishly Staged*

The old war-horse champed in the musical field of those
days. In J. A. Shipp's *In Dahomey* the elderly Negro played
by Pete Hampton, and the impetuous, rebellious child, Rosetta, by Ada Overton Walker, strongly suggested Uncle Tom
and Topsy. This ambitious opera was all-Negro, headed by

..d George Walker. William Marion Cook, ..ious work was a grand opera based on *Uncle* ..n, supplied the score.

.. another operetta, *When Johnny Comes Marching* ..ne, a comic adventurer, Jonathan Phoenix, was much of Lawyer Marks and a little of something else. The second act opened with a darkey chorus led by Uncle Tom singing, "Ma Honeysuckle Gal." In *A Girl from Dixie* the same mirth-maker of a lawyer was interpreted by George A. Schiller, whose catchline was, "As your legal adviser I advise you to be calm!" Uncle Tom appeared as one of the characters in the 1921 all-colored revue, *Shuffle Along*.

When comic opera was in vogue during the early part of the century, the sturdy perennial kept up with the tempo of the period; in 1903, it was given at Koster and Bial's, to the music of Arthur Pryor. When vaudeville came into favor, condensed versions usurped the boards. Corse Payton, famous in his own right as "America's best bad actor," played Marks in one of these emaciated dramatizations. with his wife, Etta Reed, as Topsy. Payton plugged the drama until 1927 with his group of twenty-five players, special scenery, hounds, and donkeys, including a street parade — all within the narrow confines of Keith's vaudeville "time." Sim Williams' tabloid version in burlesque form, with the Ercell Sisters (Anita and Louella as Topsy and Eva) made the rounds of the Columbia Circuit. In Chicago was seen *The Spirit of Uncle Tom*.

A musical comedy, *Topsy and Eva*, was specially prepared by Catherine Chisholm Cushing for the Duncan Sisters. Rosetta was the impish cut-up in burnt-cork, and Vivian the dainty songstress in blond curls. It first saw the foot-lights in San Francisco during 1923, then moved to Chicago, on December 30th, to the Selwyn Theatre, where it played for about fifteen months. A year later, on December 23rd, it came to the Sam H. Harris Theatre in New York, as a holiday attraction. Although this entertainment was said to be "based on *Uncle Tom's Cabin*," it was practically impossible

for critics to discover the base. One said, "Simon Legree is a whip, a whisker and a whiskey bass. Uncle Tom is a burnt cork, a Bible and a baritone." Indeed, Simon Legree was there — but only to crack a rhythmic whip to the London Palace girls' burnt-cork routine. Uncle Tom hobbled on, now and then, and crooned a few bars of "Swanee River" or "Old Black Joe." Eliza was also in circulation, and executed a few jazzy steps, perfectly oblivious to any ice. And the playbill listed Erasmus Marks, the first time that dignitary rejoiced in such a learned name. The versatile Duncan Sisters composed the music and lyrics, and sang, "Uncle Tom Cabin Blues," "Um-Um-Da-Da," and "I Never Had a Mammy." When the two sisters warbled operatically, "Onion Time in Bermuda," rampageous Topsy flung onions into the audience, and was the hit of the show. She first appeared with her toe tied up in a dirty old rag, and when the play ended, there she was in an unusual "Ascension" — riding to the proscenium by hanging on to the curtain.

The barnstorming tribulations of a tenth-rate Tom show were recounted in a comedy by Kenyon Nicholson in 1928. Originally a one-acter, *The Marriage of Little Eva* was enlarged with John Golden's collaboration to *Town Hall Tonight*; the play went on the road but the small towns passed it up as a local announcement, so the authors changed the title to *Eva the Fifth*. The comedy opened on August 28th at the Little Theatre, New York.

Eva the Fifth concerned a troupe stranded in Meehoopany, Pa. The town's richest man, Newton Wampler, a furniture dealer with undertaking as a sideline, wanted to adopt Little Eva (Claiborne Foster) but when he discovered that she was past thirty, he substituted a proposal of marriage, and was promptly accepted. While the wedding was being set in the dingy village hotel, the Uncle Tom, really in love with Eva, who would have nothing to do with such a shiftless ham actor, put on a benefit Tom Show in the Knights of Pythias Hall. The bride-to-be no longer available, her little sister (Lois Shore) was thrust into the part, and became Eva the fifth in the Hartley dynasty. Professional jealousy gripped the original Eva, and jilting the local patron and foregoing the opportunity of sitting up nights with late lamenteds in the parlor of his pretentious house, she went to battle. Deliberately, she gorged her sister with many tempting sweets. During the death scene, the child became stricken with a pain amidriffs, and ad libbed that she was dying, "no kidding." The former Eva quickly adjusted the traditional wig of heavy blond tresses, and jumped into the familiar role. And the audience was quite satisfied — with two Evas! Then Eva the fourth accepted Uncle Tom as her spouse. And there followed the backstage aftermath of Little Eva the fifth being forcibly fed castor oil.

At the time *Topsy and Eva* and *Eva the Fifth* were seen, the hardy perennial was thriving. During 1924-25, the Triangle Players revived the old Aiken version in New York. In May, 1925, both the Prince of Wales and the Grand Theatres in Sydney, New South Wales, were showing the play. In Honolulu, a month later, the State Theatre announced with widest publicity, "its first showing."

At least a dozen companies hit the road during the summer of 1927, among them: William J. Harvall's, John F. Stowe's, Mason Bros.', Harmount's, Sterling's, Harrington's, Newton, Pingree & Holland's, Terry's, Mort Steece's, Stanton-Huntington's, George S. Clark's, Capt. Roy L. Hyatt's Water Queen (a showboat)...The strongest was the forty-year-old Harvall's, stumping along the rural routes, the Black Hills of South Dakota, and Northern Nebraska and Wyoming. Three years later it traversed more than 8,000 miles through the Pacific Northwest, leading up to the Hood River, Oregon. The company was owned by William Valentine, manager, and J. W. Harpstrite, former advance agent of John Stowe's. As for the Stowe outfit, now in its thirty-eighth season, it played that Spring through Michigan with fifteen trucks and passenger cars. However, the Mason Brothers' held the longevity record, with fifty-seven years of Tomming; it began decades back as Mason & Morgan's, and was now owned by Thomas Aiten.

Harmount's was scooping 'em up. In Texas, early in 1920, "Tad" had abandoned his company to invest his savings in ninety acres of land adjoining the famous Beaumont and Humble oil fields. Now Clarence B. Harmount, his brother, outfitted the show at its quarters in Williamsport, Ohio, with eight trucks all beautifully painted yellow and white and magic red lettering. The big top broken in at the end of the decade was 80 x 160 ft., which gives some idea of the size of the audiences Harmount played to each season in Ohio, Indiana and Illinois.

Sterling's, under ownership of Thomas L. Finn, just about rounded out a quarter of a century at the close of the Twenties. It had a 60x90 khaki top, and looked more like a circus than a dramatic show. Half an hour before the play opened, an additional side-show displayed freaks to the small towners. When others began to motorize, Finn sold his twenty head of fine horses, and replaced them with five trucks, four sedans and a trailer.

E. A. Harrington's, with headquarters at Kansas City, was another die-hard, which retained the street parade in all its glory as recently as 1929. The fleet of a dozen trucks penetrated at least fifteen states during the season. The following year, Mr. Harrington, after trouping for nearly forty years, met with misfortune. He expected to clean up with *Abie's Irish Rose,* which had a successful run of several years on Broadway, but when he produced Mrs. Nichols' play in his favorite Kansas territory, alas! it did not pull 'em in like *Uncle Tom's Cabin.*

Many old Tom managers had retired from the business, and were now independently wealthy: Witherell, Doud, Davis, Martin, Darling...Dick Sutton, settling down finally in Butte, Montana, became a theatrical magnate, the first big showman of that section. Jim Shipman, before his death in

1921, put his profits into a hotel at Winchester, N. H., where his cuisine and Tomming stories made the Shipman House famous among Eastern tourists. In Pine Bluff, Wyoming, lived C. E. Beryle, the former operator of Burke's U. T. C. Company, now a wealthy banker and ranch owner. He was the first to install an electric light plant under canvas, such a striking feature at the time that mobs jammed his Tom show just to see how the lights worked. Charles York, who put out a show from Carbondale, Pennsylvania, invested his Tomming fortune in chain stores in that state. C. G. Phillips, with a show out of Cortland, Ohio, became a banker and street railway magnate there. Andrew Downie amassed a fortune from his wagon Tom show in Canada, but lost it through the failure of the Bank of Medina. John and Mike Welsh, who cached Hobson's U. T. C. Company, experimented with a movie of the play, and showed it through New Jersey and Long Island at the close of the Twenties.

However, many of the retired old-timers found the Tomming lure tugging away at them. Joe Barnum, who had enacted Marks over 8,000 times, and became known as "the 72-year-old kid," was asked to stage the old reliable for the Columbia Theatre in Ashland, Kentucky, and eagerly hobbled up to do it. . . Frank E. Griswold had been living quietly in Warren, Ohio, for a number of years, a respected member of the community; his wife, who once made 'em scream at Topsy's wild mischief, was now Grand Worthy Matron of the Ohio Order of the Eastern Star, and his daughter Dorothy, once Eva, was happily married. Upon his wife's death, the wanderlust, after a half century of Tomming, suddenly seized him. He built a trailer, and for twelve glorious months made a circuit of Lake Erie, tacking South in the autumn, when he took the old Tom trail to the Gulf of Mexico. . . Leon W. Washburn, who had organized Stetson's Company in 1880, retired about 1910. He purchased from Tom Hargrave's estate the Grand Opera House in Chester, Pennsylvania, remodeled it, and renamed it The New Washburn. He offered vaudeville and movies. After fifteen years of this sedentary existence, the old trouper, aged sixty-nine, became determined to travel over the familiar Tom route. He sold his small theatre, and took to the road again, hugging the folk play. He played throughout Michigan, but at the close of the season Washburn was in a wheel chair.

With the new spirit of the age came a complete modernization in Tom shows. When the Railroad Administration took over all available equipment in 1920, it was impossible to lease cars, and Tom managers figured that motorization would enable them to make almost any jump. By the end of 1929 the daily street parade was completely dispensed with because motorization was too hurried and mechanized. However, the illuminated trucks at night made a striking appearance on the lot. A calliope, mounted on a truck covered with large lithographs, was substituted for bally. C. B. Harmount used two of the steam demons, one tooling in advance, and the other with the show. His partner, C. W. Shartle, Jr., was a stunt flyer, and from a plane christened "Little Eva" he scattered heralds over the towns billed.

Tommers stuck to the most lucrative territory. Many troupes bunched in the North Dakota section: Terry's, Steece's, Newton, Pingree & Holland's, and a Canadian outfit, all playing within 200 miles of Columbus, during June, 1926. Harrington's, at that time, began its summer road tour of Northern Missouri and Nebraska, opening in a suburb of Kansas City, and— lo!— under the auspices of the Mt. Washington Fire Department. On the Ohio River, "Doc" Bart, closing his medicine show at Gallipolis, offered *Uncle Tom's Cabin* on a floating piece of architectural gingerbread, the "Ark Showboat."

The play had a perpetual American appeal. Mrs. Stowe's son estimated, in 1912, that it had been given about 250,000 times. He may have arrived at that figure by assuming that since each Tom show played the year round, an average company — that is, a single troupe

— would have performed it about 25,000 times during the 68 years, and as there were never less than 10 companies, hence 250,000. But Charles E. Stowe was too modest, for during the '80s the average year beheld from 20 to 50 Tom troupes; the '90s reached the saturation point — 50 to 500. And he did not consider performances abroad, especially in Great Britain.

Whether or not the play had lost any of its favor with the American public by 1927, can be discerned in the account of the Dover (Ohio) *Reporter* of that year:

> Little Eva died for the ten millionth time since Harriet Beecher Stowe wrote *Uncle Tom's Cabin* and started the Civil War; Eliza escaped across the river on swirling cakes of ice, pursued by one bloodhound — count him — and Simon Legree was as mean as ever when the "greatest and best mammoth *Uncle Tom's Cabin* production ever seen" played under a tent at the Dover fairgrounds Thursday night.
>
> And the tent was packed — get this, you highbrows and modern theatregoers. Harry Stowe, who claims to be a relative of the author, played Uncle Tom with pathos marred only by the cries of the tent vendors. He has been playing the part thirty-seven years and nothing can disturb him. Little Eva sold her photo for ten cents, then went on the stage and died amidst shouts of "Pop Corn, ten cents a bag," and after the curtain dropped and was raised again she appeared as an angel in heaven, wings and all. She'll do the same thing again tonight in some other town, but under the same old water-proof canvas.

Many a Tom troupe ran into misfortune that summer. Stanton-Huntington's company, in Ohio, had its tent blown down in a storm. Ora Martin's, bristling through Iowa, was nearly destroyed by fire the year before; now it encountered a "bloomer," because of the heavy rains and poor, muddy roads. When William J. Harvall's made a sortie in Idaho, at the end of May, illness in the company forced an inordinate doubling of parts, and the review in the local newspaper described the performance:

There was, methinks, a protest from the spirit of Uncle Tom, who lies moldering in the grave down in Alabama, when the play of that name was put on in Meridian last Friday night. And when the gentle Harriet Beecher Stowe gave the remarkable book to the world to help the cause of the North, she did not anticipate such a desecration as Harvall's *Uncle Tom's Cabin* Tent Show would inflict upon an innocent public. The good-sized tent was crowded.

Crowded is the word — as the seating of the audience was limited to narrow hard-wood planks. This was the 'reserved seats' mind you! The other seats were — well, Marshall Spencer would not let us use such a word in *The Times.*

The entire musical program was a bass drum and a trombone, played by Marks, the lawyer, and Simon Legree behind the curtain of a small stage. When they were engaged in putting over their parts there was no music.

There was nothing especially noticeable about Little Eva except that she forgot to wear any stockings, and as she was old enough to have played the part 20 years ago it was quite shocking. In fact, one Meridian resident was called down good and plenty by his wife when he became so engrossed in the story Eva was telling Uncle Tom that he fell off a high seat.

Speaking of reserved seats, it was 50 cents to get in, 25 cents for a reserved seat, and 10 cents for the concert. This is not a high price as shows go, but in this case it was robbery, pure and simple.

In the transition scene when the cruel Legree whips Uncle Tom to death, and the latter is supposed to enter the pearly gates, Uncle Tom acted as though he was willing to go to either place, so as to get through the act quickly.

You have heard of doubling in parts — well, all help, including six or eight people, trebled in parts. Uncle Tom acted as usher, as Uncle Tom and one other. Aunt Ophelia was ticket taker, Eliza and the strict New England aunt. Marks, the lawyer, was everywhere in different makeups.

George Shelby was the husband of Eliza, also a cruel slave buyer and a general utility man. Topsy was also Uncle Tom's wife and ticket taker.

Some of the time of the play was taken up in selling candy with prizes inside, and announcing the concert. Yes, it was interesting if you did not weaken and decide that your backbone would stand no more of the narrow seats and rough jokes.

Often the emblazoned "12 sheets," on both sides of the calliope, beggared the truth, indeed. Newton, Pingree & Holland's was at one time afflicted so hard that the public suspected some sort of hoax, and could hardly believe the situation as summed up by one of the players: "Sickness seems to have hit the whole show. First, 'Cap', the big Dane, caught the flu and died. Then Ruddy Stuhr's wife became ill and had to go home. Glen Radcliff took sick but managed to stay on the job. Verdoon Radcliff caught the measles. Bill Hammock was visited by the mumps. Frank Flint, doing Tom, lost his voice. Evelyn Wiltse fell under the weather. F. D. Whetten caught a cold and a bit of the flu. Al Regan is all in— trouble unknown— and the chief is not smiling either." Of course, he insisted that the troupe continued to pack 'em in, "fracturing" a number of house records along the route — despite the severe handicaps.

Chapter XVII

UNCLE TOM GOES TO THE MOVIES

T *is for Topsy, impish and wild;*
    Only sweet Eva can tame this poor child.
O's *for Ophelia, a spinster unblest;*
    An angel to Eva, to Topsy, a pest.
P *is for Platform, where Tom was on sale,*
    And also where Eva saved Topsy from jail.
S *is for Shelby, a gallant young blade,*
    Whom Topsy and Eva helped win a fair maid.
Y *is for Yore, the old cabin days,*
    In Topsy and Eva, *the brightest of plays.*
E *is for Eva, who pined to get back*
    Topsy her playmate so ragged and black.
V *is for Vivian, whose "Eva's" the pal,*
    For Rosetta's "Topsy", the "wickedest gal."
A's *for Amusement, which mounts to a shriek*
    In Topsy and Eva *arriving next week.*
        —Throwaway cards

Dr. H. D. Rucker's Korak Medicine show was a blaze of gold-leaf fretwork, traveling in grand style. The living car had eight state rooms, furnished in black walnut, silk plush upholstery and German silver metal work; each compartment had modern hotel conveniences, including a commodious bath. The other car held baggage and stock and the musical instruments of the twenty-one men in the Black Hussar Band. Dr. Rucker's company was immeasurably prosperous because the stage director, Donald Franck, had presented for the first time, in November, 1899, his original electric allegory, a feature not seen in any other Tom show.

With the use of a newly patent cineomatographic device and colored gauze drops, Franck lent great reality to the Eliza chase, although only the ice background was reproduced on the drops, flickering throughout. And when the jittery allegory was projected on the tinted gauze screen, audiences were convinced that St. Vitus himself ruled the pictured heaven. Despite the mechanical crudeness, it was a step ahead of the magic lantern, and even the Kleine Optical Company, which at that time rented out a series of a dozen slides on *Uncle Tom's Cabin,* realized it. Franck's contrivance relegated to limbo the huge panoramas so popular previously, and their mournful handlers became itinerant organ-grinders.

The rise of the nickelodeons was similar to that of the favorite American folk play: low admission prices, and performances in lowly surroundings — cheap halls, slovenly basements, empty stores — while clergymen and editors thundered against the "sinks of sin." The *legitimate* profession shunned the bawling infant, but the movies attracted Tom show actors. H. B. Morgan, of the famous Mason & Morgan's, was one of the first managers to venture into the new field, casting his fortune with the Essanay Studios in Chicago.

Curiously enough, many of the early movie comedies were either about the decline or at the expense of the *legitimate.* In the first category belonged: *The Old Footlight Favorite* (Geo. Melies, 1908), *The Old Actor* (Kleine Optical Co., 1908), *Memories of an Old Theatrical Trunk* (Edison, 1909), *The Old Actor's Vision* (Kleine, 1912), *The Stranded Actor* (Melies, 1910), *An Old Actor* (Selig, 1913), *The Actor's Christmas* (Imp, 1913)...

But it is the second group that interests us. We recognize immediately in the chief protagonist none other than Lawyer Marks, who ridiculed the tradition-bound, moribund profession. In *The Crushed Tragedian,* (Lubin, 1908) he was called Mr. Dandaly, but his makeup was similar to the

Markses in thousands of Tom shows. Here our hero was engaged for the part of another Mark — Mark Antony, but the engagement ended all too soon. He plodded into the rural sections, where his art enthralled the women folk, but incurred the enmity of their husbands. The latter had no earthly use for "them actors," and when he attempted his "legitimate drama" at a picnic, they cooled his ardor in a nearby pond. Then he counted the ties of the railroad; a train gave him a lift, but the stranded thespian found himself catapulted into a coal pile, from which he emerged — with uncrushed spirit — as a ghost at a dinner given by colored folks, where he had everything his own way.

Two other films of 1913 satirized the thespians of the old order, *Othello in Jonesville* and *Alas! Poor Yorik*. In the latter, a tall, cadaverous tragedian, the most conspicuous patient in a sanitarium, escaped from his keepers. Since he would naturally go to the theatre, all managers were warned. When an impoverished actor of the old school applied for a job, his vociferous manner excited suspicion at once, and he could not understand why he was detained *without* a contract. Then the manager was notified that the real lunatic had been recaptured.

Nor were Tommers above criticism in the early cinematic efforts. In *The Troubles of a Stranded Actor* (Lubin, 1909), a Mr. Shakespeare attempted Little Eva, but the unappreciative citizens of Windsor greeted him with over-ripe tomatoes, and ran him out of town. The last seen of him was in Mr. Bug's Sanitarium, where he enacted Little Eva with impunity. In *An Uncle Tom's Cabin Troupe* (Biograph, 1913), a local proprietor was so impressed by a Tom show that he gladly swapped his hotel for it, but the hardships entailed in the enterprise made him admit later, in a subtitle, "Evil the day that I became an actor!" A more favorable view was presented in *The Open Road* (Reliance, 1913), wherein a millionaire's disinherited son took to the highway and got a job pasting posters for a Tom troupe. Under the

The Earliest Movie
(Edison—1903)

Museum of Modern Art Film Library

influence of the bracing life, he regretted his dissipated youth, and married one of the pretty Tom show actresses.

In *The Death of Simon Le Gree* (Universal L-Ko comedy, 1915), a group of barnstorming Tommers hit the town, and Simon Le Gree completely captivated a little country maid who was thrilled when he tossed her a rose from the stage. Her jealous swain, Fatty, obtained a copy of the play, and began rehearsals at the opera house. The whole town turned out for his debut. But Little Eva's ascent to Heaven was ruined when the property man (Billie Ritchie) slipped on the rope hauling her up, and landed on the stage himself, all ending in side-splitting fashion. Similar mischief was later seen in a Paramount-Mack Sennett comedy, *Uncle Tom without the Cabin*.

The famous American play came to the screen in 1903, when Edwin S. Porter produced it with revolutionary devices for the Edison Company. It ran 1,100 feet, and was considered the longest and most expensive film yet made, comprising a prologue and fourteen scenes. The producer vouched: "The story has been carefully studied and every scene posed in accordance with the famous author's version." Further, "A departure from the old methods of dissolving one scene into another has been made by inserting announcements with brief descriptions." This may have been the same film which the Kinetograph Company rented out in 1904. The nearest competitor to Porter's masterpiece arrived during the summer of 1907, when Lubin made a 700-foot adaptation.

But by 1910 the rivalry was such that two film concerns released photoplays the same day, July 26th. The Vitagraph company advertised, "The Most Magnificent, Sumptuous and Realistic Production Ever Attempted of *Uncle Tom's Cabin*." It was in three parts, of one reel each (1,000 ft. to a reel), for the movie industry then could only release the film piecemeal, several days elapsing before the public saw it in its entirety. The rival picture, announced as "The

Prize Thanhouser Classic," claimed a tremendous triumph in so far as it was "Not a Tedious Drawn-Out, Continued-in-Our Next Affair, but COMPLETE IN ONE REEL." This one-reel masterpiece was complete in 1,000 feet, with Frank Crane as Uncle Tom and the "Thanhouser Kid" as Little Eva.

Three other productions were made in 1913. Imp filmed a three-part movie, with some interesting "shots" of George Harris and slaves hauling logs out of a swamp, and the death of St. Clair in a saloon brawl. Kalem made a "Special" in two parts, with Anna (Q.) Nilsson as Eliza. The third, a four-reel, super-super-special by Universal, was the most pretentious up to that time. Many of the scenes were taken on the Sacramento River, with the ice "shots" at Mt. Wilson. Prominent players were Robert Z. Leonard (Legree), Eddie Lyons (Marks), and Gertrude Short (Eva).

The next year, the World Film Corporation offered a five-part reeler, with seventy-two-year-old Sam Lucas, the Grand Old Man of the Negro Stage, as Uncle Tom. Marie Eline, the "Thanhouser Kid," was again Eva, with Irving Cummings as George Harris. During the filming of the scene where Eva is rescued by Uncle Tom, a strong undertow drew both players under the stern-wheel steamer, and Little Eva, contrary to the story, had to hold up the septuagenarian until aid arrived.

Another photoplay, adhering closely to the novel, came in 1918 from the Famous Players-Lasky studios. Here the camera's superiority over the stage was apparent in the re-production of the "underground railroad," and the thrilling sequences covered many States, from Louisiana to Canada. J. Searle Dawley, the director, traveled thousands of miles for the actual localities; the company went to Louisiana to "shoot" on the original site. Eliza's escape, always a memorable bit of stage technique, was even more thrilling on the screen. The lens reproduced closeups of the hounds plunging and struggling to gain a foothold on a slab of ice on the frozen river. Frank Losee, long identified in Tom shows with Simon Legree, was the pious Uncle Tom.

Thru the use of double exposures, Marguerite Clark was both Topsy and Little Eva.

Harry Pollard, the Uncle Tom in the 1913 Universal super-super-super special four-reeler, was by now a noted director for Universal, and Margarita Fischer, who had then appeared as Topsy, was his wife. Many of the scenes in the 1913 picture were taken outdoors, and Pollard could recall how they were hampered by unfavorable weather. The Eliza sequence, for instance, petered out when the ice thawed on location, and they had to resort to canvas-covered soap boxes on rockers. The sets, too, had been crude, the painted drops substituting for the St. Clair mansion, a cotton field, etc. The whole arrangement had been boxed-in, dominated by the influence of the stage. And for fourteen long years Pollard cherished the hope of doing the movie realistically.

His opportunity came when Carl Laemmle decided to transfer the folk play to celluloid. The $2,000,000 budget set for it broke all records; the 1913 super-special had cost only $15,000. This vast undertaking won for Laemmle the nickname, "Uncle Carl," and his was the highest price the slave ever brought.

A large number of technicians were dispatched to the many towns and places enumerated in Mrs. Stowe's two-volume work. They traveled eight months all over the South, and painstakingly jotted down all available data bearing on the period; they delved into the dusty archives of pre-Civil War days. There were 66,000 individual items of hand props listed, minutiae that might escape the critical eye of the most captious, such as the slaves' drinking cups hollowed out from gourds, twisted papers over the fireplaces used as tapers to light the morning fires...

Later, the exact replicas of buildings described by Mrs. Stowe were erected. The St. Clair home was constructed at a cost of $70,000, the Shelby home at $62,000, and the Legree plantation house (in its run-down condition) at $40,000. They were completely furnished with period furniture, and included a number of genuine and valuable Louis XV pieces, and a crystal chandelier from an historic New Orleans home decorated the St. Clair living room. The first two houses followed faithfully two mansions in New Orleans, the Belle Chase mansion and the Wogan residence in the old French Quarter. The Shelby estate had the "slave street," with its parallel rows of squalid cabins, authentic even to cobwebs and the quaint utensils inside the huts, and the wharf at the end of the street piled high with cotton bales. Over one quarter of a million feet of lumber was used, and more than one hundred tons of plaster went into the walls. There was no "grass matting," usually used for exteriors, but from the mountains of Southern California were hauled 1,000 full grown trees, and from the Mississippi came 50 bales of Spanish moss. The 10,000 artificial magnolias, oleanders and other varieties were intermingled with tens of thousands of jasmine, Spanish dagger, all the flowers native to the old South.

Pollard and his company journeyed over 26,000 miles to capture the various points of interesting locale. He went to Plattsburg, New York, for his ice sequences before the Spring thaws melted the floes in the Saranac River, and chased an ice jam four months, which took in over 4,000 miles of territory. He filmed Eliza at the very edge of the river, close to a raging torrent, where Phineas Fletcher saved her from the falls. The well-known flight required hounds, but Pollard insisted on "real bloodhounds," not great Danes or mastiffs. He paid a record price of $20,000 for a team of registered bloodhounds of the Ledburn strain, from England, whose ancestry trailed back to Virginia slave days.

In the early Fall, a second trip was made, this time into the deep Southern locale. Most of the animated river scenes were "shot" on the noted old side-wheeler, "Kate Adams," last survivor of the legendary river palaces once plying the Mississippi; chartered, Pollard changed her name to the "La Belle Riviere" of the novel. A few weeks after the filming, an explosion and fire burnt her to the water's edge.

To render the characters more authentic, Pollard eliminated the types seen in the Tom shows. He cast a robust, forty-year-old Negro, James B. Lowe, as Uncle Tom, true to Mrs. Stowe's original. The Legree of George Siegmann underwent nineteen different kinds of makeup before the director was satisfied; and to allow the proper repugnancy, Legree was seen storming out of a dining room, the food drooling from his mouth onto his Yankee beard. Arthur Edmund Carewe, as Harris, spoke in screen subtitles that were a departure from the educated character on the stage. The Marks of Lucien Littlefield was altogether unrecognizable — a scheming, cowardly, pettifogging lawyer. And Topsy's wickedness (Mona Ray) had to be imagined, for it was left out.

The two-million-dollar movie was completed after nineteen months, with 977,000 feet of film exposed for a record breaker — twelve reels! The average Big Production up to then required eight or nine different sets, but Pollard had sixty-five. Altogether, 5,000 players were in the massive production.

Although Pollard claimed that every play or picture done before had absolutely ignored Mrs. Stowe's novel, his twelve reels unwound abuses hitherto unknown — abuses of the camera. Various views of Little Eva's (Virginia Grey) deathbed were shown from different angles. As Margarita Fischer, the Eliza, was Pollard's wife, he gave her all the closeups. Uncle Tom seemed quite secondary, and throughout the first half he came in only for a couple of long shots. The scenario carried the plot to the end of the Civil War, although Mrs. Stowe wrote her book in 1851-52. Some of the new situations — purely cinematic — revealed a brief flash of Lincoln, and Sherman's march to the sea, with Atlanta under shell fire and in flames; then a martial finale, when the General stopped long enough in the internecine strife to rescue Eliza and Cassy from Legree's clutches; startled by the sudden appearance of the Union Army, Legree fell out of the window. Someone suggested that Pollard's epic should have been called *The Exploits of Eliza, or How Eliza Was Saved from a Fate Worse than Death by the Union Army.* Despite all that labor and expense (even Uncle Tom's purchase price was raised from $1,200 to $1,800), the motion picture fell short of the novel's spirit.

In 1927, United Artists screened the Duncan Sisters in *Topsy and Eva.* As a play it had grossed well over nine hundred thousand dollars a year, playing in twenty-three American key cities for three and a half years. Del Lord, a director for Mack Sennett, was given the new assignment, with continuity by Scott Darling. The stage version was "clocked" with 347 laughs (Hollywood went in strenuously for statistics, just then), and new scenes showed Topsy sitting on a pin cushion, exclaiming (subtitularly) that she had suffered tire trouble. In this film Eva did not go to heaven, perhaps because medical science had advanced so remarkably since 1851; incongruously, again, the old South of "befo' de Wa'" days was heavily snowed under. However, the director did not have any difficulty with his locale material, for he found, within fifty miles of Hollywood, pre-Civil War cabins, mansions fronted by white, Southern Colonial pillars and spacious porticos, and even snow-capped mountains.

Topsy and Eva went through many hilarious adventures: Simon Legree, money lender, foreclosed the Shelby estate; but in the auction no one was willing to bid for Topsy, so the becurled Eva bought her for a solitary nickel. Aunt Ophelia undertook her correction and scrubbing, but the mischievous imp chewed tobacco and crawled around tripping up people. Then Shelby's fiancee, Marietta De Brie, the ward of Legree, discovered her father's will which proved that she was not a pauper as Legree insisted. When the St. Clair cotton crop burned that Christmas, Legree, in lieu of St. Claire's unpaid note, drove off with the slaves, including Topsy. Eva ran after the wagon, but fainted in the snow. Topsy escaped, pursued by Legree and his servants, who

ran her up a tree close to the window of the imprisoned
Marietta, who handed her the will and told her to take it to
Shelby. When Legree beheld his ill-gotten fortune disappearing, he ordered his pack of bloodhounds — an affable
St. Bernard — after Topsy. The fleeing madcap found a
pair of skiis, made a fast trip downhill, and landed on a
horse with snowshoes. She reached the river's edge, stepped
on a cake of ice — and floated away. Legree almost caught
her, and the two, Keystone-fashion, jumped from one cake
to another, but he slipped and was carried over a waterfall.
Landing, Topsy wandered into a graveyard, where strange
hands clutched at her ankles; they belonged to a number of
runaway slaves who had sought refuge on hearing the dog's
barking. Topsy arrived at the St. Clair mansion, where hope
had been abandoned for Eva's recovery. The dark romp fell
to her knees, and prayed to the subtitle, "Oh, Lord, don't
take little missy! Take me instead. You got plenty of
white angels. Have a black one!" Eva instantly recovered.
So happy was Aunt Ophelia at the miracle that she placed
Topsy in bed beside Eva, and the pair fell asleep in an af-
fectionate embrace. Closeup!

About this time, *Eva the Fifth* was screened as *Girl in
the Show* (MGM), with Bessie Love as the young ups'art.
But the precocity of Evas was well known to movie fans.
There was Pearl White, of a thousand breath-taking, death-
defying exploits in serials, who had made her debut at six,
in a Tom company in Greenridge, Mo., when the Eva was
down with the measles. Lillian Gish, like many Evas before
her, had an awful time trying not to giggle when the straps
under her robe tickled her, and her little ribs could hardly
stand the strain. Belle Bennett, earlier in her career, played
the sainted child, and at one performance could not be found,
but was eventually discovered curled up with a delinquent
bloodhound, both sound asleep. Helen Holmes, at the tender age of eight, first showed the spark in a Tom show, and
later fanned it into full glow in Kalem railroad pictures.

Dolores Costello enacted the part in the Edna May and Cecil Spooner Stock Company, at the Bijou Theatre, Brooklyn. Another famous Eva, Mary Pickford, first learned her lines in 1896, at the King George Opera House, Toronto, where Joe Barnum coached her on his knee.

To glamorize themselves, many film stars deliberately concealed their early Tom show beginnings. When the Fox publicity department, in 1917, launched a new star, Sonia Markova, the public was informed that it was necessary to shoot her new picture aboard a cruise ship, where the star was recovering from nervous prostration because her Russian relatives were in dire peril in Petrograd. Miss Markova was none other than Gretchen Hartman, of Chicago, where as a child she had made her début as Little Eva in the Bush Temple Stock company.

The movies drew abundant talent from Tomming companies. Harry Carey came from Sam Livingston's show, after playing the trolley parks for peanuts; Guy Kibbee was St. Clair in Al. W. Martin's; Frank McHugh topsied with the Ralph W. Chambers Associate Players in and around Pennsylvannia; Spencer Tracy enacted George Harris with the Wright Players in Grand Rapids, Michigan...

Even a very old Tom joke found its way into the movie industry. When Famous Players filmed the epoch-making attraction in 1918, there was a press release to the effect that Legree had bullied Uncle Tom, demanding, "Ain't yuh mine, body and soul?" as per the lines in the book, and that Frank Loose replied solemnly: "No, massa, mah soul belongs ter God, but mah body belongs ter—Adolph Zukor!" Well, years before, another Legree had propounded the same question to another Tom, and on that occasion Louis James, leading man in Jacob Litt's summer stock company, had replied in stentorian tones: "No, massa; mah body may belong ter yuh—but mah soul belongs ter Jacob Litt!" The jest could be traced to the Pullman strike in the summer of 1894, when a few actor-deputy marshalls on duty in Valparaiso decided

Shirley Temple as Little Eva

(20th Century-Fox, 1936)

to combine business with pleasure by giving *Uncle Tom's Stateroom* between trains at night. The Uncle Tom made a hit with the audience when he answered Simon Legree: "Mah body may belong to you, Massa Legree, but mah soul—mah soul belongs to George M. Pullman!" But even before that time it had been heard in the Washburn troupe, as "No, Massa, my body belong to you, but mah soul—mah soul belong to Leon Washburn!" We may accept W. W. Stout's word that the stock jest of the Tom world dated way before Washburn's time. Mr. Stout claims that Welsh Edwards, enacting Tom with Dan Shelby's troupe at the Academy of Music, Chicago, spoke the line of Dan Shelby, and that it may not even have been original with him. Perhaps the third-dimensional, technicolor movie of the future will use it again as fresh publicity for their newest production of *Uncle Tom's Cabin*.

The screen utilized early Tom show advertising methods, such as Draper's innovation of distributing cards to school children. When *Topsy and Eva* was shown, throwaway cards were printed with verses and pictures of the principals; these special rhymes formed a set of eight, and when all the cards were handed in at the box-office the holder was given a free ticket. A man dressed as an ante-bellum auctioneer, outside the movie-house, bellowed, "An irresponsible li'l imp of Satan an' the angelic daughter of wealth... Burnt cork vyin' with blond curls, the licorice an' marshmallow pair... One black, one fair — both noble 'neath rags an' laces..."

Twentieth Century-Fox Pictures, in 1936, shaped the early history of *Uncle Tom's Cabin* into a vehicle for Shirley Temple. *Dimples* related the story of a broken-down old rapscallion actor (Frank Morgan), whose little granddaughter attracted a young producer who was launching the memorable play at the National Theatre. The film showed the sequences of Little Eva and Topsy in the attic room; in a later scene old Tom and Eva went through the famous discussion of the new

(MGM, 1938)

Judy Garland as Topsy
in EVERYBODY SING

Jerusalem; then the deathbed, with Shirley propped u_
veniently to deliver the rhetoric, "I can see those great
made of pearl, and they're opening wide— and there are
angels— they're calling me! I'm coming! I'm coming!"
There was a bit of backstage humor, too, reminiscent of the
Double Mammoth days, when the grandfather, after palming
off a fake watch on his hostess (Helen Westley), tries to
evade the police by blacking up as Uncle Tom, and the
audience at the National Theatre was regaled by two Uncle
Toms entering the stage from opposite wings!

That movie producers were interested in what the Methu-
selah of plays had to offer, was evident by these forays. A
modern note enhanced the old situations, as in the musical
picture, *Everybody Sing* (1938), where Judy Garland, as
Topsy, rollicked:

> *Uncle Tom's got a new routine,*
> *Eliza crossed the ice in a limousine,*
> *While Simon Legree shakes a mean tambourine...*

That was hardly the way Lotta Crabtree interpreted it
seventy-three years ago, but more fitting to the age of swing
music. In *Can This Be Dixie?* (Twentieth Century-Fox,
1936) Jane Withers, as Eva, sang, "Uncle Tom's Cabin Is
a Cabaret Now." The same treatment was given to the
double Topsies of Betty Grable and June Haver in *The Dolly
Sisters* (Twentieth Century-Fox, 1945).

Recalling former showboat presentations, however, *The
Naughty Nineties* (Universal, 1945) had Abbott and Costello as Simon Legree and Eva, and that old mishap of the
rope breaking climactically in the block and tackle flight to
heaven.

With the triumph of the animated cartoon many take-
offs were seen: in *Uncle Tom's Crabbin'* (Educational,
1927), Felix the Cat outwitted Simon Legree; in *Topsy
Turvey* (Paramount, 1927), Krazy Kat was the hero; in
Schlessinger's Merrie Melodies, the same riotous treatment

Jane Withers Sings "Uncle Tom's Cabin Is a Cabaret Now"

(20th Century-Fox, 1936)

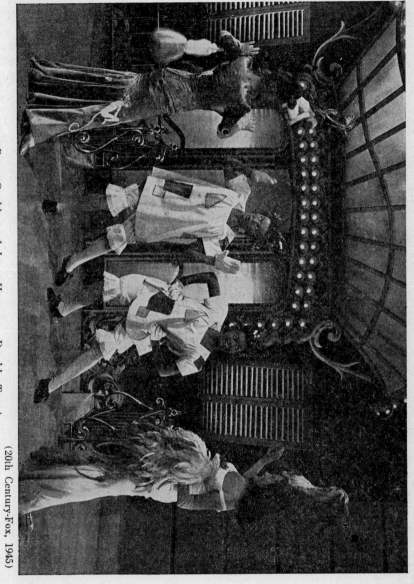

*Betty Grable and June Haver as Double Topsies
in* **THE DOLLY SISTERS**

(20th Century-Fox, 1945)

went into *Uncle Tom's Bungalow* (Vitaphone, 1937). Recently, *Pickaninny* and a Walt Disney, with the old title, caricatured the folk play.

The movies in their advance from the Kinetoscope, or peepshow machine, have outstripped every other art as the medium for popular expression. They are now the folk theatre of America.

CHAPTER XVIII

A GOOD PLAY NEEDS NO EPILOGUE

Farewell, O ancient Tom
We'll miss thee, and with reason;
Farewell forever—or until
You're reproduced next season!
— Anon., "Farewell to Uncle Tom"

INCREDIBLY, ALL THE NEWSPAPERS in 1931 carried a report that after a continuous run of seventy-nine years — the longest in history — the immortal American road show had at last scuffled off the boards! This news was based on an article in a theatrical magazine, "Uncle Tom Is Dead." But that same week, letters poured in from all parts of the country pointing out that there *was* a Tom company in town.

The hardy perennial's passing away had been rumored as far back as 1852, and regularly every theatrical season thereafter. Two years after the latest "demise," the drama enjoyed a most brilliant series of performances. The Players' Club, founded by Edwin Booth, had inaugurated annual revivals, and with the twelfth, in 1933, they chose an American institution — *Uncle Tom's Cabin*. Would it surmount the cynicism of a modern audience which expected a spoof revival of this favorite of the tank towns? Well, the Players decided to give it "straight."

A. E. Thomas revised the ramshackle Aiken text, and eliminated the high-flown phrases that had become obsolete in eighty-one years. He made at least two important contributions to the slave auction scene: First, the introduction of Aunt Hagar, who pleaded to be sold to the same master as her son Caesar; both characters were in Mrs. Stowe's novel, but hitherto neglected. The real reason for this interpolation was solely to provide a role for eighty-year-old Kate Mayhéw, who had played Eva to Lotta Crabtree's Topsy, in Indiana, in 1865. The other innovation was the sale of Topsy to Aunt Ophelia, also true to the record; but Topsy's biting of the auctioneer's finger, with her final impudent gesture to Simon

Courtesy of N. Y. World-Telegram

The Players' Revival of the Perennial (1933)
Drawn by Ken Chamberlain

Legree, who bid fifty cents for her, was purely creative. In Aiken's text the auction lasted several minutes, but Thomas's ran about twenty, and was one of the most vital scenes.

When the play opened at the Alvin Theatre, on May 29, the great cast read like a Who's Who of the Theatre. Otis Skinner was Uncle Tom, nor was it the first time he had undertaken the rôle; he had made his début at nineteen, in a little stock company at the Philadelphia Museum, and recalled, "I blacked up twelve times in one week playing Uncle Tom every afternoon and night and was happy." Fay Bainter was "the wickedest gal on de plantation," and did the breakdown with astounding authenticity, since her first appearance on any stage had been made twenty-seven years ago, as Topsy, behind the kerosene footlights of the local op'ry house in El Paso, Texas. Mingling with the distinguished performers was the pick of the Litchfield County Kennels, $20,000 worth of pedigreed hounds, and the sol-

Pollard Crowder

A Stylized Production
Gate Theatre, London (*1933*)

emnly-blinking donkey, "Jerry," also an old trouper, for he had played in *Pagliacci* with the Metropolitan Opera Company for six years.

The Alvin Theatre was packed to the doors with celebrities who came to pay tribute to the play. The critic, Percy Hammond, observed wet eyes around him, and detected dampness on the cheeks of the acrid cartoonist, Rollin Kirby, Edna Ferber, Fanny Hurst, Daniel Frohman,

Mr. and Mrs. Rea Irvin, Mrs. Skinner, Mary Nash's mother, his own son, John, and Katharine Hepburn. The noted columnist, F. P. A., found the line, "Sold to Simon Legree for twelve hundred dollars!" the most humanly moving moment in the play. Theatrical business on Broadway was topped that week with a gross of $22,000, and a great number of theatre-goers were unable to gain admittance. Orders for

In Leningrad (1933)
*Adaptation by A. Brushstein and B. Zon at Theatre of the
Young Spectators*

tickets poured in from all over the country, one party wiring reservations from Roanoke, Virginia. Against the precedent set by twelve years, the Players' Club was forced to extend the run another week; this proved insufficient, and another fortnight was added.

Then it went on tour. Many of the actors had other engagements, and reluctantly left; among the replacements were a new Topsy by Queenie Smith, the Eva by Betty Lancaster, and the Legree by Brandon Evans. The play, after

Queenie Smith

"Golly, I'se Wicked!" Gloats Topsy
to the Unending Dismay of Aunt
Ophelia Who Tries To Save Her
Black Soul

its phenomenal success in New York, was seen in Hartford, Boston and Philadelphia.

The opening in Boston took place on October 9th, at the Colonial Theatre. That evening, there sat in a first-tier box an eighty-five-year-old woman, whose snow-white coiffure contrasted vividly with the darker heads about her. She came from her home in Belmont, and brought with her a quaint, other-world charm.

Her visit to the theatre, that night, was high adventure. Tensely, she watched everything in that animated world behind the footlights. Her enchantment must have been similar to Mrs. Stowe's, when, in 1854, she was induced to enter a box at the Boston National Theatre, and heavily veiled, gazed at Little Cordelia Howard. Enraptured, the little woman watched the present Eva. She almost lived the part again. And when it was over, Mrs. Cordelia Howard MacDonald put away her handkerchief, donned her wrap, and filed from the theatre with the rest of the audience.

Then George Abbott, in 1936, expressed the belief that the famous play was sorely in need of "a more compact plot structure," and that it was about time for a brand-new script. When *Sweet River*, symbolical of Eliza's flight, opened at the Fifty-first Street Theatre, on October 28th, the program stated that it did not pretend to be an honest version, that it was "true to the original neither in the letter nor the spirit." The characters Mr. Abbott didn't particularly care for were left out, among them: Lawyer Marks, George Harris, Gumption Cute, Shelby, Deacon Perry. He eliminated, also, Little Eva's death, the Apotheosis, the onstage whipping of Tom. Topsy was tamed down, furtively darting in and out, and Legree was a paunchy, choleric, moustacheless fellow.

In Abbott's so-called realistic treatment no burnt cork was used, and all the slaves, with the exception of Eliza, were Negroes. Oddly, Walter Price, who enacted Tom, had never seen *Uncle Tom's Cabin*. The seven-year-old Betty Philson (Eva), from Philadelphia, spoke with a Southern accent — Abbott's bid for authenticity. Theatregoers were promised real ice floes in the "Ohio" River, but these turned out to be artificial frosting, a synthetic, frozen material. Most authentic of all were the dogs — real bloodhounds, no doubt inspired by a letter that Charles Washburn received during rehearsals, which he turned over to Abbott: "You don't know me, but my father worked for your grandfather, Leon Washburn, in a *Tom* show. He had charge of the dogs.

Courtesy of Charles Scribner's Sons

Sold down SWEET RIVER (1936)
Drawn by Fritz Eichenberg

My reason for writing is to warn you and Mr. Abbott to be sure to use real bloodhounds and get dogs that never were with a trouping show. Great Danes aren't the things for Broadway and I'll tell you why. They have inherited the urge to troupe and would run like mad to the railroad depot after the first performance." So wary Mr. Abbott didn't take dogs with previous experience.

The play's sets were designed by Donald Oenslager, who had endowed the scenery for the Players' revival with the quality of a Currier and Ives print, but now went strictly modern. The theatre had an uncommonly deep stage stretch-

— 417 —

Parade in BLOOMER GIRL (1944)

ing some fifty feet back, and permitted the production to be set on a turntable 45 feet in diameter, on which the settings revolved; these scenic devices alone ate up $150,000.

Notwithstanding the great modern investiture in scenery, there was an inherent weakness throughout because of Abbott's insistence, "It compelled a change in point of view — it became impossible to state the case so strongly." The drama's entire vitality was extracted in the extensive revision, so that the characters became self-effacing, and constantly aware of their unimportance. The play no longer had the old hot fury; it meandered along when it should have been a cataract. It closed after the fifth performance.

There was inaugurated, not long after, the roving Portable Theatre, five trailer trucks, each with a Washington label on its side, that served New York's millions. And the first experiment was *Uncle Tom's Cabin.* Although the players were confined in their movements, their voices were heroically amplified to reach the last ear of the ten thousand crowding each performance. No sooner had the sun set on the metropolis, then the six spotlights of the portable theatre — together with a strip of three-colored sectional border lights — were switched on. Crowds had to be roped off nightly, and if you left your seat you lost your seat. The park benches were often filled twice over, with additional excited spectators crammed in tight rows on the grass, while half-naked boys shinnied up the branches of trees.

This was the very spirit at a folk play. The actors carried on as in the days when Tom troupes traveled with horse and wagon. Scenery was stacked conveniently against the nearby trees, and the open door of the dressing-rooms disclosed the players hurrying about, anxious about their cues, and putting the final touches on their makeup. In the semi-darkness, Uncle Tom joined the crowd to watch the show. Little Eva, during the waits, lit a cigarette offered her by Topsy. As in countless Tom shows before, the two beagle hounds, "Jack" and "Jill," could not bay at all; another, a trained collie, had to be kept by his trainer below the stage, and did the barking. On many evenings, the two dogs joined in a spirited chase not after poor Eliza (who stopped to call them back), but through the inviting aisles of the park benches. The play wound up with the performers parading across t h e stage in ye olde time manner, and Simon Legree drew hisses and "Bronx cheers." Then eddying a n d pushing, with baby carriages jammed, the ten thousand taxed the energies o f Mayor La Guardia's police. A score of women lost t h e i r pocketbooks, or a shoe each; a dozen children p a r t e d from their families in the mad scramble, and mothers scream-

Courtesy of N. Y. Herald Tribune

ed for their strays. Then as each child was found, the announcement came over the amplifiers. That was modern Tomming in the metropolitan parks during the hot summer nights, when Eliza crossed the Ohio ice with the New York thermometers registering about 90 degrees.

Tom troupes are still pitching along the countryside, but the many State laws that levy prohibitive fees on traveling shows have almost destroyed the tent industry. Florida licences amount to something like $120 a day, and in New Orleans the tax is $400 a week. Each of the remaining Tom managers claims that he is the last man left in the Tom game, letting the ominous pronouncement sink in as a come-on to the public. Somewhere in Ohio, Harmount's is billowing along. Up in Hoosick Falls, New York, the early Spring usually finds Tom Finn shining up that wonder of the modern century, the $2,000 calliope, which can be heard distinctly two miles up the road, and he shuns city newspapers, for only the small towns interest him. Another, John Huftle, after giving it to handkerchief wielders in op'ry houses, barns, town halls, and under canvas, for more than fifty years, believes he is the last survivor. He purveys ten-cent matinees in schools around Rochester, New York, and his show is a family affair, with as few as five people and the family pups. He is Simon Legree and Phineas Fletcher; his son, Thomas, plays Uncle Tom and Marks; his wife enacts Topsy, and fills in as needed. Three of his daughters have warbled Little Eva's lines, and grown up for Cassie, Emmeline and others; his grandson then took over the part of Eva, but his legs got too long.

Billy Bryant's bull-whistled showboat, as it catches the high tide, heralds the famous play up and down the Ohio. A rival, Capt. T. J. Reynolds' Majestic, pulls in S. R. O. business, en route to its established string of towns along the Tennessee River.

So poor Tom's a-old. Yet new managers are coming to the fore all the time, and are inattentive to rumors that the "darkey" is slipping. Critics still insist that there isn't much plot in the clumsy form, or that there is too much; well, perhaps only time tied the events of the play together. The grizzled, old reliable is termed a "fad" of the day — as if the frightful depravity of slavery could ever cease to be poignant. In the play's raw crudity was stuff in tune with the American background; indeed, the weather-beaten, time-honored native American folk play never belonged among the potted plants on the doorstep, but in the backyard.

After it stirred a whole nation, it continued to burn — a beacon-light through the decades. Never had its naturally discursive history seemed so concentrated on a single theme. And, today, *Uncle Tom's Cabin* comes along in trailers.

APPENDIX

ACKNOWLEDGMENTS

The main body of material in this book has been built around a vast amount of research in old handbills of more than 500 Tom show companies, the newspapers and theatrical journals of nine decades, and the many letters of veteran Tommers.

For their friendly interest, the writer extends thanks to George Freedley, Curator of the Theatre Collection, New York Public Library; to Dr. Lawrence D. Reddick, Curator of the Schomburg Collection, 135th Street Library, New York; to Dr. William Van Lennep, Curator of the Theatre Collection, Harvard University; and to George F. Willison, Fred Hamlin and Louis Scall.

The author wishes to express his thanks to the following publishers for their permission to quote from these sources: Harry Watkins' journal, 1845-1863, edited by Maud and Otis Skinner, in *One Man in His Time* (University of Pennsylvania Press, 1938); Jefferson De Angelis and Alvin F. Harlow's *A Vagabond Trouper* (Harcourt, Brace & Co., 1931); Stephen Leacock's *Here Are My Lectures* (Dodd, Mead & Co., 1937), and Vachel Lindsay's *Collected Poems* (Macmillan Co., 1925).

APPENDIX

EDWARD WILMOT, *a young mechanic in bondage*	MR. W. G. JONES
UNCLE TOM	MR. C. W. TAYLOR
BURLEY HAMMOND, *a slave trader*	MR. N. B. CLARKE
MR. JOSEPH SKEGGS, *a village auctioneer*	MR. J. HERBERT
RORY MARKS	MR. TOULMIN
ARTHUR SEDLEY, *Uncle Tom's master*	MR. J. M. COOKE
JOE ADAMS)	MR. S. M. SIPLE
SAM SPRINGER) *slave drivers to Hammond*	MR. STAFFORD
BILL RAWSON)	MR. CARTER
LITTLE ARIEL, *Wilmot's son*	MASTER J. MURRAY
SAM JENKS	MR. R. MARSH
ANDY SMUTT)	MR. FREDERICKS
JAKE JARVIS) *slaves on Sedley's plantation*	MR. CLINE
SETH CRANK)	MR. MACK
LANDLORD	MR. MITCHELL
MORNA WILMOT, *wife to Edward*	MRS. H. F. NICHOLS
CRAZY MAG *of the Glen*	MRS. W. G. JONES
MRS. ARTHUR SEDLEY	MRS. BANNISTER
AUNT CHLOE, *Uncle Tom's wife*	MISS THOMPSON
EMMELINE LE THOUX, *a rich widow*	MISS BARBER

The action of the play at the National Theatre, in New York, is disclosed by the synopsis of scenes, thus set forth in the "small bill:"

ACT I.   Exterior of Uncle Tom's Cabin on Sedley's Plantation. Negro celebration; Chorus, "Nigger in de Cornfield"; Kentucky Breakdown Dance; Innocence Protected; Slave Dealers on hand; Chorus, "Come then to the Feast"; the Mother's appeal; capture of Morna; interior of Uncle Tom's Cabin; Midnight Escape; Tom driven from his Cabin; Search of the Traders; Miraculous Escape of Morna and her Child; offering Prayer, the Negro's hope; Affecting Tableau.

ACT II.   Family Excitement; Dark Threatenings; Ohio River Frozen over; Snow Storm; Flight of Morna and her child; pursuit of the Traders; Desperate Resolve and Escape of Morna on floating Ice; Mountain Torrent and Ravine; cave of Crazy Mag; Chase of Edward; Maniac's Protection; Desperate Encounter of Edward and Traders on the Bridge; fall of Springer down the Roaring Torrent; Negro Chorus, "We Darkies Hoe de Corn"; Meeting of Edward and Morna; escape over Mountain Rocks.

Act. III. Roadside Inn; Advertisement Extraordinary; the Slave Auctioneer; Recontre between Edward and Slave Dealers: interposition of Crazy Mag; arrival from the West Indies; Singular Discovery; Mountain Dell; Recognition of the lost mother; Repentance and Remorse; Return of Tom; the Log Cabin in its pride; Freedom of Edward and Morna; Happy Denouement and Grand Finale to Uncle Tom's Cabin.

(p. 25) THE NEW YORK HERALD'S EDITORIAL, Sept. 3, 1852:

Mrs. Harriet Beecher Stowe's novel of *Uncle Tom's Cabin* has been dramatized at the National Theatre, and, being something of a novelty, it draws crowded houses nightly.

The practice of dramatizing a popular novel, as soon as it takes a run, has become very common. In many instances, and particularly with regard to the highly dramatic and graphic novels of Dickens, these new plays have been very successful, giving pleasure and satisfaction to the public, and putting money into the pockets of the chuckling manager. But in the presentation of *Uncle Tom's Cabin* upon the boards of a popular theatre, we apprehend the manager has committed a serious and mischievous blunder, the tendencies of which he did not comprehend, or did not care to consider, but in relation to which we have a word or two of friendly counsel to submit.

The novel of *Uncle Tom's Cabin* is at present our nine days' literary wonder. It has sold by thousands, and ten, and hundreds of thousands—not, however, on account of any surpassing or wonderful literary merits which it may be supposed to possess, but because of the widely extended sympathy, in all the North, with the pernicious abolition sympathies and "higher law" moral of this ingenious and cunningly devised abolition fable. The *furore* which it has thus created, has brought out quite a number of catchpenny imitators, *pro* and *con,* desirous of filling their sails while yet the breeze is blowing, though it does appear to us to be the meanest kind of stealing of a lady's thunder. This is, indeed, a new epoch and a new field of abolition authorship—a new field of fiction, humbug and deception, for a more extended agitation of the slavery question—than any that has heretofore imperiled the peace and safety of the Union.

The success of *Uncle Tom's Cabin* as a novel, has naturally suggested its success upon the stage, but the fact has been overlooked, that any such representation must be an insult to the South—an exaggerated mockery of Southern institutions—and calculated, more than any other expedient of agitation, to poison the minds of our youth with the pestilent principles of abolitionism. The play, as performed at the National, is a crude and aggravated affair, following the general plot of the story, except in the closing scene, where, instead of allowing Tom to die under the cruel treatment of his new master in Louisiana, he is brought back to a reunion with Wilmot and his wife—returned runaways—all of whom, with Uncle Tom and Aunt Chloe, are set free, with the privilege of remaining upon the old plantation....

In the progress of these varied scenes we have the most extravagant exhibitions of the imaginary horrors of Southern slavery. The negro traders, with their long whips, cut and slash their poor slaves about the stage for mere pastime, and a gang of poor wretches, handcuffed to a chain which holds them all in marching order, two by two, are thrashed like cattle to quicken their pace. Uncle Tom is scourged by the trader, who has bought him, for "whining" at his bad luck. A reward is posted up, offering four hundred dollars for the runaway, Edward Wilmot, (who, as well as his wife, is nearly white,) the reward to be paid upon "his recovery, or upon proof that he has been killed." But Wilmot shoots down his pursuers in real Christian style, as fast as they come, and after many marvellous escapes, and many fine ranting abolition speeches, (generally preceding his dead shots,) he is liberated as we have described.

This play, and these scenes, are nightly received at one of our most popular theatres with repeated rounds of applause. True, the audience appears to be pleased with the novelty, without being troubled about the moral of the story, which is mischievous in the extreme.

The institution of Southern slavery is recognized and protected by the federal constitution, upon which this Union was established, and which holds it together. But for the compromises on the slavery question, we should have no constitution and no Union—and would, perhaps, have been at this day, in the condition of the South American republics, divided into several military despotisms, constantly warring with each other, and each within itself. The Fugitive Slave law only carries out one of the plain provisions of the constitution. When a Southern slave escapes to us, we are in honor bound to return him to his master. And yet, here in this city—which owes its wealth, population, power, and prosperity, to the Union and the constitution, and this same institution of slavery, to a greater degree than any other city in the Union—here we have nightly represented, at a popular theatre, the most exaggerated enormities of Southern slavery, playing directly into the hands of the abolitionists and abolition kidnappers of slaves, and doing their work for them. What will our Southern friends think of all our professions of respect for their delicate social institution of slavery, when they find that even our amusements are overdrawn caricatures exhibiting our hatred against it and against them? Is this consistent with good faith, or honor, or the every day obligations of hospitality? No, it is not. It is a sad blunder; for when our stage shall become the deliberate agent in the cause of abolitionism, with the sanction of the public, and their approbation, the peace and harmony of this Union will soon be ended.

We would, from all these considerations, advise all concerned to drop the play of *Uncle Tom's Cabin* at once and forever. The thing is in bad taste— it is not according to good faith to the constitution, or consistent with either of the two Baltimore platforms; and is calculated, if persisted in, to become a firebrand of the most dangerous character to the peace of the whole country.

(p. 67) PURDY'S NATIONAL THEATRE CAST, July 18, 1853:
Mr. G. C. Germon (Uncle Tom), G. C. Howard (St. Claire), C. K. Fox (Gumption Cute), G. W. L. Fox (Phineas Fletcher), Siple (George Harris), N. B. Clarke (Simon Legree), Toulmin (Wilson, the Quaker), Lingard (Deacon Perry), Herbert (Marks, the Lawyer), Rose (Old Shelby), H. F. Stone (George Shelby, the son), G. Lingard (Tom Loker), E. Lamb (Haley), Mack (Sambo), McDonnell (Jumbo, slave driver), Henderson (Alf Mann), Thompson (Skeggs), Mitchell (Adolph), Cline (Waiter), Smith (Doctor), Master Murray (Harry, the child), Cordelia Howard (Eva), Mrs. G. C. Howard (Topsy), Mrs. Bradshaw (Aunt Ophelia), Mrs. W. G. Jones (Eliza), Mrs. Bannister (Cassy), Miss Barber (Emmeline), Miss Landers (Marie St. Claire), Mrs. Lingard (Chloe).

Toward the close of the historical run, the cast with the exception of Cordelia Howard, was completely changed. After the first three days, Mrs. Bradshaw's Aunt Ophelia was replaced by Mrs. E. Fox's. Germon, who created the rôle of Uncle Tom, left on August 23rd, and J. Lingard succeeded him. The latter was also Deacon Perry, but G. L. Fox relieved him later by doubling it with Phineas Fletcher. When Mr. Howard was forced by the pressure of business to give up his St. Clair on September 1st, Siple played it, and J. J. Prior stepped into the latter's part of George Harris. At the same time Mrs. Bradshaw accepted Mrs. E. Fox's Aunt Ophelia, and H. F. Stone (her son) took C. K. Fox's part of Gumption Cute. This new arrangement remained unchanged for weeks. By about October 18th, Mrs. W. G. Jones withdrew, and Mrs. J. J. Prior succeded her as Eliza. At the same time J. B. Howe became the new St. Clair, superseding Siple. Mrs. Mack then played Topsy for one month. Mrs. Howard resumed her great characterization on December 5th, and held it thereafter, except for a brief period of illness.

(p. 84) CORDELIA HOWARD'S LAST APPEARANCE: On the return from the triumphant tour abroad, the Howard family was featured at Barnum's Museum. That July, 1857, little Cordelia enacted other roles besides Eva, in *Ida May, The Manager's Dream, The Lamplighter*, and in *The Youthful King* she was Charles II. The following year, 1858, George L. Aiken dramatized *The Scarlet Letter, or The Elfin Child*, in which she attempted Little Pearl, her mother Hester and her father Dimmesdale. She later enacted Jean Valasquez in *The Page of History*. Her last appearance at Bernum's came on June 11, 1859, as a farewell to the Howard family. She was seen, once again, in *Fashion or Famine, or, the Strawberry Girl*, which was — as advertised — the "Very Last Chance to see, and Really Last Appearance of the popular actress, Little Cordelia Howard!"

Cordelia's precocity was the marvel of the 1850s. As the New York *Evening Mirror* described, "There is something in the tones of this wonderful child, Cordelia Howard, that vibrates to the innermost heart, and melts the *hardest adamantine* into a state of unwonted liquidity."

When Cordelia reached young girlhood her matured voice outgrew her little figure, and in 1860 she retired at the ripe old age of twelve. She entered school for her formal education, returning to the stage but once, when her father had a benefit at Troy, on which occasion Cordelia revealed a distressing lack of dramatic ability.

Mrs. G. C. Howard, her mother, never ceased to be the public's ideal of the darky hoyden — never born, but "jest grow'd up." Mr. Howard had his heart set on managing, and leased the Adelphi in Troy in 1857. A year later he acquired the Springfield Theatre in Massachusetts.

(p. 87) BARNUM'S AMERICAN MUSEUM CAST, November 7, 1853:

Mr. Sylves'r Bleeker (Mr. Shelby), Miss Sallie Bishop (George Shelby — 1st Act), Mr. George C. Charles (George Shelby — 5th Act), Mr. Wentworth (Haley), Mr. Charles (Tom Loker), Mr. Harry Cunningham (Marks), Mr. Simpson (Mr. Wilson), Mr. J. L. Monroe (Uncle Tom), Mr. F. A. Monroe (Drover John), Mr. George (Landlord), Mr. Thompson (Sam), Mr. George Clarke (Andy), Mr. H. F. Daly (Simon Legree), Mr. Henry (Skeggs), Mr. Thomas Hadaway (Penetrate Partyside), Mr. Brown (Bob), Mr. W. Cunningham (Pompey), Mr. Howard (George Harris), Mr. C. W. Clarke (St. Clair), Mr. A. Andrews (Adolph), Mr. G. Clarke (Sambo), Mr. Jenkins (William), Miss Smith (Little Mose), Master Smith (Peter), Mrs. J. L. Monroe (Mrs. Shelby), Mrs. Burroughs (Aunt Chloe), Miss Emily Mestayer (Eliza), Miss Rowene Granice (Aunt Vermont), Miss Chiarini (Eva), Miss Bellamy (Cassy), Miss Marie Ann Charles (Topsy), Miss Jackson (Marie), Miss Burroughs (Dinah), Miss Thurston (Little Polly), Miss Flynn (Rose), Miss Palmer (Jane), Miss Brown (Mammy), Miss Morton (Lilly), Miss Wilson (Lotty), Miss Hall (Clara).

(p. 109) THE PHILADELPHIA CHESTNUT STREET THEATRE CAST,

September 26, 1853: Mr. & Mrs. John Gilbert (Uncle Tom and Aunt Ophelia), August W. Fenno (George Harris), Rensselaer A. Sheppard (St. Clair), S. Parker (Phineas Fletcher), Louisa Parker (Eva), George Mason (Legree), A. H. Davenport (Haley), Lizzie Weston (Topsy), John S. Clarke (Marks), William Loomis (Wilson), Miss C. Cappell (Eliza), John Jack (Alf Mann), Uhl (Old Shelby), W. Briggs (George Shelby), Allen (Skeggs),

Martin (Deacon Perry), Mr. and Mrs. Joseph Jefferson (Gumption Cute and Marie).

With the exception of a short break, the play ran to the end of March, 1854. It may have lasted longer, but for the reduction of salaries, and those who withdrew organized a troupe. That Spring, they travelled through the interior of Philadelphia. It was managed by Martin and Mason, with Cappell as treasurer. The latter's wife was Aunt Ophelia, his elder daughter, Cordelia, Eliza, and a younger daughter was Eva. Co-partners in the profits were Jerry and Rose Merrifield, respectively Cute and Topsy. Owen Fawcett made his debut as young Shelby, on December 17th, at Morristown. Others in the company were James Martin (Uncle Tom), George Mason (Legree), and T. S. Cline (St. Clair). Scenery was painted by Joseph Jefferson.

(p. 114) COLONEL R. E. J. MILES' PRODUCTION, IN CINCINNATI, December 5, 1853: In it appeared two members of the original Troy cast, G. C. Germon as Uncle Tom and W. L. Lemoyne as Deacon Perry, supported by the Marsh Family and Troupe. Little Mary Marsh was the Eva. Harry Hotto and Mrs. Whiting, mother of Joseph Whiting, were the better known members of the cast that since has lost itself in the anonymity of time. At Melodeon Hall, Harry Watkins dropped in, and to woo the Eliza, Harriet Melissa Secor, he joined the company, and enacted George Harris. The daughter of their marriage, Amy Lee, won great renown later in Tom shows.

(p. 118) CLIFTON W. TAYLEURE'S SOUTHERN VERSION, IN DETROIT, October 2, 1852, had the following support: The Cappell family, Cordelia (Eliza), Josie (Eva) and Mrs. S. Cappell (Mrs. Shelby); Lancing K. Dougherty (Uncle Tom), W. Powell (Haley), J. B. Tozer (Sam), W. C. Dunnavant (Shelby), Miss Jackson (Topsy), C. W. Tayleure (George Harris).

(p. 118) GEORGE L. AIKEN'S PRODUCTION, IN DETROIT, October 2, 1854: L. D. Ross (Uncle Tom), F. Phillips (George Shelby and Deacon Perry), G. A. Pratt (Fletcher and Cute), W. Tirrell (Haley), Mulholland (Legree), A. Phillips (Loker), A. Tirrell (Marks), Mary Mowry (Eva), Mary P. Addams (Eliza), Miss Selah (Cassy), Miss Armstrong (Marie), Mrs. La Forest (Ophelia), Miss Jessyline (Topsy), J. H. Hackett (St. Clair), G. L. Aiken (George Harris).

(p. 120) J. H. McVICKER'S CHICAGO PRODUCTION, 1858: Mary McVicker (Eva), John D. Dillon (Deacon Perry), A. D. Bradley (Uncle Tom), Mr. and Mrs. S. Myers (George Harris and Marie), G. F. Cline (George Shelby), G. D. Chaplin (St. Clair), E. L. Tilton (Fletcher), J. B. Uhl (Wilson), F. G. White (Shelby), Harry Hawk (Haley), W. H. Leighton and wife (Legree and Topsy), F. Kellogg (Loker), J. A. Graver (Marks), H. R. Frost (Quimbo), W. Marble (Sambo), Master Martin (Harry),

Mrs. Lotty Hough (Eliza), Miss Woodbury (Cassy), Mrs. Taylor (Chloe), Mrs. Anna Marble (Aunt Ophelia).

(p. 121)   THE WHITE SLAVE OF ENGLAND: As debates grew fiercer over the Nebraska-Kansas bill, and the latest inequities burst upon the awakened national conscience, repercussions were felt in theatres. Early in 1853, on February 28th, an offset appeared at the Broadway Theatre, depicting English mothers and wives carrying baskets of coal; one of them, a halter about her neck, was sold for twenty shillings at a white slave market. In the last act, a British lady was announced by a darky: "Here comes her habolitionist highness, de Duchess of T'other Land!" She was shown the comparative happiness enjoyed by blacks in the Southern States. The play's rhetoric was such that it unintentionally became burlesque. One white slave, a miner, with a frightfully carbonized face, was freely booted about by Lord Overland; then advanced further by Grind, the overseer, who kicked all coal miners with his heavy top boots and goaded them with a cudgel tipped with twopenny nails. The ending was most unusual, and is reproduced here for the amusement of modern readers:

> LORD O.   *Now, Grind, what art thou after*
> *Why dost thou let these slaves of mine*
> *Their sinews rest? I must have money —*
> *And their blood must yield it!*
> *What are these brainless cattle for*
> *But to supply the nobles of the land*
> *With fatness.*
>
> GRIND.   *My Lord, I pray thee trust me.*
> *I have today already broken five*
> *Hard skulls, and jerk'd three shoulders*
> *Out of joint — have branded seven serfs*
> *With irons hot as ever Devil's hook,*
> *And still they disobey me — still complain*
> *Their lot is hard.*
>
> LORD O.   *Their lot be blow'd —*
> *To blazes with 'em* (Exit)
> GRIND.   *Did I, my Lord, conceive*
> *Aright, "Their lot be blow'd —*
> *To blazes wi 'em!"*
> *It must be so — 'tis well and right,*
> *And right 'tis well! I hate*
> *The horrid scum; and even now*

Revenge will take for insults long endured.
A light — a light — my kingdom for a light!

(*Exit — Scene changes to the interior of a pit —*
GRIND *is seen at the mouth of a shaft, letting down
a torch.*)
FIRST SLAVE. *So help me, Davy, we are lost!*
SECOND SLAVE. *Let's mizzle.*
THIRD SLAVE. *Here'll be a mighty flare up!*
(*Terrific explosion of coal damp, red and green fires
in succession — the slaves blown to atoms — several
heads and limbs fly about the house and fall into
the pit.*
Enter LORD OVERLAND *and* GRIND)
LORD O. *Ha! ha! ha! ha!*
GRIND. *Yah! yah! yah! yah!*
(*Curtain falls.*)

Spectators left the theatre shuddering, but none drafted a letter calling on
English women to do their part towards enfranchising their coal miners. That
would have been, indeed, a smart rejoinder to the Address to the Women of
America from the Ladies' meeting at Stafford House; for Mrs. Stowe was just
then in England, winning support for the Negro.

(p. 140)   BOWERY THEATRE VERSION, January 16, 1854: T. D. Rice
(Uncle Tom), Jas. C. Dunn (St. Clair), John Winans (Drover John), William
Hamilton (Aunt Chloe), Reed (Adolph), Mr. W. Reed (Wilson), Whitlock
(Julius), Ryan (Symes), Myrick (Everlasting Peabody), William H. Hamblin
(Mr. Selby), Collins (Haley), Stone (Legree), Stout (Loker), Lamb (Marks),
Sam Glenn (Van Krout), Robert Johnston (George Harris), Gertrude Dawes
(Topsy), Mill Gallott (Little Harry), Miss Walters (George Shelby), Mr. S.
Byrne (Sambo), Mr. Calladine (Quimbo), Mrs. Broadley (Mrs. Shelby),
Mrs. Yeomans (Ophelia), Miss Walters (Emmeline), Mrs. Howard [not
Mrs. G. C.] (Cassy), Miss Hiffert (Marie St. Clair), Caroline Whitlock
(Eva), Miss Woodward (Eliza). With the play's popularity new parts were
added, with Miss Fanny Herring (Jerusha Jenkins), and Mrs. James Dunn
(Mrs. Van Krout). Its last days found W. R. Kerr (Tom Loker) and T.
Wemyss (Aunt Chloe).

(p. 146)   THE EARLY RIVALRY IN LONDON: The first dramatization
appeared at the Standard Theatre, Shoreditch, on Sept. 13, 1852, and the
Olympic became a rival on Sept. 20th. The Victoria was third in the field,
with a two-acter, on Sept. 27th. This play reached its 100th performance on

January 17, 1853, and as audiences demanded more than could be encompassed in two acts, a new drama was prepared, *The Slave Hunt; or, The Fate of St Clair, and the Happy Days of Uncle Tom; including Cassy's Story, and the Death of Little Eva*. The Victoria was in the managerial hands of Miss Vincent, the first woman to achieve that distinction there. Thirteen years before, she had appeared in *Simon Lee; or the Murder of the Five Fields Copse*, by George Dibdin Pitt, in which were heard such Harris-like lines as, "I wish to injure no one, but by the heavens above, if any man attempt to lay a hand upon me, I'll shoot him thru the heart!" One scene anticipated the Rocky Pass, with the baying of bloodhounds on the track.

At the Royal Park Theatre, November 8, 1852, C. M. Tideswell's dramatization differed materially, although Mrs. Stowe's exciting language was judiciously preserved. The Adelphi drama, of November 29th, was prepared by the editors of *Punch*.

(p. 197) ONKEL TOM'S HÜTTE: With the all-compelling subject debated in the Verein halls in New York City, and at the Shakespeare Hotel especially, its dramatization was soon suggested. The German-Americans who frequented the Deutches Theatre, better known to native Americans as the St. Charles Theatre, saw *Onkel Tom's Hütte*, by Olfers, on October 20th and 24th, 1853.

Philadelphia gave two adaptations: Birch-Pfeiffer's, at the Melodeon, on May 31, 1856, and the von Megerle version, on March 23, 1857. The latter was revived at the Volkstheatre, on September 15-16, the following year.

On the eve of the Civil War, Herman Muhr's *Zuavenstreiche in Amerika* had such characters as Tom, a "Neger"; Blaque, another servant; Freeman, a merchant; and a lawyer called Sharp.

In 1883, Harrigan and Hart satirized, in the opening scene of *Cordelia's Aspirations*, an Uncle Tom combination that returned busted from Berlin. The Germania Theatre, in New York, produced on April 15, 1901, the musical comedy, *Der Kartoffelkoenig*, with the playwright, Adolf Philipp, enacting a young wigmaker who put on the famous American play in German for his patron, the potato king.

(p. 197) THE IRISH INVASION AT NIBLO'S GARDEN, March 13. A skeletonized summary of the play, given in that old manner of theatre programmes of 1860, yields the following:

UNCLE PAT'S CABIN

OR LIGHTS AND SHADES OF LIFE IN IRELAND

Mickey Malone, *a broth of a boy, out of doors, out of work, out at elbows, out of all civilization, but a light heart and heavy shillalah, with the Song of "Limerick Races,"*   MR. BARNEY WILLIAMS

Widdy Casey, *keeper of a Shebeen House,*   MRS. BARNEY WILLIAMS

Uncle Pat, *a free Irish tenant, free to starve if he cannot break the bonds of want and oppression*   MR. G. FARREN

Lanty, *his son, an exile from his home, in search of that denied him there, bread and shelter*   MR. FENNO

Grindem, *Blake's agent, an unprincipled scoundrel,*   MR. CANOLL

Gruff, *a bailiff*   MR. EVANS

Middleton, *a young American from South Carolina, on a tour through Europe*   MR. WALL

Peregrine, *his friend and companion*   MR. RUSSELL

Brian   *Two*   MR. PARKE

Hugh   *Ruffians*   MR. LEIGH

Lace Sleeve, *servant to* Blake   MR. ....

Bob, *a Negro belonging to* Middleton, *accompanying his master*   MR. J. O. SEFTON

Norah, *wife to* Uncle Pat   MRS. JOHN SEFTON

Kathleen, *their niece*   MISS EMILY MESTAYER

Biddy, *the* Widdy's *maid of all work*   MISS MARSHALL

Granny, *mother to* Uncle Pat   MISS McCORMICK

Guests, beggars and servants, etc.

THE SCENE IS IRELAND

ACT FIRST — Exterior of Uncle Pat's Cabin — Grindem, the Middleman — Inventory of Property — No Cow — The Proposal — Exterior of Sheebeen House — Whiskey and Wittals — The Widow Casey at Home — Mickey Malone, the Poor Irishman — Bob, the Colored Gentleman — The Devil — Food for Uncle Pat's Family — Cornmeal — Interior of Uncle Pat's Cabin — Tableau — The Sick Child — The Absent Son — Succor for Uncle Pat — The Negro's Charity. ACT SECOND — The Manor House — Uncle Pat's Cabin. The Widdy — A Letter from the Absent Son — Hope — The Middleman — The Distraining — Mickey and Grindem. ACT THIRD — Arrival of the South Carolinian — The Executor — Bob Again — Kathleen's Story — Aid for the Irish — The Beggars — The Ruffians — The Scramble — The Bargain — The Escape — Kathleen in Danger — The Rescue — Lanty, the Absent Son —

Mickey Kilt Entirely — Grindem — Scene last — The Dreary Heath — The
Dead Child — Poor Granny — Meeting of Lanty and Uncle Pat — Relief for
the Poor Irish. 500 — Determination to Emigrate to America — "America the
Land of Liberty," the Irishman's Refuge — Grand Picture — Hail Columbia.

(p. 291) TOM COMPANIES OF THE '80s: Among the better known were:
Abbey's, A. C. Adam's, J. R. Allen's, Anderson's, Avery & Wilson's, Chunn
& Henderson's, Clifford & Webber's, Davis', Draper & Wright's, Draper's,
J. V. Farrar & C. H. Clarke's, Stephen Fitzpatrick's, Charles Forbes', Minnie
Foster's, Gibson's, T. R. Gilbert's, Giles & Potter's, J. Newton Gotthold's,
Gray & Stephen's, Grimes & Jackson's, F. E. Griswold's, J. W. Harpstrite's,
Harris & Morgan's, Hatch's, Hathaway & Ellis', J. A. Harverly's, Hender-
son's, Holland's, Hooley's, Charles Howard's, Frank Howard's, Hugh's,
Johnson's, John Keating's, Harry Keene's, Laisdell & Bryant's, Charles W.
Langstaff's, Marshall's, B. B. Marti's, H. B. Morgan & E. A. Mason's, Max-
well's, Miller's, McCall & Shelton's, Neff & Ockerman's, New York Mastodon
Company, James Nixin's, Owens', Peck & Fursman's, C. Pelham's, Phillips
& Griswold's, Frank E. Piper's, Sackett & Wiggins', Senor & Webber's,
Seymour & Stratton's, Chris. Simmons & Fred Mower's, O. P. Sisson &
Cawthorne's, Slavin's, C. H. Smith's, Chas. Stedman & Geo. E. Gouge's,
Smith & Edwards', Smith & Barlow's, Sparks Brothers', B. T. Stacy's, John
Stetson's, George A. Stevens', A. R. Stover's, Stowe's, Dick P. Sutton's, J.
W. Talbot's, Tremaine & Benham's, F. C. Walton's, Washburn & Stetson's,
Webber's, Witherell & Davies', Frederick R. Wren's, Yacton's, Frank L.
Yearance's . . .

(p. 346) BETTER KNOWN TOM TROUPES OF THE '90s: W. N. Adams'
Pavilion, Al Fal Fa Double, Anderson's, Aymar's Big Spectacular, Bailey's,
Barbour & Moore's, Bock & Stuart's, The Boston Ideal, S. W. Boone's, Boyer
Brothers', Brown & Rathburne's, Burke's, G. Burtch's Pavilion, Sam Bryant's
Wagon Show, Burdette's, Carpenter & Mack's Standard, Chester's, I. E.
Cohien's Spectacular Pavilion, Coles' Big Spectacular Pavilion, The Colum-
bia Eureka, The Columbia Excelsior, Pete Conklin's Big Spectacular, John
F. Cordray's, Cummings & Alexander's, S. F. Darling's, Davidson & Lane's
Pavilion, Ed. F. Davis', Wm. Davis', Alf Dean's, De Forest Davis', Dick's,
Dobbins Brothers', W. C. Down's, Downing & Goodrich's, Albert Draper's,
W. A. Eiler's, E. E. Eisenbarth's, Fitzpatrick's, Foerster & Gollin's, Forrests',
T. R. Gilbert's, Gilmore's New Spectacular, Glenford's, E. F. Gorton's
Mammoth, F. E. Griswold's Mammoth Pavilion, J. P. Harris', Hart's, Hatch
Brothers' Pavilion, Haynor & Langstaff's, Haverly's, Haverley & Hoe's,
Henderson's, Hobbs & Company's, Hobson's, Howard's Mammoth Pavilion,
B. J. Jackson's, Jeavon's, Johnson's, Jones Brothers', D. R. Keith's Mammoth
Pavilion, C. W. Kidder's Big Spectacular, Dell Knowleton's, C. W. Lang-

staff's Pavilion, Lincoln's Triple, Lloyd's Big Pavilion, The Lyceum's, Mack's Pavilion Spectacular, Madison Square, W. E. Marney & B. G. McGowen's, Daisy Markoe's, Marretta's, H. B. Marshall's, Mason & Morgan's, Sam McCutcheon's, McFadden's, A. McFee's, McKenzie & Erwood's Pavilion, T. D. Middaugh's Original New Orlean's, Mills', Moore & Castner's, Morgan & Sherman's Pavilion, Murray's, Ogden Brothers', Owens, Mammoth Pavilion, Palmer's Big Spectacular Pavilion, Wm. Parsons & Fred E. Pool's Famous Ideal, Peck & Fursman's, Pfaff & Goodman's, Phillips & Griswold's Grand Colossal Pavilion, F. E. Piper's, G. A. Raymond's, Mrs. Jay Rial's, Rice's, Harry Rich's, Riel & Abbey's, E. O. Rogers' Original, C. M. Roscoe's Mammoth, Rusco & Swift's, Russell & Christie's, Salter & Martin's, Saulter's, Scribner's, John Shea's, J. W. Shipman's, Smith & Andrews', H. C. Smith's Mammoth & Specialty Show, Somerby's Pavilion, Star & Vosburg's, J. P. Stenson's Mammoth Pavilion, Stetson's Pavilion, G. W. Stevens', A. R. Stover's, John F. Stowe's Original, Dick P. Sutton's, G. L. Sweet's Mammoth Pavilion, Swift Brothers', F. E. Terry's Pavilion, Thearle's, True & Young's New Railroad Pavilion, Twitchell & Robbins', Vosburgh's, Vreeland & Middaugh's, Walker Brother's Colossal, Warren & O'Day's, Webber's, Welsh Brothers', Wentworth, Wilbur & Logan's Mammoth, P. T. Williams', C. O. Willis', Witherell & Doud's Pavilion, Young Brothers', Zelma & Thorp's... A complete list would fill many pages.

(p. 377) LONGEVITY OF AN OLD TOM COMPANY: In 1925, the Tom company Leon W. Washburn had made famous advertised, "Fifty-Fourth Annual Tour of Stetson's Show." It was owned by the Charles F. Ackerman Estate, and the title was used with Washburn's permission. Ackerman passed away a year before, after having played Simon Legree for thirty-four years. He had begun as a lowly musician in the Stetson troupe, and after fifteen years became company manager and a fullfledged actor; he served later as righthand man for Ed. F. Davis' troupe, then for Jim Shipman's. When Ackerman heard that "Major" William Kibble, the famous lightning gun spinner in the Stetson parade, had broken with Washburn (the "Major" had been manager under Stetson, then used the Stetson title on his own), he became interested in the fortunes of his former band leader. Kibble, foregoing the Stetson name, bought out Al. W. Martin's, and as Kibble & Martin's the company went on the road for several seasons, when he dropped the Martin title. Ackerman became affiliated with that company, with headquarters at Mt. Clemens, Mich., and was put in charge by Mrs. Kibble when her husband died in 1922; after Ackerman resigned, she ran it herself for one season, then retired. Ackerman fortunately regained the Stetson title, and carried on the famous name.

"Wildcat" Tom Aiton, an associate of Ackerman, broke away, and become business manager for Earle Newton & David Livingston's, which went out on its first season in 1922. When Ackerman bought the imponderables from Peck & Jenning's "Stetson's U. T. C. company," in the Spring of 1923, Aiton closed the deal for the scenery, wardrobe, band uniforms, and parade equipment, which were then distributed between the two Newton & Livingston's companies. A year later, Aiton became joint owner with Mr. Livingston, and they featured the Stetson affinity in their advertising. In 1926, the company was owned and managed by C. E. Yarnell and F. D. Whetten, and was called Newton, Pingree & Holland's Famous and Original Stetson's U. T. C. Company.

Meanwhile, "Wildcat" Aiton secured the Mason Bros.' title from Walter Brownlee and Claude Reed (Brownlee had managed Washburn's Western Tom troupe during the early Twenties), and did a bang-up business through Ohio, Indiana and Pennsylvania. In November, 1930, Aiton took out the old Stone & Stetson show, and opened in South Bend, Indiana. Associated with him were Billy Blythe, his former partner, and John Stone, of Tom fame. The latter's ill health prevented him from taking an active part in the enterprise. After two months on the road, due to the great depression of the times, it folded in January, 1931. That brought to an end the famous Stetson title, in its sixtieth year.

(p. 385)   THE SAGA OF TERRY'S TOM TROUPE: On February 19, 1890, Terry's set out from Little Sioux, Iowa. The first performances were given in opera houses, but proved unprofitable. Then the troupe acquired 22 head of stock, and unfolded the play under a 60-ft. top with a 40-ft. middlepiece. It claimed that the show was the first to introduce a bale of cotton to the natives. The following year, Fred Terry, the Little Sioux barber, sold his half interest to his partner, O. Q. Setchell. The latter's wife handled the pasteboards at the front door, while "Professor" Si Setchell swung the baton, and two other Setchells, Ollie and Rose, had other duties.

In 1904, Terry's was a big two-car railroad show, with a colored band of eight pieces, buck and wing dancers, cake walkers, lady drum and bugle corps. It was managed by J. D. Chunn through Missouri, Arkansas, Oklahoma, and Kansas. By 1921 the only remaining charter member of the show was Mrs. W. G. Dickey, mother-in-law of Elias D. Terry, who enacted Eliza and Emmeline. The troupe's Uncle Tom was a Negro, John W. Beecher, with the company for twenty-seven years, having joined it in 1902.

Setchell, one of the organizers, was now living in retirement at National City, California. With Terry, Mrs. Dickey managed the company in its 40th consecutive season, in 1929, and it was well in step with modern times. The winter quarters were in Aurora, Illinois. Completely motorized, the show traveled with fifteen trucks and four sedans, and ran on the principle of the actors bringing and living in their own cars; the management supplied the necessary gas, oil and repairs.

(p. 421) WITH THE INCEPTION OF RADIO: Winged over the air was
the crackling interpretation by the Ohio State University, over the Blue
Network, NBC, in February, 1937, with *The Gray Spirit*. Meredith Page,
its director, reproduced the early background of the famous play, which
depicted the reaction of Pre-Civil War audiences to the dynamic scenes.

Set loose on the ether were many travesties, the most delightful that
of Roland Young as Uncle Tom, on WEAF in November, 1937. Never more
British, his lines had a clean-cut terseness that adroitly underplayed the
large scale chromatics and juicy sentiments. The fun was enhanced by the
superb manner in with he stepped out of character to clarify the details of
his Southern accent, and Sheila Barrett, as Little Eva, played it to tht hilt
in the Katharine Hepburn manner. Earlier in the season, in September, Al
Barrie's Mellerdrammers gave *Uncle Tom's Cabana* over WNYC in modern
slang. The following year, in June, the NBC-Blue network had Ryan and
Noblette in their travesty, with a Topsy who piped in the upper register,
a Simon Legree who boomed in a thick Russian accent, and bloodhounds
that bayed in the background. WOR performed it straight in its "Rainbow
House" hour, the same month. The "Star Spangled Theatre" on NBC-Blue
(WJZ) charged the ether, on August 10, 1941, with Al Jolson as venerable
old Tom.

And with television's bold, first full hour musical, on July 25, 1939,
the Duncan Sisters gave *Topsy and Eva* to the ether world.

(p. 421) THE FAVORITE MARCHES ON: There is a modern defense
of Tom shows in Edmund Wilson's play, *Winter in Beach Street*. The same
interest is manifested in the following: Ben Hecht's comedy, *Actor's Blood*,
where two decrepit-looking hounds from a Tom show track down poor old
Widow Cagle's murderer; Jack Bechdolt's novel, *The Vanishing Hounds*,
which has the old folk play setting; August Derleth's *Sweet Genevieve*,
which narrates the vicissitudes of a Mississippi Tom Show boat; William
G. Burleigh's novel, *Uncle Tom's Mansion*, in which the former Uncle Tom
and Eliza of a Tom troupe reveal the perils in re-enthroning King Alcohol.

Vincent Minelli's *The Show Is On*, in 1936, ended climactically its first
act with a Tom Show arrival, and this idea was carried on in *Bloomer Girl*,
but with additional scenes from the historical play. In *The Darktown Jam-
boree*, by James Reach, the finale highlighted "Uncle Tom's Harlem Cabin;"
today, in sophisticated night clubs, Dwight Fiske is singing "Uncle Tom's
Cabana." Indeed, no end of smart-looking restaurants are named after Tom's
impoverished domicile; out on Long Island, for example, a rival, Topsy's
Chicken Roost, encourages gourmets to eat fried poultry with their fingers.

The modern tempo, moreover, is caught in *Uncle Tom's Cabin in Swing*,
by Al Borde, which is offset by the experimental manner of E. E. Cummings'
pantomine, *Tom*. The grand opera by Leslie Grossmith, *The Immortal Slave*,

— 439 —

has in contrast to its formal style Yasha Frank's ebullient *Topsy*. In Henrietta Buckmaster's dramatization an attempt is made to strip away the barnacle of time from the play, and Eslanda Goode Robeson fashions the "American folk-music drama" in a manner that stresses modern connotations with leanings toward social significance.

The lusty, familiar version is still on the road, carried by such old under-canvas troupes as L. Verne Slout's, which plays in its established Michigan territory.

A half-dozen plays or more have appeared simultaneously, with Mrs. Stowe as the pivotal character, among them: *Harriet*, by Florence Ryerson and Colin Clements; *Hattie Stowe*, by Guy Bolton; *Let My People Go*, by Ian Hay and Milton Shubert; *An American Incident*, by Melvin Levy; *I Walk in Liberty*, by Guy Endore, De Witt Bodeen and William Copeland; *Hattie Stowe*, by Betty Smith; and one by Mrs Fremont Older.